Emily of Oz

by

Steven R. Garfinkel

First Edition 1.00
Paperback ISBN: 979-8-89587-034-1
Hardcover ISBN 979-8-89587-031-0
EBook ISBN NA

Library of Congress Control Number: 2024919116

Written by Steven R. Garfinkel
Illustrations by Jonathan D. Inkvell

Published by:
Ellipsah LLC
28 Thrumont Road
West Caldwell, NJ

Contents

Part I
Mirror Mirror

Chapter 1   Aunt Maybel

The bus hits my wake-up pothole, which gives me a nice shake and lets me know I will be at my bus stop soon. I'm not sure what I would do if they ever fix that pothole, but there doesn't seem to be much risk of that. Rain had drizzled slowly during most of the bus trip. Now it had stopped. Hopefully it will hold off for a bit, but the clouds looked low and ready to burst.

I have a few minutes to pack up my stuff and turn off my music before I arrive. My aunt Maybel will be standing first in line to greet me. She pronounces her name May Bell. She doesn't get upset when people mispronounce it, but it helps to get it right. And, if you meet her, you can let her know you're a friend by calling her Aunt Maybel. She's my aunt, but everyone in town calls her Aunt Maybel no matter who they are. You can be five years old or 95 years old, White, Black or Asian, Hindu Monk or Orthodox Jew. They all call her Aunt Maybel.

The bus door opens and after the line clears, I climb down the stairs.

"Hey Emily," Aunt Maybel says.

"Hey Aunt Maybel," I say as we hug.

"I was thinking of hugging you up and spinning you around."

"Thanks for not doing that."

"Well, you used to like it."

"Yeah, and I used to crawl too."

She gives me one of her smiles and a chuckle.

"Point taken." We hop into her pickup truck. "How's your parents?"

"All fine," I say. "Busy with work."

"And Jacob?"

"He's good. He's about as much a boy as a boy can be with his trucks, construction sets, and balls. He likes me to read him books about dinosaurs too."

"That's nice. And how are you? Any poems for me?"

"Oh, I'm fine. Same old same old. School, soccer. I was working on this one on the ride over, but I don't think it's done."

I take my notebook out of my backpack and begin to read.

My pencil careens across my page,
Cartwheeling over hills and around sharp corners,
Chasing my thoughts but never catching them,
Only watching their taillights speed away.
Sometimes we pause and stop,
And at others, back up and erase,
But whether to sky, or sea, earth or eternity
We course forward to an undiscovered country.

"Quite Shakespearian," Aunt Maybel says.

"Huh?" I reply.

"Shakespeare used 'The Undiscovered Country' as a metaphor for the future."

"Nice. But I mean something less big, only a new place to find."

There was a bit of a pause and then Aunt Maybel says, "I am so glad you're here. We're expecting two big truckloads in the next few days and we need to move

4

some pieces to free up the room. Otherwise, the warehouse will be so crammed we won't be able to work."

She owns a furniture store just a short ride from the bus stop, "Aunt Maybel's Antiques and Fine Furniture." She has scouts all over the country, friends from her time in the army, who buy up things and send them to her. We get trucks from all over.

That's part of the reason why I'm here. I visit her when I can to help sort through and clean up the furniture, which I like to do. It's fun. Also, I like to have money of my own.

Even the best of old furniture needs some cleaning up, and sometimes we find a really nice piece. It seems kids have been sticking gum under tables and desks for some time. I guess since these are antiques, I should start a museum for antique bubble gum. Mostly things need a good cleaning, to get the grime off them, and then a polish, but some are a bit on the gross side. Dried vomit flakes for one, or a melted lipstick, or spilled glue, or a combination of all three. Sometimes they need some carpentry, or refinishing, but that's someone else's job.

As we pull up at the parking lot Aunt Maybel says, "You have good timing, we didn't get wet at all. I didn't think the rain was ever going to let up. Time for ark building you know." We rush through the door just as thunder claps and the rain resumes.

"You don't have good timing, you have great timing. Anyway, you'll be working on your own. I'm busy as a squirrel when the nuts ripen," Aunt Maybel says as we walk through the showroom and into the front of the warehouse where there is an old metal desk and a few chairs. We sit down. "Here's your snack, just the way you like it."

I'm happy that Aunt Maybel has remembered my favorite snack. But then she pats my arm and says, "I was thinking that you're getting old enough so that we should talk about the facts of life."

I am not sure I want to hear what she is going to tell me. My uncomfortable-ometer needle swings way past ten.

"Your mom and dad and all your family want to protect you, and keep you safe, so you can be a kid for as long as possible," she says. "But you need to know that sometime in your life you are going to need to have courage. It won't give you a warning. You'll be walking along minding your own business, you will turn a corner, and it will be there, right in your face. And it's better for you to know this now, rather than being caught unprepared. You will never know when it will happen, but sure enough, it will. Courage will beckon you. You need to be prepared to answer."

"Oh," I say slowly, "that's all. That's, that's nothing." My uncomfortable-ometer needle settles back to a more moderate three, maybe four.

"That's because you haven't really heard what I told you. You sit with that and I will catch up with you during your break." She gives me a kiss on the forehead and walks away.

Aunt Maybel saw some tough things in the army. If I ask her about it, she changes the subject. But she can't hide it totally, because her right foot is a prosthesis. She was hurt pretty badly. When she got back to the states, she was in the hospital for a long time, and then in rehab for longer. My dad says that she will talk to me about it when she thinks I am ready. But she may never think I am ready. And maybe I never will be ready. How would I know? And when I am, will we make the time to talk this out? Or perhaps we won't and I will never get to know her better. I just must wait.

The rest of the warehouse part of the store, where I work, has all the usual things a vintage furniture business would have: a loading dock, a small wood shop, a few desks and computer workstations, lockers, coatracks, bathrooms and a break room. But Aunt Maybel is disciplined, so all the tools are locked when not in use, everything is neat, and the floor is clean enough to eat off of. It wouldn't be my first choice, but I could do it if I had too.

That's not to say it's grim. There are pictures and decorations here and there, and in one corner is an enormous bear carved out of a tree trunk. I'm not sure where Aunt Maybel got it, but everyone calls it Benny. It's fearsome, except for the broad brimmed hat that someone put on its head, a hat with flowers and bird feathers. And except for the large handbag that hangs off one of his arms. For a while someone had put one of those talking fish in its outstretched claws, but the batteries soon disappeared, and in time the fish did as well. After the first Thanksgiving that Benny was there, people started hanging bags full of food for the community food bank on his arms. Those bags are there permanently now, along with a large box in front of Benny. Every month they bring the donated food to the food bank.

After I stick my snack in the fridge I get suited up. I have coveralls to keep my clothes clean, and I have my 'Superhero's Utility Belt,' as Aunt Maybel likes to call it. It has almost everything I need for work.

When I'm all dressed up, I go out to the main area, where all the furniture to be worked on is kept. Each piece of furniture has a tag which lists the steps needed to get it ready. I start with a dark oak desk that has a lot of intricate wood working. It is nice looking with a front drawer, three side drawers, and a pull-down cover, but it's so covered with grime it's sticky. The draws drag and jam. I get to work cleaning it. There's a piece of melted hard candy stuck inside one of the side drawers.

That's how things go until I start to get hungry, which means it's break time for me. It's really too early for my break, so I must not have eaten enough breakfast. I get my bag from the fridge and head up to the top of the highest piece of furniture. Aunt Maybel is not so happy that I like to eat my snack up here instead of in the break room, but she doesn't stop me. I bet she would climb too if she were me.

It's like climbing on the tops of buildings, but you have to be careful not to knock the buildings over. I find my perch and start to eat my sandwich, super chunky peanut butter and strawberry jam on bread with seeds and nuts. While I eat, I look around the warehouse. That's the whole point of climbing to the top. I can see what is really going on. A few more bites from my sandwich and I spot something. It's carefully wrapped in heavy brown paper. That's not what's interesting. What's interesting is that there is a tear in the paper, and underneath it is something bright green, like an emerald, showing through.

I take another bite and climb down from my perch, holding the rest of my sandwich in one hand. It takes some maneuvering, but soon I reach my target. Someone took some time to wrap this thing up so carefully. There are three rope ties around it. I put my sandwich down on a nearby table and I remove the ties and the paper cover, revealing an emerald satin cloth wrap. That must have been what I saw through the tear in the outer cover. The emerald wrap has three ties around it also, but these ties are thick braids of emerald colored cord and have fancy tassels.

All that peanut butter has made me thirsty. I take a pause to get some soda with ice from the fridge. And what was Aunt Maybel trying to tell me about courage. Does it mean I need to be ready to fight all the time? Is that what she learned in the army? Is that a lesson I want to learn?

When I return, I remove the emerald cords. I toss them down on the table. Then I push back the emerald wrap.

It's a mirror, about half my height, in a heavy wooden frame. Nicely finished. It has some decorative carvings in the frame and looks like it is made well. But I see a lot of old mirrors pass through the warehouse and this one is not exceptional. I am surprised that someone took so much care wrapping it up so well. It must have been very special to someone. But the reflection looks very sharp and the glass looks very smooth, although under a fine layer of dust. I take a polishing cloth and give the glass a rub.

Stepping back, I give the mirror another inspection. As I look at it, from a point near the center, the reflection starts to change, expanding out like the waves a pebble makes when it hits a puddle of water. There's a path, and a park bench with some type of sculpture on it. How strange. It doesn't look at all like anything that should be reflected.

I take one final bite of my sandwich and put the remainder on the desk. I touch the glass. I can smell flowers and, all of a sudden, I feel ill and my legs are weak. I stumble forward. It feels like I am being yanked through the mirror by the bottom of my stomach.

Chapter 2   A Sculpture

I crawled forward and sat down on the park bench next to a sculpture of a metal man. How did I get here? I took out my phone and looked at it. I swiped at it, poked at it, and pushed at it, but it didn't do a thing. Looking around at the trees, and the mirror, and the field in the distance, and the sun high in a deep blue sky, I wondered what was going on. Birds flew by, bright green birds with yellow heads and wing tips and long thin necks. How strange.

What happened? I repeated the swiping, poking and pushing at my phone. It would be really nice to be able to call Aunt Maybel, or maybe my mom or dad. This second round with my phone was accompanied by some shouting, and then some loud yelling, and then some rather rude unpleasantries. It's good you couldn't hear me. I looked at that phone one last time. It was the same phone as an instant earlier, but nothing worked. The screen was blank. It may as well have been a stone for all its usefulness.

I heard a little squeak come from the sculpture so I stood to give it a good looking over. What a strange thing it was. Some parts were almost human like, while others were crudely made of sheets of metal bent, rolled, crimped and soldered.

Where am I? The sun didn't look like it was in the right place. It's mid-morning, so the sun shouldn't be directly overhead. And where are the clouds? There was only the highest blush of clouds in the sky. Weather can change fast but it felt wrong. I sat back down beside the sculpture.

And this useless phone. I should just chuck it. I went to throw my phone at the mirror. The sculpture's arm shot up with a grinding sound. My hand smashed into it. And now my hand was bleeding. I rolled around on the ground with my fingers in my mouth. Two of them had little chunks of skin missing and blood seeped out. I sat once again and using some bandages I had in my belt, tried to patch myself up.

The sculpture had moved! Now, it swung its eyes left and right, up and down. Perhaps it was a signal, but a signal to do what? "What are you?" I asked. I don't normally talk to sculptures you understand. But I don't normally get pulled through mirrors either. I grabbed the sculpture's arm and pushed it back down to where I thought it had been. The arm made an awful screech as I moved it. The sculpture kept circling its eyes, and swinging them left and right and up and down.

What can I do? I got it. I have a small pump bottle of penetrating lubricant in my belt. It comes in handy when metal things are jammed up and don't move freely, and this looked like one of those times. After a few sprays at the shoulder joint I moved the sculpture's arm up and down. I let go and the arm kept moving! This tin thing is alive! I jumped back.

"Well, that seemed to work," I said as I looked it over. It moved its arm up and down and moved its eyes about until it stopped. It got tired I guess. I decided I needed to help this thing, whatever it was. I stepped closer and gave its elbow joint a spray. With a screech it moved its arm so it was pointing to its mouth. I sprayed the sculpture's mouth. In a low voice it screeched out, "Don't break the mirror."

12

"Why?"

"It may be the only way for you to get home."

"Where am I?" I asked.

"The land of Oz," he said while doing mouth exercises. "Please spray my fingers." I did. "If you don't mind, may I use your spray?" I handed it to him. He went about spraying himself, joint after joint, moving and stretching this way and that. "And I'm the Tin Man, he said. "Wow, this is great stuff."

"It's yours. I've never heard of the Land of Oz, and I am really good at geography. How do I get from Oz to North Carolina?"

"Is the land of North Carolina," the Tin Man asked, "near the land of Kansas?"

"Not close, but it's in the same country. How am I going to get home?"

"I don't know how to get you home, but I know where to go for help, the Emerald City. The Witch's Council will soon meet. I'm sure we can get help there. Dorothy used to be sent back by Glinda the Good Witch when she came to Oz, but they are both gone."

"What do you mean 'gone?'"

"The lives of flesh people are so short," he said, as he began to sob. "All my old friends are gone. Even the Scarecrow, who was not flesh, is missing. It's my curse to have to live alone."

"Please don't cry. I need you to get me home to see my family."

The Tin Man lifted his funnel shaped hat and took out an old-fashioned handkerchief. He wiped away his tears.

"Who is Dorothy?" I asked.

"Dorothy first came to Oz in a cyclone, when she was a young girl about your age."

"How did she get back home?"

"The first time she used the silver slippers she got from the Wicked Witch of the East."

"Where are the silver slippers?"

"They're gone, lost forever on the way back to Kansas."

"Are there any more silver slippers?"

"No. No more silver slippers."

"But how about the other times? You said Dorothy came to Oz more than once. How did she get back home those other times?"

"The second time, when Dorothy came to Oz on a ship wreck, Glinda, the Good Witch of the South, sent her back using the mirrors. She gave Dorothy a mirror, just like this one, so she could return to Oz whenever she wanted."

"I guess that explains how I got here," I said, although it didn't really explain anything at all. This was so confusing. I have no idea where I am, and I'm talking to a man made of tin. "I came through a mirror that looked just like this one." Then, witches? "What do you mean, a witches council?"

"Like any other activity, those who participate like to meet. In Oz, we have a council for witches."

"With real witches?"

"What other kinds of witches could there be besides real ones?"

"There are no real witches in North Carolina. Some people play at it, and some act like evil witches, but there are none that truly are witches."

14

"That's exactly what Dorothy said about Kansas. Take my word for it, there are real witches in Oz." The Tin Man paused in thought. Then he continued. "You must have used the mirror Glinda gave to Dorothy. We need to go to the Emerald City to ask the Witches' Council for help. But first I need to visit some friends." The Tin Man stood up, stretching this way and that. He put an axe in a carrying sling on his back, and began to walk down a gentle slope covered with tall grass. After a number of steps, he turned around and shouted back, "You won't get home by watching me. You're going to have to do your own walking, unless you're some powerful witch and can fly."

"I'm not a witch," I said. "What do you mean fly? Do your witches fly?" I struggled to catch up.

"Of course, generally on brooms."

We walked down to the edge of the field where a row of three trees were growing. The Tin Man was quiet, slowly looking the trees over. He turned to me and said, "It's the custom in these parts to mark the burial sites of loved ones by planting a new tree. Dorothy loved this place and she asked to have her uncle and aunt buried here. She wanted to be buried beside them when it was time, and so they rest together. I often visit them when I am lonely, or uneasy and not sure why, or when I need to make a difficult decision."

We walked closer to the trees. The first tree was the smallest and was covered in blue, pink, yellow, and green blossoms. "If you listen you can hear the hum of the humblebees as they go from flower to flower," said the Tin Man. I watched them as they buzzed about. The bees hummed a happy melody as they worked, working in pairs, two on each blossom, helping one another. I got in close to one cluster of blooms, close enough that I

15

could smell their fragrance, and close enough so I could see much better. The humblebees ignored me.

"Do they sting?"

"No. Not unless you provoke them. Left alone, they don't hurt or bother anyone."

Just to my left, one flower began to grow and change. First it looked like an apple, and then it changed to a notebook, and then a small backpack. The backpack continued to grow and the branch was bent toward the ground so that I feared it would break. I lifted the backpack, which continued to grow. When it stopped growing it came off in my hands.

"We don't have trees like this in North Carolina."

"Dorothy used no magic in her life," the Tin Man said, "but Oz is a land of magic. So, it seems that she has given you a special gift."

I looked at the backpack, not knowing what to expect from a backpack that grew on a tree. Inside the backpack I found a dress, a pair of shoes, a large apple, and a handkerchief. That apple looked really good and I was still hungry so I began to eat it. Nice and crunchy. I really need to eat more for breakfast.

The next tree was an oak.

"This tree was planted for Dorothy's uncle Henry," the Tin Man said.

I guess I was hoping for something unusual, since that seemed usual here, but nothing happened. I was disappointed. I guess sometimes in Oz, a tree is just a tree.

The last tree was a maple.

"And this tree was planted for Dorothy's Aunt Em," said the Tin Man.

I walked by and my shoulder brushed against a low branch and the branch began to sprout. As the sprout unfurled it grew into a pair of socks.

"Again, I don't recall Aunt Em ever doing any magic, but magic is a funny thing."

"What do you mean?" I asked.

"Oz is a land of magic. It's here, all over, in this place. You only need to want it to happen," he said.

"Do you mean all I need to do is wish I was home?"

"It's not quite that simple," he replied, "but it could be that simple for you. If you are a witch."

"But I don't want to be a witch."

"And that's not that simple either."

My coveralls were making me hot and my feet were cooking. I found privacy in some nearby bushes, and changed into my new dress, which fit perfectly (as if by magic, of course). Just to be clear, I put them on, I didn't change into a dress, shoes and socks. I have enough problems without changing into clothing. The dress needed a belt, so I put my tool belt back on. It was out of place, but it was all I had. I put on my new socks and shoes and stuffed everything else into the backpack.

"You're wearing Dorothy's favorites. She loved that style of dress and shoes and she often wore them."

We set out, strolling along, me munching on my apple and the Tin Man taking care of the talking. The shoes were nice and comfortable, much better for a long walk than my work shoes.

"I was once a man of flesh, a woodsman by trade, and my name was Nick Chopper. It was so long ago that few would know me by that name now. There was a girl I loved. But an evil witch put a curse on me and I

17

became a tin man. Now, everyone calls me the Tin Man. I don't think there are any others, so I guess I am one of a kind."

He spoke of some of the adventures he had with Dorothy, and his many other friends in Oz. I listened as I walked and ate.

"I am most proud of my heart. The Wizard gave it to me. It is the most caring heart in all of Oz. I may be tin, but I am more alive now than I ever was when I was flesh. Would you like to see it?"

"No," I said. "That's okay."

He looked a little disappointed but after a short pause he began again, continuing his stories of adventure and magic.

Oz is one strange place. Evil witches. Good witches. Flying couches. Living jack-o'-lanterns. Magnified bugs. When I had eaten all of the apple I could, I wrapped the rest in the handkerchief and returned it to the backpack. Too bad there hadn't been two apples.

We seemed to walk on forever. The day had passed and the sun settle low on the tree tops. The stories kept my attention but I was tired. The Tin Man must have noticed. "Let's find a place where we can sleep. You need a good night's rest because we have a long way to go." We walked on until we came to a bend in the path. As we rounded the bend I noticed a large tree off the side of the path. "Look over there. If we have to sleep outside, under that tree looks about as good as any spot we've seen." The tree looked very inviting.

The sun was setting and parts of the sky were lit in bright red and orange. We walked to the tree and as we got closer, we both started to yawn. We couldn't go much further. A breeze with a snap of cold gave me a chill.

When we got closer, I could see that under the branches of the tree were sleeping bags all laid out on the ground. The sleeping bags looked soft and warm. I crawled into one. With half closed eyes I noticed that the Tin Man was in a sleeping bag nearby. I said, "Good night Tin Man," fighting to keep my eyes open. The Tin Man made no reply, he had already fallen asleep, and in a few heartbeats, I gave up my fight and closed my eyes.

Chapter 3   The Sleeping Bag Tree

The floor was tipping side to side and the walls spun slowly. The small house had exposed rough cut wooden studs and unpainted wooden walls. On one of the walls was a framed needlepoint that said "Home Sweet Home." It swung side to side. The floor fell out from under my feet and then rushed up, smashing me against it. I climbed a simple ladder that was nailed to the wall, one hand holding a small black dog, the other fighting to hold on. At the top, I stepped off and went through a door that led to a small bedroom. The dog leaped out of my hand and began running around in circles, barking and growling. The room had only a bed and a bare desk with a chair, all which slid back and forth as the house tipped and spun. I slammed the door shut and looked out the window. We were flying. I couldn't see the ground. The wind blew and shrieked so loudly that even with my hands over my ears the sound was deafening. I jumped into the bed face down and held onto the bedframe to keep from being flung onto the floor. The dog jumped onto the bed and snuggled against my side.

I must have blacked out because the next thing I knew I was waking up to the little dog licking one of my ears. I stood and shook myself off. Bits of dirt and pieces of wood fell off me. The sun poured through large holes in the roof. The floor was tipped to one side, so I climbed the slope to get to the door to escape. I tried to open the door and I could hear things scraping. I forced the door open enough to peak out and see a tall pile of wood and debris blocking the way. I pulled the door closed.

The shutters on the window were barely on, hanging crooked. No glass remained in the window. I opened the shutters and one fell to the floor. I looked out and saw that the window was only a bit more than half my height above the ground. The bottom floor of the house had been flattened when the house landed, but the attic area, where my bedroom was, had saved me. I knocked the window frame out with a push and climbed out of the window. I stepped onto what had been the side of the lower half of the house, which now sloped from the floor level of the attic to just above the ground. The little dog jumped out of what had been the window and ran down to the ground, turned to look at me, and started barking. I climbed down to join him. I could hear people talking at the other side of the house. I went to see what was going on.

"A very powerful witch must have sent that house to kill her."

"Look at the silver slippers, the Wicked Witch of the East never took them off. And so she lived, and so she died."

When I got to them, everyone grew silent and took a few steps away from me. I took another step closer and they backed away again. One asked, "Is this your house?"

"Yes, it's my house," I said.

"Well then you killed her," he replied.

"I didn't mean to kill her, I'm sorry," I said.

"Meant or not meant, if that's your house, then you killed the Wicked Witch of the East."

"I promise, I didn't mean to. I, I couldn't help it. The cyclone did it, not me," I said.

Another person yelled, "She was as evil as can be and now we are free!"

Four official looking people came toward me, walking slowly and cautiously. All were shorter than me, though they were older. Two were men and two were women. One of the women was much older than the rest and dressed all in white. The others dressed all in blue. They all wore round hats that came to points on the top, with tiny bells hanging from the brims that tinkled as they walked.

That dream faded and without pause another began. I was mopping the floor in an old castle. The walls and floor were all made of stones set in mortar. On one side of the room there was an enormous lion, with its front and back legs bound together. He was hung on a horizontal pole so that his back hung high above the floor. In another corner sat the Tin Man sobbing, with his head in his hands, in a cage made of heavy metal bars. In another corner a man made of straw was in a prison of fire. He darted back and forth constantly to keep away from the fire, while trying to snuff out the sparks that hit him.

A woman dressed all in black, wearing a black pointed hat appeared. She said, "If you would only give me the silver slippers, I will set you and your friends free and you can be on your way. Those shoes were my sisters, and now they are mine, rightfully mine."

Just then the lion let out a roar of rage and shook furiously, trying to break his bindings. He fought until he was exhausted and then went limp and silent.

The woman said, "Perhaps you will be more reasonable after a few more days with no food. It looks like your friends are suffering. You can set them free, if you only cared for them. If you would only show your friends some compassion, you would give me the shoes, that are mine, mine, and then you could all go free. Doesn't their pain bother you?"

The lion once again erupted in a fit of roars and violent shaking, and then went quiet.

The woman stared at my shoes and then left.

I looked at my shoes thinking how easy it would be to give them to her. I moved my shoes left and right, seeing how the light reflected from them, so that sometimes they appeared to be a shade of radiant red and other times to be shining silver.

A monkey, who had large folded wings and wore a vest and a cap, walked up silently and placed a crystal ball on the table. He left without a word.

My attention drew me to the crystal ball and I gazed in. A fog filled the ball, but it soon dissipated to reveal that woman.

"Yes, I will set you free, you and your band of misfits. I will set you free of your miserable lives. I believe the lion's skin will make a nice door mat. And the Tin Man a nice set of tin cups. And the Scarecrow, he is not even fit to start a fire. And the girl, when I am done with the girl, she will beg to have an end like her foolish friends." Then the woman laughed a hideous laugh.

The crystal ball returned to fog. I turned my head away in disgust and rage. I was furious, so furious I could not think. My hands were shaking. The woman was lying, lying. Evil. I got so angry my whole body shook with rage.

I slowly mopped the floor, without thinking.

The woman returned.

"Get moving. There are many more floors for you to wash."

My anger was spitting spewing lava. It flowed down to my knees, to my feet. It flowed to my fingertips. Fire rose from my shoulders and my face flushed. I picked up the bucket of mop water and threw it in her face. She started to fume, sputter, and melt. She deserved it for all her lies and pain she caused. She deserved no pity and I gave her none. I watched in fury as she melted. I thought of how evil she had been, and how much she deserved to die. I stirred her remains about with the tip of one of the silver slippers. I watched as she fumed and melted to nothing. And then, then I was surprised at how much anger and hatred I felt. I took a deep breath and went to release my friends.

My dream faded away and a third began. In this one, I was myself. The girl from the other dreams was holding her little black dog, and trying to tell me something. She wore a dress just like the one I was given by Dorothy's memorial tree. She repeated what she said again and again, but I couldn't hear her. Or maybe I couldn't understand. She started talking louder, yelling at me. She was upset and she started waving her arms and shouting, but I still didn't get it. Finally, the little dog jumped from the girl's arms and bit me on the heel.

"Ouch," I yelled. It felt like I had actually been bitten. I bent to touch my heel, but the sleeping bag was tight around my body, like an unwanted hug I could not break free of. The bag had pulled me upright during my sleep, so that I was vertical. My head and face were totally covered. It was hard to move and difficult to breathe. I remembered my knife. Thankfully, I had been so tired when we reached the tree that I hadn't taken my tool belt off before getting into the sleeping bag. I pushed out hard with both knees, which gave me some space to move my arms. Now I could reach down and get my pocket knife. I pulled the blade open and slashed my way out of the sleeping bag.

"Damn it," I yelled. "What evil."

I looked at where the Tin Man had slept. His sleeping bag was hanging vertical, like mine had been. I ran to where he was trapped. I grabbed his sleeping bag and shook it roughly. "Wake up Tin Man, wake up." I took my knife and stabbed forward and pulled down. The blade hit his metal body.

"I'm so sorry. Are you all right?" I asked the Tin Man as I helped him free.

"I'm fine, though it looks like I had emergency surgery," he said as he looked at his lower torso. "It is good you were so well prepared and had that knife, or who knows what would have become of us."

The Tin Man turned to stare at another sleeping bag hanging on the tree. I saw the fear on his face and sprinted to the sleeping bag.

I shook the bag fiercely and yelled "wake up, wake up." Then I shouted, "I'm going to cut you free. Push your knees out so I have some room to stab my knife without cutting you." Whoever was inside moved so there was room to cut safely. This time I cut slowly. I cut a vertical slit into the sleeping bag. Then I stepped back, not knowing what to expect.

Feet first, a little boy slipped out of the bag. He was dressed like a jester. His coat had alternating stripes of the brightest yellows and blues, and reds and oranges. His hat had floppy points going here and there. As soon as he was free, he ran over and gave me a hug.

"Thanks for saving me," he said.

"You're blue, like blueberries," I said.

"And you're brown. Do you taste like chocolate?" he asked.

Normally, if someone would say something like this to me, I would have gotten angry and given them a piece of my mind, but I didn't have the time. Since when he had hugged me, the boy had done a flip off the tree and started drumming on the Tin Man's stomach. So I just said, "No."

"Have you checked recently? You shouldn't assume things you know," he said as he drummed on the Tin Man.

I started to raise my arms to object and, in an instant, the little boy cartwheeled over, grabbed my hands, and started dancing with me. He asked, "May I have this dance?" Then he spun me around a few times and cartwheeled back to the Tin Man.

"Hey Can Man." He ran around him and started drumming on him again.

"Oh, I'm getting called away. Call me when you need me," he said. There was a popping sound, like the sound you make when you hit your partially open mouth with your hand, and he was gone.

"Well," I said, "What was that?"

"No idea" said the Tin Man. "I've never met the boy, and as for the tree, it must have been planted for someone very evil, or had an evil enchantment placed on it. I hate to hurt any living thing, but I must make sure that no one ever again is trapped by this tree."

The Tin Man pulled a large axe from his sling and began to chop the tree down. He swung his axe fast and true, and in a short while the tree was lying on its side. He chopped off any sleeping bags that were growing on its branches just to be safe.

I gathered my backpack and we began to walk again. The Tin Man asked, "What woke you up? I am not sure I would have ever woken if it wasn't for you."

"I was having a dream of a white girl holding a small black dog. She was trying to tell me something that I wasn't understanding. And then the dog jumped down and bit me on my heel, near the top of one of the socks Aunt Em gave me. That woke me."

"That must have been Dorothy and her dog Toto," said the Tin Man.

"I had two dreams before that," I said. "In the first one, I was in a house flying through the air. It crashed on top of the Wicked Witch of the East, crushing her to death."

"That dream was about how Dorothy and Toto first came to Oz. They were carried here during a great cyclone. Dorothy got the silver slippers from that witch, and she later used them to return home."

"And in the middle dream I threw a bucket of water on a witch and melted her."

"In that dream you saw how Dorothy destroyed the Wicked Witch of the West," the Tin Man said.

"I saw an enormous lion, bound with ropes, and a straw man in a prison of fire, as well as you in a cell of iron bars."

"Yes, that is just as it was. We were all imprisoned. The witch so wanted the slippers she would have killed us all just to get them. But she knew that if the wearer was forced to give them up their magic would end, so she plotted and schemed to convince Dorothy to hand them over."

"Who are the lion and the straw man?"

"Those are my friends the Cowardly Lion and the Scarecrow. The Cowardly Lion is no more. He returned to his kingdom, the great forest, long ago. My friend the Scarecrow is missing. He could be on an adventure, or studying something somewhere, but I fear he is in danger. It is not unusual for him to be gone, but it is unusual for him to be gone so long with no word."

After a pause, the Tin Man returned to telling stories of high adventure. We walked along. Now I had a story too. But who would ever get to hear it? And who would ever believe me?

Chapter 4   Robotville

We hiked through the remainder of the morning and a good part of the afternoon until we came upon a high wall that crossed our path blocking our way forward. It looked like it went on forever in both directions. We walked along the wall until we saw a door. Over the door was a sign that said "Robotville."

"Have you ever been here before?" I asked the Tin Man.

"No. It looks like it would save us time if we could pass through though," he replied as he inspected the wall, trying to determine if there was a way around.

We knocked on the door. Immediately, a voice asked us to come in. Once we were inside, a metallic man locked and bolted the door behind us. In some ways he resembled the Tin Man, but he walked slow and jerky, unlike the smooth fluid movements of the Tin Man. He wore a name tag that read 'James005.'

"Only robots may enter Robotville," the robot said. "You must prove you are a robot by passing this test. It consists of a number of mathematic and logic questions. It is an accepted fact that only robots can answer these types of questions."

The Tin Man looked nervous, but I motioned to him to sit down and take the test. In school, this is where I shine. And how does he get off saying only robots can do math and logic? This should be a piece of cake.

James005 handed tests to us and said not to help each other. The first question was a box to be checked off that said: "I am a robot." I do not like to lie, but I wanted to get home fast, and preferably while I was still in one piece. The rest of the questions were basic math and logic problems which I answered with ease. I was done in a minute. I hoped the Tin Man was good at math and logic. I watched as he worked his way through the test. He was slow and methodical, carefully writing out each answer. I wondered if the Tin Man would finish in time.

Just as the Tin Man put his pencil down a bell chimed and the robot returned to retrieve the tests.

"What happens if we fail the test?" I asked.

"You sit in jail," replied James005

"For how long?"

"No one has ever been released from jail," he replied.

The Tin Man's knees started making a racket banging together.

James005 said, looking at the Tin Man, "Friend robot, you should have your vibration dampers inspected. They must be starting to fail."

He guided us down a hallway. When he came to a room on the left, he lifted a large chain of keys from his metal belt, selected an odd looking key, and opened the door. He took the tests over to the far side of the room, where papers were neatly stacked from the floor to just below the ceiling. He brought over a ladder, climbed to the top, and slipped the tests onto the nearest pile.

"When will our tests be graded?" I asked.

"The tests will be graded when enough are here for grading with optimum efficiency. Are you okay? It should be obvious that optimum efficiency is preferred.

Perhaps some of your gears and cams are damaged. You should get looked at. You both appear to need some maintenance. I know that many do not like to ask for help, but a fix in time saves nine, you know. Of course you do. Also, are you brushing your gear teeth at least once a day? Remember, only brush the gear teeth that you want to keep."

"Thank you, James005, for your efficient assistance," I said.

"You are welcome fellow robots. May you operate well and long."

We hurried to leave the testing building, relieved to escape.

"I hope we are very far away from Robotville when the tests are graded," the Tin Man said.

"Me too," I replied. The test was easy but still I wanted to be far away. As I was about to close the door I turned and saw that James005 was sitting motionless in a chair by the entrance.

We walked to the end of the lawn and looked out on the rest of Robotville. Robotville had four square blocks, with the four blocks arranged in a square. Each block was surrounded by a paved road. In the center, at the main and only intersection, was an enormous old fashioned traffic signal, with red, yellow, and green colored triangle shaped signal flags, though no cars drove on the road. The only thing on the roads were robots walking in long lines. As they passed each other in the intersection, they greeted each other, some bowing and some tipping their hats. Some robots walked alone, others walked in pairs, and still others pushed baby carriages. When the signal flags changed the robots traveling along one street stopped and the robots traveling on the cross street began walking and greeting each other. The lines of robots circled completely around each block. We watched as they repeated their mechanical dance. And if that wasn't strange enough, there were pieces of wood, lumber, placed at regular intervals across the streets, forcing the robots to step over, or stumble, or stop to lift a carriage. After a few cycles of the signal we moved on, since it seemed like they would go on and on and never stop. None of the robots on the street took notice of us.

Near the traffic signal at the main corner there was a tower with a large clock. I noticed the time. The clock hands had just reached 4:30. Immediately, all the robots stopped and stood like statues. The entire town became silent. Then a short stout man scurried over.

"I'm so glad that you came to help me. It is so hard to wind up all these robots each day. With all the winding, I don't have enough time to do my design work." He handed large winding keys to me and the Tin Man. "If we all work together, we can get them wound quickly. Then we can all have a good dinner. Does that sound okay?"

We nodded our agreement in silence. "Young lady, if you would please wind the robots on this block, and if your metallic friend would be so kind as to wind the robots on that block, we can quickly get them all wound for tomorrow." The man took a pause to look both me and the Tin Man up and down. "I have so many questions to ask you both. So few people come to visit me."

The winding went quickly, and, once we were done, the man ushered us into a large log cabin with three chimneys. Through the windows I could see that behind the cabin were fields and gardens.

32

"I must apologize," said the man. "I am not used to having guests. I haven't introduced myself. My name is Johan de Brohan. As you can see, I am a master designer of robots. The world's best, if I do say so. Though you," he nodded at the Tin Man, "are truly a work of art. How I would love to see how things work inside you, I really would. But I am being rude. It's not polite to ask someone you hardly know to let them take you apart. While I prepare dinner why don't you tell me your stories?"

The Tin Man gave Johan an abridged version of his story. Johan was disappointed when he learned that the Tin Man was magic, and not gears, cams, and springs.

I and the Tin Man took turns telling of our recent adventures as Johan chopped and sliced and cooked and boiled different things, but I couldn't tell exactly what they were. Some kind of vegetables but nothing I'd ever seen in the grocery store.

"All finished. Do you eat?" Johan asked the Tin Man.

"No," the Tin Man replied. "I don't, though I sometimes remember being hungry, and the taste of my favorite foods."

"Then it will be just you and I, young lady," Johan said. He took out a pair of bowls and served a bowl to me and to himself. The food had steam drifting off it and smelled good. I wondered what time it was at home. I was ready to eat. He also set out slices of dark brown bread with some butter. I was hungry.

After I ate the food, which was a vegetable stew, and some of the bread, which was so fresh it must have been baked that day, I wiped my mouth and pushed my chair back. "I hope you saved some room for dessert," Johan said as he took a melon out of a wooden box that somehow kept things cold. The melon was pink with blue circles on it. He handed a small slice to me and took one for himself before returning the rest to the refrigerator box.

"What type of melon is this?" I asked.

"It is one of my favorites, a bubble gum melon."

It looked like a very small slice, but when I took a bite, my mouth was filled with bubble gum, perhaps a bit more than I wanted. It was sweet and juicy with hints of watermelon and blueberry.

After a bit Johan started blowing large bubbles. He was an expert. He blew bubbles in different shapes, like someone who can twist balloons into animals.

Then Johan noticed it was getting late.

"Emily, perhaps you would like to bathe before bedtime. I can have your clothes washed while you bathe."

"That would be nice," I replied, since it had been a long road from when I first put on those clothes. Johan showed me to the bathroom and brought me a bathrobe and a towel.

"Before you start, I need to explain how the sink and the shower work. Do you know how to fly an airplane?" Johan asked me.

"No," I replied. I thought, "What does flying an airplane have to do with taking a shower?"

"Have you ever been in an airplane?"

"Yes. Once when my family went on vacation."

"That is so exciting," Johan said. "Where you come from must be truly magical. I have never seen an airplane. There are none in Oz. When I was very young, I met an old woman who talked constantly about airplanes. Those stories and her descriptions of airplanes were so exciting to me that I listened for hours and hours, even though people said that she was crazy. I was so interested in them that as a young man I spent much time unsuccessfully trying to build one. When I designed this house, I used some of the spare parts from my prototype airplanes. Just look. To increase the flow of the water from the faucet, pull up on the yoke, and to decrease the flow, push down on the yoke." He pointed to something a bit like the steering wheel of a car that was mounted above the sink. "To make the water hotter, roll left. To make it colder, roll right. When you are happy with it, let the yoke free. When you are done, push down on the yoke until the water stops completely. Remember, it doesn't control how the water is, but rather how the water is changing: faster, slower, hotter, and colder." He demonstrated, pulling back, pushing in, turning counter clockwise, and turning clockwise on the yoke. "If you roll left, the water will continue to get hotter until the water is steaming hot, and you could be hurt. If you roll right and hold, the water will continue to get colder until the pipes freeze. Please don't do that."

I nodded. I sort of got what he said. "Do I need to know anything special to use the toilet?"

"No, it works like a normal toilet," Johan replied. I was concerned about how a "normal" toilet worked in Oz. I also was concerned about how toilet paper worked in Oz, but I didn't want to find out the answer. I just hoped there was no surprises.

I was happy after I tried everything. I could operate the sink, shower, and toilet even though they were very strange.

A few minutes later I came out from the bathroom, my hair still a bit wet.

"You showered so fast I haven't had time to get your clothes clean," he said. Johan took my clothes, placed them into a wooden box, added a few leaves that he picked from a nearby houseplant, and turned a lever on the side a few times. The box jumped about and made quite a lot of noise and in a few seconds stopped.

He opened the box and took out my clothes. They were washed and dried and folded neatly. "Follow me," Johan said as he walked into one bedroom and laid my clothes down on the bed. "This will be your bedroom," he said to me. Pointing to another bedroom across the hall he said, "And Tin Man, that will be your bedroom."

"Oh, you will need a toothbrush too. But you are in luck, toothbrushes are in season, so you can have a perfectly fresh and ripe toothbrush. Let me just run out and pick one for you."

Johan was back in no time and handed what looked like a standard toothbrush to me.

I went back to the bathroom and ran a little water over the toothbrush. Some toothpaste appeared on the bristles. I started brushing my teeth like I do back home, but I found that the bristles of the toothbrush worked on their own, twisting and squirming between my teeth, and scrubbing the surfaces. I ran my tongue over my teeth and they felt as clean as they do right after they're cleaned by the dental hygienist.

I went back to my room. I didn't have any pajamas so I put the dress from Dorothy's tree on. When I got back I asked Johan, "I have a bit of other dirty laundry. Would you please wash my work coveralls?"

"Of course," he replied.

I took my work coveralls from my backpack. Johan put them into the laundry box with more leaves and turned the lever a few times. The box jumped around as before, but this time it seemed to huff and puff with strain. While it was working I asked, "Why are there pieces of wood across the streets? It seems to give the robots trouble."

"Yes, but I've had some difficulty with hooligans, and the wood keeps them away. Please don't let it bother you."

After a short while the washer stopped. Johan removed my coveralls and handed them to me.

"They were pretty dirty," Johan said. "But now they are as clean as new."

I looked at them. Johan was right! They were as clean as new though they were well worn. The ink smudge and the dried glue, which had never come out before, no matter what was done to them, were gone.

"Thank you, Johan," I said, returning my coveralls to my backpack. A yawn sneaked out.

Johan said, "I believe that it is time for bed."

The Tin Man walked me to my bedroom. "Good night Emily," he said as he shut the door. It wasn't until much later that I learned he stood watch over me all through the night.

I crawled into bed and pondered Oz. I thought of all the things I had to be thankful for in my life before Oz. I said a short prayer that I would see my family again, and soon. The blanket was warm and fluffy and in a short while, I fell into a sweet, cozy sleep.

Chapter 5   The Wall Without End

I rolled over in bed, rubbed my eyes, and then let out a scream. It was so loud that even I was surprised. The door swung open with a bang and the Tin Man burst into the room, looking left and right.

"Are you in danger?" the Tin Man asked.

"Sorry," I said, "it felt like I was back in my bedroom at home. I was scared through and through when I woke up and didn't recognize where I was. But I'm fine."

The Tin Man tested the window lock. "Locked," he said. "No one under the bed. No one in the bathroom. The closet is empty."

Johan appeared in the doorway and the Tin Man eyed him suspiciously. Johan said, "You're totally safe here, Emily. Now that we are all awake, why don't I prepare breakfast? Let's give you some privacy so you can get ready."

The Tin Man interrupted. "Have any of your things been moved?"

I looked around the room. "No, nothing has been moved."

The Tin Man looked over everything once again, under the bed, behind the furniture, and in every corner. After he was satisfied I was safe, he and Johan left the room.

Once I got out of bed I put my tool belt on again; it helped save my life once and I feared I would need all the help I could get in this strange and dangerous land.

I brushed my teeth with the odd new toothbrush Johan had given me. Then everything went into the backpack. I wanted to get to the Emerald City and on to home. I thought, "What would the Emerald City be like?"

In a short while we all gathered in the kitchen. Johan served me a nice breakfast, one fitting for a new day of adventures. At least I would start the day clean, fed and well rested.

It was already past 8 O'clock when we got outside, so the robots were all walking around, wishing each other good day, bowing, and tipping hats to each other.

Johan pointed to the traffic signal. "I had to make the traffic signal super large because the robots, for some reason, have a real problem seeing them. It's probably a design defect but I can't find the cause."

Something in the garden area caught my attention. It looked like a herd of horses was approaching.

"Oh no," Johan lamented. "Run for it."

Johan broke into a run and the Tin Man and I joined him. I ran to the traffic signal and climbed up on its base to see what was coming. They were rocking horses. With each rock back and forth they leaped forward. I looked closer. On each side, by the back of their rockers they had a wheel, and a big coil spring, and a few levers so that with each rock the spring was tightened and released pushing them forward. They couldn't cross the lumber, so they avoided it where possible. But some got stuck on the lumber and others got tipped over and struggled to right themselves. The robots joined the mayhem, leaving their normal path and running to and fro, sometimes running head on into each other. The horses chased them. The robots ran around erratically, and Johan and the Tin Man ran around with no more sense than the robots.

A few of the horses came to look at me. Seeing that I wasn't going to run they left and found someone else to chase.

After watching for some time I could see that the robots were slowing down. Some came to a halt and fell over. Johan was still running but he was panting hard. I climbed down. A few horses came at me but when I didn't run they went back to chasing Johan, the Tin Man and the robots that still moved. A rocking horse galloped by and I hopped on. We raced around the edge of the mayhem. The rocking horse didn't seem to mind me, it seemed to be happy I was riding it. I rode up beside Johan and yelled, "Stop! Stop your running!"

Johan stopped. He bent over with his hands on his knees trying to catch his breath. I rode over to the Tin Man and told him to stop running. He stopped running and walked beside me and my horse to Johan. Some of the horses came over too. From close up, I could see that some of their paint had peel offed, and they had mud and mold on parts of them. They didn't look like they were well taken care of.

Johan said, "I don't want these rocking horses here. See what mayhem and destruction they caused! Now all the robots are fully wound down, not like the daily use, but fully wound down. It will take a long time to wind them and set them upright again. And look at the mess in the lawns! Ruts, and holes all over."

A horse spoke up. "We just want to run on your road, but you blocked us with all this wood. We don't like living in the forest or in the grass lands. We can't run free there. We need a smooth paved road to run our best."

Johan said, "The streets belong to the robots. They need it for their walks."

"Couldn't the robots take a break?" I asked. "Maybe each afternoon they could let the horses use the road for a while."

"And what would they do then? Where would they go?"

The Tin Man said. "I bet with all that lumber I could build a bleacher so that the robots could watch the horses race."

"Oh yes," the horses rejoiced. "Make stands so they could watch us. We like that."

"And give out ribbons for fastest, and most colorful, and things like that."

"And for nicest, and most helpful."

Johan said, "If it brings peace I will agree. Let me make some sketches of the design of some bleachers." Johan returned to his house. The Tim Man and I spent the time standing up some rocking horses and winding some robots. Johan shortly returned with some drawings in his hand.

Johan and the Tin Man conferred over the sketches. When they agreed Johan gave the sketch to the Tin Man.

"Do you think you can build from this sketch?" Johan asked the Tin Man.

"Yes. I should be able to. If I find something I will mark it on the drawing," the Tin Man replied.

Johan left but quickly returned. He brought some other robots, including James005, and they gathered the lumber from the streets.

I started winding robots. Each robot was fully wound down, so it took far longer than yesterday. The rocking horses began to help wind the robots. It was clumsy looking, but by holding a winding key in their mouth they could do it. And two or three of the horses working together could set a robot back on its feet.

The Tin Man began building. Using a tape measure, a square and a pencil he marked the wood for cutting. Then he carefully sawed the lumber and placed the pieces into neat stacks. Then he began nailing the pieces together, stopping now and again to looked at the sketch, until he had assembled a section of the bleachers

Johan looked at it. "This is very fine. I have a few minor changes to the design that will make the remaining sections stronger and easier to build." He pointed to a piece of paper that was taped to a drawing board. The Tin Man looked closely at the drawing and nodded his approval.

A T-square and a triangle rested on the drawing board. It reminded me of the time my mother told me about how things where designed before there were computers. She had said that there would be long columns of drafting tables, perhaps twenty in each column, and many columns. Each designer had a drafting table and a book case built into the front of the drafting table behind them. This was how everything was designed, by hand, with paper and pencil. Even the first ships that took astronauts into space were designed on drafting tables. There may have been computers, but only enough to perform calculations for navigation. That reminded me, "I need to get home."

Johan said, "We need seven more sections so all the robots can have a proper seat. It looks like —"

I cut him off. "I need to get to the Emerald City so that I can meet with the Witches' Council and get back home. What is the quickest way from here to the Emerald City?"

"Don't you want to stay and build the bleachers? Don't you want to cheer on the rocking horses as they race?"

"That sounds like fun but my parents and friends don't know where I am. I need to get home."

"I see," Johan said. "That's fine. The Tin Man can help me."

"I go with Emily," the Tin Man said, putting his tools down. "You have plenty of help between your robots and the rocking horses. And there is no need for all the bleachers to be done in one day."

"Hmmph," Johan said. "You are both going to abandon me." Then he pointed toward the west. "The Emerald City is in that direction, but you can't possibly leave Robotville. The wall around Robotville goes on as far as the eye can see in both directions. It is too high to climb and topped by dangerous wire. Come and see."

Johan started to walk to the wall.

"Hold on a bit so I can get my backpack," I said as I ran off.

When I returned Johan led me and the Tin Man toward the far end of the town. When we finally got to the wall I leaned my head back far to see where the wall met the sky. Johan was right, the fence was very high, too smooth to climb, and there was barbed wire running along the top.

"I'm sorry," Johan said, "But there is no way to get to the Emerald City from here."

An idea popped into my head. The room where the robot tests were kept had piles of papers that reached the ceiling, yet there was no one else in Robotville but me, the Tin Man, Johan, and the robots Johan had designed and built, and now all the rocking horses. Lots of others had entered, so lots of others must had left, so there must be a way out.

I walked up to the wall. It really did seem to go on forever. I looked to the left, and to the right. At first, I felt overwhelmed with disappointment, but then I noticed something odd. What looked to be an enormous bird landed on part of the wall that was very far along on the right side. When it landed the wall shook.

"I'm going to take a closer look at the wall," I shouted as I started to run in the direction of the bird. I ran until I was breathing hard and then slowed down and stopped. It was tough running with the backpack on. I caught my breath while I looked at the wall again. The wall did not look quite as high as it had been when I started running. I gathered myself together and ran again.

I repeated my run, running until I was breathing hard, slowed, and stopped. Sure enough, the wall was lower here than where I had just been.

I thought, "This is just a trick, like in the dioramas at the Museum of Natural History. It's made to look large, even though it's small." I tried to yell back to the Tin Man, but I was already too far away for him to hear. I motioned with my arms but I could not catch his attention.

Running again brought me to where the wall was only up to my shoulder, and what had looked like barbed wire was now just lines painted on a board. After another run the wall was up to my waist. I ran again and the wall was only as high as my knees. I stepped over it.

On the other side of the wall was a large grassy field, dotted with some roaming animals, green bushes, and tall trees. I could hear birds singing in the distance. I watched as a flock flew off. I started to walk into the field hoping to be able to get a better look at the wall from this side.

Suddenly, the ground shook once, so hard I almost fell to my knees. There was silence. There was a pause, like everyone was waiting to see what came next.

I scanned the field. The ground began to rumble and shake again. Turning to the direction of the rumbling, I saw that the earth was churning up, forming a huge wave that was rushing toward me. The animals in the field began running to try to escape the oncoming wall of earth. Even more birds lifted off with shrieks of fear. A small herd of deer bounded off, speeding away from the oncoming wave. A group of maple trees were engulfed and disappeared. I heard bushes and trees snapping, breaking, and being crushed. I heard cries of small animals that had been caught by the oncoming wall of earth. I turned and ran.

The rumbling was louder, closer, but out of nowhere a wall of mist formed in front of me. From the mist came a faint crashing sound, barely audible over the cries of animals, breaking of trees, and rumbling of the earth. I turned to look back, but the wave of earth was almost upon me. I could not wait an instant longer. I turned back and sprinted toward the mist with all the strength I had in my heart.

As I entered the mist, the situation became clear. I was running toward the edge of a cliff that overlooked a great waterfall. I wanted to stop and think, but there was no time, no time to choose.

The sun and the mist painted a beautiful rainbow part way down the falls. I leapt out, over the edge, and over the rainbow. My eyes caught a brilliant glimmer of green that cut through the mist from far off in the distance, and I started to fall.

Chapter 6   Kaylahs

Moliere smiled to himself. He looked out from the ledge that he was on, half way up the cliff face, and admired the great falls. It was truly a magnificent natural beauty. On the other side of the falls were more cliffs, almost vertical, much as on his side, with ledges here and there where large boulders had fallen to the ground. How long had he been here? He had lost track of the days. And in all that time he saw not a single soul, none of his own kind, and no creature of any sort. "There must be a spell on this place," he thought since he had seen many animals and birds but none had ventured to visit him. "Not one soul," he mused in his loneliness. "This is what it is like to be truly alone."

He thought longingly of his family. Sadness welled up in him when he considered the future of his people. So much work to be done. And he could not help. It will fall heavily on others. He hoped they could bear its weight.

"Veeron had done well selecting this as my prison," Moliere said to himself, "perhaps too well. On one side unscalable walls, and on the other side, a cliff that would mean certain death to anyone unable to fly. And that is the point, isn't it? I can't fly. At one time this would have been a nice place to picnic, or perhaps to take a short nap, but now it was my prison. Yet, the fact that I can look out over the cliff and imagine myself flying, brings me a kind of pained solace. It reminds me that I am a broken person, and yet it allows me to imagine being whole."

Moliere looked out over the cliff, and then over the falls, once more. He heard the thunder of the water as it poured over and pounded on the rocks below. He caught a glimpse of the rainbow that flickered in and out of existence, as the sun sent bright light through the water droplets surrounding the falls. He was about to step back from the cliffs edge when he heard a deep rumbling sound, though he could not place where it was coming from. In an instant the rumbling grew loud enough to drown out the falls, and he could see that pieces of the cliff face across from where he was imprisoned were falling off and dropping to the ground. He heard some rocks falling nearby. "So be it," he thought. "If this is to be my end, so be it." But something on the other cliff face grabbed his attention. He watched closely. A young dust eater appeared. She ran off the edge of the cliff.

Moliere leaped off his ledge to fly to her, beating his wings, broken as they were, furiously. He fought to gain control of where he was going and of his speed but he was too fast, much too fast, to catch the girl. Despite his efforts he slammed into the girl with a great force. The wind was knocked out of him but he continued to fight as they hurdled toward the ground. He knew they would crash, so he pushed himself until every sinew of his body screamed at him. Still, he could not slow them down enough. Just above the ground, realizing that he had failed, he wrapped his wings around the girl. He slammed to the stones, and lost consciousness.

In time, Emily let out a deep moan and rolled herself over onto her hands and knees. She took a few deep breaths to clear her head, but it was spinning and her ears buzzed. The creature who had saved her was struggling to breathe. It reminded her of the winged monkey she had seen in her dream, the one who brought Dorothy a crystal ball, except this monkey had sharp shards of black glasslike rocks protruding through its chest, each edge glistening with a thin coating of blood. And its wings, which lay open on either side of him, ended in rough stubs, with discolored bone ends that jutted through the flesh. They looked awful. She wondered who this was, who would leap to their death to save someone they did not know.

Emily knelt beside Moliere and cried. He had given his life for her. Her tears flowed and her sobs rang out, though they were easily drowned out by the crash of the falls.

If you had been nearby, perhaps a sallymander or a stanleymander in the water beside them, or perhaps a humble bee flying among the ferns growing along the bank, or perhaps even a small brown mockingmonk looking down from a tree, taking a break from throwing acorns and nuts at passing targets, you would have seen something to make you pause. For each of Emily's tears found its way to one of Moliere's wounds, and each drop hissed and steamed when it landed.

Moliere groaned as Emily's tears dripped down on him. He spoke in a halting voice, "Thank you for your care, but you must leave now. When Veeron finds I have escaped my prison he will send his men to investigate and you will not be safe. You must flee now if you value your life."

Emily looked at him and said, "You saved me."

"Yes, you are alive, but not if you stay here. I will not live for much longer, even with your magic, so you must run. Please heed my advice and go. Go now."

"You flew," Emily said.

"If that was flying, then stones fly. Not too long ago I would have plucked two of you out of the air with no effort. But this is Veeron's solution to anyone who speaks out against him; cut off their wings, so that Flyers must be like the dust eaters. I mean, you who walk on the land."

"Why would anyone do such a horrible thing?"

"Veeron disbanded the parliament and moved to become dictator of all Flyers. Some of us tried to stop him. Since I was a judge and an outspoken leader, I was selected to be punished as an example. Not being able to fly is worse than death for my people." Moliere blinked slowly; his eyes watery. "I have many questions I would like to ask you, but since I will be gone soon, I can only hope you will listen to me and escape from here before one of Veeron's patrols comes and capture you."

"Your people are called Flyers?" Emily asked.

"Yes, many call us flying monkeys, but we call ourselves Flyers, because that is our gift. But please don't give a thought to me. You must leave," he said, his voice breaking.

"I will leave in a short while," Emily said. She listened to Moliere's strained breathing and watched his chest rise and fall with each breath, each breath which sent his body shaking in pain and painted grimaces on his face.

Moliere spoke in a soft and faltering voice, "If you take a deep breath you can smell the kaylahs, which are just ripe. If you are hungry, you can climb that tree," he said, pointing, "and will find some kaylahs that I am sure you will like."

Emily did not want to leave him, but she felt uncomfortable just sitting by as he suffered. She decided to climb the tree. She shimmied up the first section of the trunk, but then the climbing became easy since the branches were nicely spaced, like a ladder. She saw the kaylahs, which looked like large lime green bananas, and reached out to pluck one from the tree. She needed her hands free, so she held the kaylah in her mouth as she climbed down. Once she was back next to Moliere, she pealed the kaylah,

"Would you like a piece?" she asked as she took out her pocket knife.

"Yes, that would be nice," he replied, his sentence ending with a choking cough.

Emily put a slice in Moliere's mouth. She cut a slice for herself and had a taste. It was delicious, like a piece of key lime pie. She cut herself another larger piece and started to eat it. Then she looked to Moliere.

Moliere had passed. His eyes were closed and his chest was still. Emily folded his wings and picked him up as gently as possible. She was surprised at how small and light he was. She put his body down by the trunk of the kaylah tree and then she searched for a tool to help her dig a grave. Along the bank of the water she found a large clam shell. There was an empty spot not far from the Kaylah tree. The earth was sandy and easy to dig, and soon Moliere was laid into his resting place. After Emily covered his body with the sand from the grave, she found flat rocks and lay them over top. She remembered what the Tin Man had said about the customs here in Oz, and she took the apple core from her backpack and buried it by his head. Perhaps an apple tree might grow here in his honor.

She thought back to when her grandfather had died. She was very young and she hardly remembered him. He was the only one she knew who had died until now. She had never been so close to someone as they died, and she had never touched anyone who was dead. Moliere had given his life to save her, someone he didn't know. She felt lost and couldn't think.

She looked back at the falls and the cliffs. Climbing up was not possible. She had no idea what would come next, so she put her backpack on and climbed the kaylah tree to pick some for her next meal. From the branches of the kaylah tree she searched and thought. The air felt warm and moist. She saw the cliff that she had jumped from, the roaring falls, and the river that flowed on into the distance. She could not see the place she had buried Moliere, what lay ahead, or a path that would lead her back to the family she missed so dearly.

Emily was picking her fourth kaylah when she heard some voices below. She paused and listened carefully. Moliere had warned her not to stay, was her chance to escape gone? She could not make out everything that was said, but this is what she could understand.

"Who would bury that filth Moliere?" one said with a snarl in his voice.

"We should dig the bag of dirt's body up and drag him through the mud like the dust eater that he was," said another, his voice high-pitched and squeaky.

"It is abhorrent to defile a grave, even of someone you despise. How can you even think such a thing? It is against everything we believe," came a third voice.

"We could pay a dust eater to do it. They will do anything for gold," said one of them.

"You make me want to vomit," said the third voice again. "How can you even consider doing this?"

Emily felt a breeze and turned to see what had caused it. A Flyer was so close that she startled and lost her grip. The Flyer caught her from falling with one arm and covered her mouth with the other. He bent close and whispered into her ear, "Stay here until after we have all left. I will return before dark. Stay here and stay quiet." The Flyer took to the air so smoothly that the branch he was sitting on did not shake. He flew down below and landed near the other Flyers beside the kaylah tree.

"I have searched the trees," Emily heard him say below her. "Whoever was here must have been clever and walked off through the river, covering their tracks. We could follow the river, but without tracks we have no idea how long a head start they have or even if they went that way."

"Veeron will be very angry that he did not get to make Moliere a further example. I hope he is in a good mood when we return and I am glad I won't be the one who has to tell him."

The discussion continued in bits, but after a short time the Flyers flew off. Emily waited in her perch for what seemed a very long time, and her arms and legs ached from having to stay still yet hold on tightly. Emily realized the true danger she was in and despite the words of warning from the Flyer, she climbed down and decided not to wait at the kaylah tree. Now she wanted to flee and to be as far away from the kaylah tree as possible.

Emily headed off, keeping under the cover of a row of trees for as long as she could. She did not want to be seen by anyone from the air. She walked until she needed to rest and then sat down with her back to a large stone. Her best guess to the time was mid-afternoon. She was looking up at the sky when she saw one of the Flyers descending fast toward her. She could see that she would not be able to outrun the Flyer, so she sat and waited, watching the Flyer as it glided down.

As the Flyer landed Emily asked, "How did you find me?"

"The kaylahs," he said. "We can smell them at great distance. Which is why I advised you to stay in the kaylah trees. The smell is so overpowering to us that none of the Flyers could smell you. Normally, our sense of smell is very precise."

Emily nodded. She decided it would be a good fact for her to remember.

"Thank you for burying Moliere," the Flyer said.

"He saved my life. How could I leave him?"

"You might ask that, but others in these parts would never consider such kindness." The Flyer stared into Emily's eyes trying to understand her. "What can I do to say thank you?" he asked.

"I need to get to the Emerald City so that I can be sent back to my family. Can you help me?"

"I can carry you for some of the way, but I will need to return so that no one notices my absence. If you are ready, we can begin. My time is limited." The Flyer smiled. "I'm Archimedes, by the way."

"Nice to meet you Archimedes. Emily," she said as she extended her hand in greeting.

Archimedes took her hand and shook it. It was the first time in his life he shook the hand of a land walker.

Emily tugged her backpack on. Archimedes crouched down and Emily clung close on his back as he lifted off with strong flaps of his wings. Shortly they were high in the sky, and Emily could tell that Archimedes had begun to float on the air, rarely having to move his wings.

"What did Moliere tell you?" he asked.

"He said that Veeron had taken over and dissolved the parliament, that he was a judge, and that he had his wings cut off because he spoke out against Veeron."

"Yes, all true, but to call himself a judge is an understatement. As always, he was too modest. He was the Chief Justice of our Supreme Court. We looked to him to save us from a future of trouble. He was our last hope for a return to democracy through negotiation. There is great hardship and there will continue to be great hardship for my people. No peaceful resolution is in sight. So many suffer."

They continued to have periods of discussion broken by long silences. Emily looked down on the surrounding land, which was full of farm fields, and pastures, ponds and parks, dotted with houses, grain silos, and other buildings. They flew on until the light began to fade.

Archimedes' breathing ceased abruptly and they began to fall. Emily screamed as the tumbled down. She fought to keep hold of Archimedes as they spun and flipped. Just as abruptly, Archimedes regained his breath and brought them under control. Emily asked, "Are you okay?" Archimedes wheezed out a low gasped and they began to fall once again.

The ground was fast approaching. With only a short distance left before a collision with the earth, Emily rolled off of Archimedes' back to one side, hoping to avoid a hard crash on top of him.

She slammed into the ground and rolled a few feet. As soon as she was able to stop rolling, she sprinted back to Archimedes. He was gasping hard and pointing back toward the way that they had come. Emily picked him up and ran off. She ran as fast as she could, until sweat dripped into her eyes, and she ran on. While she was panting from exertion, she could hear that Archimedes' breathing had improved. He said in a weak voice, "Just a little further please."

In a short while he signaled to Emily that she could stop.

"There is some evil enchantment on that land," he said. "I don't know why, but you are unaffected. That's good, because I don't think I could have survived much longer. I could not breathe. Thank you."

"Of course," Emily said. "Are you okay now? I can carry you further away if you need me to."

"No," Archimedes said. "I am fine, but I had hoped to carry you closer to the Emerald City. You are still far from it, but you will need to continue on by yourself, as I cannot go further. Continue in the direction we were going. And since I cannot help you, I will leave here as soon as possible."

"Thank you for your help Archimedes," Emily said.

"I hope that those who watch over travelers protect you and keep you from harm," Archimedes said, as he lifted off. In a breath he was far away, rising swiftly into the sky.

Emily turned and began to hike on. After some time, the sun left the sky and the stars showed in a burst of glory. She did not remember them being so distinct and bright back home. She continued for a short distance until she came to a field of brush. Among the dried remnants of life were a few corn stalks.

"This must have been a field of corn," Emily said to herself, "but it must not have been planted this year since nothing is growing."

She decided to stop there for the night. She collected a pile of dried corn stalks and other brush and made herself a bed. It was getting chilly, so she put her coveralls on over her dress.

As she looked up at the stars, she tried to find the constellations she remembered. Her father had shown the constellations to her and her brother during a family camping vacation; the Big and Little Dipper, Orion with his belt, and Cassiopeia. She could not recognize any of the constellations that she could see that night. She could not find the North Star, or even guess why things looked so different.

She imagined being very tall, so tall that she could cross the entire earth in a few steps. The earth had a pole sticking through it and the earth rotated around this pole. The pole stretched on and on and at one end of the pole was the North Star. At the other end she imagined a South Star. If she stood in the northern hemisphere and looked north, she could see the North Star. If she walked to the southern hemisphere and looked south, she could see the South Star. Perhaps she was in the southern hemisphere, which would have different constellations from any she knew. Or perhaps she was someplace totally different. She imagined herself walking back to North Carolina, lying down, and falling asleep.

Emily lay down on her bed of cornstalks and took some kaylah out of her backpack for a snack. When she was done, she put her backpack under her head as a pillow, closed her eyes, and thought about seeing her family. Though her stomach was full, she still ached with longing to be home.

Chapter 7   Treed

"Wake up dear," my mom said in my dream. "Your alarm didn't go off and you need to get up for school."

"Wow, my dreams are getting pretty strange," I thought. "A tree that tries to kill you, a town full of robots, jumping off a cliff, and finally being saved by a flying monkey."

"Wake up, wake up, please. You need to get up."

I rolled over in the direction of the voice, still mostly asleep. I felt something brushing against my face, I propped myself up on my elbows and opened my eyes with a yawn.

"Tiny pigs," I blurted. "I'm surrounded by tiny pigs." It looked like there were about fifty pigs, each the size of a plump squirrel, all looking at me.

"Well yes, we are indeed tiny pigs, however inelegantly you have put it. You need to get up because we need your help."

I stood up and pulled some twigs out of my hair. Seeing that I was quite far above the tiny pigs, I sat back down cross legged so I could be closer to their height.

"We need your help as we are not good at climbing trees. Some bad birds have tossed our friend the Scarecrow into a tree and, well, we need your help getting him down," said the lead tiny pig who wore a dainty crown upon her head. She spoke with a distinct British accent and sounded like someone impersonating the Queen of England.

"Which tree?" I asked with a yawn.

"The third tree in that line over there," the Queen pig said, as she motioned toward the far side of the field.

Just then a flock of black birds flew in low, causing the pigs to scatter. The birds circled, some flying just above my head.

I walked toward the tree. I saw some cloth hanging from a branch and figured that must be the Scarecrow. He was not very high in the tree, so I just started climbing. When I got to the first solid branch, a bird flew in and landed right near me.

"Na-na-na pooh-pooh, I'm not scared of you-ou," the birds squawked.

"Na-na-na pooh-pooh, I'm not scared of you-ou," the birds squawked at me again. Staring at the bird, my head began to pound. Was this real? Was I awake? My vision tunneled so that all I could see was his shiny beak and black eyes. I felt a pop in my ears and I grabbed him in my hand.

I said in a slow voice, "If you ever bother the tiny pigs, or the Scarecrow again, I will turn half of you into worms so that every time you eat you have to wonder if you are eating your brothers and sisters." I opened my hand. The bird sat on my hand with its beak buried against its breast and its eyes closed, motionless and totally silent. A moment later the bird said in a low voice, "I understand," and flew off. There was some noise among the birds in the trees and then they all took off. I watched as they circled the field, squawking and chirping, as more birds joined them. They left in the direction of the sun.

After I was a few branches higher the Scarecrow was in reach and I carefully started taking him down from the tree. He didn't have much stuffing left in him, but he was able to speak. "Well, you can be scary," he said.

I climbed down with the Scarecrow hanging over my shoulder. I guess I can be scary. I wonder where that came from. I was as surprised as the bird to see him in my hand, but when it was happening, it seemed like I had all the time in the world. It seemed like I could have grabbed the bird five times before the bird moved.

I lay the Scarecrow out on a flat spot and the tiny pigs started collecting straw and corn leaves from the field and stuffing it into the Scarecrow here and there.

"You're the Scarecrow, the straw man I saw in my dream," I said. "I had a dream where there was a large lion, the Cowardly Lion, tied up in ropes, the Tin Man in a metal cage, and a straw man in a cage of fire. You're that straw man. And Dorothy threw her mop water at a witch and melted her."

"You dreamed of when Dorothy melted the Wicked Witch of the West," the Scarecrow said. "Your dream is very detailed. I am not sure how you could know these things without having been there."

"My clothes and shoes were gifts from Dorothy's and Aunt Em's memorial trees."

"That must explain it. They wanted you to know what happened, but I'm not sure why." He stood up and offered me his hand while saying, "Thank you so much for your help. What should we call you?"

"I'm Emily," I said, "but I need to get home. The Tin Man said that I need to go to the Emerald City and get help from the Witches' Council."

"That is an interesting coincidence," said the Scarecrow as he massaged his head so it was a bit less bulging. "Or is it a co-interesting incident?" he said as he put his hand to his chin in thought. "I am on my way to the Emerald City myself. I have some business I must attend to there."

The Scarecrow got down onto his stomach so that he could speak directly to the Queen pig. "Queen Minerva, my old friend, thank you again and again. May your reign continue forever in peace."

"Always at your service." The Queen curtseyed as she walked closer to the Scarecrow and whispered into his ear. As she stepped back, she added, "Now that I know you are safe, we must leave. There are concerns in other places that must be addressed." With that the tiny pigs all vanished.

"Where did they go?" I asked. "Are they magic?"

"Queen Minerva did not tell me her destination so I have no idea, for question one, and no, they are not magic," replied the Scarecrow. "While it looked like they vanished into the air, they just move extremely fast, faster than you expect, and they travel by tiny tunnels that crisscross Oz and other lands as well." The Scarecrow paused and looked at me. "I'm afraid my friends woke you abruptly. I apologize."

"It's okay," I said. "If that's the worst thing that happens to me today, I will be happy. I have met the Tin Man, and I know you are the Scarecrow. What can you tell me about the Cowardly Lion?"

"It's a shame that you will not get to meet him," the Scarecrow said. "He has long since passed away. But I am friends with his descendants, who rule the jungle."

"Was he really cowardly?" I asked.

"Oh, dear me no," the Scarecrow replied. "He was the bravest creature I have ever known, though even the bravest sometimes have fear. At first I think being called the Cowardly Lion bothered him, but he grew to be proud of it. He took it as a challenge to be courageous."

"I was also helped by a Flyer," I said. "He helped bring me here, but he was stopped by an enchantment placed upon this land."

"The Wicked Witch of the West enslaved the Flyers, and Dorothy freed them," the Scarecrow said.

"The Flyers don't particularly like us, do they?" I asked. "They sometimes call us dust eaters."

"No, they don't," the Scarecrow said. "They were fine until the witch enslaved them. The witch treated them with extreme cruelty. And they knew that she had come from one of the towns in the land of the Quadlings, which is part of Oz."

"Their problems haven't ended," I said.

"No, they have not," the Scarecrow said solemnly. He paused. "A lot has happened to the Flyers since they were freed from the slavery of the Wicked Witch of the West. Not all of it was good."

Then the Scarecrow said, "We are going for a long walk. You may want to take some time to get ready."

I looked down at my outfit. I had my coveralls on over my dress and they were crusted with dirt and mud. My hands were filthy. I pulled out some bits of corn stalk and leaves from my hair. My stomach finished my thoughts with a growl.

"Got it," I said.

I began to attend to myself, wiping my hands off on some nearby grass. I bent over and shook my head trying to shake out the last bits of debris. I ate the last kaylah while I thought of Moliere. I was as ready as I was going to be. I stowed my coveralls and everything else in my backpack.

"Ready," I said. "The quicker I get to the Emerald City, the quicker I see my parents."

The sky was overcast but the breeze was pleasantly warm. The path was covered in spongy green moss, providing a cushion for my feet. And though the route had some gradual hills and dips, the walk was very pleasant. Things felt right, and safe, and I was excited about the new adventures that the rest of the day would hold.

We walked on, the Scarecrow guiding the way and pointing out things of interest, like kinds of bushes, or a bit of unusual moss, or a bright blue fungus growing on a tree. He seemed to know everything about everything. At times he was so involved in talking that he stumbled and fell. It didn't bother him in the least and, besides the short interruptions, he continued happily.

I got to talking. I spoke about my time in Oz, with the Scarecrow mostly rubbing his chin and saying "hmmm." When I would ask a question about Oz, he answered in detail.

"Exactly how far is it to the Emerald City?" I asked.

"I can't tell you exactly," replied the Scarecrow.

"But you know how to get there?"

"Yes, generally," he said.

"Do we need a map?"

"It wouldn't really help. We had a mapping project once, and in a way, it was a success. We always suspected, but had no proof, that things move around in Oz. The general relationships between things stay the same, but all the fine details change. Like this path, which winds and bends. When it was first made it probably was perfectly straight."

"Well," I replied, "I guess I shouldn't be too surprised considering all the strange things that have happened to me in Oz."

"Do you mean things don't move where you live? Strange indeed. Well, it does make it interesting laying out a garden," the Scarecrow said. "If you put in some stakes and lines you need to make sure you do your planning pretty soon. Wait too long and some of the strings will be slack while others will be broken from stretching. On the other hand, sometimes it works out nicely. The yellow brick road that leads to the Emerald City, for example. When it was first built it was straight. Now it meanders here and there, full of bends and spirals."

I was getting tuckered out and the Scarecrow notice I was falling behind. He seemed to be able to walk forever. And I was getting hungry. The Scarecrow smiled when we turned a bend in the path and came to a neat cottage set back from the road. A small sign said S. Stronnie, Flower Arrangements. The path to the door curved here and there, and the small gardens along the way looked like they hadn't been tended for some time, with disorderly brown stalks, lonely flowers, and sprawling weeds.

"Please wait here while I see if we can find you some food," he said as he careened down the path to the cottage door. The Scarecrow could run quite fast, even though he sometimes stumbled and cartwheeled.

A tall thin woman came to the door. "What brings the great and renowned Scarecrow to my little cottage?" she asked.

"We are a pair of weary travelers looking for some food and some rest." He winked at the woman, who seem to understand his signal, though it only made me wonder what it meant.

"I was just about to sit down for lunch. Please come in and give me some company," she said with a warm smile.

"Emily, come, this fine woman has invited us for lunch."

He waved me forward and when I arrived by the door, the Scarecrow asked the woman her name.

"My friends call me Suki," she said.

In short order we were all seated around a thick wooden table and some sandwiches were served. When the sandwiches were done, Suki opened the oven and took out some muffins. "You picked a good time to drop in," she said. "Toffelberry muffins for dessert." She took the muffins out of the tin and put one in front of me and one where she had been sitting.

"Thank you," I said. The muffin was very nice, though it had a flavor that I can't really describe. Not like anything I had ever eaten, but it tasted good.

The room was nicely decorated with paintings, mostly of gardens, and some cute nick knacks, but there were no flowers. I felt a little shy, but I couldn't stop myself. "Your sign says flower arrangements, but I don't see any flowers."

"Yes, it has been awhile since I did a new arrangement here," she said. "Isn't that the way it goes, flower arrangements for others but none for myself. My work requires a lot of travel, so my little place sometimes gets neglected. Let's go outside and I will see what I can do."

Suki stepped outside in front of one of the gardens. She took out two sticks and began waving them about, the way orchestra conductors do. "Crocuses, I can't see you. More color please, thank you. And you white Irises, please pull yourselves closer together and stand taller. Tulips, tulips, your color is just a bit off. Please try to harmonize. Harmony please, not dissonance. Thank you."

As Suki motioned and gave directions, the flowers grew, bloomed, and moved themselves. She stepped back and gazed across all of her gardens. Then she began to walk, conducting as she went, and flowers appeared and arranged themselves, in the path to her cottage door and in all the gardens along the way. A tree just to the left of her lowered small blossoms from its bottom branches. Pink, yellow, green, and blue pastel petals grew out radially from the center. Once they stopped growing, patterns of black lines appeared across their surface. Next the petals grouped together in pairs, and then began to fall to the ground. After a few seconds they fluttered into flight, becoming a swarm of beautiful butterflies that flew among the flowers, though some landed on my shoulders and on my ears and head. They tickled my ears. They did the same with the Scarecrow and Suki.

The clouds separated and the sun shone brightly down. The colors were vibrant, rich flaming reds and brilliant blues. Colors that should not normally go together seemed to be just what was needed. I couldn't help notice that a number of small animals popped up to view the gardens. They all smiled in appreciation. Suki continued to conduct, and in a few minutes the flower bed was a grand panorama of hues covering the entire spectrum, all part of a single grand concert of color. It was breathtaking.

"Wow!" I said. "So beautiful. But in our garden, the flowers bloom at different times."

Suki replied, "Perhaps you do not ask them nicely enough. They can be very sensitive, very sensitive indeed. It takes a long time to fully gain their trust, and without trust you can't collaborate well."

"These flowers are so beautiful," I repeated in awe. "And the butterflies are amazing."

Suki said, "Thank you, Emily. I studied with one of Oz's greatest teachers, who arranged many of the flower gardens in the Emerald City. Most of my gardens are patiently planned, but in my home gardens I prefer to improvise. I think it gives it a more natural and inviting look, one that ask people to rest and be at peace."

Though I had never seen anything like Suki's garden, the mention of the Emerald City reminded me of why I was here. I straightened myself up. The Scarecrow must have seen how anxious I was to leave so he flattened his shirt and gave his head a push here and there. He cleared his voice, which sounded a bit husky, perhaps from all the corn stalks, and said "Suki, thank you for your hospitality. I think we need to be getting on our way."

"Emily, Scarecrow, please visit me again the next time you pass this way," Suki said.

I gave her a hug. She's a strong hugger. Suki gave the Scarecrow a hug and nearly flattened him. The few butterflies that had remained on me and the Scarecrow flew off. I watched as they fluttered to the ground.

We started once again on the way, refreshed and inspired by the beauty of Suki's flowers. Not to mention good food and toffelberry muffins.

We walked along the path for some time and then I heard a small voice in my left ear. "Emily, if you would sit for a while on that large stone ahead to the left, I would appreciate it."

I put my hand by my left ear and one of the butterflies from Suki's garden jumped to my finger. The Scarecrow watched in silence.

"Thank you so much for letting me hitch a ride on you Emily. I am so far from my tree. And I have seen so many things. What a grand adventure for a tree butterfly," the creature said, "but I am afraid I don't have much more time."

"What do you mean, don't have much time?" I asked.

"We tree butterflies don't live very long. But it was such a thrill accompanying you on your walk."

"Do you mean you are going to die? It seems all that happens in Oz is that people die."

"Yes, that's what I mean. But that is not all that happens in Oz. Please don't be sad."

I couldn't help it. Moliere and now this butterfly. I began to cry.

"My life is at its completion," said the butterfly, "and I would rather you be happy then sad."

"Okay, I'll try," I said, sniffling but trying to control my sadness.

"Let me taste one of your tears so I can see your future."

I took a tear on my fingertip and brought it to the butterfly who took a tiny taste.

"What will happen in my future? Will I get home?" I asked.

"Never trust anyone who tells you details about your future," the butterfly said. "Only people with bad intentions would ever tell someone specifics about their personal future."

"But what can you tell me?"

"You will live a long life, full of adventure," the butterfly responded. "You have much to do in Oz."

"Why am I in Oz?" I asked.

"You were called here," the butterfly said in a wavering voice, and that was the last words it spoke.

I watched as the butterfly's wings began to fragment and blow away in the light breeze. After a few puffs only a shell of its body was left, and in a few more that too was carried away, leaving my hand empty.

Chapter 8   New York, New York

I stared at my hand in silence.

The Scarecrow said in a low voice, "We should continue, we can mourn the loss of our new friend on the way. We need to walk so that we can find a safe place to spend the night."

"Okay," I said softly.

We walked along a footpath, passing farm houses and cottages. The buildings were getting closer together and the path was getting wider and easier to walk on. We walked until I heard something in the distance. I stopped to listen.

"Scarecrow, do we need to run?" The sound was getting louder. I could see a cloud of dust rising from the ground in the distance.

"No," the Scarecrow said, "these are friends."

We watched as a herd of horses, real horses, not rocking horses, galloped toward us, the riders making whoops, shouts, and yells. Each horse carried a large oat O, like the cereal but much larger. These oat O riders perched atop the horses and, even though they had no arms or legs, or heads or faces for that matter, they rode confidently. Some perched on their horse's back, some on their horse's head, some moved back and forth between the two, and some jumped around atop their horse, but all were wearing large cowboy hats.

The troop rushed to a halt. The leader leaped from his horse and bowed in front of the Scarecrow, waving his hat with a big flourish.

"My liege," he said.

"My friend," replied the Scarecrow, as he bowed down in return. He bowed so low that he lost his balance, teetered on the brink of falling, and then fell over. His face hit the ground but he was unbothered. He raised himself and stood up, brushing his face off.

"I am here to report that all is quiet in Munchkinland. The Riddle Writers Association send their regards and this riddle. What stands upon four columns, seats three to the left and three to the right, and has been empty far too long. Additionally, the Hopscotch University requests that you speak at their next graduation ceremony. And the Shore Line Institute would like you to review their recent research concerning why the shore loves the coastline so much that it constantly hugs it."

"Thank you," the Scarecrow said in an official sounding tone. "Your report is accepted."

The leader of the riders jumped back onto his horse, waved his hat above his head, and with a whooping yell, all the horsemen galloped off in another direction.

"What, or who, was that?" I asked.

"Those are the Oat *O*'s Errant, protectors of all of Oz"

"The riders look like super-sized versions of the cereal I eat."

"These are one and the same with those that you eat. You probably have spilled your cereal before. Some of the *O*'s that are spilled are picked up, and some are not. Of those left on the table or floor, only the bravest and most resourceful make it to Oz where they grow to their full size and potential."

I had to think about that. Did that mean I should be more careful when I poured my cereal, or less careful, and so help more oat O's gain their freedom?

As if reading my mind the Scarecrow said, "You do not need to change. Whether they make their way to freedom is a matter of bravery, as well as magic."

"What about the horses? How did those cereal O's get horses?"

"They are wonderful together, are they not? The horses love the adventure and the Oat O's Errant are very light loads for them. The oat O's also take great care of the horses. If you were an oat O, you would not want to have your horse be too hungry, you see."

"Yes, that makes sense," I replied. "And what about the riddle?"

"So easy. I prefer it when the Riddle Writers work harder and make it tougher. My throne, of course," said the Scarecrow.

"Your throne?"

"My throne sits upon four legs, and there are three chairs to the left and three chairs to the right of it. And I have been away for some time. Whether my throne has been empty for too long is a matter of opinion however."

We walked for some time in silence. The land was covered in rolling hills and the houses were even closer together than before, and closer to the path. The path had widened so that now it was more a road than a path, and a number of people could walk side by side, and they did, talking to each other and saying hello to us. Everyone seemed to know the Scarecrow.

As we rounded a bend in the road, there was a sign which said, "To New York."

"Are we close to New York?" I asked. I had never been to New York, but I knew it was a large city in the north.

"We are indeed close to New York," said the Scarecrow. After just a short walk we were standing before an expanse of tall buildings. I spotted a statue of a girl with long pigtails. She held one of her hands on her hip and stretched the other in front of her defiantly, holding a large red knit sock. The girl was staring sternly at a statue of a large rabbit who stood upright, towering over her. He wore a bowler on his head and a plaid vest around his furry shoulders, and he carried a shiny silver cane. I walked over so I could take a closer look.

Just then a group of people rushed by. One of them shouted over their shoulder, "Trading has started. You do not want to visit New York without seeing the trading."

We joined the group and followed it to a tall building, which had a large sign that read "New York Sock Exchange."

The group headed into the building, so we did as well. Someone nearby said, "You should have seen the trading floor back in the old days, before it went online."

Above us there were balconies on all the upper floors. Clothes lines were strung from one balcony to another, and socks were coming in on lines through the windows from all directions. They were being taken off the clothes lines, circulated around, put into pairs, and sent back out again. Cats were working at each line, and sometimes a cat would leap from floor to floor to make a sock trade. Mostly it went smoothly, but some cats were napping, so their lines were inactive. And then there was some snarls and a cat fight erupted.

Closer to where we stood, a few old timers on the trading floor carried briefcases full of socks that they held up, yelling to grab the attention of other traders.

It was way too noisy for me so I tapped the Scarecrow on the shoulder and pointed to the exit. Outside it was much quieter, and we sat down on a bench.

"The sock exchange?" I asked.

"What did you think happens to all those lost socks?" the Scarecrow replied with a smile. "They make their way to Oz where they hope to be reunited with their mates."

I couldn't help but smile. It was odd, but then in Oz odd was normal, so it all made sense.

The Scarecrow added, "There was an experiment with going wireless, replacing the clothes lines with pigeons, but then some of the pigeons that transported the socks went missing under suspicious circumstances. After that the program was cancelled. Apparently, some of the cat sock traders confused the pigeons with the meal delivery service."

I looked up at the Sock Exchange building. There was clotheslines going from each of its windows to the nearby buildings. And each of the nearby buildings had a network of clotheslines that spread to a cluster of buildings further away.

We walked to a large park and sat down on an empty bench that was by a large lake. Boats, rowed by many different types of people, skimmed fast upon the water.

Some went so fast that they seemed to fly on the water, and some actually did fly above the water.

In a field on the far side of the lake there were children flying kites. The kites were bright and colorful and flew high in the sky. Once, during a trip, my family had gone to a field so I and my younger brother could fly kites. How long ago and how far away that all seemed now. And yet, the children, who looked so different from anyone I had ever seen, ran and played the same as we did, and they laughed while flying their kites the same as we did.

The sun was high in the sky and I felt its warmth. I was lost in thought for a bit, but I was brought back when a ball rolled to my feet. I gave it a nice kick, sending it back to a group of children that had been playing a game that looked like soccer. The ball sailed over some of their heads into the center of the field.

"Please come and play football with us," the children shouted. "We need another player to make proper teams." I joined the children in play, and the Scarecrow watched from the park bench.

One of the players gave me a blue vest to put on so I would know what team I was on. "You're a striker," he said. "We're short a striker, so you're a striker."

What was confusing was that there were children with blue, and with yellow, and with green vests playing, so there were three teams on the field, not two. And the field had three goals, one for each of the teams. And you could score points in two places, but also two teams were trying to score in your goal. Maybe it wasn't as much like soccer as I thought.

Each team had a goalie who tried to prevent other teams from scoring goals. There were three defenders, who helped the goalie, and two strikers, who tried to score goals for the team. The field, called a pitch, was circular and had a diameter about three-fourths the length of a soccer field. In the center was a circle of about half the diameter of the pitch where no defenders could go, only strikers. The defenders and the goalie where restricted to an arc-shaped area in front of their goal, which was slightly smaller than the goals used in soccer.

I'm pretty fast, but I soon figured out I would have to play harder and run faster than I had ever played to keep up with what was going on. The game was one-part super-fast soccer and one-part Ozian chaos, with the ball moving across and around the pitch in a blink of an eye. It was wonderful!

The game moved like lightning and there were no time outs. I noticed that things got more physical. People seemed to bend the rules. Then the whistle blew and the referee called out, "Halftime."

I jogged over to my team's bench and got something to drink. "What's with all the pushing and shoving?" I asked.

"There are no penalty kicks after the time is over at halftime and at the game end. Kids take advantage of it by breaking the rules right before," someone replied. It seemed like too short a break but the whistle blew and the referee called, "Second Half." I barely had time to finish my drink.

We took the field and the play resumed. Time flew by as I raced all over, in front of one opposing team's net, to the other opposing team's net, back to mid field bringing the ball forward. I was at the left corner of one team's net when I noticed a yellow player obviously interfering with the goalie. "So much for sportsmanship," I thought. Another yellow player was taking her time setting up her shot on the empty net. She kicked. I intercepted and curved the ball to our other striker who was in the yellow zone. I dashed to the yellow net and our striker passed the ball to me. It was wild. I jumped and headed it cross net back to him and he kneed it in. I leaped into the air.

I noticed that the oaf that had been interfering with the goalie was now running at me at full speed. Thankfully, what the oaf had in size he lost in agility. I went from my leap to a tight ball and he flew over me. As he passed I pushed up hard and he went flying heels over-head, landing on his back with a thud. The whistle blew ending the game and I skedaddled to the Scarecrow.

"That was something," I said.

"Yes, it was," the Scarecrow replied. A bunch of players came over.

"We always get pizza after games. Please come with us."

"May I have pizza with my friends?" I asked the Scarecrow.

"Of course," he smile back.

I hustled to join my new friends. We walked together and turned right onto a side street. When we could see the pizzeria, the line was crazy long, reaching outside the door and part way down the block. One of our group said, "We're never going to get served, and my parents expect me home on time." We were all disappointed and some started to say their goodbyes. But the Scarecrow, who must have been following along, walked past us and into the pizzeria. A moment later a group of workers came out and started setting up a special table for us.

"You are friends with the Scarecrow!" a boy whose name I had learned was Tunny, said in surprise.

"Yes, I met him earlier today."

"Wow, that's 'mazing," Tunny said.

Pizzas floated into the room over the heads of people seated at the other tables, who paid no attention to the flying food. They landed on the table, followed close behind by plates, utensils, glasses, and drinks. We had a great time, laughing and joking, and telling stories about what happened in the game. Someone told the story of the oaf that tried to smear me but who got flattened himself. There was a great story about a point that was headed three times and then sent to the net by bouncing off the back of an opposing team player. And the pizza was delicious, really delicious. I have to remember that New York has great pizza. At least the New York in Oz.

In time, the families of my new friends arrived at the restaurant, and the children said their goodbyes.

"I need to go," Tunny said to me. "Please come and join our game again. You are a really good player, though your tactics are a bit unusual."

"If I am by this way again I will." I waved as he left. I thought, "How could I explain? It would be nice to visit, but I hope I never do."

Soon all the children were gone; it was just me and the Scarecrow.

"It seems that everyone knows who you are," I said. "You seem to get reports on things far and wide. And I remember someone calling you 'my liege'. And what about the riddle about your throne. Is there something I should know?"

"Well, I am the regent, the acting king, of the land of Oz." the Scarecrow said.

"That's all? Just the king?"

"Yes. I really didn't qualify to be wizard, so when the Wizard left and Ozma went missing so long ago, the people asked me to be their leader."

"Should I call you 'Your Majesty'?"

"No, just Scarecrow is fine. If you must, the Scarecrow. I really try to avoid all the pageantry of being king. I might stay in the Emerald City more if it wasn't for all the attention I am given. Sometimes I like to sneak away and stand quietly in a corn field, in a place that no one knows me, and just think."

I stood up and took the Scarecrow's hand. "Perhaps we should be on our way, back to your city, and closer to my getting home."

The Scarecrow looked around, sniffing the air.

"I have found that while I get musty when I am exposed to dampness, meat people get a bit musty after periods of hard exercise, such as a game," he said.

"Are you telling me I smell?"

The Scarecrow grasped his chin and thought for a few beats. Then he said, "Yes, I believe I am."

I gave him a gentle push. "Then we better find me a place to wash up. There should be someplace in this big city where I can do that."

We walked a few blocks, the Scarecrow leading the way. We turned on a broad street that was lined with elegant hotels. As we passed the doormen and doorwomen noticed the Scarecrow and entreated us to stay at their hotels. "Our Royalty Suite is ready for your use sire," I heard one plead. "We'd be honored if you would stay with us your majesty," yelled another.

After passing a few hotels the Scarecrow must have been satisfied and we walked toward the entrance of a particularly grand one. "This will do."

We walked into a beautiful entry room decorated in natural woods, with rich carpets upon the floor and dazzling chandeliers hanging from high ceiling. In the center of the main room stood a grand piano. A short woman, dressed in a multicolored gown, played slow jazz.

"The Monarch's Suite?" asked the concierge, who had rushed to us as we entered.

"Yes, thank you," replied the Scarecrow.

The concierge guided us to a hidden elevator that brought us directly to the Monarch's Suite. The suite covered the entire floor of the hotel, and included six enormous bedrooms, each of which had an attached large and elegant bath. My whole family could easily have stayed in any one of the bedrooms and the baths were each more than twice as large as my bedroom at home. I took a few minutes to explore. I never saw anything like this. Each bedroom was overwhelming.

"Which one will you take and which one should I take?"

"I don't require a bedroom so I won't take one. Please pick anyone you would like," the Scarecrow said.

I picked the first one for mine. I walked through the bedroom and into its bathroom. When I closed the door I saw that hanging on the door back was a thick white bathrobe. I put my dirty laundry on the bed. I was relieved to find that the tub and the sink did not require a pilot's license to use. Everything I needed, and more, had been provided. There was an assortment of brushes, combs, toothbrushes, toothpaste, soaps, and shampoos.

When I stepped out of the tub and returned to the bedroom, I found that there were two beautiful dresses laid on the bed, one of white satin and another of emerald green satin. They were both a bit too oofy poufy for my taste, with frills and puffy sleeves and shoulders, but I decided that the white one would serve.

When I finished dressing I returned to the central room. It was empty, so I looked around the suite. I found the Scarecrow in the library, quietly reading.

"It's already late afternoon, and this is a nice place for you to spend the night. If you would like we can go out and be tourists for a while," the Scarecrow said.

"If you think it best to stay here for the night."

"It is still far from the Emerald City, and the next town is further away then we could reach by sundown, so yes, I think we should stay the night."

"Okay, I would rather sleep here than in another cornfield."

"Each to his own," said the Scarecrow. "Do you like museums? Perhaps the Museum of Natural History would be nice."

"That would be fine. Maybe I will have something interesting to tell my little brother. He's a big fan of dinosaurs."

"As I am. Off to the museum. Let's use the subway," the Scarecrow added.

In a few minutes we were standing by a small subway station, along with a group of people waiting to get on. The station platform faced a rectangular pool of water. The pool of water had a roof and side built around it, protecting it from weather. Two uniformed workers sat on chairs on the left and right sides of the pool. They wore high boots and there were puddles of water under their chairs.

"What is the water for?" I asked.

"It's for the sub," replied the Scarecrow.

Just then some bubbles came billowing up from the water and a small submarine rose above the surface. The workers lowered chains down from the ceiling, hooked the chains onto metal loops atop the submarine, and started hoisting the submarine up out of the water. When they stopped, one of the workers banged on the submarine and the door rotated and opened. The passengers filed out, thanking the workers, and the people waiting to board got in.

We boarded and sat down on one of the wooden benches. The floor of the submarine was a metal grate through which I could see the bottom of the submarine, which had some water in it. Once everyone was seated, one of the workers inside the submarine closed and tightened the door with a large wheel. When the door was secured, he banged on the submarine wall and the submarined started to be lowered into the water. The workers sat down on bicycle seats. One of them moved a lever and water started to fill the bottom of the submarine, stopping just below the floor grate. Then they moved levers by their seats and started pedaling. The submarine started to move forward slowly.

"I've never been in a submarine before."

"You don't have subways in North Carolina?" the Scarecrow asked.

"None like this, not anywhere in the land I come from." I watched through a portal as fish past by outside, some looking in and waving to me. Signs went by as well. One said Hampsterdam Avenue.

We must have reached the next stop because the workers moved their levers and pedaled hard, slowing the submarine down. One called out, "Onion Square, Museum of Natural History." Then they moved their levers once more and continued to pedal. The sub made a sudden lurch.

"What's going on now?" I asked the Scarecrow.

"They are pumping out the water in the sub so it will rise." I watched as the water below the floor grate slowly receded. It felt like the submarine was rising. I could hear some clanking of chains and the submarine rose further with a bit of a sway. One of the workers began walking down the center aisle.

"Here is a subway token, as a token of our appreciation," the worker said while handing one to each passenger.

"Thanks," I said. First time I ever got something for using something. The token looked like a coin, but it had an *N* and a *Y* cut out of it. I put it in my pocket.

There was a bang on the submarine wall and the other worker opened the door. In a few moments we were outside walking down a street lined with museums.

"There it is," said the Scarecrow, pointing to a large building with Museum of Natural History cut into the stone above its many doors and columns. We walked up the stairs and into the museum.

Right in the entry way there was a complete set of Tyrannosaurus bones, like in the dinosaur book my little brother Jacob likes.

"Wow, this is amazing." There was no barriers protecting the displays. Children were climbing on the skeleton bones, like it was a jungle gym. I watched in awe. It looked like fun but I couldn't bring myself to climb on dinosaur bones. They're so rare and protected back home.

I noticed people standing near audio players, pulling strings, and holding headphones to their ears. I found an unused audio player, put the headphone to my ear, aligned the pointer on the player to what looked like a large squirrel, and pulled the string. When I let go of the string it started to play. As the string retracted, the pointer spun around and I could hear a voice in my ear.

"Some people believe that this skeleton is the skeleton of an ancient squirrel. If true, this squirrel would be as tall as a four-story building, and it would need four houses full of nuts stored away for winter."

I moved the pointer to a picture of a fierce looking rabbit and heard this:

"Some people think this is the skeleton of and ancient rabbit. If so, this rabbit would have ears that were over two stories high, and would eat about one ton of carrots each day."

I looked at the other choices - house cat, mouse, gerbil, and guinea pig. I put down the headphones and looked around. I best not mention this to my brother. Or anyone else for that matter. Sabre tooth guinea pig?

In a nearby room was a skeleton of a Pterodactyl. I looked at the audio player and saw choices of stork, bat, egret, spoonbill, and parakeet. I decided not to listen. I tried to imagine an enormous terrifying parakeet but it just didn't work.

"I guess I've seen enough," I said to the Scarecrow. "Museums can be very tiring."

"That's good. We can walk back to the hotel."

We stopped to listen to people singing in four part harmony. They sang a sad and poignant song about their mothers. They all had long hair down to the floor that completely hid everything but their faces.

"Where I come from this would be called a barbershop quartet," I said. "But it is obvious that they have never been to a barbershop."

"What does singing have to do with hair cutting?"

"People meet and socialize at the barbershop. I guess they started to sing with each other there. And in the long past people would go to the barbershop to get their blood drained."

"You come from a seriously strange place," the Scarecrow said with a look of disbelief on his face. I decided it would be best not to go further into the practice of bloodletting.

We continued leisurely along and in a short time we were back at the hotel and in the Monarch's Suite.

"I understand they have a fine restaurant here," said the Scarecrow. "Would you like to dine?"

"Yes." Suddenly I was famished. We left the suite and shortly were seated in a secluded back section of the restaurant. There was music playing. From our seats we could see a small corner of the dance floor. Young people were coming and going as songs ended and new ones began. They looked to be enjoying themselves a great deal.

"I thought that it would be good to keep to ourselves," the Scarecrow said. "I am not sure why Oz has been so dangerous for you, but it might be good not to attract too much attention."

I read the menu and ordered something I hoped would be good. As I put the menu down I asked, "What of the Tin Man? Scarecrow, shouldn't we be trying to help the Tin Man? Is he okay?"

"Don't trouble yourself with worries for the Tim Man. He is well built, well-armed, and very resourceful. I am sure his stupendous heart will lead him on the right path. And now he has a cause, helping you, to guide his adventures."

I sat thinking of the Tin Man and hoping he was safe. We, I should say, I, was served. The food turned out to be delicious and I ate with gusto from all the exercise I had gotten today. The Scarecrow sat silently as I ate, at times lost in thought, and the sound of the music playing filled in the silence.

A boy about my age walked up to me. "May I have the honor of a dance?" he asked.

I looked to the Scarecrow for guidance. He smiled with approval so I said, "Yes." I learned later that the Scarecrow was concerned but thought it would be more conspicuous if I said no, especially if it started a long discussion.

When the dance was done, the Scarecrow said, "I believe we should go. It appears that every young person here would like to dance with you."

We left through a back way and returned to the Monarch's Suite.

"I have ordered some breakfast for you, and some food for our trip," the Scarecrow said, "but I would like us to leave at dawn tomorrow so that we can get out of New York before people arise. With luck we can avoid attracting more attention."

I set about getting ready for bed. The Scarecrow sat in silence in a chair in the main room. He looked to be in thought, but of what thought I have no idea.

"Goodnight Scarecrow," I said as I closed the door of my bedroom. I slept long and comfortably. I dreamed of playing soccer, kicking and heading the ball, and leaping above the heads of the other players.

Chapter 9   A-mazing

I awoke and looked out the window. The sun was still below the horizon and the sky was dim, but I could just make out in the distance a river. In the middle of it stood a figure that looked like the Statue of Liberty. Could there be a Statue of Liberty in Oz?

It was before I normally would get up, but the Scarecrow had said he wanted to get an early start, so I got myself dressed, brushed my teeth, and packed my things away, ready for the start of a new day. I left the dress I wore last night on the bed. It was beautiful but not mine and not something I wanted to carry on a long walk through who knows what.

When I finished, I went into the main room and found the Scarecrow exactly where he had been the night before.

"Good morning. It's good you're an early riser. Here's the food I asked the chef to make for you. I hope you like it." He handed a paper sack to me. "If we are expeditious we will be gone before most people start their days. I hope you had a good sleep and are well rested because we still have a long way to go."

"I did," I replied. I looked through the bag and took out a nice large muffin and a bottle of something that turned out to be similar to orange juice. I put the remaining things into my backpack.

"I can walk and eat." I took a bite out of the muffin and washed it down with a gulp of juice. Quite good.

"Okay," the Scarecrow said. Shortly we were on the still deserted streets of New York, starting our journey to the Emerald City.

We walked out of the hotel district and past a large stone building. There were two enormous stone lions on either side of the wide staircase that led to the entry doors.

"This is the main branch of the public library," the Scarecrow said.

I looked closely at the grand stone lions. I did not need to ask if they were statues of the Cowardly Lion, as they had the end of their tails in their mouths and front paws and wore fretful expressions.

On the next block was the Museum of Post-Modern Art. And further along was the Palace of Post-Modern Art. And further still was the Free Library of Post-Modern Art.

"What is the Free Library of Post-Modern Art?" I asked.

"If you create a piece of art, you can donate it to the library. Other people can borrow it so it gets to circulate around the community," the Scarecrow said.

"Interesting. So the drawings that my parents had proudly displayed on their refrigerator when I was in grade school could be in a museum. If the people of New York had refrigerators and had refrigerator magnets, they could have the best decorated refrigerators in the world."

The Scarecrow wore a puzzled look but remained silent

"MOPMA, POPMA, and FLOPMA!" I blurted. "How cute."

"You might think that was what the people of New York call their art museums, but you would be wrong," the Scarecrow said. "They are a bit more creative. Mopsie, Popsie, and Flopsie. No one knows why they call them that though."

"Perhaps they are named after some bunny rabbits? I said."

The Scarecrow again remained silent, though he looked even more puzzled than before.

New York turned out to be smaller than I thought it would be. Only a few minutes later we had left the built-up area and were walking on a path with meadows on both sides, houses dotted here and there. The paved streets were replaced by gravel paths. "Two butts width," I could hear my dad say, that's how wide the path is. Just wide enough for two horses side by side.

We came to the bank of the river and I saw that the statue I had seen from my hotel window was much shorter than the real Statue of Liberty. There was a line of stepping stones in the water that led to the statue's platform, a small grassy raised area in the middle of the river. I hopscotched my way over to the statue with the Scarecrow following behind.

"She's my height!" I said. I raised my arms up to see if I could touch the torch that the lady was holding. I looked into the eyes of the statue and saw that there were tiny images of people staring back at me. There were even some tiny figures of people sitting on the lady's crown and around her torch.

I hopscotched my way across the remaining stepping stones, arriving at the far side of the river. I turned to look back on New York and the Statue of Liberty.

"What are your thoughts?" the Scarecrow asked.

"I was just thinking how many different people live there, and they seem to get along."

"They do. It's quite a nice town."

"And we need to get going. I don't want to waste any time getting to the Emerald City and back home."

We set out, walking through the sand of a small beach until we found a path that led up a hill and through a handful of majestic old trees.

As we got further away from New York, the houses got further and further apart and the path was reduced until we could only walk single file. I led on, with the Scarecrow behind. After some time, we passed the last house. The footpath meandered through some small hills, and the ground around us was wild, with high grasses, bushes and scrub trees scattered about. The path itself was earth and rocks, with moss growing here and there between the rocks, but on either side it was lined by beautiful flowers. They look just like sunflowers, but with light blue petals instead of bright yellow.

As we walked on, the flowers that lined the path grew closer together and taller. And as we continued down the path I noticed that the petals of the flowers grew darker. They felt menacing. There was something sinister about them. Now, they were even taller, so that they blocked the sun.

I kept walking and the Scarecrow followed close behind. After a short while I began to have a strange sense that we were being followed. "Did you hear that?" I asked the Scarecrow.

"Oh my, yes, I did," he replied. "I didn't want to hear it, but I did."

I sped up, walking along, faster, hoping to avoid whatever was following us. The flowers were even taller, and thicker, in dense inescapable rows lining both sides of the path. We pushed on, picking up the pace. After a bit I turned, motioned to the Scarecrow to be silent, and tried to listen carefully.

"I definitely think we are being followed."

The Scarecrow didn't reply, but he was trembling, making a rustling sound. I sped up further. We were moving fast. The path curved to the right and, as soon as I rounded the bend, I stopped short. The Scarecrow slammed into me.

"Sorry," he said.

"No problem. What do you think this is?"

"What do I think what is?"

"This thing right in front of me."

"What thing right in front of you? I don't see anything." he replied. His shaking was worse.

"You don't see it?"

The Scarecrow moved closer. He looked around, forward, to the left and right, and back at me. "No, I don't," he said. "Describe it too me."

"It's vertical, like a door, but it looks like the surface of a pond, with shimmering ripples streaming out from random places."

"I don't see anything," he said.

I turned around, walked past the Scarecrow, took another step, and stopped short again.

"Now it's blocking the way back. Whatever it is, it wants to stop us."

The Scarecrow stopped in thought and then added, "It seems to want you to go through it. I can't see it, so it must be for you alone."

"But I don't want to go on alone," I said. "I don't want to and I will not."

"Perhaps if you hold tight to my hand as you go through, I will be able to accompany you."

I got a firm grip on the Scarecrow's hand crushing it a bit, took a deep breath, and stepped into the shimmering surface.

It felt like I was falling. The Scarecrow's hand felt like it was on fire, burning me, but I squeezed harder. Then the Scarecrow's hand felt like it was icy cold, numbing my fingers, but I held tight. Then it felt like an electric shock so that my entire arm both ached and felt numb, from my finger tips to the top of my shoulder. I held firm. I was not going to go on without him.

We fell onto a cold stone floor, which was dusty, dirty, and littered with dried leaves, bits of earth, and bits of old cloth.

I let go my grip on the Scarecrow's hand, got up, and brushed myself off. The Scarecrow did the same giving himself a push here and a tug there. He did his best to fluff up the hand I squished.

"Any idea where we are now?" I asked.

The Scarecrow gazed around slowly. "This is Glinda's castle," he said.

"It doesn't look like anyone's been home for a while."

"No one has been in Glinda's castle for years. And no one, in fact, has even seen Glinda's castle for some time. She left us, and every trace of her left with her."

We walked along a deserted hall, peaking into the equally deserted rooms as we passed. Some mice scurried along the edge of the hall.

"A few mice, I can deal with that."

"Let's hope that's all we find," said the Scarecrow.

"What do you mean, no one has seen Glinda's castle?" I asked.

"Glinda's castle was once very grand, almost as grand as the palace in the Emerald City. And Glinda had an army of fierce warriors, all young women trained in all things martial, who drilled constantly. They were a force unrivaled in all Oz, and since Glinda was good and fair, Oz was safe, for few people with bad intentions dared to face her army. When Glinda sought to retire from her responsibilities, she disbanded her army. This is a secret, but since we are in Glinda's castle, you should know that it turned out Glinda's army was far smaller than anyone had imagined, a small group of warriors only. The rest of the warriors were a creation of Glinda's magic."

"For many years Glinda hid from the world and lived like a hermit, never being seen and never taking visitors. Even the possibility of Glinda's intervention kept all mischief doers silent. I might get a short message from her occasionally. Then, all that she had, everything that was hers, disappeared. People returned saying they could not find her castle. Search parties were sent out to be sure, and they returned to say the same; the castle, the grounds, the fields, even the nearby houses, all were gone."

"Wasn't there a sign that something was missing? How can so much space disappear without a trace?"

"Glinda was a great sorceress, so how she did it none can tell. No one since has commanded magic like Glinda. She had many apprentices, but the best possess only a small part of the skill of magic that she had. She was in a class by herself."

"If she was a great sorceress, how come none of her apprentices advanced further?"

"Many came to Glinda to study, but most left after a short period in frustration. They wanted a step-by-step guide, and Glinda would not give it to them. I once heard her tell an apprentice, 'Magic is not like making pancakes. There is no ingredient list, and there is no list of steps. Don't waste your time making pancakes, unless your goal is breakfast.'"

We continued to walk along the corridor.

"Where are we going," I asked.

"Almost there. We are going to Glinda's throne room. Here it is," said the Scarecrow.

We entered into a great room. There was a single throne in the center of a platform, with two lower, more modest thrones on each side.

"I can understand their frustration," I said.

"Her guidance was obscure," said the Scarecrow, and then he paused in thought. "When we get to the Emerald City, you will see the Witches' Council. Some of them were Glinda's apprentices. None longer than Gings, who is their leader."

"You say none are as powerful as Glinda. Do you think they can help me return home?"

"I don't know. But you will never find a more powerful group of witches in one place than at the Witches Council."

We walked slowly toward the center throne.

"People say that Glinda wrote other books on magic, but none of her apprentices ever advanced beyond the first book, which Gings keeps and protects. Many copies have been made. Perhaps you will have a chance to read one when we get to the Emerald City. We are not sure if there really are more books, and, if they exist, where they are."

"What is that on Glinda's throne?"

"What's what?" asked the Scarecrow as he felt his hand over the seat.

"It's right where you had your hand."

"Show me."

I reached forward and picked up a short sword, encased in a leather scabbard attached to a leather belt. In the center of the scabbard was a raised insignia, and the edges of the scabbard were lined with small jewels that twinkled even in the dim light. At the end of the handle a short gold chain swayed under my hand.

"I see it now," said the Scarecrow. "That is Glinda's sword. Clearly Glinda wants you to have it."

I pulled the sword from the scabbard and slowly swished it side to side. It glimmered in the dim light. I couldn't help myself, I made a "zuzz" buzzing sound with my mouth. I imagined being in a space adventure. The Scarecrow watched with a puzzled look on his face. That was enough so I put the sword back into its scabbard. I put the scabbards belt above my work belt, so that the sword was on my left hip. It just felt natural to reach for it there.

"Is Glinda's castle closer to the Emerald City than where we were?"

"No," replied the Scarecrow, "much further away."

I sat down on Glinda's throne with my head in my hands. "Now I'm further from the Emerald city than before, probably the furthest I've ever been from getting home. How am I ever going to get out of Oz when everything pushes me back?"

"Have courage Emily. The road to home may have many turns. But don't lose hope," The Scarecrow said.

He sat on a nearby throne. All that could be heard was the sound of a slight breeze moving the leaves on the floor and the scurrying of mice.

I closed my eyes to think, and an image of a young woman appeared. She was dressed in a brilliant white gown studded with tiny gems that twinkled like stars. Next to the woman was a young man, a few years older than the woman, who had a pale complexion and wore a short mustache. He had short jet-black hair. The woman held the young man's hands in her own. She said to him, "When you are ready, a door will open that will invite you to more advanced magic. Until that time, you must be patient. Magic cannot be rushed." The man replied, "It is taking too long, at this speed I will be an old man before I can do anything of use with magic." The image dispersed and I reopened my eyes and stood up.

"Okay, let's go. Slow is better than never, and I am not so fond of mice anyway."

"That's the spirit," the Scarecrow added.

We left the throne room, the Scarecrow taking the lead as he had visited Glinda in her castle many times and so knew the way. As we turned a corner in the hallway, we were again stopped by a shimmering object blocking our path.

"Do you see that?"

"Yes, this time I do," said the Scarecrow.

I grabbed hold of the Scarecrow's hand and said, "I think we are meant to go through."

"Through we go," said the Scarecrow, and on the count of three we stepped through together. This time I felt no pain in my hand.

We found ourselves in a small clearing, surrounded on all sides by tall, dark blue flowers. They were the same as those which lined the path outside of New York, but these were even more ominous. The flowers towered over us so that only a small bit of blue sky could be seen. I looked around for a way forward. I found a small break in the flowers, just wide enough to walk through. I stepped in.

"It looks like a maze. It leads in both directions, but it is jet black in there. I cannot see a thing."

"Maybe we should call for help. There could be someone nearby who can help us," the Scarecrow said. The Scarecrow cried out for help in a pitiable voice. I joined him. We called for what seemed forever. We heard no sounds in return.

"If there were people nearby, they could not hear us, or were too fearful to help," I said.

"Perhaps I could help you," came a small voice from the Scarecrow's shoulder. "I am really good at mazes, captain of my school's maze running team."

I turned to the Scarecrow and saw that a very small mouse was perched on his shoulder.

"It sounded like you were playing an exciting game," the mouse continued, "and my life is always so boring, so I stowed aboard this straw man. It looks like I was right. This is fun. I would be happy to help, and, as I said, I am good at mazes. My name is Paesanella."

"Nice to meet you Paesanella," said the Scarecrow.

We agreed to follow Paesanella. Paesanella jumped down and darted through the opening. In just a few moments she returned.

"Okay, follow me! Take a left at the entrance," Paesanella said.

Paesanella gave directions and we followed in the total darkness, left here, right here, left again, straight on. My head swam with all the directions. Paesanella did her best to stay close, but not get stepped on.

Finally, Paesanella said, "Please stop. This is as close to the edge as I can bring you. The flowers have sealed us in."

The Scarecrow started to fret and mutter. "We will be stuck here forever, and you will never get home."

It was total darkness. I put my hands on my hips and I brushed Glinda's sword. "Glinda told one of her students that when you are ready, a door will open. Sometimes, you have to cut your own door."

I unsheathed Glinda's sword, crouched low, and swung a broad stroke, cutting down a swath of flowers. Each flower cried out in pain as it fell to the ground. The rest of the flowers bent to try to avoid the blade, but all fell to the ground. After a few strokes I could see that we were only a single step from the edge of the maze. I slashed a wide path so that we could walk out side by side and still not need to touch the flowers. The sap of the flowers had a pungent stench. I was careful not to touch it.

One of the cloths used to polish furniture at the antique store would do the trick. I took one out of my work belt and wiped the foul sap off the sword blade, leaving the cloth covered with drops of dark blue sticky liquid that smelled like skunk mixed with rancid vomit.

"Whew, this stuff reeks." After I put the sword away I went into the maze, dug a small hole with my heel, and buried the cloth. "I sure don't want to be carrying that around."

The color of the fallen flowers slowly changed from dark blue to bright yellow.

Paesanella, who had climbed back up to the Scarecrow's shoulder, said, "This looks like a nice field, so I am sure I will find some of my cousins I would like to visit. Thank you for the adventure, but (as she looked straight at me) I am not very fond of girls, especially those swinging swords." With that, she jumped down and disappeared in the nearby grass.

We walked a short distance from the flowers and sat down on a large rock. We had been pushing on relentlessly since morning and I felt tired. "It seems Glinda's sword was no mistake," the Scarecrow said. I finished whatever food I had left and rested. The sun warmed me. Looking back once more to the maze that we had just escaped I said, "Thank you, Paesanella," to myself. I heard a tiny "Your welcome Emily," from somewhere in the nearby grass.

Across the field was a road. A horse drawn bus was slowly approaching. The bus stopped and the driver rang a bell and yelled out, "Bus to town, bus to town. Get yourself up and get yourself down, to the town."

There were people walking to the bus. "Let's go. Let's get on that bus," I said.

We hurried toward the bus and climbed on. There were bench seats on each side, and an aisle down the center. We took a seat together as other people climbed aboard. A young man who looked quite confused sat down next to me. Everyone boarded and sat down. The bus started to slowly plod along the road, swaying side to side slightly with each step of the horse.

The young man turned toward me and asked, "Dorothy?"

The bus stopped abruptly and there was some commotion up front. An old woman dressed all in black called, "Tippetarius, you lazy selfish boy. You know I need you to walk the dog." The young man next to me slowly walked to the front of the bus. Before he stepped off the bus, he turned back to look at me with a confused and questioning look on his face.

"Why would someone call me Dorothy?" I thought.

The bus continued slowly along the road as I watched the young man and the old woman fade from view. I turned forward just in time to see the bus pass the very same young man walking a jet-black dog along the side of the road. My head spun back and forth wondering how he got in front of the bus, where the dog came from, and where the old woman went.

"Most peculiar," the Scarecrow said.

"I'd say," I said.

The bus plodded its way into a town. When it came to a stop, we followed everyone into a large room with bench seats and a stage at one end. The sign on the stage read "Weather Report Today." I overheard a man say to his neighbor, "I always look forward to the weather report. I just love it and I cannot remember the last time they got it wrong."

Chapter 10 New Friends

A tall woman came to the center of the stage and said, "You all know him and love him, so without further delay, here is Cirrus Thunderwail."

A man stepped forward and immediately started presenting the weather report. He had charts and maps. He drew frantically on the maps, and then erased them just as frantically. "Last Tuesday, the day was bright and sunny. The high temperature was 94, and the overnight low was 70. The winds were calm throughout the day. And the next day, last Wednesday, the weather was cloudy, and we had light rain during most of the day, ending just after sun down. After sundown winds picked up with strong gusts"

He continued like this for quite some time. I looked around the room. The people in the audience applauded at times and said things like, "This is just wonderful," and "My word, last Friday's report was absolutely inspiring." They all were delighted by the presentation. The speaker apparently came to the end of his talk. He said, "And yesterday we had mild temperatures and it was partly sunny. Now that the report is complete, I would like to thank all those who provided the critical information that I used in my presentation. Everyone that helped by providing reports, please stand."

At this, pretty much everyone in the room, except me and the Scarecrow, stood up. Cirrus continued, "Please let's give them a hearty round of applause."

All the people applauded loudly, some whistled, and some stomped their feet as well. While the applause continued, people carrying pitchers passed by each table, setting out and filling mugs with some fizzy drink. I sneered at my mug. "I hope this isn't beer," I said to the Scarecrow. "I tasted beer once and I don't like it."

I took a little sip. It tasted sweet, with hints of vanilla and cinnamon. "This is delicious!" I said, but my voice came out high-pitched and funny sounding.

The Scarecrow replied, "Oh, wonderful," in a high-pitched voice, obviously making fun of me since he could not drink, and therefore had not had a drink of whatever was in his mug.

The people around us were drinking and talking funny, laughing at each other, pointing, and good-heartedly goofing around. A large woman from the row ahead turned around and in a high-pitched voice asked the Scarecrow, "Friend, it you don't plan to drink that, me and my chums will gladly take it off your hands." Without a sound the Scarecrow slid the mug to the woman.

I took a few more sips and then set my mug down. It was good but the voice thing I could do without. I noticed that some people were already leaving the hall.

"I think we should get going," I said.

The Scarecrow responded "I agree" in an equally funny voice.

Once outside I asked, "Where do we go next?" pleased that my voice had returned to normal.

"We need to skirt the edge of the jungle," the Scarecrow said. "It's still a long way to the Emerald City and it would be faster to go through, but the jungle is much too dangerous for flesh people like you, and even too dangerous for me."

We walked out of town. At a crossroad, there was a sign with an arrow that read "Jungle, Beware." Soon we came a short distance away from a dense forest. We followed along the edge, keeping the forest always to our right. I could hear the sounds of birds punctuated by the screeches of animal calls. I tried to look into the forest, but the trees were too close and all I saw was darkness. The sounds told me that many creatures were nearby, but I could see none. We continued along a short time until we reached a tall tree.

"Let me climb this tree and see the best way for us to go," said the Scarecrow, and he jumped to the tree and started climbing. I sat down and leaned against the tree to rest.

I listened carefully. I could hear some noises in the forest; bird calls, growls, cries, and squawks. And something was moving through the grass. The wave in the grass darted to me and before I could get up, a tiny tiger kit and a tiny lion kit stood before me.

"We've been tracking you and now you are our prey," said the tiny lion kit in a squeaky voice.

"Our mothers have been giving us lessons, and you are the first thing we have caught," said the tiger kit.

I could not help but smile since they looked adorable. "What are your names?" I asked.

"My name is Roya," said the lion kit.

"And my name is Trusheet," said the tiger kit.

"And mine is Emily," I said. "Shouldn't you be in the forest? Is it okay with your parents that you are here?"

"Oh, our moms will never know," said Roya. "They never leave the forest." The two kits came up to me and sat down on my legs. I rubbed their heads.

Roya turned around and asked, "Where is your mommy, Emily?"

I was quiet thinking about where my mom might be right this second. "My mom is far away, in another land, and would have no idea how to help me, even if she knew where I was."

"Oh, but our moms will help you," said Trusheet. They are big and powerful."

Roya put her front paws into my hand. "Ouch, you cut me," I yelled. I pulled my hand back. A tiny drop of blood came from my palm.

"Oh, I am sorry. Really sorry, but please don't tell my mom," Roya said. "She yells at me if I am not careful with my claws. 'Roya, pay more attention. Roya, you need to be more careful. Roya, you must not hurt others.' I know. I know. But I sometimes forget. I am sorry Emily. I really am."

"That's okay," I said. "It's not much of a cut and it doesn't hurt at all."

Just then two enormous creatures bounded out of the jungle, a tigress and a lioness.

"Children, are you okay?" asked the lioness. She prowled around me, looking at me from one side and then the other. Then she bent close, so close I could feel the moisture from her breath. She took a deep inhale to smell me.

"This is our new friend Emily," Roya declared.

"We are great," added Trusheet. "Emily is lost and needs to find her mom. Can we help her? Please, Mommy? Please?"

"What are you holding behind your back Emily?" asked the Lioness. "Let me see."

"I cut my hand earlier today, that's all."

"Please let me see your hand," asked the lioness once again.

I took my hand out from behind my back. The Lioness carefully grasped my hand in her paw. Her paw was as big as my head, and the claws were so long they could go through my arm with ease.

"You say you got this cut earlier today," the lioness asked, while looking at Roya. "You would not be stretching the truth to protect someone, would you?"

Before I could answer, the Scarecrow made his entrance.

The Scarecrow climbed down from the tree.

The Scarecrow fell down from the tree.

The Scarecrow fell head first, down from the top of the tree. His head, being filled with bran, needles, pins, and other things that helped him to be the sharp intellect that he was, was much heavier than the rest of his body, which was made of straw and cloth and could float on the air. So, his head hit the ground with a thud.

He landed near my knee. He sat himself up and then tried to smooth out the flat spot in his head caused by the fall. After a few attempts he got his head more or less back to normal. It was always a bit lumpy anyway.

The lioness and the tigress called out to their babes, and they all backed away a few paces and sat down on their back legs with their stomachs on the ground and their forepaws forward.

The Scarecrow came forward. "Orlanda and Ungeira, my dear friends, it has been far too long since we last talked. What brings you to this far corner of the jungle?"

The tigress spoke. "We are in this area in response to some reports of problems. But what brings us out of the jungle is that our kits were making friends with Emily."

"Well they have good taste," said the Scarecrow. "Emily and I are going to the Emerald City in hopes of returning her to her home. She comes from near where Dorothy grew up. The shoes and dress Emily wears were given to her by Dorothy's memorial tree. Also, Dorothy and Toto came to Emily in a dream and saved her from a tree that would have entombed her. Our friend the Tin Man and another innocent person were trapped in that tree with her, and Emily saved them. And then later she saved me from a flock of cruel birds."

"Quite a lot of adventure. How did she save you from the birds?" asked the lioness, Orlanda.

"She grabbed one and then told them all to leave and they flew away," said the Scarecrow. "I believe she said something like 'I will turn half of you to worms so that you never know if you are eating your brothers and sisters.' Something like that."

"Oh" and "Ah" said the mothers, as they both looked me over once again, this time even more carefully. I didn't like the feeling of being inspected like this.

"And how did you come to be trapped in a tree by birds?" asked the tigress, Ungeira.

"I was walking along a bank of a small creek," said the Scarecrow, "observing some sallymanders and

108

stanleymanders swimming in the water and hiding among the stones, when a flock of blackbirds swarmed upon me and lifted me into the sky. I watched the scenery go by below me as the birds flew. Then they began pulling some of my straw out and I thought, how nice, my straw will be used in some of their nests, but they just dropped it to the ground. They did not stop, and in time I had no more straw and thus could not hold my head up. All I could see was the front of my clothes, which are sewn together with great skill I might add."

"They dropped me in a tree that stood in a field which had just been harvested. I thought that in time someone would come and save me, but there was a spell on the field so that no other creature or person could come close. The birds returned again and again to watch me and heckle me."

"But how is it that Emily saved you?" asked Orlanda the lioness.

"The spell did not affect Emily, nor did it affect the subterranean miniature porcines," said the Scarecrow.

"Interesting," added Orlanda. "Emily is not from Oz and the porcines travel to many worlds."

I had been listening carefully. When I heard that I blurted out, "Do you mean that the tiny pigs could take me home?"

"No," the Scarecrow said. "There tunnels are much too small for you and digging tunnels large enough for you would take much too long."

"But they could send a message to my family?"

"Perhaps, But they keep hidden in most worlds, for their safety, you understand. And if they did send a message, who would listen? Who would believe them?"

"Yes, I see." I felt sad that there was no quick way to return home, or even tell my family that I was alright, that I missed them, and that I was on my way.

Orlanda looked into my face. I turned away not wanting to show her how sad I was. She spoke. "Ungeira, please take care of the children. I will help these travelers along their way." Turning to the Scarecrow and me she continued, "It is much faster to go through the jungle, but it would not be safe for you alone, so I will take you."

Turning once more to Ungeira she added, "I will be gone a number of days. I believe that I hear the sounds of kits with empty stomachs." Then she addressed her kit. "Roya, I am leaving you under Ungeira's care. You are on your best behavior. Do you understand?"

"Yes, Mommy," Roya said. "Oh this will be a great adventure!"

"I will take care of them my friend," said Ungeira, the tigress, to Orlanda.

"It is a long way," Orlanda said. "You will need to ride atop me. Emily, since you are heaviest, you should be in front. I will go very fast so you should hold on firmly. Do not fear hurting me, hold me tight. Once I begin I will not stop so make sure you are ready."

I gathered myself and climbed to the shoulders of the great lioness, and the Scarecrow climbed up behind me and wrapped his arms around my waist.

"Bye Emily. Come back to play with us soon," said Roya.

"Yes, please, please come back soon," wished Trusheet.

"Good speed," said Ungeira.

"Thank you all." I knew I would miss them, but I also hoped I would get home, and likely never see them again. I was about to say something but when I grabbed onto the fur of the great lioness she shot off like the wind, bounding forward through the jungle, over bushes, stones, and fallen trees. She seemed to fly forward, and at one point my grip failed and we nearly fell off. I grabbed on harder, and in response she charged ahead even faster, so fast that I was terrified. I grabbed on harder yet, and the lioness must have decided that I had learned my lesson and was holding on firmly enough. She slowed slightly from her fastest, still so fast that I held a constant fear in my heart.

Startled animals fled from us, caught off guard. Those who Orlanda might at times hunt scattered in all directions, happy to see that the great lioness had no interest in them this day.

We left the dense trees of the jungle behind and entered into wide areas of grass. We passed a lake where creatures of all sorts bathed. There were hippopotami, and giraffes, wilder beasts, and fisher birds, zebras and wort hogs. One creature looked like a walrus, but it was as large as a hippopotamus, and apparently fond of sunning by the edge of the lake.

The landscape flew by and we returned to a section of dense trees, where monkeys swung and leaped branch to branch. There were squirrels as large as house cats that jumped and glided from tree to tree. And the lioness sped on and on.

We returned to grass land. There were enormous trees separated by wide fields of high grass, each tree easily twice as high as the tallest oak tree, or any other tree, I could remember. And the trees were not just tall, but wide, with branches that went on and on. Each tree was so large that it was like a forest in itself, and jungle beings of all sorts lived and played among the branches.

And the lioness sped on. We once again returned to dense forest. It was so dark I could not see, but I could hear the sounds of startled beasts, scurrying away and making calls of alarm.

After such a long time that I feared I would fall asleep, the lioness slowed. Light came through the trees in front of us, and in a few more steps we stepped out of the jungle. The lioness walked a few more paces and stopped.

"This is where I will leave you. We have left my domain, and I cannot protect you further as I must consider my own subjects."

The Scarecrow jumped down in his own clumsy way, but he soon was standing up straight once again. I climbed down as well.

The Scarecrow said, "Thank you, Orlanda, for all your help."

I bounded forward and threw my arms around her neck, though my arms were far too short to meet at the other side. "Thank you, Orlanda, I will never forget you," I said, and then I stepped back to stand beside the Scarecrow.

Orlanda scrutinized me once more. Then she said, "I will give you one final thing, Emily." She came closer and rubbed her left forepaw on my shoes. "I have placed my scent on your shoes. No creature who knows me and enjoys life will do you harm, and many who are my friends will help you if they can. But do not assume that this gives you leave to enter the jungle. Do not. The jungle is fair but it is rarely kind. Remember this and stay safe. And now I must leave."

She stood up, turned, and bounded back into the forest. In a heartbeat she was gone, and all sounds of her movement were gone. No sounds came from the forest, or from the sky, or from the ground. All was quiet.

Chapter 11 Emily in the Sky with Emeralds

"She sure doesn't go for long goodbyes," I said.

"No, Emily. Orlanda is not one for goodbyes," the Scarecrow replied.

"How long have you known her?"

"Her entire life. Since she was smaller than Roya is now."

He stood in silence.

"What's the matter?"

"This is very close to the place I said my final goodbye to the Cowardly Lion. It was so long ago, but it seems like it was just yesterday that he returned to his home in the jungle. It still saddens me. A lifetime ago and yet so present."

The breeze was soft and gentle so that some tiny flowers waved back and forth. The sky was dotted by high clouds that looked like marshmallows floating lazily along. The Scarecrow was lost in thought again. He was watching one particular cloud that was shape like a donut drift slowly through the rays of sunlight.

"Your thoughts?"

"Do you ever watch clouds?" the Scarecrow asked.

"Sometimes."

"I do as well," he replied. "And I wonder, what combination of heat, and humidity, and breeze comes together to make this specific shape at this specific time? And then everything changes. How does it all work? What mathematical equations govern all this?"

"Oh," I said, though I didn't really know what to say.

"And how are you, Emily?" the Scarecrow asked.

"I'm good."

"Excellent. You must be made out of good strong stuff considering all you have been through."

"I've never thought of it that way, but yes. I guess I am made of good strong stuff. And I want to get back to my family who made me that way. Which way to the Emerald City, Scarecrow?"

"Just follow me."

I followed and we resumed our walk toward the Emerald City. There were hills here and there. The Scarecrow started to hum a tune.

"You seem happy."

"I am," said the Scarecrow. "Soon I will be returning to my throne and my friends."

"Scarecrow, why did Orlanda say that it would take her so long to return to Roya, Ungeira, and Trusheet?"

"After that long run Orlanda was exhausted. She will need a few days to recover before she can travel again."

"But she seemed fine when she bounded back into the forest."

"She would never show you that she was tired, it is not her way. Having known her all her life, and her family for far longer, I can tell you it is not their way to show any weakness. But she is not a machine and not magic but made of flesh, like you, and so she tires. She will likely sleep most of the next day, and then wake up famished. Then she will hunt and rest again. And then she will start the return trip. Even then, the jungle is her land, so she may be called upon to help some of her subjects."

"I couldn't tell at all," I said. "She ran as fast at the end as she did at the start of the trip. How large is the jungle anyway?"

"Very large. Vast. I have seen only a small part of it. Our trip was through a tiny corner of the jungle. Anyway, the creatures of the jungle fear outsiders. When outsiders enter, often those who live in the jungle suffer."

We came to the top of one of the hills and could see the spires of the palace in the Emerald City far off in the distance. We stopped to look.

"It's very beautiful, but it will take us many more days to get there, won't it?" I asked.

"No, I don't think so," the Scarecrow said. "I believe we are very close to one of the terminals of the Yellow Brick road."

We walked down from the top of the hill and I could see a spiral of yellow bricks.

"And I am right," the Scarecrow said. "There's a start of one of the spurs of the Yellow Brick road. The Yellow Brick road has round terminals, and then the road spirals out from the terminals for a few revolutions, and then the road curves off, heading to the Emerald City."

"Why do people walk around in circles before they head to the city?" I asked.

"When the road was first made, these roads were all straight. But, as I mentioned before, things in Oz don't stay put. So now we have spirals, which I quite prefer anyway. They are much prettier, don't you think?"

I nodded. It made sense. I hoped I wasn't going to have permanent brain damage from accepting all this crazy stuff.

"But we won't be walking anyway. We have an ongoing program to upgrade the transportation system and it looks like this terminal is one of the first to get service. I've never tried it myself, having been away for some time, so this will be a bit of an experiment for me."

We walked to the middle of the terminal, and in the very center of the yellow bricks was a bright silver post. On the top of the post was a small bell, made of emerald glass.

"Let's call ourselves a JetBroom," the Scarecrow said as he rang the bell. "Our ride should be here soon." The bell made a bright tinkling sound.

I heard some booms from the sky and I looked up.

"Run for it," the Scarecrow yelled. He grabbed my hand and we scattered from the fast-approaching shape.

The flying object crashed hard into the grass outside the paved area. A young man nearly flew from his broom, which lay planted firmly in the ground. He rolled and tumbled across the grass, and when he came to a stop he lay on his side, groaning and moaning, not far from where we stood.

We ran to him. He shimmied himself up to a sitting position and blinked a few times. "Yes. I'm okay," he said with a sad tone. He worked on getting his arms free from the long scarf that had wrapped around him as he rolled across the ground, so that now he was rolled up like a mummy. "I'm just not getting the landings." Besides the long scarf he wore a pair of goggles over his eyes, a leather cap with a small brim, a leather jacket, leather pants, and leather gloves. "I can't land properly and the autowitch is on the fritz because it can't find enough crystal balls to get a good position."

Then he looked around all over and said, "Thankfully there are no flight inspectors around. I would be in big trouble if that landing was reported. You won't report me, will you?"

I shook my head no.

"No," the Scarecrow said. "But how come you are not getting enough connections? There are so many crystal balls in Oz."

"All the witches are either in the Emerald City or on their way there," the young man said, "and they all brought their crystal balls, naturally, so they are not far enough apart to be useful. I just finished my course on Crystal Ball Navigation. The Highly Magnified Wogle Bug, who first proposed using crystal balls as reference points for navigation, warned that the crystal balls needed to be separated sufficiently so that they were independent in terms of location, or the trigonometry would not provide a precise location. I have his paper *Crystal Ball Navigation, the Future Beckons* in my dorm if you would like to read it."

"No, that's okay," the Scarecrow said as he rubbed his forehead. Some of the pins that stuffed the Scarecrow's head were sticking out and he tried to push them back in. "I can review the paper later in the palace library."

The young man had a name tag on his leather jacket that read "Josh, WIT IV." He was looking over the broom, rocking it back and forth, trying to free it from the ground.

"What's that?" I asked pointing at what looked like a little guitar with arms and legs coming from the body and a mouth where the hole should be. It had its hands and legs wrapped tight around the broom handle and was shaking like a leaf in a brisk wind.

"That's my music app, but it's going to need a lot of time to recuperate before it wants to play any happy songs again. Poor thing. I don't mean to mistreat it but I am afraid that my flying…" His voice trailed off. He continued rocking the broom side to side hoping to get it unstuck.

Josh raised his eyes and realized who he was near. "Oh my, the palace. You're the Scarecrow and you just watched me crash my broom."

"That's okay," the Scarecrow said. "Your secret is safe with me."

"Thank you, Mr. Scarecrow, I mean your highness, I mean…," Josh's voice trailed off once again.

"It's okay. Just call me the Scarecrow. I prefer to be informal."

Josh finally freed the broom and then cleaned off the small crystal ball, which was sized to fit into someone's hand. It was attached to the broom handle with a mount that allowed it to be adjusted for better view.

"Everyone on," Josh said. He got on closest to the front of the broom, so he had a good view of the crystal ball, then the Scarecrow climbed on behind him.

"This is safe?" I asked hesitating before I got on. "I escaped death a few times already in Oz. I don't want to die crossing the street."

The Scarecrow said, "Perfectly safe," though his tone of voice was not encouraging. Josh didn't answer. I got on anyway.

"Why don't you leave the autowitch off? I can give you directions," the Scarecrow said. "Anyway, I want to show Emily the Emerald City from the air, and you need some practice flying."

Josh grunted his agreement and the broom lurched up into the air, testing the grip of everyone onboard and sending the music app into a fit of sobs.

"Try to relax Josh. Don't think of grasping the broom, think of the broom flying through a gentle breeze. If you are tensed you can't let your body fly the broom, your mind will take over and your mind will always overreact."

The broom slowly rose in the air. The Scarecrow pointed and Josh took us off in that direction. Things went smoothly for some time, but then a bird flew by and must have scared Josh, because we pulled hard left and did a loop de loop before returning to straight and level. My hands were clenched so tight they ached.

"Sorry about that," Josh said. "I got startled."

With time Josh settled down, much to my relief and that of the music app. Besides a few short screams, I took the ride pretty well. The Scarecrow seemed to enjoy the acrobatics. What did he have to worry about after all? He was probably trying to estimate how fast he would hit the ground right now as we flew. If he fell to the ground it would hardly be noticeable. I however gulped a bit with every change in direction, even the minor ones.

As we approached the Emerald City, the Scarecrow gave Josh more directions. First we flew low above the outskirts of the city where there were pastures and fruit orchards. Then we went higher and circled closer to the center of the city, where there were buildings close together, circular ponds, and great parks. Finally, we climbed higher and circled the tall spires of the great palace of the Emerald City. The spires glistened in the sunlight, with the emeralds that decorated the roofs and pinnacle sparkling like green diamonds.

"I can see why you call this the Emerald City," I said.

"Yes indeed," the Scarecrow said. "Oh, I'm so glad to be back home. See that series of low buildings over there. They're my workshops. I have many things I'd like to show you when we have time." Then he said to Josh, "Why don't you set us down over there?" pointing to a grassy area in a park, which also happened to be empty of people and obstacles. "Good choice," I thought, "just in case of a mishap." But Josh landed smoothly. The music app was relieved and I took a few deep breaths trying to relax all the muscles I had been holding clenched.

There was a small group of pigeons nearby, who flew over and landed around us.

"Excellent landing," one said in a high pitched and cracking voice. "Bravo," said another as they all pecked around Josh and his broom.

Josh turned to me and said in a whisper, "I really need a clean record, so I am glad the flight inspectors were here to see a good landing."

"Thanks for the ride," I said as I shook Josh's hand. "Good luck on your witches training." If I never get on a broom again I wouldn't be sad, but I didn't say that to Josh.

"Thanks." Josh looked down at the crystal ball on the front of the broom. He must have gotten a new ride request. "Okay, gotta fly," he said as he lifted off once again.

"Well, he is certainly brave," I said as we started walking to the palace. We had not taken two steps when a carriage drawn by four horses stopped to carry us on. Like many things, the carriage was glistening with emerald stones and brilliantly polished gold and silver.

"Please take us around to the kitchen entrance," the Scarecrow requested. Turning to me he said, "I have been away some time and I am sure there is a long line of people waiting at the main entrance who want to talk about everything in Oz with me. I hope to defer as many discussions a possible. I have found that no answer is always better than a hasty answer. And often time, no answer is the very best answer of all. If you ever become a leader, you may want to keep this in mind."

The kitchen entrance was a tall and broad double door. The doors were open and I could see that a carriage pulled by a team of horses could fit inside. We walked into an area where all sorts of kitchen items were stored; many bags of flour, each as large as a cow, great bins of potatoes, carrots, and apples, crates full of tomatoes, sweet peppers, and Brussels sprouts.

"I see that Brussels sprouts have infected Oz."

"Emily, I take it that you do not like them."

"You are well taken."

"Don't give up on them. I hear our chefs are excellent, though I have no personal experience."

We walked further along and entered the baking area of the kitchen. Many workers of all sizes were busy pushing dough around on long tables. On the first table they were kneading the enormous dough that covered the table. On the second and third tables there were cloths over what I assumed were other doughs. On the fourth table a number of workers were weighing and cutting the dough into pieces. On the next table workers were making the blobs of dough into rounds. There were a bunch more tables as well. A creature that looked like a large frog walking on his hind legs carried loaves of bread that were on thin wooden boards into and out of a room that had steam pouring out its door when it was opened. There was a long oven, with many individual doors that creatures that looked like large iguanas worked at, putting just risen loaves in and removing loaves baked beautifully light brown.

One of the workers called out a song and they all joined in. Part of it went like this:

Hey baker, bake me some sunshine
Hey baker, bake me some sunshine
People got to eat so bakers got to bake
Hey baker, bake me some sunshine.

The song continued with bakers baking all sorts of things, some things that were actually baked, and just about anything else one could think of.

The Scarecrow said, "There is bread right out of the oven. I can get you some to eat if you are hungry."

"That would be nice," I replied. After a short walk we had entered a dining area and I was eating some hot fresh bread with butter and washing it down with milk.

Between bites, I asked "Do you always have so many bakers? They must be making hundreds of loaves of bread."

"Not usually, but the Witch's Council is a big event. Lots of witches and many dignitaries from all over Oz attend. It can be quite wonderful, and quite tedious. Did I mention that it could be quite tedious?" He said with a glum look on his face.

I took my last bite, "You have great bread in Oz."

"I hope this is enough to hold you to dinner Emily," the Scarecrow said.

"It might," I said.

After I finished drinking my milk, the Scarecrow and I walked down a wide hallway decorated with colorful wall hangings, large pictures of all sorts of people and creatures, who I assumed were historic figures in Oz, and sculptures as well.

I followed the Scarecrow into an office and he sent a messenger to find some witches. With no delay the witches walked in and began to discuss with the Scarecrow what they needed to do to send me home. It was like going to a doctor's appointment; everyone talking about me as if I wasn't there, or was a chair, or perhaps the rug. Thankfully there were more people waiting to speak with the Scarecrow so the discussions were cut short. By short I mean already way too long for me and they hadn't even gotten warmed up with the blah blah blah.

As soon as the witches filed out two people walked into the office. The first, a large woman with bright blue hair said, "Scarecrow, my team and I can't meet the deadline for the road bed preparation for the extension of the Yellow Brick Road. We just don't have enough people."

And the second, a stout and muscular man said, "And even if the bed preparation was complete right now, my team can't possibly lay the bricks in time. It just can't be done."

The Scarecrow asked them some questions and they said that the road needed to be finished in two weeks, but that the bed preparation would take two weeks, and then another two weeks for the brick laying.

"Are your teams fully committed to getting the road finished on time?" the Scarecrow asked.

"Yes," they both said. The woman added, "We may be able to pull in the preparation a bit, perhaps a day or two, but without more help that's the best that can be done."

The man added, "Same with my team, but that leaves us still about two weeks late."

The Scarecrow turned to the man, "Is your team busy now?"

"No," the man replied, "we can't start laying bricks until the bed is ready."

"So why don't you and your team work with the bed preparation team?"

"Okay," the man said, "it's not what we usually do, but I think we can do it. That solves the road bed preparation problem, but what about the brick laying?"

The Scarecrow then turned and faced the woman, "Is that okay with you?"

"Yes, that should be fine. My team is very experienced so we can train them as we go."

"And can your team help the brick laying team after the bed preparation is done?" the Scarecrow asked.

"Yes, that should be fine as well. We were scheduled to work on the preparation for two weeks, so we should have a week were we are free."

"So that settles it," the Scarecrow said. "Thank you for dropping by," and he shook their hands. The man and woman stood up and the Scarecrow quickly ushered them out of the room together and closed the door. After the door was shut the Scarecrow turned to me and said, "They might even realize that the brick laying doesn't need to wait until the entire road bed is completed, but I leave that for them to discover."

I could see that the Scarecrow was a good manager of people. Perhaps having a leader stuffed with straw was not such a bad thing, and perhaps in some cases it may be an improvement.

The Scarecrow read a paper on his desk and then said, "I need to step out for a few moments. It should not be long, so please wait here."

I was left to sit in the Scarecrow's office, which was pretty similar to my mother's desk where she works, except there were no computers, or phones, or any electronics.

An older witch entered the room. She wore a collarless shirt and pants that had horizontal stripes that were colored like the rainbow. Around her neck the shirt was red, and at her wrists and ankles the cloth was blue. The buttons on the shirt were colored to match the cloth and the shirt extended down to mid-thigh, so no belt was visible. The most striking thing about her were her piercing blue-grey eyes.

"Emily, I was in the recent meeting where we discussed how to send you home, so I know some of your story. But I have more questions. How you are sent home may depend on how you came here. Everyone calls me Gings," she said.

"Hello Gings," I said, standing up and offering my hand.

She shook my hand with an uncomfortably tight grip. "Please tell me exactly what happened before you came to Oz."

126

"There was a mirror that I was looking at. I cleaned it off with a polishing cloth. The surface shimmered and then I saw what I now know was the Tin Man sitting on a park bench. When I touched the mirror's surface I came through somehow and I stumbled out onto the ground in front of the Tin Man. He had been sitting in front of a mirror that was identical to the one I had touched," I said.

She sat down and thought for a while. Then she stood once more.

"Emily, I need you to follow me." She began to walk briskly out of the office and I followed as requested, struggling to keep up. We went through another door, up a few flights of stairs, and then down a hall, and then I lost track of where we had gone.

She took a key out and we entered a large room. From a cabinet she took down a wooden box that showed Glinda's insignia. Gings took out a key and opened the box. Inside were a book and a small crown.

"These are everything that we have from Glinda. I would like you to place Glinda's sword inside, as I believe it is safer for you not to carry it with you. It would be best if I did not touch it either."

I took the sword and its belt off and placed it inside. "What was Glinda like?"

"She was, as I am sure everyone you have asked has said, a powerful sorceress. As a person, at first, she was cheerful, but with time it seemed that concerns weighed heavily on her. When Ozma went missing, Glinda never recovered. She never smiled with joy or laughed with glee again. Even Dorothy, who was Ozma's closest friend, was able to move on in time, but Glinda never did. And she devoted her life to protecting Oz, and she knew that she would not be here to protect it forever. I think this weighed on her most of all."

As she talked, Gings closed the wooden box and locked it.

"She was my teacher, and though there were times we were not close, she was a true friend to me through everything."

"It was frustrating to me, as a student, not being able to understand Glinda's use of magic. I thought she was hiding things from me so that she would always be most powerful. It was only after, long after, that I understood that there was nothing to hide, or in fact, that could be hidden."

She returned the box to its place in the cabinet and turned so that we looked into each other's faces.

"Once, she said to me, 'Magic comes naturally from purity of intent and integrity.' I flew off in a rage, thinking she had insulted me. In time I realized that she was right and I was only being proud. That time I lost can never be replaced. What she had said was exactly true, but knowing it is not enough. Magic is not simply a matter of knowledge."

Gings motioned toward the door and we headed out of the room.

"Why didn't you want to touch the sword?"

"Touching something implies a relationship of ownership, when it comes to certain things. Clearly Glinda intended that sword for you."

I said, "It's been a long day. I hope I'm going to get a place to sleep."

"That's where we are heading next," replied Gings. We walked down a long hallway, turned into an alcove and entered a small bedroom.

"There are so many folks here for the council that all the normal rooms in the palace are taken. The larger rooms are packed to overflow. This room is rarely used, since it is so small, out of the way, and in an area of the palace normally used for storage. It should have all you need however. I had some pajamas sent down for you and we can look after your clothes tomorrow."

"Thanks," I said. It was a small room but since all I wanted to do was to take a shower and sleep, it would be fine.

"You need to use the AI to turn off the lights. Its name is Valdamorta," Gings said with an exaggerated roll of the *R*. "It's sensitive. If you don't roll the *R* it will ignore you. You are familiar with AIs?"

I looked at what she was pointing at. It looked like a small crystal ball with a bunch of minute ears floating on its surface. When it heard its name it lit up with a faint blue glow. The ears flocked to whatever direction there was something to hear. It was creepy. "Yes," I said.

"Fine," Gings said. "I'll give you some privacy. I know it's been a long day for you." She turned and left without delay.

As soon as Gings left, I took a shower, changed into the pajamas, and jumped into bed. I looked around the room. It was very small, only containing a bed, a tiny desk, and a plain chair. It looked like someone had been sweeping up but got interrupted. There was a broom and a dustpan full of sweepings against one wall. The wall near the head of the bed was covered by a heavy curtain that went from the ceiling to the floor. The curtain was deep ruby red and it had vertical pleats. Besides the AI, there were a few books left on the desk, and it looked like more dusting was needed. Knowing how opulent things were in the palace, I thought that it was an odd room for me to end up in.

Even though I had already changed into pajamas I didn't feel ready for sleep. I got back out of bed and sat down at the desk. One of the books was a copy of Glinda's magic book. I opened the cover and was surprised. I could understand it, yet it wasn't in English; it was some language I couldn't quite place, but definitely not English. Some of the characters in the alphabet were different as well. *How strange. And how was it that I hadn't noticed the language of the sign at Robotville. Was the sign at Robotville in English, or was I just too distracted to notice?*

I paged through the magic book and read some of what seemed to be simple stories. I read a story about a young girl who lost a key. She searched everywhere for the key and couldn't find it. The next day, as she was walking with one of her friends, she stumbled over something on the sidewalk. She looked to see what she had stumbled over, and it was the key she had been searching for.

I closed the book. How about a bit of exploration? I left the room and searched around trying to figure out some of how the palace was set up. In no time I was good and lost. Then I recognized the door of the room Gings had put Glinda's sword in. That was far enough. I was getting tired. I walked back the way I came and quite by surprise I found my room. Outside the door was a tray with some food. It had a note on it that read. "Emily, here is some dinner for you. I apologize for not being a better host but I have many things to see to. Scarecrow."

I picked up the tray and went back into the room. I was hungrier than I thought and I scarfed down every bit of food on the tray. Now I was tired and ready for bed. I growled out a long yawn. I brushed my teeth and tumbled into bed. "Valdamorta, lights off," I said, with no response. It's sensitive all right. "Valdamorta, lights off," I said remembering to roll the R, and the lights turned off. Then it said, "I also found this article titled 'The Many Ways Valdamorta is Superior to Hey Shmeagle.' Would you like to hear it?"

"No," I said.

"Are you sure?"

"Yes."

"Really sure?"

"Valdamorta off."

Chapter 12 Oz's Armada

The next morning, I woke up and, without anything else to do, I went back to paging through Glinda's magic book. It fell open exactly to the start of the story about the girl who lost her key. I read on for a bit and then I heard a knock on the door.

I opened the door and a tiny woman walked in. "I'm sorry to bother you so early, but I need to measure you for clothes for tonight. I'm the royal measurer, and my name is Marta. Nice to meet you," she said quite business-like.

"Nice to meet you," I replied. "My name is Emily,"

"Well I would hope so," She said, "since I am here to measure Emily."

She pulled out a cloth tape measure and began measuring me. She switched back and forth between measuring and writing things down on a clip board.

"The request looks incomplete, but don't worry, I will make sure you are fitted nicely," she said without a pause.

She measured me all over: my head, my feet, my hands, my arms, my top and my legs. She knew more about my size than anyone has ever known. She measured how fat my fingers are, how long my forearms are, and the size of my biceps. At times she needed to climb on top of the chair, and at other times she needed to climb onto the desk. She apparently was used to this climbing furniture, a bit like me in the antiques store.

She was finishing up, muttering to herself, when there was another knock at the door. I opened the door and the Tin Man was standing there, smiling from one ear to the other. "Good morning Emily," he sang out.

"Good morning," I said as I hugged him. "When did you get to the Emerald City?"

"Very late last night," he said. "Oh, hello Marta, how are you today?"

"I'm fine and I will be on my way. One day is insufficient time to make formal clothes, so I cannot dilly dally. Duty calls." She exited the room muttering "dilly dally, dilly dally."

"And how did you get here?" I asked the Tin Man. "It's good to see you, and to see you are safe."

The Tin Man nodded his thanks. "After we got separated in Robotville I realized that we might need the mirror to get you home, since that is how you got to Oz. So I backtracked to retrieve the mirror. I got help from some of my Winky friends and we had a slow and uneventful trip here."

"And how did you get out of Robotville? There was supposed to be no way out."

"I just walked out the way we came in. James005 didn't even notice me."

"Sounds a lot safer than the way I left Robotville."

"Yes," the Tin Man said. "Anyway I thought I would spend some time with you today. Perhaps you would like some breakfast?"

"Breakfast sounds good, but first, can you explain this book? It's written in a language I don't recognize, yet I can understand it. I thought everyone in Oz spoke English."

"Oh no, how did you get that impression? This is Oz. Why would we speak English? We all speak Ozish. Don't you?" asked the Tin Man.

"No, I speak English."

"Well, it sounds like Ozish to me, and Dorothy and the Wizard all could understand us, so we assumed that everyone spoke Ozish."

"If Dorothy came from Kansas, she spoke English, or at least American. Apparently in Oz we can all understand each other," I said.

"Do you mean where you come from people don't understand each other?" the Tin Man asked.

"Yes, frequently we don't understand each other, and it gets even worse if we are talking in different languages."

"How inconvenient," he said, "and how baffling. I think you come from a civilized land. That must be why you can't understand each other. Oz has never been civilized, so we have no need to be confused. Anyway, Gings sent me here with some clothes for today. If you leave your pajamas on the bed, they will be clean when you return."

I took the clothes into the bathroom and changed. I laid my dirty clothes on the bed and put on my utility belt. "Better to be prepared," I thought.

We headed to an eating area where I had some oatmeal with some fruit, and an egg on a slice of toast. You just can't beat that no matter which world you are in.

We left the palace and walked through a park with a series of circular ponds separated by paved paths and grassy areas. There were young children playing and running around. People were seated on park benches, some reading newspapers and some talking.

We walked by the first pool. A crowd sat around the sides of the pool, laughing and joking with each other. It seemed very pleasant, so we sat down.

"I'm sorry about the scratch I made on you," I said.

"Oh, don't think about it. I have come to quite like it. Don't you think it makes me look dangerous?" the Tin Man asked. "Of course, I don't tell people that I got it while being rescued from an overly tight sleeping bag."

We sat in the sun for a few minutes and then I heard some muttering from the next pool over.

"The Royal Armada has been scuttled, and now it will be lost to crumble and scale in the deep blue seas," an older man wailed. He was dressed in a bright blue satin uniform, with many patches of rank and many medals on his chest, and fancy epaulettes on his shoulders with golden cords. On his head he wore a black hat with points to the front and rear and medals on both sides, with gold braids that matched those on his shoulders.

"Can I help?" I asked.

"No, I think not," he said. "The Armada is lost. It is a tragedy of unthinkable proportions. In fact, I just can't think of it."

"Is that the Armada?" I asked, pointing at three small wooden ships that were below the surface of the water toward the center of the pool.

"Yes," he said, with tears streaming down his face.

I took my shoes and socks off and waded into the pool. I tipped each ship over and poured all the water out and then handed them to the man. "Here you go," I said.

"Thank you, thank you," he said. "I will recommend you for a commendation for meritorious service to the Oz Royal Navy."

"Anytime," I said.

I whispered to the Tin Man, "Why didn't he just go in and get them?"

"When the Wizard had these pools built, he forbade anyone to enter them. Besides that, the admiral is probably scared of water."

"How sad," I said. I sat there kicking my feet back and forth thinking of how hot a day it was already, how nice it was while I was rescuing the ships, and how nice it would be to cool my feet in the pool. I stood up on the bench and yelled out, "I, Emily of North Carolina, friend of the Scarecrow, declare that anyone who desires may cool their feet in these pools."

The children shouted out in glee. I swung around and stuck my feet back into the pool. Many of the children kicked their shoes and socks off and did the same, and many of them sat down next to me and said hello. We sat there swinging our feet for a while and then I noticed a bin which contained a large stack of newspapers. I grabbed a paper off the pile.

The first headline read, "Scarecrow returns to the Emerald City," and below it was a sketch of the Scarecrow and me sitting inside the carriage that had brought us to the palace. The subheading said, "Emily of North Carolina's Courageous Rescue of HRM." Just below that was an article titled, "Witches' Council meeting tomorrow." There were articles about the weather, and farming, and business, and music as well.

There was a cartoon, but I didn't understand what it was about, so I couldn't tell if it was funny or not.

I was about to put the paper down when I changed my mind and carefully tore the article on me and the Scarecrow out. I folded it up and slipped it in a pocket. Then I took some pages of the paper, folded them into a boat, and gently glided the boat into the pool. The boat sailed slowly out to the center and then drifted to the edge in a breeze. This caused quite a commotion.

"Hey, can you fold me one?" a girl asked. "Me too, please," said a boy.

"I can do better than that," I said. "I can show you how to fold your own boats, and how to fold your own admiral's hats out of newspaper."

"Watch now," I said. "This is the way my mother taught me to fold boats during one of our family trips." After I taught the children how to fold paper boats, I showed them how easy it was to change a paper boat into a paper hat. Some could not master the folding, but the older children were happy to help their younger friends.

I folded one last paper boat and handed it to a child who was sitting on a park bench nearby, watching all the activities by himself. "This one I made especially for you," I said. He took it from me and scampered off to the nearest pool.

Many of the children were wearing admiral's hats, pushing paper boats about, and walking in the pools.

Everyone was happy except the Admiral of the Royal Navy, who muttered that his position of authority had been usurped. The admiral packed up and walked away with his ships.

I sat down by the Tin Man who had been watching.

"I don't think I will get my commendation," I said.

"I think not," the Tin Man said. "If we can't find a way to send you home, you are certainly well loved here."

"I need to get home. My friends are there, my family is there, everything I love is there," I said.

I realized that I had been speaking rather loudly, and that the Tin Man had tears in his eyes.

"Please don't cry," I said. "I was wrong, not everything I love is there. I will always remember you and my friends in Oz. Please dry your tears. I can't bear the thought of you rusting again."

The Tin Man dried his eyes. Then he said, "Today is a day for Deenranja. Let's go watch."

I followed the Tin Man to a quiet section of the park where there were round tables, surrounded by three chairs each.

"This is the ancient game of Deenranja. It has been played in Oz for centuries," the Tin Man said.

The game used a board with hexagonal spaces and the board was hexagonally shaped as well. Three players had a set of pieces on the board and took turns moving their pieces. The pieces looked a bit like those used in chess.

"Is Deenranja a type of chess?" I asked.

"I am not familiar with chess so I can't say. If you watch perhaps in time you will be able to answer your question."

"Chess is a board game, but only two players can play at a time. And the board is square, not hexagonal."

"Interesting," he said.

"What are the different pieces?" I asked.

138

"There are hats, spires, wands, and crowns," he said as he pointed to them. "Each piece type moves in its own way. Each player plays until they lose their crown. It is a game of strategy and concentration. Many people play it regularly."

"It sounds a lot like chess," I said.

I watched as the players began the game. The crown could move in any direction for any amount of spaces. If it hit a board edge, it could change direction and continue on. The game had some similarities with chess, but seemed much riskier. Each player had two opponents. I wondered, "How do you play against two people? You don't get to immediately respond to a threat! And you could have two threats to deal with, and only one chance to move."

We watched the game play continue. One player in the game had their crown captured so they no longer moved. That person's pieces still scattered the board, sometimes helping, sometimes hindering the play of the other players. The second player's crown was lost and the game ended. They bowed to each other. The winner stayed at the board waiting for the next opponents.

"Do you play?" I asked the Tin Man.

"I do, but I am not a very strong player. The Scarecrow plays a very good game, but of course, being regent, he does not have so much time to play when he is home. That reminds me," he said. "I need to bring you back to your room in time for lunch. It's a bit early but are you ready to go? You'll have some time to rest in your room."

"I'm ready," I replied.

We walked back through the area with the pools. The children had moved on to other games.

"It would be nice if these pools had some fountains in them," I said.

I remembered some fountains in a water park I had once visited. The fountains shot bursts of water from one area to another so that it looked like the water was jumping from one pool to another.

Suddenly, at the farthest pool, a burst of water shot out and flew to a nearby pool.

"I guess a witch must have heard me and agreed with me," I said.

"I think you are right," the Tin Man said. "A witch must have heard you."

We continued on and I saw a Flyer on one side. I grabbed the Tin Man's arm and said, "I don't want to be seen by that Flyer."

"Let's go this way then," he said, leading me off into a crowd of people. They were gathered around the entrance to a roller coaster. There was a sign that read, "The Cyclone, M. B. Yus Proprietor."

The cars on the roller coaster were turning the final corner as the roller coaster came into view. It didn't look like the cars were going that fast. The roller coaster wasn't that high and really didn't look scary.

I said, "Maybe I can hide on the roller coaster."

The Tin Man replied, "Are you sure you want to? I've ridden it. It can make flesh people sick in their stomachs."

"I've been on loop de loops, and I've been on corkscrews, and this one just doesn't seem that high or fast," I said.

"Okay, I warned you," said the Tin Man. "I hope you have a strong stomach."

"Okay, I'm warned, but it just doesn't look that special."

It did look modern though. The twin tracks were supported by massive metal towers on the left and right of the tracks. The area between the tracks was empty.

We climbed the stairs up to the loading platform as people exited the cars and left through a different staircase. Some people looked a bit sick and walked a bit wobbly. I tried to hide myself on the far side of the Tin Man. We passed a man with hair that looked like multicolored curly fries. He was seated in front of a control panel with a number of levers and switches.

"Make sure that all the securing devises are snug and that your head is properly supported," the ride attendant said. "We don't want anyone losing their head."

We sat down. I positioned the thigh supports over my legs, and the shoulder clamps into place, then the head supports. The attendant walked through making sure everything was snug. She called out, "Moe, everyone is locked in and safe to go."

Then the ride started. It gave a hard lurch forward and then we slowly climbed a long hill. Once we reached the top the cars sped up and took a sharp right turn, then on into a loop de loop. Another hard-right turn out of the loop de loop into a long corkscrew. It was a nice ride but nothing to scream about. After the cork screw we did another hard-right turn, then a flip, and a hard-left turn.

"Oh!" I yelled. The flip put us upside down so we went underneath the loading platform and climbed the hill hanging upside down in our seats. The blood immediately went to my head and my head started pounding. Then we took a hard left and entered the loop de loop. I clamped my arms firmly over my stomach. At the bottom of the loop de loop, my head was a bit too close to the ground for my comfort. At the top I could look out far into the distance. My stomach did not appreciate the ride at all. Then another upside down hard left turn into the corkscrew, with our heads flying passed the ground and hoping that the thigh and shoulder clamps held tight. At the top some people were waving at people in the other cars. I caught the eyes of the Flyer who was evidently following me. So much for staying hidden. I closed my eyes after that, hoping I wouldn't vomit on the Tin Man.

Another sharp left and a rotating flip put us right side up again. The blood slowly returned to where it belonged. I was thankful it was almost over. We did a final hard right turn, slowed, and approached the boarding area.

"So, how was that?" the Tin Man asked.

"Pretty cool. I hope my stomach catches up with me soon," I said trying to sound okay. The Tin Man helped me keep from falling over.

"I didn't see that half flip and I really underestimated the ride. I can see why people get sick. Taking those loop de loops upside down is something. On the other hand it's really clever. It was tricky that you could go around the whole track twice, but do different things each time. But I'm afraid it didn't help keep me hidden. The Flyer was watching us during the ride."

As we walked my stomach settled. I didn't tell the Tin Man but I resolved never to take that ride again. I looked around for the Flyer, but he or she was nowhere in sight.

"I guess the Flyer must have left," I said.

We turned and headed back to the room I was staying in.

"I have a poem for you," I said to the Tin Man. "I can't write Ozish, so you will have to write it down for me."

The Tin Man found a pad of paper and a pencil and said, "Okay."

"Here it is," I said.

"Through the looking glass, Alice went
and other girls it seems.
To a land of magic and mystery
and messages in dreams.
And though there is no place like home
I can surely say,
of my friends both dear and true in Oz
I will think of every day."

"Thank you," said the Tin Man, brushing back a tear.

"You may be made of metal, but you are an old softy inside," I said.

"When the wizard gave me a heart, he chose very well," the Tin Man replied.

We started to walk around the palace to the main entrance. "How old is this palace?" I asked.

"Not very old," the Tin Man said. "There was an old palace that was here, but the new palace is much larger and grander. I believe that the new palace was built around the ancient one, so that parts of the present palace are actually from the old palace. Those parts are very old."

The Wizard of Oz was a humbug, but he was a master at putting people to work. The Munchkins hailed him as their leader after seeing the magic of his hot air balloon. And while he had no magic, he did have the Munchkins build the new palace, and the pools, and the parks, and the new library, and many other works that they all love and enjoy. So, I would say that the Wizard had magic, but a different type of magic than witches have."

"He sounds like quite a character," I said.

"Yes, but looking back, he did a great deal of good. Dorothy, the Scarecrow, the Cowardly Lion, and I did not like going off to kill the Wicked Witch of the West, but in the end, she is gone and everyone is better off. The Wizard's methods were not always fair, and he was selfish at times, but he left Oz much better than it was when he arrived."

The Tin Man brought me back to my room, and I found that my clothes were cleaned and folded on the bed.

"I'm going to leave you to rest here for a while," he said. "I am not sure who will be taking you to lunch, but I am sure the Scarecrow has it all arranged."

When the Tin Man had left, I tossed the book on the bed and plunked down beside it. It fell open to a page with a drawing of women in chariots. There were three chariots across, and in the middle chariot stood a young Glinda, wearing her crown, with her short sword at her right hip and a small shield on her right arm. She had a calm smile on her face. In her chariot was a young girl, younger than me I think. The girl looked like a very young Gings. She had Gings eyes. The drawing must have been made a long time ago. The chariots on both sides each had an archer and a swordswoman. The all wore light armor and they all had fierce expressions on their faces.

Each chariot was pulled by a pair of large horses, each horse wearing armor on its back and sides, and a helmet protecting its head. None of the horses had bits in their mouths, and there were no reins.

After I thought about what it must have been like to fight with Glinda to protect Oz, I began to flip to other pages. The first one I came to was a description of how to fly a broom. It seemed pretty straight forward, but considering the trouble Josh was having flying, it must have been harder than it looked.

I flipped to another part of the book and I came to a story that was about a girl who reached through a window to pluck a distant flower. I closed my eyes and tried to imagine it. I was in a cottage, looking out through a kitchen window that was over a sink and had short light blue curtains. Outside the window there was a green lawn, and a small group of yellow and white flowers planted among the roots of a large old tree. The flowers were very tiny, and shaped like bells. I reached out to one. It felt like I could feel the flower in my hand. I bent over to smell the flower and took a deep breath.

Chapter 13 Witches' Council

I was brought back to the present by a knock on the door.

"Emily, I'm here to take you to lunch." It sounded like Josh. I darted to the door and there he was.

"The Scarecrow was planning to send Gings to accompany you to lunch but the Tin Man thought you might want to spend the time before the council with people closer to your age."

"Thanks, that sounds nice," I said.

We walked to a cafeteria that looked busy. I got a tray and began to select food. Everything was pretty similar to lunch at my school cafeteria.

I picked what looked like a stew, with potatoes and green beans, and for dessert, some kaylah pudding. I may as well eat it now because I am not going to get it at home.

We sat down at a table full of young witches. They were eating and goofing around, tossing food in the air and then catching it in their mouths. Of course, being witches, the food didn't fall straight down, but danced and darted around, bobbing here and there.

"Who is your new friend?" one of the witches asked Josh.

"This is Emily, from, I'm not sure."

"North Carolina," I said.

"Where's that?" someone else asked.

"I am not really sure," I said. "Not close."

"Hi, I'm Teresa," said one of the witches, and we shook hands. Another said, "Hi, I'm Ptano." And then I got introduced all around, but there were too many names for me to keep track of.

"What a great belt you have. Do you carry your powders and magic ingredients in it?" asked one witch.

"Let's see," I said as I went through the compartments. "I have a pocket knife, a couple of paper clips, a few wipes, a marker, a few sticky bandages, and a lot of dirt, it seems."

"It looks great, and really useful," one witch said. "I really want one."

I spotted the Flyer who had watched me while I was on the roller coaster. I was nervous as he came over to me and introduced himself.

"Welcome," he said. "I hope the Emerald City is meeting all your expectations. I saw that you got to ride The Cyclone. How did you like it? I'm Zhang,"

"Yes, it's, it's a once in a lifetime experience, meaning I never want to do it again," I said nervously.

"It often has that effect on people," he replied.

I was worried about how my conversation with the Flyer would go, but someone called him away. We shook hands before he left, and I felt something sticking to my palm; a little piece of paper. I closed my hand around it so no one could see.

"I'm going to the bathroom," I said to Josh as I stepped away.

When I was safely sealed inside a bathroom stall, I read the note. It said, "Veeron knows you are here and has your description. Protect yourself."

I decided not to leave any trace of the note behind so I tore the paper into little pieces, then I put them into my mouth and chewed until they became mush. Then I spread the mush over some toilet paper and flushed it down the toilet.

After washing my hands and rinsing my mouth out, I came back out and finished up my food. Folks were beginning to get up and leave.

"Emily, why don't you come with us back to the dorm?" asked Josh.

"Sure," I said. I thought it would be safer if I stayed in a big group. And it didn't hurt that they were witches. We walked out of the cafeteria and turned down a hall.

I recognized that we were near the kitchen. Josh and I stopped at a group of witches crowded around a large cauldron.

The witches were dressed in their own personal styles. Some were dressed all in black with black pointed hats and that characteristic bend in the top, and some others were dressed in white lab coats. Another group wore jeans and pastel colored tops, and had flowers in their hair and painted on their faces. Still others were dressed all in black leather with chrome diamond studs, and some were dressed in sweat pants and sweat shirts. They were all stirring, chanting, and tasting the thick liquid that bubbled up and steamed.

"What's that?" I asked. "Some kind of magic potion?"

"Why yes, it's the spaghetti sauce," Josh replied as we walked along. "This is one of the most important parts of the Witches' Council meeting, the cooking of the sauce for the pasta dinner that follows. They seem to be getting along this year. Last year there was quite a to-do over how spicy the sauce should be," he added.

"Why don't they just use magic to make it?" I asked.

"You can't eat magic. I mean, you can, and it will even seem like you are eating. But a moment later you will be hungry. Also, the rule is that no magic is to be used in preparing for and during the council meeting. There were too many problems in the past when everyone was working magic."

We all shuffled into a big common room that was part of the dorm area.

"Let's give Emily a lesson in flying on a broomstick." one of the witches proposed.

"Yes! Emily, you will need to fly a broom if you want to be a witch," another said. "And we can help you."

"I am not a witch and I don't want to be a witch," I said.

"That will make it even more fun. I always wanted to know what would happen if someone who wasn't a witch decided to fly a broom," another chimed in.

Josh said, "This has to be totally up to Emily. Emily, do you want to give it a try?"

I am never going to get to do this at home, I thought, so I may as well try. "Yes," I replied.

"First you want to get back on the broom so that the bristles are under your butt," said a witch who I later found was called TP. "For protection of sensitive parts, you understand, especially while learning."

I sat back upon the broom.

"Now, I'm going to lift you a bit off the ground," TP said.

And the broom lifted about waist high so my feet were just off the ground. By leaning right and left I could move the broom side to side.

"Good, so you move the broom by shifting your center of gravity. Lean forward and you go forward, lean back and you go back. You already got left and right down," TP said.

I moved the broom around slowly left and right, forward and back.

"Okay, now things get a bit more complicated so just listen. If you tip your hips to the right, you will rotate right. I'll give you a bit more height so you can try it without whacking your head on the floor. Hold on tight!"

I got a good hold of the broomstick and wrapped my legs tight around it too. I tipped my hips to the right. I began slowly rolling over clockwise, to the right, then down, then left, and then back up again. I did it a few times.

"Cool," I said though being upside down reminded me of my recent ride on The Cyclone. I tipped my hips to the left, and I started rolling over counter clockwise.

"I'm not going to let you do this, because the room is not high enough, but normally if you tilt your hips forward, you are going to rotate down and if you tilt your hips back you will rotate back. This is how you control the pitch of the broom. If you fidget around, you can do loop de loops, whether you want to or not."

"And the last piece is vertical control. It's hard to describe exactly, but you use your abs. Pull your stomach in and you go higher, push your stomach out and you go lower."

I tried as she said. It was a bit of a strange feeling, and I bumped my head into the ceiling once, but after a few attempts I had some idea of what to do. I started slowly circling the room. It was too much fun to resist, so I rolled a bit over and sped up. I guess I got carried away, because I began hurtling around the room. I took out a few tall plants along the way as well.

"Go girl!" they were shouting. "You fly girl!"

Then there was a loud knock on the door. Everyone quieted.

"I already warned you once. You know you're not supposed to fly around inside." It was Gings, and she sounded like she wasn't happy.

I jumped off the flying broom and slammed into Josh. It's good he is pretty big, because I would have knocked over one of the smaller witches. The broom flew into a corner, and the plants I bowled over righted themselves just in time for Gings to open the door and step in. I saw that my hands were red from gripping the broomstick, so I hid them behind my back.

"Emily, which of these witches was flying around in here?" Gings asked me.

"None of these witches were flying around," I said.

She came closer to me, looked me straight in the eyes, and asked me again.

"Okay, tell me the truth. Which witch rode the broom?"

I said, "None of these witches rode the broom," feeling a great deal of discomfort.

"I don't understand it, but even though I heard someone flying a broom, I can see that you are telling the truth. At least most of it. All of you, be warned, you are flying in stormy skies."

Gings looked around once more. She left the room and closed the door with a slam behind her.

Then there was another knock on the door. A young man stuck his head in and called out, "Emily, I have your clothes for you for the council meeting. I need you to go to your room and start getting ready."

It seemed too early, that time had flown by. I said goodbye to the witches in the dorm and, after a lot of handshakes and hugs, I followed him into the hallway.

He said, "Here are your clothes," as he handed me the box. "Do you need help finding your room?"

"No," I replied. I had a good enough idea of where I was, and I wanted to do some more exploring. I stopped to examine the box he had handed me. It was very fancy. When I looked up, he had already left.

It only took me a bit to find my room. I put the box on the bed, and then I wondered what was behind the ruby curtains. I pushed through the curtains only to find my way blocked by a pair of heavy wooden doors. I opened the doors with a shove and stepped out onto a balcony, a "where art thou Romeo" kind of balcony.

Outside, clouds had moved in. The sky was dark and ominous. I could look out over the park area that the Tin Man and I had walked through earlier in the day, which now was empty and quiet. I could see the Scarecrow's workshops far off in the distance. I was about to go back into the room when I heard some voices.

"This is her room. We need to get in place to take her. Here's her description: medium tall, taller than you, shorter than me, athletic build, dark chocolate skin, black hair in tight curls. Got it?"

"Yes, I got it."

"Push the gag in her mouth, and stick the powder under her nose."

"Got it."

"When she turns into a bird, stuff her in the bag and into your pocket, and then go."

"Got it. What kind of a bird will she turn into?"

"A small blackbird."

"Okay good. I mean, I don't want to have to carry around a stork, or a vulture. So you're sure about that? A small blackbird?"

"Just a small blackbird. Done with questions?"

"Yeah done. But what if she turns into an enormous bird, with a large beak and claws? What if she is taller than me, with bright yellow feathers and a long beak?"

"She won't and stop asking questions. I don't want any mistakes. If we do this right Veeron will pay us enough so that we will be sitting pretty."

"I got it. What's Veeron doing with her?"

"You don't want to know, but he wants her unhurt. He wants to do all the hurting himself."

"Okay, I will go down to the left end of the hall and wait for her to come."

"And remember to put your mask on so you don't get changed into a bird."

"What do we do if she has company?"

"Throw the powder into the air and change them all to birds. Take Emily and do whatever you need to do to anyone else."

"Okay, I'm ready."

The door shut. A few breaths later I came out from behind the curtains.

I took the desk chair and jammed it against the door so that it could not be opened from the outside. At first I figured I would wait for help, so I got dressed for the council meeting. The dress was elegant, and I had long white gloves, and a fine hat, and nice shoes, but my thoughts were on other things. That's when I realized that if I waited, whomever was sent to take me to the council could get hurt. My eyes found the broom and dustpan. I had a lesson on flying a broom so I thought I could do it.

"Okay, Mr. Broom, I am going to take you for a ride," I whispered.

I have to say that when I got on the broom on the ledge of the balcony, it looked a whole heck of a lot higher off the ground then it had been just before. But I was going.

I rose up so my feet just couldn't reach the ledge. It looked even higher now. I flew against the wall of the palace, creeping along and sometimes banging into the wall pretty hard. But with each bang I was slowly getting closer to the ground. The witches in the dorm must have been helping me a lot when I zoomed around the room, because this time I struggled to keep control and not fall from the sky.

When I finally got to the ground, I got off, said "Thank you, Mr. Broom," and ran to the nearest palace entrance. I rushed along the hallways and barged into the Scarecrow's office, where he was talking to Gings and some other officials.

"There are people outside my room who want to kidnap me," I said, breathing hard from the run.

"What?" asked the Scarecrow.

"Some spies want to kidnap me and take me to be Veeron's prisoner."

"How did you get past them?" Gings asked.

"I flew," I said.

"Like a bird?" she asked.

"On a broom," I said.

"I see, and now I understand," she said, giving me a stern look.

"Gings, please send some of your friends to take care of this," the Scarecrow said.

Gings got up to leave. "Wait, wait," I yelled. "You need to know that they have powder that, if you inhale it, will turn you into a small bird."

"Okay," Gings said. "Wait here."

The Scarecrow and I waited in a heavy silence. Time seemed to stand still as we hoped that the spies would be captured and no one hurt.

After a long quiet the Scarecrow asked, "Are you fond of geometry Emily?"

Before I could answer Gings reentered the room.

"Two spies taken into custody," she said. "One tried to escape by turning into a bird, but we have him in a cage."

"Thank you, Gings," the Scarecrow said. "Why don't you get ready for the council meeting and then come back to stay with Emily? I don't want her left alone."

In a short while Gings returned and the Scarecrow went to change for the council meeting. Gings now wore the typical work clothes for a witch, black all over with a black hat, but it shimmered like silver in sunshine. She helped me brush off and straighten out my dress. She cast a spell and it looked almost new. "I need to go to the hall," she said as she left me alone in the Scarecrow's office. I counted out the seconds as I wondered what the council meeting would be like.

A few measures later the Scarecrow walked in wearing a plush ermine cape and a crown on his head that made his head crunch up on one side. He looked as regal as a Scarecrow could look.

"Take my hand," the Scarecrow said. We walked out of his office, down a hall, and toward two great doors with doormen who looked like large playing card. As we approached the cards bowed low and opened the doors. Another card announced, "The Scarecrow, Regent of Oz, and Emily, of North Carolina."

We entered an enormous hall where there were crowds of people on both sides of the aisle. We walked through, hand in hand, as they cheered. And then past the crowds to where there were long tables, though not one chair was filled. At the front was a raised stage with a grand table. At the center of the table there was a large throne. As we got closer the Scarecrow released my hand and we walked to opposite sides where there were short flights of stairs leading up. The Scarecrow sat on the tallest throne at the very center, and signaled me to sit to his left.

Next the Tin Man and Gings were announced and entered. The Tin Man sat to the Scarecrow's right and Gings sat to my left. The Tin Man was polished to a bright shine, though I could still see the mark I made on him with my knife.

Then General Scaredenof and Admiral Drownski entered and were seated. And many more dignitaries followed. The local witches' organizations were announced and seated. First came the Witches of East Harrumph, followed by those from Long Whatsit and Lower Whocaren. There were many local witches groups. Finally, everyone was seated.

Some announcements were made and a long meeting began, starting by a reading of the agenda and then by discussions of witch education, support for local communities, and big challenges in the Emerald City and across all of Oz. Gings acted as the moderator, with various witches standing up when they wanted to speak. In time the agenda was completed and the meeting was adjourned.

A great party began, with pasta and sauce, hot bread, Brussels sprouts (double yuck), green peas, yams, beets, and carrots. That's at least what I thought they were. A lot of other foods, well, I couldn't even try to guess what they were. Some moved about in the serving bowls. And the pasta sauce was excellent. There were many delicious drinks, one that tasted like kaylah juice. Since the Scarecrow mentioned it, I decided to taste a Brussels sprout. First, it was much softer than I remember them to be. They must cook Brussels sprouts longer in Oz than back home. It wasn't really that bad, but still not my favorite food. I was also happy that no spaghetti sauce stains showed on my white dress. Now that's magic.

Storks flew about removing all the used dishes, in perhaps a less than perfectly hygienic manner. After the food was eaten there was music and dancing. Then desserts came and many tasty things were served, many not even big enough to fill one mouthful, but when they touched your tongue the taste exploded from the top of your head to the bottom of your feet.

It was like the most wonderful birthday party, and it was everyone's birthday. I knew that even though I would leave Oz tomorrow, I would remember it with love for my entire life.

The Scarecrow stood up and signaled me that it was time to leave. I stood up as well. I slid in my chair and took a last sip from my glass.

My vision swirled. I reached out to the Scarecrow, pulling him down as I fell to the floor.

Chapter 14 The Cold Spring

"How long do we have?" the Scarecrow asked Gings. "Gings is as wise a witch as we have in Oz," he thought. He hoped her wisdom would be enough to save Emily.

Gings looked at the floor. "I don't question your decision to use the Cold Spring, you had no choice. But the Cold Spring exacts a price, nothing is given for free. So while it will keep her alive we have no way of knowing what that price will be. For that we can only wait. Since she is not from Oz how she is affected could be more, or less, than those of Oz. Either way, she may be alone when the fee is exacted."

"Yes," the Scarecrow said. "It is a great risk, but there was no other option. All that is in the future, right now, how long does Emily have?'

"Emily is young and strong, so she can stay safely in the Cold Spring for a week, perhaps longer, and the Cold Spring will keep her alive. But we cannot help her fight the poison, and we cannot bring her out of her sleep, that will be up to her. And we do not know who or how the poison was given to her. Whoever poisoned her is cunning. The poison was placed in Emily's glass right in front of everyone at the Witches' Council. He or she could be here, in this very room with us. Emily must be closely guarded," Gings said.

"Do we have enough trusted and experienced witches to have four on guard, outside the room, and one on guard inside the room, with Emily?"

"Yes," Gings replied. "When they saw what happened many of the witches at the council volunteered to stay in the Emerald City and help."

"And how will we know if the guards can be trusted?"

"I have a test that will reveal any frauds."

"And how do I know that you are not a fraud?"

"I am afraid that you must trust me."

"And I do," said the Scarecrow. "When the rotations are set up, I would like to meet with you and the Tin Man in private."

A short while later the Tin Man and Gings entered the Scarecrow's office.

"The schedules are all arranged," Gings said as she placed them before the Scarecrow.

"Good." He looked over them. "Fine." He turned to Gings.

"Gings, is there anything more we can do? How are we to protect Emily from someone so powerful? And why do they want to do Emily harm?"

"I don't know. It doesn't make sense, she is an outsider. Apparently she brought Veeron's ire from her action, which is uncalled for but at least linked in some way to something she did. I don't believe Veeron has support among any witches, let alone such a powerful one, so I can't understand this attack."

The Tin Man spoke. "Emily was given significant items from Dorothy and Aunt Em's memorial trees. This was the first and only time they brought forth anything of magic. It was like they were aware of her danger."

The Scarecrow added, "And Glinda left her sword for her, specifically for her. Somehow she knew."

There was a long silence as the Scarecrow reviewed what had transpired.

"Thank you," the Scarecrow said. "I need to think and I do that best in private." The Tin Man and Gings left his office. The Scarecrow closed the door behind them and then went to stand in an empty part of the room with his face to the corner. He stayed just so for a long time.

Early the next morning the Scarecrow walked by the Cold Spring room and found all as expected. There were four witches posted by the door. When he went into the room he saw that the white curtains were in place. Vera, one of Gings most gifted students, was inside the curtained area.

"How is Emily?" he asked through the curtain.

"Scarecrow sir, Emily seems to be resting easily," Vera replied.

It was a nice thought, but he knew that for Emily, this would not be restful or easy.

I was walking along a path, following two people. I wanted to catch up to them but my legs didn't work. I tried to move them and they wouldn't move. Then without moving my legs I leaped forward on the path bumping into some strange sunflowers, making them rustle. Everything became silent, the people I was following must have stopped so I waited. How unusual the sunflower plants looked. The center part was pale white and the petals were black. I stared into the center of one of the flowers. Did it make a face at me?

The scene was replaced by a new one. I was sitting on the bus again. The Scarecrow was to my right. And a young man got on the bus and sat down to my left.

He turned toward me, and asked, "Dorothy?"

Just then the bus stopped and there was some commotion up front. An old woman, dressed all in black, said, "Tippetarius, you lazy selfish boy. You know I need you to walk the dog." The young man slowly stood and walked to the front of the bus.

Before he stepped off the bus, he turned to give me a final look.

"Why would someone call me Dorothy?" I thought.

The bus continued slowly along the road. I watched the young man and the old woman fade from view. I turned forward just in time to see the bus pass the young man who had called me Dorothy walking a jet-black dog along the side of the road. How did he get there?

I jumped out of my seat and ran to the front and then leaped out of the bus. I rushed at him.

"Get away from here. Go, leave me alone," I screamed straight into his ear. He kept walking, ignoring me, as if he had not heard me. He and his dog walked slowly away from me.

"Show yourself," I yelled at the young man and the dog. "Show yourself now."

They blurred and shifted. When my vision was clear again, the black dog was now walking on two legs and the young man was walking on all fours, his neck in a leash that the black dog yanked in all directions. The dog reveled in the boys torment.

"Show yourself," I repeated once more. "Show your true self."

And again, the image blurred and shifted. And now the black dog was replaced by a man dressed all in black. He had the palest skin, a short black moustache, and short jet-black hair. The blackness of his hair and mustache made the paleness of his skin more striking.

"I see you. I know you. You can't fool me, not again," I yelled.

The pale man yanked hard and viciously on the leash and the young man was pulled to the ground. The pale man savagely kicked his prisoner. Then he looked at me and laughed. He snapped his fingers and he and the boy disappeared.

What a strange dream, I thought as I sat up. There was water up to my waist. I was in an area surrounded by white curtains. The area was empty except for a single chair by the entrance. I pushed off the platform I had been laying on and the water went over my head. I stared down at a faint light far below. The water was very deep. The sides of the pool were made of large rocks except for the part near the top, which was built from bricks that had an Oz design. I gave a few strokes and came up to the surface. I was totally naked, not a stitch of clothes on. I climbed out of the pool and was surprised that I wasn't wet at all. The water, or whatever it was, touched my skin but never wet it.

I found my clothes neatly piled by the chair. I was famished, so I wanted to go to the kitchen to see if I could get something to eat.

Once clothed I walked out of the curtains and out the door of the room. There were four empty chairs lined up beside the door. I walked down the hall and at the end there was a staircase. After climbing up three flights of stairs I recognized where I was. I had seen these tapestries before. I turned to the left. The hall was quiet. I remembered where the cafeteria was so I started in that direction. I wondered how I had come to be in that pool. After a bit of walking I entered the cafeteria. I looked toward the kitchen. The lights were out and it seemed empty. When I got closer, I noticed a dimly lit area where one of the cooks was putting some food away.

"Emily, my dear, you startled me," she said.

"Sorry," I said. "I'm very hungry. Is there anything left over from the council party that I can eat?"

"Of course, dear. Here is a nice piece of kaylah pie," she said, putting a slice on a small plate. "I know you like kaylah pie."

〰〰 〰〰 〰〰 〰〰 〰〰

It was the Scarecrow's time again to check on the guards, so he walked down to the Cold Spring. After he left the main floor of the palace, he found the rest of the way empty - he passed no one. That was fine since the Cold Spring was in the very lowest level of the palace, well below ground level, and it was concealed from view, by design and by magic. Only the most trusted people even new it existed.

He was shocked to his core when he saw that all the guard seats were empty. He jumped into the curtained area and found no one inside; no guard, and no Emily. He bolted from the room and began banging on the gong that was mounted on the wall across the hall.

"Where could Emily be?" He asked himself. His great brain churned, and quickly he knew. Emily had
164

been in the Cold Spring for more than two days without food, and if she was under her own mind, she would go to the kitchen.

The clanking sound of metal on the palace stones echoed down the hall as the Tin Man descended the stairs, three at a time. The Scarecrow saw the Tin Man and yelled "To the kitchen, Emily is gone," and they both sprinted in that direction.

The Tin Man sprinted up the stairs followed by the Scarecrow and various witches who joined them as they dashed along. The Tin Man quickly outdistanced everyone and careened into the kitchen, where Emily stood posed to take a forkful of pie.

He shouted, "Stop!"

Emily turned to him and paused with her fork right before her lips.

In a sprint the Tin Man shouted, "Don't eat it!"

"You are hungry dear, it's fine," the cook said enticingly."

Emily put her fork down on the plate.

"Go ahead, it is delicious," the cook tempted.

The Tin Man ran full speed to Emily and slammed the pie onto the wall and turned to face the cook. "I don't recognize you," the Tin Man said.

"Fool," the cook said. In an instant she had slid a few paces away and transformed into the pale man, all dressed in black, the man that Emily had seen in her dream. The man's face was pallid with a grey cast, like someone who was dead. He gestured and a bolt of blood red light and fire flew toward Emily, who was knocked to the floor. The Tin Man stepped between Emily and the man, shielding Emily. He screamed and writhed in pain and agony.

The Scarecrow entered the room, with the witches right behind. He threw his body between the pale man and the Tin Man. The witches began to chant and gyrate, trying to counter the spells of the pale man, with no success. The Scarecrow began to smolder and smoke.

As Gings entered the room she gasped, "Sebastian." The pale man recognized her and let out a hideous laugh.

A young witch moved his hands back and forth, and what looked like an enormous soap bubble moved to enclose the pale man. The fire and light went right through the bubble.

The Scarecrow's body burst into flames.

The pale man laughed, "You fools! You are powerless. Pay careful attention to this lesson. Perhaps you may, quite by mistake, learn something."

The blasts of flame continued, consuming the Scarecrow's body. His head fell to the ground. The Tin Man leaped in front of Emily. Fire engulfed him and he shrieked in agony.

The bubble began to close in around the pale man and as it shrunk, less and less of the fire pierced the bubble. The pale man stopped his laughing as the bubble became impenetrable and tightened around him. As the bubble squeezed in, for an instant, a look of fear appeared on the pale man's face, and then he was gone.

Gings darted forward and took the Scarecrow's head. "Emily, are you alright?"

"Yes," she said. "Besides the bang on my elbow from being knocked to the floor I'm fine."

Gings cut her off, "Fine. All of you, protect Emily," and she dashed off.

The witches all circled around Emily, looking desperately in all directions in hope of seeing any attacker before he could strike, but what could they do against so powerful a sorcerer?

⌁⌁⌁ ⌁⌁⌁ ⌁⌁⌁ ⌁⌁⌁ ⌁⌁⌁

Gings returned. "The last thing the Scarecrow said to me was to return Emily to her home. It is our first and only task. We will be going to a hidden place that many of you are not permitted to see. I will lead you there, but you must all be blindfolded." She moved her hands and blindfolds appeared on all faces, except for hers and mine. All the remaining witches, and even the Tin Man, had their eyes covered. I wanted to ask why I alone was not blind folded, but she stopped me with a motion of her hand.

We walked hand in hand down halls, back hidden passageways, and down even more halls, some of which looked the same to me. I doubt I could find the way to where we were going. No one with their eyes covered, even someone perfectly familiar with the palace, could find the way.

We went through another hidden passageway and stopped in what appeared to be a hallway. Gings felt along the surface of the wall, which was made of solid stone, and at a certain point she reached her hand through the stone and turned some hidden lever that opened a door.

"Careful," Gings said, "walk slowly and thoughtfully."

167

One after another the group filed into a circular stone room. There was a staircase, which had no railings, and was barely wide enough for one person to walk. It led up to a balcony one floor above. Light flickered through two large open windows that were part of the balcony. Gings motioned and the door was replaced by a solid stone wall. The area looked ancient. Perhaps this was part of the original palace.

"We are here," Gings said. Some went to take their blindfolds off, but found that they could not be removed. "Sorry," Gings apologized. All the blindfolds disappeared.

"Emily, we are going to send you home," Gings said. She gestured with her hands and my backpack appeared. She handed it to me. "You must take everything that you brought with you and only those things you brought with you. Everything from Oz must remain in Oz and everything you brought must leave. When you get back home, you must smash the mirror. It must be destroyed. Otherwise you and your home will be at risk. You could be pulled back to Oz. Do you understand?"

"Yes," I said. "I am not even sure how long I have been in Oz; how will I explain where I've been?"

"We will send you back so that you will have only been gone a short time to the people at your home," Gings replied.

"I will get changed then," I said. I took my backpack into a small side room and put back on my coveralls and my work shoes. It seemed so long ago that I was sitting on a desk eating a sandwich. Then I noticed the mirror and my life changed. I put everything I got in Oz back into the backpack.

The witches went to work. They conjured all types of books on magic and began to read.

"Are you ready?" Gings said.

"Yes," I replied, "I want to thank all of you for your friendship and for helping me get home." I wiped tears from my eyes.

Many of the witches hugged me and they all wished me good luck. I stood in front of the mirror. First Gings cast her spell. The mirror didn't change at all as I looked into it, and when I touched it nothing happened. Then Martin, who was the next most senior witch, cast a spell, again with no effect. Then Vera, and then each witch in turn cast spells, all with no effect.

"Emily, we need a bit more time," Gings said, and the witches all went back to studying their books and scrolls.

After some time, Gings asked, "Ready again?" I replied "Yes" and Gings cast her spell. Again, the mirror was unchanged, only showing the reflection of the witches before it, and nothing happened when I touched it. Again, all the witches in turn cast their spells, and once more all met failure.

I really can't tell you how many times this went on, because at a certain point, it was all routine. They would study, I would look out the windows, they would cast spells, I would touch the mirror, and I would still be there, and it would all repeat. Sometimes I would look at the magic books, which though written in Ozish I could read, but did I really understand?

I was standing on the balcony and I thought, how do I even know that the pale man is not right here, in this room, right next to me? I remembered my dream in the Cold Spring and I closed my eyes and envisioned what

I had done. I moved my hands in a slow circle as I thought to myself, "Reveal yourself."

When I opened my eyes, I was surprised to find that nearly everyone in the room was staring at me. Some of the witches looked a little older, and some a little younger, some a little taller, and some a little shorter than I remembered them. Gings' hair was a bit whiter than before.

I turned and went back to looking out the window.

"I see we need to approach this a bit differently," Gings said to the witches.

This continued and soon the sun left the sky. I lay down in a corner with my backpack as my pillow and went to sleep. The witches, as far as I could tell, worked on through the night without a break.

When I awoke the sun was streaming through the windows. The sky was clear and a beautiful light blue. There was a touch of chill in the air and I could smell something cooking. It would be a beautiful day in Oz, though not here.

Everyone stopped for food, but the witches seemed weary.

I guess I hadn't seen her leave, but I noticed when Gings return. She entered followed by a group of witches. They were greeted warmly. I heard that they had been guarding me but were overcome. They had been found walking aimlessly in circles in an unused storage room.

More rounds of preparation, spell casting, and failure continued, through lunch and then through dinner. I resumed flipping through some of the magic books that were now haphazardly piled and tossed about. Sometimes I lay down on the floor, just to daydream. I could see the exhaustion in each witch's eyes. Some stopped to take naps, curling up in corners and against the walls. Some were so tired their speech was slurred and they stumbled when they walked.

I was standing on the balcony, looking out the window. I noticed that I had left a book of magic that I had been reading on the windowsill. Some seagulls flew by lazily, riding the air currents. The sun began to go down, and the sky lit up with fiery red streaks. The sky grew dark and the first star appeared.

"Starlight, starbright, I wish I may, I wish I might, have the wish I wish tonight," I said as I put my hands on the book on the windowsill and lowered my head to rest on my hands. Would I ever get home? Would I ever see my family? Would I ever see my school and friends again?

Chapter 15 Soda

A loud pop brought my attention back to the room. I spun around and that strange boy in the colorful clothes I met at the sleeping bag tree was cartwheeling around the room. His skin was green now and he turned to look at me.

"Hey Emily, Emily, Emily," he shouted.

I thought, his skin is the same exact color as a lime.

He smiled and he licked his wrist, "Nope," he said as he winked at me.

Then he did a back flip and some more somersaults to bring him in front of the Tin Man.

He started banging on the Tin Man's chest, bah bih chah, bah bih chah, bah bih chah boom. He looked at the Tin Man's stomach, which had the mark from my knife as well as the burn marks from the attack in the kitchen.

"You really need to watch what you eat, Can Man," he said without taking a break from his drumming.

Then he danced his way over to Gings. He plucked her hat off her head as he danced around her singing, "Gingold-ee, Gingold-ee, wise and str-ong, flies and Ping-Pong, when they made you, they broke the mold-ee." He tossed her hat back on her head.

Then I heard another pop, and a girl appeared above our heads. She was dressed all in white, and she radiated pure white light that lit up everything and everyone in the room so that there were no shadows and no dark places. Even though the light was brilliant, it was pleasant to look at.

"Hi, Sis," the lime green boy said.

"Hello my dear brother," the girl of light said as the lime green boy flipped up to give her a hug and a kiss on her cheek.

The boy said, "Sis, this is the girl who saved me from the sleeping bag tree."

"Thank you, Emily," the girl of light said as she slowly drifted to the floor. "Are you ready to go home?"

I tossed the book into my open backpack and swung it onto my back and said, "Yes."

"Then hold our hands," she said. I heard some murmuring between the witches, but I couldn't make it out. The instant the girl of light, the lime green boy, and I touched hands I heard another pop.

I fell onto the floor in Aunt Maybel's furniture store. I was right in front of the mirror that had brought me to Oz.

I needed to break the mirror. I needed something heavy to smash it with. I looked around and then ran across the room. There was an old stapler on a desk along the wall. I picked it up and turned to head back to the mirror.

Susan, the bookkeeper, stepped into the room and asked, "Have you seen Aunt Maybel? We need to go over the accounts and I think she's avoiding me."

"No, I haven't seen her," I said hoping she would leave quickly.

"Nice backpack," she added. "Khaki green canvas. It looks similar to the one my great-great-grandfather was wearing in some old pictures. Very retro."

"Thanks," I said and waited as she shook her head and finally left the room.

I sprinted back toward the mirror in time to see that Aunt Maybel was looking at the mirror.

"No! Stop!" I screamed. Aunt Maybel touched the mirror and vanished.

John, one of the sales staff, rushed into the room, followed by Susan.

"Is everything alright?" he asked.

"Yes, everything is fine," I lied, hoping that they would leave.

John turned and left. Susan said, "Tell Aunt Maybel that I know every hiding place in this building, so I will find her no matter where she hides," and she followed John out of the room.

I thought to myself, you may think you know every place, but there are some places that you can't even imagine.

If everything went well, Aunt Maybel would come through the mirror pretty soon. I did not want to think about anything else.

I took off my backpack and put it on the desk by the mirror. The backpack and its contents were another problem, one that would have to be solved some other day. I got myself ready, waiting for Aunt Maybel to return so I could break the mirror. I noticed my soda sitting on the desk in front of the mirror. Most of the ice had melted. I guess I was gone for about twenty minutes. I took a sip, and put it back down. I paced in front of the mirror with the stapler in my hand.

The reflection in the mirror blurred and swirled. I lifted the stapler ready to throw.

Aunt Maybel fell through the mirror and onto the floor as I threw the stapler with all my might. The glass shattered sending shards in all directions. I helped Aunt Maybel up as people ran into the room.

"What happened? Is everyone alright?" John shouted.

"Yes, everything is fine," I said. "I broke this old mirror, nothing more."

"Are you sure? And Aunt Maybel?" he asked.

"We're both fine," I said.

Aunt Maybel was sitting on a chair, rubbing her prosthetic foot. She looked at me, and then she looked back at the smashed mirror. She took a few deep breaths, and looked back at me, and again at the broken mirror. She stood up and took a few paces, and turned and paced again in silence.

"Emily, are you okay?" she asked me in a low voice.

"I'm fine. And you?"

"Yes, I am fine," Aunt Maybel said.

She cleared her throat. Then she spoke to everyone, "Everything is fine. Just leave this mess. Emily and I will take care of it."

Everyone was looking around, at the shattered glass on the floor, and at Aunt Maybel, and at me.

Aunt Maybel added, "Okay, shows over, nothing to see here but a broken old mirror. It's not like we've never seen something break here. Don't we have some customers to take care of?"

"Sure," John said, and he looked around once more and left the room.

Susan said, "Accounts some other time then?"

Aunt Maybel replied, "Another time."

When finally the last person walked out of the room, Aunt Maybel asked, "Why don't we call it a day? I bet you could use some peace and quiet, and perhaps a walk around the town. I know I could. Why don't we walk to the diner and sit down for a talk? I bet we have some stories to tell. What say you, Emily of Oz?"

I nodded my head yes and we started our walk to the diner.

Part II
Cold Fusion

Chapter 16 Questions

Since I've gotten home, I have had nothing but questions. How did I get back from Oz? I don't remember how it happened. None of the witches could send me back, and then, there I was, on my knees in front of the mirror in Aunt Maybel's store.

And why did I take my backpack, and all the things I got while in Oz with me? They all told me many times, "Don't take anything from Oz with you and don't leave anything you brought here." Why did I take my backpack? Why didn't Gings stop me?

But I'm glad I have them. Otherwise I wouldn't believe it. Would you? I mean, a scarecrow who is the leader of a land, a man of tin, flying monkeys, witches, and such things.

The day after I returned, I decided it was all a strange dream, only to be convinced, and then convinced again, by the things I had brought back from Oz. For days I would think Oz away, but every time I looked at these things, the backpack, the clothes, and the other stuff, it was inescapable – I had been to Oz, Oz existed, and I had proof.

But where is Oz? I mean, we have pictures of every spot on the world. How come no one knows about Oz?

And how come I, me, Emily, got pulled into Oz in the first place? Was I just unlucky (or lucky?) to happen to look in that old mirror?

And I have a burning desire to learn about magic. How does it work? Why does it work in Oz, but not here? I mean, there are no real witches here. Or are they just hiding? I can't read the book on magic I have from Oz; the words don't mean anything to me. It made perfect sense to me when I was in Oz and now it's gibberish. I can't even figure out what alphabet it uses. I want to learn about magic, at least whatever I can do at home.

I decided to ask the local experts.

"Mom, how does magic work?" She was outside digging in the garden. She likes to grow a few things every year, like an experiment. This year she was growing a number of types of pepper plants. She stood up and wiped some sweat off her forehead with her sleeve.

"That's one you should ask your dad. He used to do magic tricks when we were dating. It's been a while since then, but I'll bet he can impress you."

"Thanks, Mom." I rushed off to find my dad. He was slicing some carrots really thin in the kitchen.

"Dad, can you explain to me how magic works?"

"Sure, let me finish this slicing. Just a few seconds. I really like my fingers so I like to pay attention when I am using a knife." He finished and then rinsed off and dried his hands.

"How does magic work? Let me show you. Let's go to your computer."

When we got to my computer he sat down and found a video of an old television cartoon.

"Watch this." And when it was done, he asked, "Did you see the magic?"

"No, it's just an old cartoon about some people who are supposed to live in the Stone Age."

"Well, then the magic worked. Take a closer look," he said. I watched part of it again but I didn't see any magic.

"No magic."

"Okay, now do this. Pick one of the characters and don't let your eyes move from that character, no matter what. You are going to have to struggle to keep your eyes from moving."

I did. "When the people aren't talking, they just stand there, not moving, with blank expressions on their faces. It looks like their mouths are half open," I said.

"Now you're really looking. One other thing to note, is that all the people who are not talking are looking at the character talking. That's how magic works, or at least the trick part of the type of magic, known as sleight of hand, or legerdemain, light hands. You get people's attention to one thing, and you do your trick where they are not looking. In these old cartoons they couldn't animate all the characters all the time, since they were drawn by hand. But people only see whomever is talking, and they look at whatever other people look at, so it doesn't matter that the other characters aren't moving at all. The trick is that even though none of the people who don't talk are moving, no one notices. So, they used magic."

"Nice. Thanks, Dad."

"Any time Emms." He always uses nicknames. I think he knows my real name; I just never hear him say it.

The next day I got three books from the public library about magic. When I started reading, the first turned out

181

to be too simple. I skimmed through it in a short while and put it aside. The second book had what I wanted. It showed many tricks and explained how to do sleight of hand. I would need to practice a lot to get good, especially for the card tricks. I decided to work on one trick, making something disappear. Really, nothing disappears, it just ends up somewhere else, like in your pocket. I used a quarter and practiced in front of a mirror. I was looking forward to showing this trick to my friends at lunch time.

"Let me show you how to make a coin disappear, Dad." I found him back in the kitchen rinsing off some beans. He does a lot of my family's cooking.

"Sure," he said, as he shook his hands off and grabbed a towel.

"Watch closely. Disappear, disappear, be gone from here." I moved my hands around. "Vanished."

"Pretty good," my dad said. "It's in your left pocket, but you did a pretty good job. Let me see that coin."

I fished the coin out of my pocket. "Here," I said as I handed it to him. Clumsy guy, he dropped it on the floor.

"Now where did that coin go?" he asked.

I looked around but it was nowhere to be found.

"Oh look, its right here." He picked the coin from behind my ear.

I put my hand out and he put the quarter into it. I made sure the quarter was there and I sealed it into my fist.

"How did you get interested in magic, Dad?"

"Well, I was a few years older than you. My friends and I were going to a magic show but we got there late, really late. The show was packed, so they set up some chairs for us all the way up front, on the side of the stage. We could only see one side of the magician, and we could see things we were really not meant to see. The magician was doing a floating ball trick. The audience thinks that the ball floats in air. It's performed with the magician holding a sheet in front of him. Since we were so far up front, I could see what was going on in back of the sheet. In one of his hands the magician holds a rod as well as one corner of the sheet, with the rod hidden behind the sheet. The ball has a hole in it, and the magician holds the ball in his other hand in front of the sheet and he inserts the rod into the back of the ball. Of course, the rod is behind the sheet, and the ball is in front, so when the ball starts to float on command, the audience is amazed. I could see how the magician did the trick, and how excited the audience was. They loved it. I learned that people love being tricked. It took me a few tries before I got a ball and a rod that worked good enough to fool people, but when I finally got it, it worked great. From there I studied other tricks and one by one I mastered them. And how did you get interested in magic, Emms?"

"I saw someone doing magic."

"What kind of magic?"

"Shooting flames was one."

"Now, you're not talking about in the movies? That's all done by computers now."

"No, live in person."

"That must have been impressive. They must have had some pretty sophisticated tools to do that."

"I guess so. I'll get back to practicing," I said. I needed to practice, and I needed to end the conversation.

I went back to my room and repeated the trick again and again. After many repetitions, and hands that were starting to hurt, I decided I was ready to show my friends.

When I got up the next day, I decided, since I was going to perform magic tricks, I would wear the clothes I got from Oz. Magic is common in Oz, so it seemed fitting. I looked through the backpack that I got in Oz, which I had hidden in the back corner of my closet under some sports gear that hardly gets moved. I didn't want my mom or dad to see this stuff. The fewer questions, the fewer stretched truths.

I took everything out, the shoes, the socks, the dress, the subway token, the magic book and the newspaper article about me and the Scarecrow that I could no longer read, and laid them out on my bed. I put on the dress, the socks, and the shoes. I returned everything else to the backpack and returned it to its hiding place.

When I was ready, I went out to get breakfast.

"We have some nice cantaloupe you can eat," my dad said. He was sitting by the table eating his breakfast. My younger brother Jacob was working on some toast and jelly.

"Thanks, Dad." I took some melon and cut it into fine pieces and stirred it into my oatmeal. If you want to have a good day, it sure doesn't hurt to start it with oatmeal.

"Emms, I don't remember seeing that dress before," Dad said. "So ultra-retro."

"I got it the last time I visited Aunt Maybel."

"It's so old fashioned. I'll bet you could hunt dinosaurs in it. But it looks very nice on you. Want more toast, Yakkety Yak?"

My brother said, "No, don't talk back." It's just my dad and his goofy old songs.

As I scooped the last bit of oatmeal into my mouth, I saw that it was just about time to go. "Almost ready Jacob?"

"Yup." He put the toy car he had been playing with into his pocket.

"Be good, be safe, my dear ones," my dad said as he kissed us and put us on our way.

We started to walk to school. I drop my brother at before care and then I walk further to the middle school. We walked a few steps and we were joined by a large intimidating dog. I was frightened at first, but it never barked or snarled or came closer and we had to get to school. Jacob didn't seem bothered by it at all. It walked in front of us, sometimes stopping to sniff the air. It seemed to be busy concentrating, thinking, and observing. I don't remember a dog ever concentrating so much.

When we got to the elementary school where Jacob goes to before care and school, he saw his friends and skipped off. "See you later Emily."

I kept on walking, picking up the pace so I could get to school on time. The dog came along with me for a few blocks and then stopped to smell the air once more. Something must have changed because when he was done sniffing, he bolted back the way we had come. He really ran, like he had somewhere to go.

I hustled to my locker and got the books I needed for my first two classes, which were in the same room. There was a chance that we were going to get a pop quiz in the second class and I wanted to review my notes during the time between classes.

Well, there was no pop quiz. After the next class, and a visit to my locker, I headed off to the lunch room. I picked up my lunch and looked around to see where my friends, Susan and Daniel, my two closest buds were sitting. I spotted them in the usual place. I sat down. The food met all the minimum requirements to be described as food. Actually, some of it was pretty good. After some chit chat and goofing around, I stood up. "Now, I the great Enchanting Emily, master magician, will make this (looking around I spotted a bag of sugar on Susan's food tray) bag of sugar vanish. Disappear, disappear, be gone from here." I held the sugar in my left hand and faked picking it up in my right, following my right hand with my eyes.

Just than a boy that wasn't in any of my classes interrupted me and asked, "Can I borrow a quarter?" He was wearing a T-shirt that read "Not Grateful, Not Dead, No plans to change" over baggy pants. The laces of his fancy high top basketball shoes were loose and untied. His black hair ran wild.

I checked if I had a quarter to lend him, digging through my coin purse and counting what I had.

"Sorry," I said. "I don't have enough to loan you anything."

"What do you mean you don't have enough? I saw the coins you have."

"I need this money for later," I said. "Sorry."

"Yeah, you will be sorry," he said.

I asked Susan, "What's up with this guy?"

"He borrows (Susan added air quotes with her fingers) money from kids and never pays it back. If you don't give him money, he can be threatening."

"Have you told the teachers?"

186

"No one wants to get him angry."

I walked over to the nearest lunch monitor.

"You see that boy over there," I pointed to the boy who had moved on to another group of kids eating lunch, "He keeps asking to borrow money but he never pays it back."

"I'll keep an eye on him. This is the first I've heard of it."

"Thanks Mrs. Truly," I said as I walked back to my seat.

I finished what I wanted from my lunch and I was about to clean up my place and throw the trash away when the boy came by again, bumped into my chair, and spilled orange soda down my back.

"Oh, sorry Emily," he said with a smirk on his face. "I can be really clumsy sometimes. And sometimes things happen to people who rat on me."

I got up. "You don't scare me." I was loud enough to draw the attention of a lot of kids and some of the lunch monitors.

"Maybe you should be." He put his face close to mine.

"Scared of you? Are you trying to make me fall down laughing?"

Mrs. Truly walked over and stood next to us.

"Until next time, Emily," he said as he walked away.

I wiped myself off as well as I could. Susan and Daniel gave me their extra napkins.

"Mrs. Truly, I need to go to the bathroom to clean up the soda that boy poured on me."

"Poured on you, or spilled on you?"

"He did it on purpose," I said.

"Okay. Go to the bathroom and get yourself cleaned up." She wrote out a hall pass without looking down. I guess it was for me, the name started with an E and completed with a squiggle. She stuffed the hall pass into my hand.

I went to the bathroom. I used some dry paper towels to blot the soda up, and then some wet towels to try to get some more off. I dried it off again, but there was only so much I could do.

After I did my best cleaning up, I started walking back to the cafeteria. I was thirsty so I decided to stop at the water fountain. That boy walked over.

"Don't rat on me again," he said as he jabbed my shoulder with his finger.

"Back off jerk," I said.

"Or what," he taunted, poking me again.

"Or you are going to regret it," I said.

He smirked and poked me once more, even harder.

I looked at him in silence. He poked me once more and I stepped in and punched him flat in the nose. It must have surprised him because he fell flat on his butt. Blood was streaming down from his nose, out of both nostrils. He was good at bleeding.

"Let's go to the nurse," I said, offering him my hand. I guess he was not used to being stood up too since he took my hand without comment.

As we walked to the nurse's office, I gave him a paper towel I had so he could wipe his nose.

"What did you do that for?" he asked.

"I told you to stop and you didn't. What did you think was going to happen with you poking me?"

188

When we got into the nurse's office, Mrs. Johnson, the school nurse started working on the boy's nose.

"And how did this happen?"

"I punched him," I said. "He was poking me, so after I had enough, I smashed him."

"The Vice Principal and your parents are going to be called," she said sternly. She walked to a small metal cabinet and opened it with a key that was on a string around her neck. "Phones, in the cabinet, now." We both took out our phones and put them in the cabinet. She locked it. "Ralph, you sit there, and Emily, you sit there. Keep apart and keep your hands to yourself."

After a few minutes, the room phone rang. Mrs. Johnson said, "Emily, call for you." She handed me the phone.

"Emily," my mother said. "I am disappointed in you. What were you thinking punching someone?"

"I was thinking that I was tired of being poked."

"That's not the right attitude young lady. There are always better ways than violence."

"I know. I'm sorry, Mom."

"I'm coming to your school later today to talk with the Vice Principal. We will continue this conversation later," she said as she ended the call.

"Ralph, your father will be here in a short while," the school nurse said.

I stood up and looked at myself in the mirror on one of the medicine cabinets. There was still some sticky orange soda on the back of my dress and some little spots on my front. My hair was a bit mussed up. I pushed it a bit trying to fix it. Then I sat down.

Ralph got up and looked into the mirror. Something must have caught his attention because he raised his hand to the mirror. And when he touched the mirror, he vanished.

"Oh, my goodness," I thought. It was about two weeks since my trip to Oz, and I knew things weren't perfect. I had all those things from Oz, and I shouldn't have them here. And Aunt Maybel seemed upset, not herself, sort of bummed out. But this was a real and immediate problem. *Ralph may be a jerk, but his getting pulled into Oz is my fault. And Oz cam be a dangerous place. Probably especially dangerous to jerks.*

"Where's Ralph?" Mrs. Johnson asked.

"I think he must have gone to use the bathroom," I lied.

"I told you both to sit down and stay put. How'd he get by me?" she asked.

"I'm not sure," I said.

"I need to go to the Vice Principals office," she said. "When Ralph gets back you tell him not to move an inch or there will be consequences."

"Okay," I said.

When she left, I went to the mirror. If Ralph could be pulled through, I hoped I could follow. One of the stories I read in Glinda's magic book was instructions on how to transport yourself. I imagined that I was looking out a window, and there was a tree with a small group of flowers planted by its trunk. I could see it in the mirror. I felt the pull of Oz. I reached through the mirror and took hold of a flower. My head swam and my stomach churned, so I let go. I took a few deep breaths holding the sink with my hands. I steadied myself and reached through once again. I clenched my stomach and I pulled up on the flower. I was pulled to Oz. I fell to my knees, still smelling the flower. I couldn't get a full breath of air and I felt sick to my stomach. I rolled on my side and my head hit the trunk of the tree. I tried to inhale and I made a loud whooping sound, gasping for air. Two young women dressed for battle ran to me. They were wearing swords and leather arm guards, like in the pictures in Glinda's book of magic. They picked me up under my arms and carried me away in a run.

Chapter 17 Glinda's Castle

The world clouded over as everything I looked at faded. Lines appeared and then broke into swirling pinwheels. My head thrashed left and right and I saw that we passed through wide wooden doors. My eyes refocused and I could see dark lines in the wood. Between those lines there were finer lines and even finer pores. I could see the grains of sand in the cement between the stones in the walls. Everything blurred again, like looking through a steam covered window. Down halls lined with fogged tapestries they carried me as the world spun around. My eyes refocused once more. I could see that the tapestries were of scenes of flowers with deep blues and golden yellows. The threads in a flower trapped me. The fluff had been brushed so that the weave was hidden. We burst into a room where a young beautiful Glinda sat. Her face had a faint blue glow. She was younger than in the picture of her in the book of magic, and she had a warm smile on her face that immediately changed to concern. Drums thundered in my head. The world had bright lights racing in random patterns, vanishing and returning, joining and exploding apart.

"Please lay her on the table and leave the room," Glinda said. Her voice was urgent. I was making whooping sounds as I tried to breathe and I was feeling like I was drifting in a slowly flowing river. Those who had carried me rushed from the room and slammed the door.

Glinda took my hands in hers and said, "You don't have enough time for me to explain, but you must concentrate on something that you just did. Whatever you immediately did before now. You need to concentrate with all of your might. When you have it pictured in your mind, squeeze my hand. Do it now."

My head was spinning. I was twirling through the air. Glinda squeezed my hand so hard that it brought me back. I imagined just an instant before, looking into the mirror in the nurse's office. I squeezed Glinda's hand.

I may have lost consciousness, but when I could think again, I found myself lying on my back on a table in a dimly lit room. I wheezed out a few breaths and turned over, falling to the floor. I broke my fall with my hands. After a few more breaths I was strong enough to push myself up and look around the room. It looked like Glinda's castle. The floor was dirty and a few ants were marching along near my hands. There was an eerie silence broken only by the sound of leaves blown along the floor. My breathing slowly returned to normal but my head throbbed and ached. I got myself up and brushed myself off. I was in the same room that I was in just a moment before but, besides the table I had been on, all the chairs and table, now covered with dust, had been moved against the walls. I left the room, which led to the hallway that not so long ago the Scarecrow had led me through. Things looked just as they had been, abandoned and empty. A breeze rattled the shuttered windows. The shutters were broken enough to let random rays of sun through, enough for me to see my way. The hanging tapestries were faded and had rips and parts missing, perhaps eaten by moths

"Now that I am in Oz, how am I going to rescue Ralph?" I thought. I didn't think before I decided to return. Mom always tells me, "Look before you leap." Someday I'll remember. Someday I will remember before I leap, not after. But now that I was in Glinda's Castle, it was time to at least start to think of a plan. First, how am I going to get to Ralph?

It was strange. I remembered things I shouldn't know. I remembered that the Golden Cap that gave the wearer the ability to command the Flyers three times was stored in a room nearby. I remembered this, but it wasn't my memory. When I recalled the memory, everything in the castle was new, bright and full of life, not like the present state of decay. If I could get the Golden Cap, I could have the Flyers fly me to the Emerald City. If I could get to the Emerald City I could get help.

I turned around and headed down the hall. A few doors down on the right felt like the correct door. I opened the door only to find the room empty except for a box in one corner. It looked like it was forgotten when someone moved out, something that the owner didn't care enough about to bother taking. But something about that box drew me.

Inside the box there was a pile of odds and ends. There were some bits of paper, an assortment of thin paintbrushes, some tiny doll clothes, a small bag that held a bunch of buttons and marbles, a wooden match box with a dozen or so ornate pins inside, and a tiny wooden carving of a Flyer. It looked like a winged monkey, crouching down, with its hands held high over its head and its wings spread wide. Disappointed, I put everything back in the box.

I felt certain that what I wanted was in this room. Certain there was something here I needed. If it was, I wasn't finding it. I looked around the room once more before I closed the door.

I walked past Glinda's throne room. I needed to come up with a plan so I sat down on Glinda's throne. I looked around and imagined it filled with important people and dignitaries. I even imagined the Scarecrow, all dressed in ermine robes, with his crown mushing his face, and the Tin Man, polished to a blazing shine. I sat myself up tall in the throne and smiled.

After some silent thought I left the castle and started on my adventure. I walked along a path that separated wide meadows. Further on there was an intersection so I stopped to look around. Off the path to the left was a little hut, built of sticks and straw, that had some smoke coming from its top. I started that way, hoping I could get directions there."

When I got to the opening, I didn't know quite what to do since there was no doorbell or buzzer, or even a door to knock on. I yelled in, "Hello, anyone home?"

"Yes, of course I am home. Come in and let me take a good look at you."

I walked in slowly. The light was dim inside so it took a few moments for my eyes to adjust. Inside was a large creature with a bill like a duck, sitting in a rocking chair, crocheting, in front of a small fire that a kettle was being heated on.

"Would you like some tea? Penelope Primrose Platypus, at your service."

"No, ma'am," I said. "But I would like some directions on how to get to the Emerald City."

"And who, may I ask, do I have the pleasure of making my newest acquaintance?"

"Emily," I said. "It's urgent I get to the Emerald City."

"Ah, the Emerald City. No brighter star shines in the firmament of the heavens, nor dearer gem is found in all the lands."

"Do you know the way?" I asked.

"Does a bird know how to fly, or a fish how to swim?" she responded.

"If I go right at the intersection, would I be on the right path?"

"To be, or not to be, on the right path, that is the question."

"And?" I asked.

"And will history record this turn of events with pride, or embarrassment, glee, or sorrow?" she continued.

I looked at her in silence.

"Continue straight at the intersection, straight and proud, proud of where you came from and who you are, and march on to face the future with strength and perseverance, ready to face each challenge as it arises."

I got up, said thanks, and stepped to the entry. As I was about to leave, she called out, "Aren't you going to show me your magical item? It would be a sword through our friendship if you departed without sharing."

"What do you mean?" I said. "I have nothing of magic."

"You can't fool me, at least when it comes to magic. We platypodes can sense magical items you know."

"Well, I have nothing of magic."

"Oh, perhaps you don't know what you have," she said. "If you are going to work with magic, you really ought to learn how to tell if things are magical. But since you can't," she said with a suspicious look at me, "let me look at what you are carrying."

I emptied my pockets. In my left pocket I had my coin purse and the bag of sugar from lunch. In my right pocket I was surprised to find the carving of the Flyer, but its position had changed. Now, one hand was pointing forward, and the other was covering its mouth. Its wings were closed.

"That's it," said Penelope Primrose Platypus. "That's magical."

"Do you know what it does?" I asked.

"I do not," she said. "But it is magical as true as a sunny day will warn you and a snowy day will chill you."

"How do you know it is magic?"

"Some know magic by sight, some by smell, some by feel, and some by sound. I know magic by sound. You seem to be numb to magic," Penelope Primrose Platypus said.

"I can't sense magic. You hear it?"

"Yes, I hear the vibrations of magic, the hum of an item, the tone that each magical thing and person emits. Pay attention to the Flyer. Do you sense it in any way?"

I held it in my hand and stared at it. I did not see, or hear, or feel or smell anything. "No, I can't sense it at all."

"That's a shame. I know you can. Many people sense magic, but do their best to ignore it. Magic can be challenging. If you want to sense magic, your first step is to stop denying it and start accepting it."

I stared at the monkey. Then I put everything back in my pockets and got up. "Thank you," I said once more.

"I am here to help and it is my pleasure. To help all those who pass my way and seek aid, whether weak or strong, brave or cowardly, wise or foolish."

I left. I could hear her monolog continue as I walked back to the path. I jogged to the intersection and continued straight for a short distance. When I looked back to where I had come from, where the castle, the meadows, and Penelope's hut had been an instant before, there was a forest, full of tall trees.

I turned and started off again. With my first step I heard a shrieking sound. It was coming from my right pocket, from the carving of the Flyer. I pulled it out. Its expression was one of pain. I could feel it shake and grow hot in my hand. I dropped it and ran. There was a large bang, a burst of flames and a cloud of smoke. A breeze dispersed the smoke and a cap of golden yellow velvet, with a golden band, was sitting in the carvings place. I had a flash of memory, with Glinda wearing this cap and summoning the Flyers.

I read the inscription in the cap. It had some crazy instructions about tapping your toes, and reciting some inane words, and spinning about. I put it on my head and though I felt foolish, I followed the instructions exactly. I started to pace back and forth not knowing what to expect. In a short while I could see some Flyers coming toward me. Six Flyers carrying a palanquin landed a distance from me. Three Flyers followed, each struggling to carry a wooden chest. They landed near the palanquin. After a short discussion, one flew to me.

"Where is the lion?" the Flyer asked. "We will not comply with your wish if we are put in danger."

"There is no lion," I said. "You must be smelling the scent of Orlanda, who has marked my shoes so that all who meet me know I am under her protection."

The Flyer trembled in fear. "Orlanda," he muttered. Then he flew up, looking over the area, and then returned to the other Flyers. After a short discussion the Flyer returned. "I will carry you to Veeron," the Flyer said.

In a moment I was standing before the palanquin. Seated on the throne on the palanquin was a large Flyer wearing a crown of gem speckled gold. "So, this is Veeron," I thought. I would have trembled in fear but one of Glinda's memories informed my decision to be bold. Our eyes met and I could tell that he knew who I was. The description his spies had given him must have been accurate.

Each of the six carriers wore jet black vests, and Veeron wore a pure white robe. The clothing worn by those that carried the chests were faded and patched.

"I am Veeron. You have called us using the golden cap and we are here, in fulfillment of our obligation, to follow your command to the extent possible. We will fulfill that requirement even though you are an enemy of our people, having buried that filth Moliere. We are compelled to obey, but rest assured that I would kill you and rejoice if you were not wearing the Golden Cap."

I ignored Veeron's rant. I saw that Archimedes was one of the Flyers carrying a chest. He looked tired. "You must take me to the Emerald City," I demanded, controlling my fear and staring directly at Veeron.

"Any of these three can take you," Veeron said as he waved his hands indicating the Flyers that had carried the chests.

"I will interview them to determine who is suitable," I said.

"Fine, the quicker you begin the quicker I will be rid of you. But I will only grant you one turn of this sandglass for each of my subjects."

"The interviews must be in private. That location over there," I said pointing to a distant stand of trees, "will do."

"I see no need for that," Veeron said.

"I require it," I said. "To fulfil my request, they must be in private." I knew that none of their answers would be truthful if Veeron could hear what was said.

"Fine," Veeron said with a snort. "Your first time starts now. I will send you another to interview when your time has expired. You on the left, you are first. Do not anger me with slothfulness." He signaled to one of his attendants who took grapes from a chest and began feeding him.

The first Flyer stepped forward. "Please fly me over there," I said motioning to the stand of trees. We arrived and it was a good choice, distant enough to not be heard and secluded enough so that we could not be observed. I wanted to know more about the Flyers, their country, and about Veeron, so I needed answers, honest answers.

"This discussion must be private, so you must speak softly. How did Veeron come to be your leader?"

"He was freely elected and then became our king and beloved leader," he said.

"I have heard that he disbanded the parliament."

"With Veeron's great leadership and wisdom there is no need for a parliament. Those people can now be reassigned to work in the mines."

"And he disbanded the courts," I said.

"There is no need for courts. Veeron's word is the law and he is always just and fair."

"I thought Flyers loved to fly, why is it that Veeron is carried?"

"It is our pleasure to carry him so that he can preserve his energy for more important things. He is a perfect physical specimen. I can only hope to be as fit as he."

"When was the last time you saw him fly?" I asked. I couldn't get past that he was being carried. It just didn't seem right.

"I do not recall. I am sure that he is the most graceful flyer of all Flyers."

I was about to continue when the next Flyer, the one who carried me to Veeron, landed.

"You may ask me what you will," the new Flyer said, "and I will reply what I must." The first Flyer departed.

"Is Veeron a good leader?" I asked.

"Veeron looks after his own, unlike the dust eaters who have ground the Flyers under their heels for ages."

"He looks after his own, but not everyone?"

"I am not a fool. Veeron's interest is limited to what will bring him more power, who he can buy to get more power, and who he can step on to get more power."

"You don't like him, but yet you work for him."

"I have family. I have friends. I find a way to survive. Why would a dust eater be concerned about a Flyer?

Concerned enough to bother asking? Are you looking for a new way to torment us?"

"You prefer Veeron over dust eaters?"

"Given a choice between a dog that bites my hand, and a dog that gnaws my hand off, I prefer being merely bitten. But perhaps you would like all Flyers dead?"

Just then Archimedes landed. He turned to the Flyer and said, "Hypatia, your time has expired. Please return to Veeron."

The Flyer turned to me and said, "Good riddance dust eater," and flew off.

After she was away, I asked Archimedes, "How have you been my friend?"

"Things are tough, so I do what I can. I apologize for Hypatia. It has been especially tough for her. Some of her family have been sent to the labor camps in the mines."

"No need to apologize. I can see the hatred Flyers have for others. Is there anything I can do to help?"

"Perhaps," Archimedes said. "You now have the Golden Cap though I cannot guess how it came to you. If the curse on the Flyers was removed, freedom would be one small step closer."

"I promise you I will do all I can to break the curse. Did you have trouble after you helped me escape?"

"Everyone on the patrol was beaten and locked in prison for three days with no food. But this is a mild punishment. I have heard of much worse. And how did you fair after I left you?"

"There were some incidents. Two spies sent by Veeron to take me were captured. And I was poisoned. But it all resolved."

"Emily, Why are you here again? I thought the only thing you wanted to do was to return to your home."

"Yes. But a, uh, a friend of mine has been pulled into Oz and I need to bring him home."

"I will help you if I can," he said.

Hypatia had just landed. "Your time is up dust eater. Archimedes, you can carry her back to Veeron. I don't want to touch her again."

I got on his's back and we flew to Veeron.

"You must now decide," Veeron said.

Archimedes edged forward. I pointed to Hypatia. "I choose this Flyer to take me to the Emerald City." Archimedes tried to hide the look of surprise on his face. Hypatia did not hide her look of disgust at all.

"Fine," Veeron snarled. "Leaving your presence will be a relief." Hypatia's wooden chest was placed on the palanquin behind Veeron's throne and they lifted off.

Hypatia said, "Why did you choose me? Is it just to torment me?"

"No, I have more questions I would like to ask you."

"Should I lie, like a dust eater?"

"I hope that you will answer honestly."

She squatted so that I could get on her back. "Hold on carefully. I would not want to drop you to a viciously painful, hideously bloody death."

She took off and swiftly climbed high into the sky. There were just a few clouds and I could see in all directions for miles. I looked around trying to figure out where the Emerald City might be.

"Do you know the way to the Emerald City?" I asked.

203

"Of course, don't you?" Hypatia replied.

"No, I have no idea."

"Then it really doesn't matter where I take you."

"It does matter very much to me," I said.

"Why would you trust me, someone who hates all your people?"

"I trust that you will honor your pledge to help me."

"Then you are a fool."

"Not only do I believe you will bring me to the Emerald City but in time we will become friends."

She broke into a loud laugh. "You will be dead before that happens," Hypatia retorted.

We fell silent. The ground passed swiftly under us.

"Why are the mines so important? What do you get from them?"

"Misery. We mine misery. That is all, misery. Veeron mines for misery for anyone he hates. He hates many, so the mines are busy."

"That can't be the goal." I said.

"It is most definitely the goal, to punish all who Veeron hates. Nothing is ever brought from the mines except those destroyed by mining. Most can hardly breathe. All are physically broken, never able to fly, or even stand again. A mine is no place for a Flyer."

"Some of your family is in the mines?"

"Yes, a brother and a cousin."

"I am sorry," I said.

Hypatia grunted.

"Who cursed the Flyers and made the Golden Cap?" I asked.

"Gayelette did. It was on her wedding day and some Flyers decided to do mischief. They took her groom and tormented him. She was an enormously powerful witch and cursed us forever."

"How long ago was that"? I asked.

"Generations and generations ago. In the long past."

"You are being cursed for something that you didn't do?" I asked.

"We are being cursed for something a small group of Flyers did centuries ago. Those who did it, and their children, and their children, and their children and their children are all long gone. We are slaves to the Golden Cap. And all our young are taught the story of the humiliation of Gayelette's groom, the curse, and the eternal shame of all Flyers."

"I will destroy the Golden Cap, if it is possible," I said.

"It is better to be quiet than to lie," Hypatia replied.

"I will. It is my promise to you," I said.

"I will believe that when it is smashed into pieces at my feet."

"I promise you I will."

"Yes, you do. And yet I recall that I am carrying you on my back."

Silence returned.

"Why didn't Veeron just kill me and take the cap? Why don't the Flyers just ignore the request?" I asked.

"You need to listen dust eater. Gayelette was an enormously powerful witch. Compliance is not optional," Hypatia said.

"Oh," I replied.

"Not oh," Hypatia said. Gayelette's groom, now husband, received the cap as part of his wedding gifts. He was the first to use the Golden Cap. He was a mild and quiet man, and he asked a simple request, to be brought a glass of water. Instead of bringing him a glass of water, one of the Flyers who had tormented him, laughed at him. The result was described as universal agony. All the Flyers, infants, toddlers, children, Flyers of all ages, the elderly included, experienced unimaginable pain. Flyers with hearts of iron were on their knees in agony. Some Flyers of that generation are said to have never been the same afterwards. The only Flyer who did not experience the pain was the one asked to bring the water. And the pain continued until the task was completed."

"I am sorry," I said. "That is truly horrible."

And silence returned once more. Then Hypatia asked, "And what are you called?"

"I am Emily," I said.

"You are indeed a strange dust eater," she said.

We flew on. The houses below were just tiny dots. We were going very fast.

I caught a glimpse of the Emerald City far off in the distance. Scenes of towns, farms, and pastures passed below us. Then we started to fall rapidly.

"If you're trying to choke me you are succeeding," Hypatia gasped.

"Sorry," I said, relaxing my grip on Hypatia's neck. "I must have panicked."

"Thank you. Let the Flyer fly," she replied. We continued in silence.

The Emerald City was now just a short distance away. Then we began to descend. We approached the ground at a break neck speed. We were falling like a rock from the sky. I was terrified. At the very last moment Hypatia slowed us and we landed so softly that I didn't feel it.

Chapter 18 Gings Objects

We had set down next to the pools of water in the park beside the palace.

"Thank you," I said. "I will destroy the Golden Cap and free the Flyers from its curse."

"I will believe you only when your promise is fulfilled," She said.

"I will."

"Many things are promised, and many promises are broken," she replied. She leapt straight into the air and ascended so quickly that by the time I raised my head to look, see was just a small dot in the sky.

I walked through the park and around the palace toward the nearest entrance. A horse drawn carriage pulled beside me. "Please enter," the driver announced. "The Scarecrow requests your presence."

The carriage circled around and continued past the palace to a large single-story building. "Enter and announce yourself," the driver said as we stopped by the door. I got out and as soon as my foot touched the ground the carriage departed.

I walked in. It was filled with work benches, rows and rows of them. And on the benches were different experiments. Some had mechanical things spinning and whirring on them and some had burners heating up beakers of chemicals. One looked like a game of ping pong was being played, but the paddles were floating in the air by themselves.

"Hello," I yelled. "I was told to come in. It's me, Emily.'"

I heard nothing so in a while I repeated myself. Then I was startled by the Scarecrow, who was standing beside me wearing a brightly painted grin. We hugged.

"Emily, I am surprised to see you," he said. "It is a pleasant surprise, of course. But the last time we were together your keenest hope was to get away from here. And it was not without reason. Your life was in danger then and will likely be in danger now."

"And I am glad and relieved to see you," I said. "I was afraid that you burned to death."

"Oh no, nothing of the sort. A bit of fresh hay and a new set of clothes and I was as good as new, perhaps better. I am fine as long as my great brain is unharmed. It was time for a bit of freshening up anyway."

"How did you get to Oz?" he asked.

"One of my friends was pulled into Oz, and I came to help him get back home. He was looking through a mirror and he vanished, so I followed him, but I didn't end up where he went. First I was at Glinda's castle, but it was long ago. Then Glinda sent me to today. And then I used the Golden Cap to command the Flyers to carry me to the Emerald City."

"Oh," the Scarecrow said. "That's a lot to take in all at once. Pulled to Oz … Glinda's castle long ago … the Golden Cap …" The Scarecrow stood in silence, with a serious expression on his face. Then his expression changed to a smile and he started again. "Anyway I want to show you my latest work. I am very proud of it. It highlights the power of my magnificent brain."

We walked between the benches to a far bench. Near it was something that looked like a motorcycle.

"Here is my fusion cycle," he said.

"A fusion cycle?" I asked.

"Yes. The primary source of power is the heat generated by fusing the nuclei of copper and tin, which are abundant throughout Oz."

"It doesn't, like, blow up and destroy everything?"

"No, and that is my innovation. By fusing the atoms in a special crystal matrix the energy released is well controlled and self-regulating. The reaction continues at a temperature well above the boiling point of water, but below the melting point of most common metals, making it perfect for a source of energy for a steam powered vehicle."

"How does it work?" I asked.

"By rotating this handle," he said pointing to the right hand grip on the steering, "you control the amount of water metered into the steam chamber. The water is converted into steam, forcing the turbines to spin. The turbines are attached through a series of reducing gears to the rear tire, which propels the vehicle forward."

"Is it noisy and does it belch out lots of smoke?" I asked.

"It makes a bit of a high-pitched whine from the turbines when it is moving. No smoke, and no belching. The only exhaust is a bit of water and steam. There is also a small amount of gold created but it is easily disposed of."

The Scarecrow pointed to a white board on the desk that had "Cu 29 + Sn 50= Au 79" written on it. Below it was another equation 2Br + Pb + Je = Sw

"What's that other equation?" I asked.

"Josh was trying to explain to me the steps to make a peanut butter and jelly sandwich. Not eating leaves me perplexed by some of these things."

"Makes sense. Can the fusion cycle go very far before refueling?" I asked.

"The major limitation is water, which gives you a few hours of operation between refills. The power source should last a few hundred years."

"Can I give it a try?" I asked.

"Sure, use the helmet on the bench over there," the Scarecrow said as he pointed.

I put the Golden Cap on the nearest bench, put on the helmet, and jumped on the fusion cycle.

"Give the water a bit of a turn. There is a small lag between increasing the flow and cycle speed."

"What do you mean, a lag?"

"A time delay."

"Okay," I said.

I gave the water a small turn and I could hear a growing hissing sound. In a few moments the fusion cycle started to gain speed. Then I was riding at a pretty good clip for inside a building. I drove around the entire building and as I returned to the Scarecrow, I turned the water flow off. The cycle kept on going. After a while it slowed and came to a stop, but I was already a good walk from the Scarecrow, so I parked the cycle and jogged back to him.

"Nice, but the speed control is a problem," I said.

"Yes, it has a few rough edges," the Scarecrow said.

"Have you considered adding brakes?"

"Brakes? What are they?" he asked.

"You know. Something you step on or turn that helps to stop the wheels from turning."

The Scarecrow crumpled his brow. "Brakes. I will have to consider them."

"I need to speak to Gings. Is she in the Emerald City?"

"She should be here shortly," the Scarecrow said. "When I was told that you were back I had someone message her and she immediately started her return so she could speak to you. Let's walk back to the palace."

I picked up the Golden Cap and we started back to the palace. It was a very fast walk so I had to work at keeping up with the Scarecrow. If I paused an instant I would fall behind and have to run to catch up. The new hay they stuffed him with must be very energetic.

"How you left Oz is a mystery to us all," the Scarecrow said. "Gings told me that none of the spells had worked, and yet, you were gone. No one remembers which spell worked, if any worked, or anything about how you left. But by the time your Aunt Maybel arrived the witches had figured out the problem."

"And what was that problem?" I asked.

"The spell caster needs to know where they are sending you. To do that, they need either to have been there, or to use the memories from the other person's mind. To use that memory, they must touch the person. But the memories go both ways, the witch sees the destination, and the person being sent sees the images and thoughts of the witch."

"Do you mean to tell me that my Aunt Maybel has the memories of some witch in her head?"

"Yes. When Gings realized the need for the memory transfer, she would not allow any other witch to do it. So your Aunt Maybel has some of Gings' memories."

"I see," I said. "I hope my Aunt Maybel is okay," knowing full well that she was not. "When Glinda sent me to today, she touched me. That explains the strange memories I have."

"And, how are those memories?" the Scarecrow asked.

"Short and fleeting. Some have been useful, and some are troubling," I said. Just then I heard a boom. A witch came hurdling down toward us. It was Gings, and she landed so fast that in an instant she was walking on the other side of the Scarecrow as if she had been there all along.

"Hello," Gings said. "How and why are you back in Oz?" She was wearing a light blue top with large sleeves that billowed as she walked.

I gave Gings a quick review of what had happened. She interrupted me to ask a few questions.

"You came through a mirror by imagining the scene from Glinda's book of magic?" Gings asked. "You have no idea how dangerous practicing magic without understanding it can be. That is why witches must be instructed. You came to Oz at a time in the past. You imagined pulling that specific flower illustrated in Glinda's book on magic. And when did you think that flower grew? It was pure luck that Glinda was there, and knew precisely what to do to save you, and was also willing to do it. You cannot live in times when you were not alive. And you were lucky the place was real. You could have gone to someone's imaginary world, and be lost forever."

"I read how to do it in the magic book," I said.

"But you didn't read the preceding pages that describe the risks. The magic book is meant to be gone through page by page building understanding, not by flipping around. I don't know how you did it. You should not have been able to do something like this," Gings said in a stern, almost angry, voice.

"Anyway, I am here. I promised to have the Golden Cap destroyed," I said as I handed it to Gings. "Will you help me?"

"Not anyway. You need to stop messing around with magic. You will hurt yourself and everyone around you."

"I am sorry, but I don't think there is any other way."

"You should not ignore what I say. You will get yourself killed. You have been lucky, but even the luckiest person's luck runs out. And are you sure that you want to destroy the cap?" Gings continued. "It has been very helpful at times to be able to command the Winged Monkeys."

"The Flyers have been shamed far too long," I said. "They deserve to be freed from their curse, and I have sworn that I will destroy it."

"I will do my best to help you," Gings said. "But it may be highly protected."

"Please try," I begged.

"I will take this to my home and do what I can," she said.

"And my friend is here, somewhere. I need to bring him home with me," I said.

"Let's start by finding where he is," Gings said. We approached one of the palace entrances. After a short walk we were sitting in the Scarecrow's meeting room. We sat down in chairs at a round table.

"Let me get my main crystal ball," Gings said. She reached her right hand into her left sleeve and pulled out a small clear marble. She set it down on the table and it grew until it was the size of a bowling ball. It was crystal clear. Then Gings waved her hands above it. It became cloudy.

"Describe your friend for me," Gings asked.

"His name is Ralph. He is a little taller than me. And he is a bunch heavier than me. His hair is wild. And the laces of his sneakers are untied."

"Okay, hold on a second, things are coming into focus."

I tried to look into the crystal ball as well but I couldn't see anything.

"Oh my," she said. "Sebastian. He has been taken by Sebastian,"

"Sebastian. He's the guy with the pale skin and the jet-black hair and mustache, and the flames shooting from his hands. The one that tried to kill me the last time I was in Oz."

"Yes. He is the one who tried to kill you," Gings said.

"The same Sebastian that was Glinda's boyfriend long ago. The same one who practices dark magic so that he can live forever."

"You have some of Glinda's memories," Gings said. "But you should know that they may not be dependable."

"Yes I do," I replied. "And dependable or not, I need to know how to rescue my friend."

"You have Glinda's memories, so you know this is pointless. He took your friend just so he could lure you to him. He will kill you, or something worse."

"I don't plan on dying, only rescuing my friend and getting out of here again." I said.

"I cannot help you." Gings said. "I will not be part of this rescue. You will only be captured. It is better to return home and save yourself."

"That's not happening. It is my fault he is here and I will do everything and anything to save him," I said.

"I cannot agree to help you," Gings said.

"I am going to rescue him with or without your help. But how can you sit there and not help? How can you ignore him? Are you a coward?"

Gings was silent. I stared at her and saw that it was pointless to discuss it further.

"Okay, you're not helping me," I said. "Give me back the Golden Cap."

Gings slid the Golden Cap to me.

"Scarecrow, do what you can to destroy the Golden Cap," I said as I slid the cap in his direction.

"But I don't know the first thing —" the Scarecrow said before I cut him off.

"I need someone I can trust working on this," I said, looking at Gings.

"I will do my best," said the Scarecrow.

"I'm going somewhere to think," I said as I stood up and began to walk away. "Somewhere quiet, where no cowards are nearby."

I passed the pools, through a field, into a wooded area. I climbed up and sat on the top of a large green sandbox turtle, like the one outside in my backyard. I closed my eyes.

I thought, "What a big mess I am in. Ralph is here, I am here, Gings won't help me, and I have no plan. How am I going to get home? How am I going to get Ralph home? Would it have been better if I had just let him go? How could I have lived with myself?"

My thoughts were getting darker and darker. "Now neither of us can get home. And Sebastian has Ralph. Are there really things that can be done to people that are worse than death?" I started to cry, and then sob loudly.

I fell off when the sandbox turtle I was sitting on lurched to a halt. I must not have noticed when he had started walking. I twisted my head around and found I was staring into its face.

"Things must be very bleak for you to be so sad," it said.

"They are very, very bleak," I said.

"But you look healthy."

"I am healthy."

"And you don't look tired, or hungry, or thirsty."

"I am not tired, or hungry or thirsty."

"So, right now, you have no reason to be sad."

"I guess you're right. But so many things are wrong and I am the cause."

"Perhaps you are the cause. But you can try to fix things."

"I don't see how. I can't think of how I can even begin."

"Thinking is my specialty," said the sandbox turtle. "Tell me the whole story, and don't leave out any details. Don't stop even if I close my eyes. I am not going to sleep."

After I was done, I waited in silence.

"Well, you are loyal and reckless. You are also bold and fearless. You will need all that and more to succeed. Shortly we will have our meeting of backyard toys. We can discuss how to help you then."

The sun was beginning to fade and I noticed creatures moving our way. First came a red and white plastic horse that rolled on a wheel. Then came a blue and white plastic car, the kind you sit in and move by pushing your feet. And then came a brown plush dinosaur. And then a pink and white wooden unicorn, whose horn had been broken off. There were many others that slowly joined the group. As soon as they met, they started to talk about different girls and boys, one who skinned a knee and needed cheering up, another stuck inside with a broken arm. The sandbox turtle banged on a tree stump. Everyone fell silent.

"Today, my friends, we break from our normal meeting to help this girl before us, Emily, who has a challenge and is in need of special assistance." The sandbox turtle explained my situation to all the backyard toys.

The plastic horse with the wheel, whose name was Raspberry, and who sloshed a little as she spoke since she had been left outside so long that some rain had filled her insides said, "She could ride me to find Ralph."

"Thank you," said the turtle, "but Emily is too big for you, and it would be faster if she walked."

"I have seen the witches fly, and they fly very fast," said the plush dinosaur, whose name was Deena. "Do you know a witch that can fly you there?"

"No," I said, "I don't think so. I flew on a broom once, but I am not good at it. Maybe I could use the Scarecrow's fusion cycle. I can't just get there by magic, since I don't know where there is."

"How would you find your way?" asked the turtle.

"I don't know. Gings used her crystal ball to find Ralph. I guess I need a crystal ball. There's no crystal ball tree around here, is there?"

"No, not that I know of. What would you do if you got to Ralph? Do you know how he is being held?"

"No. I don't."

"If you had a crystal ball you could find out how Ralph is being held. Without knowing what you are up against you won't have a chance," said the turtle.

"So, I need a crystal ball," I said. "But how am I going to get one. I don't think Gings is going to hand one over to me."

"Let me see," said the turtle. "I think I know someone who might help you."

It was agreed that the sandbox turtle would investigate getting me a crystal ball. After that the toys told each other stories about what they had done since the last meeting. I sat down against the sandbox turtle to listen and I must have dosed off.

I had a strange dream about toys and then I found myself on a path in the woods watching an old woman walking slowly to me. She walked with a tall staff, and her clothes were in tatters. I watched in silence as she made her way toward me. At last, she stood in front of me and said, "I have been summoned to train you for Glinda's guard. Before I begin, you should know the training is rigorous. You may not succeed. The first step is to see if you are an acceptable candidate. Do you have any questions?"

"Who requested that I be trained?"

"I cannot tell you that."

"How long does it take?"

"That depends. In any case, you will have no memory of any of the trainings."

"What good is that? How can it help if I can't remember any of it?"

"This training is for your body, not your brain. In these things, if you have to think before you act, you are too slow. The training is for a deeper level."

"How will I even know to join the guard then?"

"You will do what is necessary without thinking. And then, years from now, you may recall the training. Now, I will test you physically."

She lifted her staff and tapped me on my shoulders.

My dream changed. The woman was gone, and I was dressed like Glinda's Guard. I had protection along my shins and forearms, and wore a skirt made of overlapping pieces of heavy leather, wood, and seashells. On my top I had a plain white shirt below similar armor. My shoulders had guards as well.

I heard a voice in my ear and I began to run.

I ran along a path through the forest. The path was steep, and then fell off abruptly. I thundered through branches of trees. At one point a large branch swung at me, knocking me flying, tossing me down on the side of the path. I got up, determined not to let that happened

220

again. The path turned sharply to the right and ended in a cliff. I leaped forward and grabbed a vine, swinging over the edge of the cliff and around the tree the vine hung from. The path resumed. I pushed on, ducking, leaping, at time seemingly flying through the air, only to catch hold just before falling.

Chapter 19 Lessons

I awoke and tried to get up. I was sore all over, especially my stomach and ribs. I was in so much pain that I had to roll on my side to push myself up. I must have slept outside where the toys held their meeting. All of them were gone. I was awake but I felt dead tired.

I walked slowly back to the castle, trying to stretch as I went along. My stomach growled. It was more of a roar really. The sun was still below the horizon so it was still very early in the morning. I walked into the castle to the cafeteria. It was empty so I peeked into the kitchen.

"It's still too early for food, but if you help us I will get you something," someone called out. "We are making pancakes. Have you ever made pancakes?" she asked.

"Yes, I've cooked pancakes for my family," I said.

"Great. We are expecting a big crowd this morning and we are short staffed. Use this grill," she said pointing to an empty spot in a line of grills that spanned the entire wall. "The pitchers of batter are over there. When they are cooked the pancakes go over there. Pay attention to what you are doing since things are crowded. I'm busy so I will leave you to it."

I grabbed a pitcher of batter and started pouring pancakes. I've only cooked a few at a time but I saw that everyone else was cooking three rows of six, so I poured them out. Then I looked around the kitchen and got myself a spatula, just in time to start flipping them. A couple got messed up so I kept them to eat. After I poured the second batch I gobbled them down. They were good.

I heard the person next to me say that members of the Taffy Pullers Association were here for a big symposium on taffy pulling technique. I worked away at making pancakes. A second shift of people came into the kitchen to take over and my shift all came around to a table in the cafeteria. When I finally sat down to pancakes I realized I must have eaten quite a few while I was cooking them because I was pretty pancaked out. I had one more. When other people started to leave I followed them.

We went outside and watched a demonstration of taffy pulling technique. The taffy pullers all were strong looking with big muscular arms. And no wonder. There was a big blob of taffy on a long marble table. There were long marble rods through the taffy. Four pullers, one at each end of each rod, pulled the taffy, stretching it the length of the table. When they got to the end, more rods were put on the taffy closer to the center, and the taffy was folded over on itself. There were two teams, one working on each side of the taffy, each team working like in a relay race, pulling, adding rods, folding, removing rods and repeating. It was hard work pulling taffy. I would have never guessed it.

I was so tired after all the making pancakes and watching all the taffy pulling I went to find a nice place to nap. I walked in the direction of the Scarecrow's workshop and I found a small garden with an inviting park bench. The air was warm and the sun was behind some fluffy clouds. I lay down and immediately fell asleep and started dreaming.

I was standing in a large green lawn, next to a path that went on into the distance. There was a blob of something on the path in the distance slowly moving toward me. As it got closer, I could see that it moved like an ameba, sending out projections that stretched forth, and flowing into them. When it got even closer, I could see it looked like the stuff that wasn't flowing was made of pancake, sending out pseudopods of what looked like pulled taffy and then settling into cooked pancake. I wasn't scared at all, in fact something about it was familiar. When it was right in front of me it stopped. "You have been approved for warriors' training. This is your first formal lesson."

"What are you?" I asked.

"What do I look like to you?" it replied. It spoke in the same voice as the old woman in my previous dream.

I described her taffyness and pancakeness, which caused her to break out in laughter. When she finally stopped laughing she said, "Really Emily, you shouldn't complain to me about your dreams. They are your dreams, not mine."

"Then, who are you?" I asked.

"I am one of your future lessons, but for now we need to get on with your training. We do not have time to waste. Today we will discuss the most dangerous aspect of our warriors' training. Do you know the most dangerous aspect of being a warrior?"

"And how come I was so beaten up after my last lesson?" I interrupted.

"This is your dream, so don't complain to me about it."

"Great non-answer. I guess it is my dream but it doesn't help me. Anyway I think the most dangerous tool warriors use is the swords."

"No, it's not the swords."

"The bows and arrows."

"No. It's not the bows and arrows."

"Then it the crossbows. I've seen them in one of the pictures of the warriors. They look really dangerous."

"No, it's not the crossbows."

"I give up," I said. "What could possibly be more dangerous than these weapons?"

"The most dangerous aspect of being a warrior is working with horses."

Something hit me on the left side of my face. It felt like I was hit by someone's hair, but it was harder.

"These horses are enormous beasts with fierce temperaments."

A warm moist voice said into my right ear, "Enormously fierce. Fiercely temperamental."

I got slapped in the face again. "Hey, stop it," I yelled. I swung my left arm out but there was nothing there.

"Some of the horses are also wise-guys."

The moist voice said, "Wise, very wise. Wise-gals and guys."

I got slapped in my face again. This time I swung my right arm out and it wacked into something. I looked to my right and there was a large horse, the largest horse I had ever seen. I didn't know they got so big.

"This is Athena. She will be training you."

"Do I have to? Really?" Athena asked. "She is so scrawny, I might hurt her." She turned to me. "Don't your parents feed you?"

"My parents feed me just fine, thank you," I said.

"But she's so small. How will she even get up? I don't come with training wheels, you know," Athena said, "or a step ladder."

Well, she was right about that. I could just barely reach the pommel of the saddle. I had to strain hard to get my foot up into the stirrup. But I did and I swung my leg over. As soon as I was in the saddle, Athena bolted forward with a gleeful laugh. "Hold on Emily, if you can," she said.

But I did. In time I was comfortable riding and in more time, leaping off Athena as she sprinted on, letting my feet hit the ground, and holding the pummel, leaping to her other side. Soon I was standing on the saddle holding the reins, and then I was standing on the saddle without the reins.

Athena slowed and stopped. "Emily, your lesson is complete. It is time for you to awaken."

"But I won't remember any of this when I am awake. I won't ever remember you."

"But I will remember you and whenever you need me I will be there."

"I don't understand," I said. "But thank you, Athena."

I woke up. From the sun I guessed it was mid-afternoon. I was tired again, more tired than when I took my nap. What is happening to me? Did I catch some kind of cold? I stood up and I had to sit back down. My head was spinning and I didn't feel solid on my feet. I thought, "I'm supposed to be helping Ralph and I can't even walk."

A flicker of light reflected off something in the distance. In a few measures I could make out my good friend the Tin Man. And in a few more beats he was smiling in front of me.

"The Scarecrow sent message that you were back in Oz. I came as fast as I could. Are we adventuring?"

"I guess we're adventuring," I said. "One of my school mates has been taken by Sebastian and I need to save him. But, you knew that already, didn't you. Even before we get to that, I seem to be sick. I must have caught a cold. I'm not steady on my feet."

"Hmm. I'm not sure what you mean by sick. Or what a cold is. Or why you would want to catch one? If you caught one, couldn't you just let it go free? But if you are not steady on your feet I can bring you to a doctor who should be able to get you looking sharp in no time."

"You don't know what being sick is?"

"No, but I do remember that Dorothy once mentioned it, but when we asked about it she refused to discuss it."

"Your nose runs, your throat is dry and scratchy. You run a fever. Sometimes your head aches."

"No, I'm not familiar. But it does sound like a lot of running. Where would your nose run to? Would it try to hide from you? And how long is a fever? Is it like running a marathon?"

"No. I'll try to explain it later. But if we could go to a doctor that would be nice."

The Tin Man pulled a whistle out of his pocket and blew it a few times. I couldn't hear it at all. It must have been too high a pitch for me; maybe it was a dog whistle. Or maybe it didn't work.

A short time later a bird landed on the Tin Man's shoulder. The Tin Man made some chirping sounds to the bird, who then flew off.

"I requested a carriage. I didn't think a JetBroom would be good for you considering your problem. It will be here shortly." While we waited I tried to explain being sick to the Tin Man.

"Well, it sounds so inconvenient, this being sick," he said as I was just about to give up hoping he would ever understand it. "And you say you can pass it around. I guess there are things you really shouldn't share. Being civilized does seem to have its down side."

Then the carriage arrived. It was a small carriage drawn by a single horse. The driver was dressed all in green. The Tin Man helped me into the carriage and we both sat down.

"Doctor Ulam, please," the Tin Man told the driver. "As fast as possible."

The carriage door closed and then reopened again.

"We're here," the Tin Man said.

"We didn't even move, I said. "Are you sure we're at the doctors?"

"Sure as can be," the Tim Man said. "These carriages can go quite fast when they please."

I thanked the driver and the horse.

The Tin Man helped me into the exam room of Doctor Ulam. After a few questions he started looking me over. He used some odd shaped implement and looked into my left eye. At a certain point he leaped back with a howl. "Well, I don't want to watch any more of that. I'll probably have nightmares for weeks just with what I saw."

After he calmed himself down he said, "I will need to use the diagnostic darts. Please stand over there, in front of the body outline."

"Did you say you are going to use darts?" I asked.

"Yes, diagnostic darts. They are cutting edge technology, from the Diagnostic Dart Company."

"Before you use them, explain how they work."

"As I said, you stand in front of the outline. I will be blindfolded. After I am spun around sufficiently to make sure my throws are purely random, I will throw darts at you. They will pass through your body and land in the area on the body outline where you are having difficulty."

"And this works? The darts don't just stick in me?"

"Never fails. It is medical sciences' leading diagnostic tool."

"Better than X-ray, or CAT Scan, or sonogram?"

"I am not familiar with any of those tools, but a cat scan sounds like it would have possibilities. Cats have extremely good senses of smell."

I turned to the Tin Man, "You think I should let him throw darts at me?"

"Yes," the Tin Man said. "Dr. Ulam is too humble. He helped the Diagnostic Dart Company develop this technique. It is now standard practice throughout Oz."

"Okay," I said with a sense of dread. I walked in front of the body outline.

Dr. Ulam took out a heavy blindfold and put it on. The Tin Man spun the doctor around, one way, and then the other, until the poor doctor couldn't stand up straight. The Tin Man helped the doctor walk to the throwing line and handed him the darts. I closed my eyes and prayed. I heard a thunk as the dart stabbed into the body outline. I was relieved not to have become a pin cushion. Then, an instant later, the doctor threw another dart.

"Hmm," The doctor said. "You seem to have a problem in the right inner ear. I am going to call in some specialists to examine your ears."

I was glad that was over. "That sounds good. How long will it take for them to get here?" I asked.

"They are already here," Dr. Ulam said, pointing to what looked like a little pile of sand in the corner where one of the tables met the wall. Out climbed two tiny ants. I got close enough to look at them. They wore tiny lab coats and had caver's lights on their heads.

"This is Dr. Vali and Dr. Gi, doctors of the inner ear." Dr. Ulam put his finger by the two ants who crawled on.

"Young lady, we will perform inspections of your inner ears and determine what, if anything, is out of order." They spoke at the same time, perfectly synchronized.

The doctor guided one ant to each of my ears. They walked into my ears with a ticklish sensation. They played a short drum piece on my ear drums. Then there was a bit of banging inside my right ear. I felt more tickles as they climbed from my ears onto Dr. Ulam's hand.

"We (they talked in unison again) inspected your ears. All was in order and your ear drums are fit and well tensioned. Substantial ear wax was noted in your ears, especially the right one. The wax was then removed. This is a possible cause of your balance problem."

"Thank you so much, Dr. Vali and Dr. Gi. You have been so helpful," I said.

"You're welcome young lady."

Then Dr. Ulam said, "I believe this will solve your balance problems. If you experience further balance problems we can call in additional specialist who can inspect your stomach, colon, and small intestine. Their inspection usually takes from 18 to 24 hours, depending upon what you recently ate."

"Thanks," I said, doubly thankful that my balance seemed good. "I seem to be fine. If I have more problems I will return."

"You know where I live," Dr. Ulam said as I exited the exam room. When the Tin Man saw me going he quickly followed.

The Tin Man used his whistle and in a few moments we were in a carriage.

"The Pondering Forest please," the Tin Man requested of the driver.

"I will leave you in the Pondering Forest. It's a fine place to consider future plans. I must continue on to confer with the Scarecrow."

I left the carriage. The Pondering Forest was a beautiful peaceful place. There were tall trees, oaks, maples, sycamores, and others, with a cushioned floor of bright green moss. The air was moist and a breeze, just strong enough to notice, kept it fresh and perfumed.

I sat down against a large ash tree to think about how I could possibly save Ralph. I hoped I could figure something out, and I hoped Ralph would hang on until then. *I can't understand Gings. She of all people knows Sebastian and his evil. Gings said he was just there to lure me in, so perhaps Ralph was safe, at least for now.*

231

I was lost in thought, watching a pair of mockingmunks running around the trunk of a nearby oak when I notice Josh walking toward me. "Emily, what are you doing back in Oz?"

"I had to return to save a friend," I said. "How did you find me?"

"I was talking to the Tin Man when Gings poked in and said you were out and needed a friend."

"One truer than herself, I hope. I can't understand why Gings refuses to help me."

"I am sure she has a good reason. She sees further ahead than anyone I know."

I filled Josh in on the details of my return.

"Gings really held back on you, you know," Josh said. "Transfer magic is very dangerous. You could have been lost, outside of normal space, or in an imaginary world. You could have died someplace that no one even knew you. If Glinda wasn't there you would have probably died right there."

"Well, I didn't. And I still have to save Ralph."

"You really can't be serious, thinking you are going to just walk up to Sebastian and he is going to let you and your friend walk away. I don't understand why he tried to kill you, but I don't think he has changed his plans."

I wanted to change the subject, so I did. "When I needed to get down from my room on a broom, I really had trouble. I think I bashed into the palace wall a hundred times. What am I missing about flying on a broom?"

"You don't think that short lesson covered everything about flying a broom? It's amazing that you made it down more or less unhurt. In that room there were more than a dozen witches helping you."

"I figured I was getting some help. Anyway, I had no choice, I could either fly on the broom, jump out the window, or be captured by Veeron. I think I chose correctly."

"You did. Now you need more training. And you need to practice to fly smoothly. You saw how I struggled the first time we met. But I think I can help you. Gings gave me this new navigation crystal ball. I don't need it and I'd rather not have to break in a new ball. This would be perfect for you. I can set you up with an account and then you can practice flying. The nav balls have a ten-level tutorial on broom usage."

"That would be a big help," I said.

Josh went to his broom and fiddled with his crystal ball. A short while later a broom descended near us.

"Let me look this broom over before you start," Josh said. "These pool brooms sometimes get mistreated by the users." Josh inspected it carefully.

"It looks good," he said. "Really good. It should suit you fine."

He took out the nav ball and put it into the holder. Then he made some adjustments.

"Emily, come over here and look straight at the ball."

I did. "What's going on?" I asked.

"I made an account for you. The nav ball is linking itself to you. I'm not sure how it works, maybe it's scanning your face, or your eyes, or even your brain, but whatever it's doing it will know you now and forever."

"Forever?" I asked.

"It is yours forever, unless the ball is voided, which takes a special procedure. Whatever you do with it is perfectly private and there is no witch that exists who can find out how you use it."

"Thanks Josh," I said.

"I set it up on level one broom usage, but I am going to have to leave you to your studies. I am already late for one of my lectures."

"Thanks again Josh. You're the best."

I jumped on the broom and started the lesson. I knew I needed to be able to fly if I was going to have any chance at saving Ralph. Josh flew off and I began to slowly go through the lesson. After a bit I found where the setting for the speed of the lessons was set and pushed it forward a few notches. I was going to have to learn to fly and I didn't have forever.

I was well into level two, and about tree height, when someone flew up on my right and startled me. The broom jerked around and then settled down.

"Hello Emily."

"Oh, hi, uh Teresa." I had to think up her name. "I'm learning how to fly a broom step by step. Thanks for the early lesson."

"You're welcome," she said. "It's very impressive that you could fly after so short a lesson. I guess it came in handy."

"It sure did. I don't think I would be here without it."

"Gings said you were out here and might like company."

"I don't understand her. Why would she care?"

Teresa didn't reply. We landed and I paused the flying lessons. I noticed she was wearing a utility belt.

"Teresa, what's with the belt?"

"It's the newest trend among some of the younger witches. How do you like it?"

"Very stylish," I said with a grin. "I need some help. If I lost something, is there magic for getting it back?"

"You asked the right person. I am always leaving things wherever I go. I don't know what I would do if I couldn't get them back. So the answer is yes, there is magic for getting things you lost back. It only works on things that are yours."

"But how would something know if it was mine or not?"

"Things know, they know who they belong too. Of course, if you have a big pile of pencils in a holder, they are not tightly bound to you, so they wouldn't come if you lost one. But if, for example, you had a special book as a child, or a special toy, it would be very tightly bound to you, and you could call it."

"Oh," I said. "But what if someone else finds it and I don't try to get it back?"

"Over time, the thing binds to its new owner. You can also help transfer the binding to a new person. If you met someone who was sad, and you gave them something that you loved to help cheer them up, that thing knows you want it to help the new person and binds with that new person immediately."

"But what if it's not mine?"

"Then it won't come."

"What if I am not sure?"

"All you can do is try. If it comes, it is yours, no matter what anyone else thinks."

Teresa explained the steps. It involved some footwork, and some incantations.

"It doesn't really need to be lost. You can use this magic to retrieve things in general."

She showed me how it was done and one of her wands appeared in her hand.

"Now you try," she said.

"Oh, I don't know," I said. "I am not sure I have anything in Oz that's mine."

"Take some time and think."

"I gave the pump bottle to the Tin Man, so that's his. The only other thing I used while I was in Oz was a magic book. I read it a few times while I was in my room before the Witches' Council. So maybe that would work. And there was that other magic book, but I took that one home with me."

"The only way you will know is by trying. Since it had been left in that room, reading it may be enough to make it yours."

I stood on my tippy toes and said "Ubbly Zoobly."

Then I leaped back and stood on my right foot and said "Zindly Grindly."

Then I put my left toe down and hopped around making clockwise circles around my left toe, two complete circles and said "Grimdly Mimdly."

I expected nothing would happen. I felt the magic book in my left hand.

"Well done, and whatever you may think, that book is yours."

"Thanks Teresa," I said.

"You are very welcome," she said. "Anytime I can help you please just let me know." She got on her broom and zoomed away. I noticed that there were three little bookmarks in the magic book. But where had the magic book been? Had it been sitting in that empty room in the dark? I guess it was mine, in part, because no one else cared. And where did the book marks come from? More questions.

I put the book down at the trunk of the tree and resumed my studies. The lesson was getting faster. I noticed that when I got startled, if I didn't control myself, the broom would kick up more forcefully.

I was starting level three when the next step was to take a flight of some distance, so I headed off in no particular direction. As I flew, I saw far below me a stone bridge over a small river. It looked interesting so I flew down to check it out. I landed close by and propped my broom against a large rock that was there. The bridge was made of stones, and it had two arches underneath it where the river flowed. To the right of the path was a large pile of rocks. I looked at the bridge from one side, and then the other, and then I decided to cross to the other side. As I approached the bridge the pile of rocks started to move and arrange itself into sort of like a person. The rock creature picked me up and smelled me. I screamed.

"No worry, not squeeze hard, no juice come out."

After it was done smelling me it put me down.

"No cross. Give something do something."

"I don't have anything to give you," I said. "What can I do for you?"

"Idea. Play game."

The creature brought over an enormous wooden chest and dropped it on the ground. The ground shook and the box twisted from the crash.

"Ominoes. Play."

The creature opened the chest. There were large stone pieces, shaped like equilateral triangles, and on each side there were from one to four dots.

The creature closed its eyes, if that's what they were, and pulled the pieces out at random dividing them evenly between us.

"Match. First."

The creature picked up one of its pieces and put it down on the ground between us. I started to flip my pieces right side up, so I could see the dots. The pieces were designed for someone who was much larger and stronger than me; I struggled to move them. I found a piece that matched one side of his piece.

"Good." The creature put another piece down.

I put out another piece and the creature added one of his own.

I picked up a piece and laid it against a side of the last piece the creature had added.

"No. No allow. No space." The creature pointed to the gap between the pieces. "No allow."

"Hmm." I thought, "Okay now I need to match on two sides." I found a piece and fit it in.

"Good," It said. We played on until the fourth level was almost complete. It was my turn, but none of my pieces fit.

"I can't go," I said.

"Lose. Nice. Again?"

"No, I really need to get back," I said.

"Like cherry?" he asked.

"I love cherries," I said.

"Good. Love cherry stones, hate yucky mushy sweet outside." He pointed to me and said, "Eat yucky outside," and then pointed to himself and said, "Eat stones."

The creature effortlessly yanked a cherry tree from the ground. He shook the tree over a big tarp, and then poured the cherries into a barrel. He replanted the tree with just as much ease as when he yanked it up.

The creature took each cherry stone from my hand and gobbled it down. I ate cherries until I couldn't eat another. They were delicious but I was stuffed.

Afterwards we sat and talked.

"Rock troll," it said pointing to itself. And as it waved his arm to point at the bridge it said, "Family bridge."

"Maw went Daw went. Long time. Stay. Sis went. Long time."

"All your family went away?" I asked.

"Left. Long time."

"I am sorry to hear that," I said.

"Good. Grand Maw Grand Daw went. Grr Grand Maw Grr Grand Daw bridge. Sleep. No talk. No move."

"I am sorry," I said again. It sounded like the rock troll was lonely.

"Time. Cross bridge," it said.

The sun was slipping behind the hills off in the distance. "It's getting dark and I really need to return to the Emerald City," I said. "Maybe I can cross the bridge the next time I see you."

"Now. Cross bridge."

I decided it was smart to take a minute and make him happy by crossing the bridge. I got my broom. As I stepped onto the bridge a bolt of fire fell in front of the rock troll. It transformed into Ralph.

"Ralph, how did you get here?" I asked.

Ralph walked toward me. The rock troll blocked his path.

"No cross. Give something, do something."

"I will do neither and yet I will cross your bridge as I please. You can let me cross, or you can die trying to stop me," Ralph said.

"Ralph, what is wrong with you?" I yelled.

The rock troll did not move. It repeated, "Give something, do something."

Ralph shouted, "I shall not," and he shot flames that engulfed the rock troll.

"No," I screamed. Ralph paused and the rock troll stood there unmoved. It seemed unaffected.

"Cross. Cross now!" it shouted at me, looking and motioning to me.

Ralph sent green bolts of lightning at the rock troll. The rock troll glowed with an eerie green halo but it remained unbothered.

Ralph swirled a tornado at the rock troll. In an instant the rock troll took the back of its hand and sent Ralph flying head over heels. He landed in a crumpled pile by the side of the path.

"Are you okay?" I asked.

"Good. Cross bridge."

"And Ralph?"

"Good. No worry."

"Thank you," I said.

"Cross bridge. Cross bridge."

I decided it would be smart to do as told, so I hurried over the bridge. When I got to the other side I turned to look back. The bridge was gone. The river was gone. I was in the middle of a large open field covered in high grasses. I knew I wasn't getting close to saving Ralph. The light was leaving the sky and I knew I wasn't getting back to the Emerald City tonight. I saw a small cabin at the far corner of the field. I flew over to it.

It was a simple cabin, made entirely of boards rough cut from trees. The roof was covered with wood shingles, warped and partly moss covered. I made my way to the door and found it open.

In one corner was a sink and pot-bellied stove. In another was a table just large enough for two chairs. In the third corner was a small desk, with some old-fashioned quill pens in a cup made from a hollowed-out branch. And in the final corner was a thin bed, just wide enough to fit a person.

I put my broom by the door. Before I put it down I checked the nav ball. Totally blank. The nav ball was not going to be any help getting me to the Emerald City this time.

The place smelled musty but it was the only hotel in town, at least the only place I was going to reach before sunset. After taking the blankets outside and giving them a good shake off, they looked clean enough. I found a thick candle and some matches. There was one bound book and a few collections of papers on a shelf that was built into a wall. I pulled some papers down. I was surprised to see that they were hand written in English script on unlined paper. I sat down at the desk to read.

The sun abandoned the sky and with its absence a chill hit me. There was some wood beside the pot-bellied stove so I started a fire. I read on, entranced by the writing. I lost track of the time, but my yawn told me it was time for bed. I put out the candle, made sure the potbellied stove was safe, and got into bed. All the adventures of the day suddenly caught up with me. I felt tired through and through. There was a lot to do and a lot to learn. All of it would have to wait for another day.

Chapter 20 Ralph

"Don't just lie there on my floor. Get up. Now. Get off the floor. Who are you?" asked a man with a thin mustache and a pale, almost translucent complexion. He spoke in a chilly monotone. It was so dark. Only dim flickering lights lit the room. All the windows were covered.

I had stumbled forward onto a faded carpet, braking my fall with my hands. As I got up, I said, "Ralph. Who are you? Where am I?"

"Only talk when spoken to," the man replied.

"What?" I asked, but I didn't get the word out before I started to choke. I gasped for air. I couldn't breathe.

"I am patient only to a point," the man said in an ice-cold voice, "but this is entertaining. Keep talking until you pass out, but don't hurt yourself too badly as you hit the floor."

I stopped trying to talk and I regained my breath.

"Too bad," he said. "I am surprised. It doesn't strike me that self-control is one of your strengths."

"What is that on your nose?" he asked pointing at the bandage the nurse had just given me.

I was hesitant to talk. He said, "Talk when spoken to, so now talk."

"I got punched," I said. The man laughed so hard his face turned gray and he started to choke and cough. After a while he regained his composure.

"Let me guess, my dear friend Emily did that to you." His voice had returned to a cold monotone. "This trap was for her." He looked me over, noticing my T-shirt.

"I think your plans have changed," he said. "She punched you. Did you hurt her properly in return?"

"No," I replied. He laughed again, coughing and gagging.

"How charming you both must be," he said. "To show you what a thoughtful person I am I will fix your nose for you." He gestured with his hands as an incredible pain raked through my entire body. I felt weak on my feet. In an instant the pain past and the bandage on my nose was gone.

"Silly me," he said with a smirking smile on his face. "I forgot to tell you that it would be painful. Not to me, of course. Now, you may go outside and do as you please. Don't worry, I like to keep my bait fresh. But don't wander too far. It can be dangerous out there. Now go and play."

I tried to talk again but I could not breathe.

"You aren't going to pass out for me?" he chided. "No more shows? Please don't disappoint me. Oh please, take a run at me. You are like a patch of pure darkness in my dreary life."

I considered trying to rush at him but it was useless. I turned to the door. The door led to a dark hallway that had no windows and that snaked its way to the outside.

I came out in a heavily wooded area, very little light fought its way through the trees to the ground. The building was a mess, ram shackled and broken down. If it had once been painted, at present, you could not guess its color. It looked like the original simple cabin had been added onto again and again with no plan, small additions slapped on here and there. There were no visible windows. A stone chimney had some pieces missing and the top was partly toppled. I walked away from the building as fast as I could. At a certain point my skin felt like it was set on fire. The creepy guy's voice sounded in my head, "Go ahead. See how much pain you can take." I stepped back from the edge. I walked along checking where my skin began feeling like it was burning. It was like a pen for a dog. If it was a pen, I hoped that it might have an escape. Any hope I had of a quick escape was soon dispelled.

I worked at finding the limits of my cage and wondered where I was. *Was this like in Hansel and Gretel? But this house wasn't made of gingerbread and pastries. And didn't that witch want to eat them? Something to eat would be nice.*

The creep wasn't interested in me, only Emily. *Maybe she hit me harder than I thought and I am bonkers. Maybe my brain got scrambled, or I'm passed out, hallucinating. That was a pretty good punch.*

What happened to the nurse's office? Maybe I better not mess with Emily. She knows some scary people. How does she know this creep? Why would he want to trap her?

And what about my nose? The bandage was gone and no blood was coming out but I couldn't really breathe. Every breath took an effort. Did that creep heal my nose? What did he do?

I continued testing my pen. There was a table, all set for dinner. It had roast turkey, and mashed potatoes, and candied carrots, and sweet potatoes, and a big boat full of gravy. At least I wasn't going to be hungry while creepzilla waited for Emily. I sat down and gathered a big plate full. It was good. I ate until I was full and I pushed myself back. I was about to start exploring my pen when my stomach growled.

I sat back down and got more food. Another plateful of turkey and fixings. After I had polished that off I stopped. My stomach growled again. I looked at the food. I took another mouthful. My stomach growled even louder. I pushed my chair back and as I was about to get up I heard super creepman in my head, "There is plenty of food Ralph. Go ahead, help yourself."

I started testing my pen again. *The creep enjoys being cruel. He is not just creepy, he is sick.*

As I walked along the perimeter of my invisible pen I came to a small brook. I bent down to check my reflection to see if my nose looked okay. It looked okay but it really wasn't. *This creep is impressively sick. Is this some kind of prank? If it is, hats off to the prankster. Well done.*

I noticed that some little fish were swimming below me. Their bluish glow caught my eyes. They swam beyond the edge that made my skin burn. I stuck my arm under the water to see if I could put it on the other side. I could. The pen seemed to only go through the air. It ended at the surface of the water. Perhaps that meant I could find freedom.

I traced out the edge a bit further. My stomach was growling fiercely. I didn't have much for breakfast and I didn't get a chance to eat lunch. And creepman's dinner didn't help. *Was there anything I could really eat in this cage?* I scanned the ground. It didn't look promising. After I had traced out the entire limits of my cage I walked back to the brook. There was a rock nearby so I sat down. It was going to be a hungry wait.

And wait for what? Did Mr. Creepy really expect Emily to try to rescue me? And how was that going to go? Did she plan to punch him in the nose? It was a good punch, but this guy is seriously evil.

I heard some crunching overhead. I looked up. There was a squirrel-like creature on a branch nearby, munching down on some kind of nut. My stomach roared out a growl, just to get attention. The squirrel sat there busily eating its nut, slowly, crunch, crunch, crunch. My stomach roared again.

"Hey there. Don't you know it's rude to stare?" came a chirpy voice. The squirrel had talked to me. *I must really have lost my mind.* But my hunger was real.

"Or are you just dim?" It was true, I was dumbfounded.

"Are you talking to me?" I asked.

"I don't see anyone else around. Who else would I be talking too?"

"I don't usually talk to animals," I said.

"You think you are too good to talk to squirrels? You don't look too good to me."

"No. It's just squirrels don't usually speak to me where I come from."

"Maybe they're snobs then. You must come from a snobby place."

"It's just —" I said but was interrupted.

"Why are you staring at me?"

"I see you are eating a nut and I am hungry."

"See that tree over there," the squirrel said as it motioned to a small tree that had many small trunks. "Hazelnuts."

I walked over to the tree. There were these things on the tree, sort of round. Each one was covered with green leaf-like wrappers. I picked one and pulled off the wrappers. Under the wrappers was a nut. I looked at the nut. "How am I going to eat this?" I thought. The squirrel must have seen my confusion.

"Just bite into it with your long front teeth," the squirrel said.

"I don't have any long front teeth," I said.

"Poor design. If you are going to eat nuts some long front teeth are useful. But there are so many poor design choices on you people. Your feet are not sharp and tough enough to climb trees, and you are so large that if they were, the bark wouldn't hold your weight and you would fall off. And where did you people get your voices? So annoying. So low in pitch. So slow. And so breathy. How can you stand it?"

"I guess I am used to it," I said. I looked around for a rock to use to break the nut open. There was a nice sized rock not too far away. With a few light whacks the nut was open and not so much of it was mashed to dirt. It was nice to eat something. I filled my pockets with the nuts and sat back down, starting to peel them and then smash them and then eat them. The squirrel came down and sat next to me.

"I guess that's the way it is. We all get use to our limitations. Otherwise we could never be happy. Do you mind if I have one of your nuts? You can pick them a lot faster than I can."

"Sure," I said. "Help yourself."

The squirrel grabbed a nut and started gnawing on it. "What's your name?" it asked.

"Ralph," I replied as I stuffed another nut into my mouth. "And what's your name?"

"My name is Nutmeg."

I went back to the tree and picked a few more nuts. I started peeling off the wrappers when I heard some scurrying. Nutmeg had run off.

"Wolves," Nutmeg called from above.

I looked around. There was a pack of terrifying wolves walking slowly toward me, their heads down, teeth flashing and eyes menacing. I watched as they approached my cage. I could see the path they were walking on and it came right by where I was standing, into my cage. I realized that they weren't going to stop. I jumped up and ran toward the house. I ran straight at the rock chimney. I hoped I would be able to climb it to get to the roof. I reached the chimney as the first wolf caught the back of my pant leg. I kicked it off and climbed up. The wolves were just below me jumping and snapping their jaws. I climbed up to the eves of the house, and then higher so that I could step onto the roof. The wolves waited below, pacing and snarling.

"Why don't you come down and join us for a meal?" one of the wolves growled.

"No, I don't think so," I said. "I don't like what's on the menu."

"Pity, you look very tasty."

A large wolf came forward as the others scrambled to get out of his way. The wolf wore a necklace of teeth and the ends of wolf tails. There was a long scar that crossed his snout. And his left ear had a piece missing.

"Tell Sebastian that I know he took my sister. Tell him I will gnaw on his bones. His treachery will be repaid. Give Sebastian my message while you can."

Chatting with the wolves didn't appeal to me so I started climbing further from the edge. I took a few steps and I fell through. Luckily I hit something soft so that besides having bits of debris all over me I was fine. Light came in from the skylight I just added. There was a candle and a small box of wooden matches on a dresser. I lit the candle and stuffed the matches in a pocket. I had fallen on a bed. *It may be where Creepman sleeps, if he sleeps.* The dresser had a thick layer of dust on it, and cobwebs were strung here and there. There was a picture of a younger version of Creepman with a young woman. There was a plain gold ring hanging on the corner of the picture frame. Some holiday cards lined the back edge of the dresser. It looked like the dresser once had a mirror in it. Now there was an empty hole, like the dresser's heart was missing. As I stepped outside the room I heard the door click. I tried the door and it was firmly locked.

I walked down the hall and opened the next door. There were different types of stuffed animals on display, a buck, a large black dog, and a wolf. There was a thing that was sort of a monkey, but had long outstretched wings. I walked over to take a closer look at it. As I looked further I saw something. I had to stop to keep from vomiting. There were some stuffed people there. I mean real people. There was an old woman and a boy who was older than me. I couldn't look anymore. *Is this what Creepman has planned for me? And Emily?*

I stepped back into the hallway and continued walking. The door to the next room was open and in its middle were two waist high operating tables. The one to the right was empty. The one to the left had a boy lying on it. I shuddered to think what that meant. The boy seemed familiar. He reminded me of the stuffed boy in the other room. I went back to take another look at the stuffed boy. They were identical. *What does that mean? What is going on?* I went back to the boy on the table. He seemed sound asleep. I gave him a shake. He didn't notice it at all. I shook him harder but no matter what I did he would not awaken. *This is one sick place. What could Mr. Creepy do with stuffed people? And why would someone look identical to someone who is stuffed. And why couldn't I wake him up?*

I was about to open the door to the hallway when I heard some footsteps outside so I picked up the candle and slipped into a small closet. I didn't want to be found. The creep enjoyed hurting me when he was happy. I didn't want to be around when he was mad. He preferred me to be alive, but I think it was only a preference, not a requirement. And I required that I remain alive, preferably unharmed.

If I blew the candle out the smell and smoke would give me away. I drew some saliva into my mouth and stuffed the candle top in. I heard a faint hiss and it hurt like hell. I could hear the door open and I held my breath. Someone walked around the room, moving back and forth. I could only imagine what was happening. I heard something get lifted up, and then it sounded like it was set down again. More steps, just outside the closet where I was hiding. Then the door opened and closed again. It sounded like the door had been locked with a key.

I took the candle out of my mouth and slowly exhaled. The roof of my mouth hurt, but I was still free. The floor inside the closet tipped when I moved my weight from foot to foot. I slowly turned the closet door knob so it would make no sound. I opened the door the slightest crack, peering into the room. The room was empty. I slowly opened the closet door, trying not to make a sound.

When I looked back into the closet I could see that the floor board of the closet had been cut away and refitted so that it could be lifted up. I could see the crawl space under the house, and in I went, replacing the floor board after me. I crawled along until one of my hands fell into the ground. It was a hole covered by some branches, cloth and dirt. I lifted the corner of the covering and peered in. It was a tunnel. Its walls were lined with rocks that gave off a muted glow. "A lot of work was done making this tunnel," I thought. "Had they been successful? Did they escape? Had they been caught?" The cover was intact, so perhaps it meant that either the attempt had not been made, or the attempt was made and yet the tunnel had not been discovered. I wondered which.

"Come here," I heard in my mind. My body began to crawl out from the underside of the house, and then make its way to the door that I had left the house through. I had no choice. I could only come to the call. I had no control of my body.

I entered. I watched as the door opened, I moved in and the door closed, my hand and body executing the motions without my assent. Then I followed the hall, and entered the room where I first saw this evil place.

"It is good that you did not go far," Sebastian said. "I need your help."

I tried to resist but I walked to him. Up close I could see that his skin had some small slits that were cleverly covered by makeup. In the few spots that the makeup didn't cover his skin looked dried, like old paper, maybe old parchment.

"And how was your play time?" he asked.

"A wolf says —" I tried to say but was cut off.

"Yes, that he will chew on my bones. But really, what should you expect from a pup. Enough socializing. I don't really need your help. What I need is just a few bits of you. You see, I have located your friend Emily and I want to go pay her a visit. Who better to welcome her than you?"

He took a pair of scissors and cut a bit of hair from just behind my right ear. Than he took a nail cutter and took a bit of fingernail from my left ring finger. Then he took a scalpel and a small glass tube. He moved toward my face.

I tried to step away, or raise an arm, or even move my head, but I could not.

"Close your eyes," he said, and I did.

He stepped in. He smelled like cleaning fluid, perhaps ammonia. The scalpel cut into the skin over my right eye. I screamed inside but could not move.

I stood like a statue. I could hear him moving around.

"Open your eyes," he said and I did. On the far wall was a wide stone fireplace with an arched and keystoned opening. Creepman walked to the left side of the fireplace where a caldron was boiling furiously. He grabbed a lever and the pot rotated out of the fireplace. He put the hair he had cut from me into the pot. The mixture fumed and let out the scent of burning rubber. I could hear him muttering something to himself. He stirred the contents and moved the caldron back into the fireplace.

He hummed to himself and then he rotated the caldron out of the fireplace once more. He put in the bit of fingernail he had cut from me. The mixture belched out rancid smoke. He returned to me.

"How careless of me," he said. "I almost forgot." He cut off tiny bits of material from my shirt sleeve and my pants pocket. He added these to the mixture which responded by settling down. The boiling ceased. Everything turned to silence. All that could be heard was my tormented breath. He made no sounds.

"Almost there," he said. He gave me a spiteful smile. He took the vial of blood. He put a drop in. "One drop," he said to himself in a whisper. I felt a thrumming sound in my head. He added a second drop of my blood. "Two drops." The thrumming grew louder. A third drop. "Three drops." It felt like my whole head was shaking. A fourth drop. I could not stand it. *Cry.* I would cry but I could not move. I prayed it would end. "Four drops," I barely heard above the thunderous noise in my head. I realized then that I was lost. *This is not a game. Not a fanciful story. Not a clever prank. This will be my end. I am so sorry, Carrie Anne, and little Johnny. So sorry Mom and Dad. So very sorry. Sorry Emily. Save yourself, I am lost.* And then the fifth drop.

Chapter 21 The Escape

I awoke on a table next to the unconscious boy. I wasted no time and shot to the closet, pulled up the floor, slid in, closed the closet door, and replaced the cover. I crawled to the entrance of the tunnel. I looked around for a digging tool and quickly found a flat rock that would serve well. In a few heartbeats I was at the tunnel's end digging. There was a muted glow along the tunnel's wall, not bright, but bright enough for me to just barely make out what I was doing. I set to, digging. With each small pile of dirt I felt I was a bit closer to freedom. I shoved another pile of dirt behind me, and another and another.

I worked furiously until I needed to take a break. I looked at the end of the tunnel. I had been working with all my might and I hadn't moved at all. *This is a waste of time. How can I fight someone who can use magic? He would win every time. What was the point of trying? I should just lay here and wait for him to make me come to him again.*

I did lay there for some time. Then, I had an idea! I backed out of the tunnel and into the closet. I put everything right and then I went to the hall. I found the room that I had fallen into. I turned the knob hard. Nothing. I grabbed the knob and pulled up. With all my might. There was a large snap of wood breaking and the door was free. Either Creepman heard me or he didn't. Either way I needed to move fast. There were some letters on the top of the chest. I took them. They would be useful. I put a chair on the bed and I climbed out onto the roof. The sun peaked through the breaks between the leaves of the trees. I tested the roof to make sure I wouldn't fall back in and climbed on. A few steps to the chimney and down to the ground. There were plenty of dry branches scattered around on the forest floor. Plenty for what I had planned. I collected up a nice pile. Three nice piles in fact. Once I started I needed to work fast. I went to one corner of the building and crumpled up a few of the pages of letters. A nice lean to of dried branches, a strike of the match, and the first fire was set. Everything was nice and dry. It was like everything was waiting for someone to light it. I ran to the next pile of branches. Another fire. I ran to the last pile of branches. Everything cooperated. It all lit and burnt. I had a few more pages of letters, and the envelopes, they went on. I ran to the first fire. The flames were climbing the wall and smoke was collecting under the eaves. I added a few more branches. I ran to the second fire. The wall was covered in flames. The flames were like orange and red ivy that was growing on the wall and would soon cover the entire building. I ran to the third fire. The eaves and the roof were burning. Sparks were drifting off. The fire popped and hissed. I watched for a moment, then I turned and darted to the edge of my cage. I felt my hand along it hoping that there may be a break. I watched the flames slowly cover the house walls as I walked the extents of my prison. Something must happen. Something soon, I hoped.

I continued along. One of the areas of burning roof fell in with a pained groan. That was it. I felt my hand go through the barrier. I turned and ran.

The branches of the trees tore at me as I pushed my way through, each step a step further from that prison. I battled on. I burst into an opening in the forest. Wolves surrounded me. Better to die from wolves than whatever Creepman had planned for me. I was brought to the head wolf.

"Did you tell him?" he asked.

"I did," I said, panting from my run. "I set fire to his house. You can smell it."

"You are cleverer than you look. I like you boy. What's your name?"

"Ralph."

"Good name, proper name, honorable name." He turned to the wolves. "This boy, you will not harm or impede in any way. He has free passage through all Wolf Forest. Anyone who disobeys will answer to me."

"Boy," the wolf said as he turned back to me, "you should leave this area. None of these wolves here will bother you but also know that wolves are independent and think for themselves, so it is best not to stay long. That way," he said pointing, "is the direction to the closest human town."

I got up off the ground. "Thank you," I said and I fled. I ran into the forest and after a short distance, stopped to consider how I was going to make sure I went the right direction. I could still see the wolves, who were sitting and talking. I picked out some trees that were lined up. If every time I went to the first tree I picked another tree further ahead that lined up, I could keep going the right direction. Or at least the right general direction. It slowed me down so I had to walk. I went on like this, all the time in dense forest. The ground started to rise and going became harder. In some places I had to pull myself up over small outcroppings of stones.

Then the temperature suddenly dropped and snow tumbled down on me. In a few moments I was walking in ankle deep snow. I started to shiver. I was dressed for school, not for a snow storm. I stuck my hands into my pockets but it was no help. The snow poured down, covering my head and my shoulders. I shivered uncontrollably. I stumbled and fell down face forward into the snow. I lay there. A voice was in my ear, "Get up or you will freeze." It may have repeated. I don't know. I began to feel a comforting warmth. "Get up, don't fall asleep." But I was so sleepy. I dropped off.

When I awoke I found myself in a warm room in an oversized soft couch, covered by a pile of fluffy blankets. I was seated facing a roaring fire and a dog was curled up to my right. A large hairy creature sat in an oversized upholstered recliner, silently reading a book. I tried to talk but all that came out was a rough grunt.

The large hairy creature stood up. "We had thought that we might have lost you, but you looked tough enough to take a bit of weather," she said. I could tell the creature was a she, though the hair covered her thickly.

"Big Foot," I said.

"Thank you for the compliment. I hope you are not jealous," she said. "They give me a great advantage when walking through the forest, or even walking through snow. We do get a lot of snow here, but this storm is not natural."

I reached out and started patting the dog. "Thank you for saving me."

"Thanks goes to Rover over there," she said motioning to the dog with her hand.

"Thank you, Rover," I said.

The dog opened its eyes but didn't move. "Oliver. My name is Oliver. I found you but that animated dust bunny carried you home."

"Thanks to you both. But the witch will come for me. He is insane."

She sat beck down and picked up her book. "Don't worry. No one but a fool would enter my home without my welcome. And soon enough the weather will break and you can continue on your way."

"Why soon?"

"Changing the weather takes a lot of energy. It's hard for even the strongest witch to hold it up for long. It drains you, wears on you, and forces you to stop and rest. After it breaks you will have a time to make your way unimpeded."

"Won't you come with me? He is insane, sick."

"No. Here I stay. I don't like bustle. Truth is, I don't like people. My cozy home, a warm fire, a nice book, and a quiet day are my preferences. I leave excitement to others. Would you like some tea?"

"Yes." She brought me some tea that tasted like oranges and lemons. I sipped it slowly. She picked some colored balls out of a wooden basket and started to juggle.

"Do you juggle?" she asked without waiting for a reply. "I find it very calming. I like to do it while I think things over. Why don't you tell me about your escape?"

I gave her a condensed version, leaving some details out, especially those that were embarrassing.

She smiled, never letting her attention waiver from the balls. "You made him drop his balls," she said.

"What do you mean?" I asked.

"Every juggler has a limit to how many balls they can keep in the air. Add too many, or if something goes wrong, things get out of control and the balls drop. Now, Sebastian is a powerful witch indeed, but even he has an upper limit. You tossed him a bunch of balls at the same time and he had to let some drop. Your cage was one of the balls he dropped. From how you described him, he has more important balls to keep in the air, like keeping himself alive. When you started those fires, he had to let some balls drop. You were very clever, setting multiple fires must have given him something to do."

"I still don't get it," I said.

"Every bit of magic he does, keeping you caged, keeping that boy asleep, keeping himself alive, and probably lots of other bits of magic we don't know of, all are like balls he is juggling. You overloaded him. He's experienced so he unloaded by dropping the least important bit, holding you in a cage. He recovered pretty quickly so he's good. And he got on with his temper tantrum of a storm, so you must have really shaken him up." As she was saying this she was juggling, and with each loop of the balls, tapping one of them so that it flew back into the basket. After a few more loops all the balls were stowed away.

The wind suddenly died down and the sun broke through.

"As I said, it is hard to sustain that kind of magic for long. Where are you going?"

"To the nearest human village."

"When you are ready I will start you on your way."

"Is your house in Wolf Forest?" I asked.

"The wolves think so, but really the forest is not theirs. They roam the entire area but so do many others. The wolves harass those they can, and ignore those they cannot. They have a reputation for being smart, but they spend so much energy in petty squabbles. If they are smart, they don't act it."

I finished my tea and got up. "I will go then. The wolf leader gave me passage but he warned me that it may not be respected by all wolves."

"It is their nature," she said. "And perhaps their squabbles are also due to their nature." We walked out of her home. From the outside I could see that it was a log cabin, built of massive trees. Around the cabin were gardens of vegetables and flowers. Nearby I could see large vines with differently shaped and decorated squashes and pumpkins hanging on. In the distance I saw corn, and perhaps pepper plants. Everything was covered with a thin layer of snow. The air had warmed, but the snow lingered. Snow in the trees sent drizzles of cold water and clumps of wet snow down along their drip lines.

She walked me to the edge of her land and looked back to her house. "I won't have to water this week. I can only hope Sebastian's outburst hasn't caused too much damage to my gardens." She turned and pointed, "That is the way on. Good luck to you young man. Continue that direction. Further on you will come to a creek. You can follow the creek into the town."

"Thank you, and Oliver, again," I said, realizing I never learned her name.

I looked at the sun and started off. In a short while I was out of the forest, walking in grassland. Most of the grass was waist high, but there were sections where the grass towered over my head. I kept away from those.

I walked for what seemed to be hours when I saw the creek in the distance. I was tired and I was thirsty, so I stopped to rest and get a drink. I found a section where the willows gave me some protection from the sun. I bent down, cupped my hands and took a drink. My pant knees got wet and muddy. *But why should I care? I know that it won't be long before psycho man comes looking for me. I should enjoy my freedom while it is mine.*

I noticed some insects floating down the creek. They used boats made of what appeared to be half acorn shells. They stood in the middle and used tiny sticks to help navigate. I use the word navigate loosely because they went where the current brought them. The sticks only helped free them from obstacles. They were spun around and tossed mercilessly. I don't think I could take it. But they seemed to enjoy it.

And then I could hear their voices. They laughed with glee. I decided to follow them down the creek. The current was moving pretty fast, and the banks of the creek were steep, full of slick rocks and soft ground that tried to pull my sneakers off. I kept up, but I spent a good part of the time slipping and falling into the mud. I could feel my feet squishing in my sneakers. I scampered along, sometimes leaping from one side to the other, watching them as they floated. I must have lost myself watching them because when I paused to look around, I was in front of a town. I looked at myself. I was a mess. So much for trying to keep my fancy sneakers clean and new. My hands were covered with mud from breaking my falls and my pant knees were wet and muddy. I tried to wipe my hands off on a nearby tree trunk. When I looked back at the creek, the insects were gone, carried away by the current. I felt sad. I liked those little bugs, and now they were gone. *It's funny how something so short and passing can cheer you while it is happening, and sadden you when it is over.*

I walked slowly into the town. Some people stared at me. Some people moved away from me after they looked at me. I guess something about me scared them.

I walked down the sidewalk until I came to a bench in front of a store. I sat down and began to think. *What was the point of running away? I know he will capture me, and he will be angry. Angry and psycho. What could I do against him? Are there witches stronger than him, one strong enough to help me?*

I tried to ask someone where I could find a witch. She hurried away from me. I walked into the store and blocked the door. Some people gasped when they saw me. I yelled, "Is there a witch in this town? One who can help me fight Sebastian?"

Everyone was quiet. I cornered a man and yelled out my question. "No, no," he whimpered. "I can't help you. I won't help you."

"Tell me where there is a witch! When I am captured I will tell Sebastian how all of you helped me! Imagine what he will do with you! Imagine your agony! Where is a witch?"

Someone said in a low voice, "Esmeralda, on Spruce Street. Fifteen Spruce Street. She is our witch."

"Where is Spruce Street?"

"Down four blocks on the left. Two blocks and then a right gets you to Spruce Street."

I stormed through the door and thundered down the street, crossed and followed left. Two blocks and right

263

onto Spruce Street. I ran down the street, counting houses and looking at the numbers. I found number fifteen. There was a sign outside the house, much like the sign a dentist or a doctor would have outside their office. Except it said witch.

I walked in. The front was empty except for some potted plants and chairs. I heard some noise in the back. I rounded the desk and opened the door to the consultation rooms. I saw someone running for the back door. I hurried down the hall. I got outside in time to see someone flying off on a broom.

I went back in and sat down on one of the chairs in the waiting room. *That didn't help. If not a witch, who would help me. Who would not fly away?* I walked back to the main street.

I pushed into another building. It was a restaurant. The people reacted much as before.

"Where is your town's leading scientist?" I shouted. "If you do not help me, and do it fast, I will make sure Sebastian knows of how you are plotting against him."

Someone fainted. An old man said, "You will find her on Canal Street. From here, cross the street. Go this way (as he pointed) five blocks, go left three blocks, and take a right. Number 26. Now please leave us in peace young man."

I left them. After a short walk I was outside a house with a large brick building near it. I heard the sound of movement inside and I went in. I found the scientist in goggles and a face shield, heavy gloves and a heavy coat, holding a blow torch, bent over some pieces of metal, doing what looked to me to be welding.

"I need your help," I yelled. Loudly. Loud enough to be heard over the sound of the torch. She ignored me for a moment and then turned her torch off. She place her torch in a holder and began to take her protective gear off. She motioned me to follow her and we sat down in a small office.

"What can I do for you young man?" She asked.

I told her of my situation.

"Sebastian," she muttered. "He is a nasty piece of work. He has taken some of the townspeople and there is nothing anyone can do. I am not surprised Esmeralda flew off. She confronted Sebastian once and suffered greatly for it."

"Is there anything you can do to help me?" I asked. "Or should I just try to enjoy myself until he captures me again."

"If you plan to wait for him, please do it somewhere else. We all will be punished simply because you are among us. But I may have something that will help you, perhaps only a bit. Follow me." She walked back where she was welding and picked up a cloth pouch and a hand trowel. We walked out of the town to an empty lot.

"When I discovered this I bought this bit of land." She waived her arms left and right. "I have not had a chance to do any tests but it appears that the blue grains of sand have some anti-magic properties. Witches and magical being keep far away from this area. The blue grains are just a small part of the sand, so I can't say how effective it will be as a weapon. But you are welcome to what you can dig."

"Thanks," I said. I looked around. There were a few places that showed concentrations of blue sand. I searched out the one location that was the bluest and started to dig.

"Good luck young man," she shouted. She had already put a lot of distance between us. "Make sure you leave the town when you are done."

I dug until I came to a vein of very blue sand, almost pure blue. I filled the pouch and began to walk out of town.

Chapter 22 Amelia Who?

I stood on a path. I had seen this path before, each time at the start of a dream lesson. This time, off to the right was a grass runway. A flying machine was moving parallel to the runway. It had blades like a helicopter. At the front was a propeller. Its body was like a plane, with a small wing just above the wheels. The flying machine turned right and flew past the end of the runway. Then it turned right once more and began to approach a landing pad. As it approached the landing pad it slowed and began to descend. The breeze made me raise my arms to shield my eyes. The machine lowered and settled into place. The pilot climbed out, not waiting for the blades to stop. They wore a flight suit that covered them from ankle to neck. They tossed a cap and gloves into the cockpit and jumped to the ground. The pilot gave their head a good shake tossing their hair here and there.

The pilot walked briskly toward me. They were thin. Even in the flight suit they looked thin. Their hair was cut short, in waves and curls, and it was tussled. Their smile beamed. As they came closer I could see that their face was lined, but not lined by care. They were relaxed and comfortable. That's it. They were comfortable. And I had seen her before, in a book.

"Emily," she said. "We are now beginning another section of your lessons."

"You're Amelia Earhart," I said.

"As I have noted previously, this is your dream. It's like a play. I know the script. You provide the props, the scenery, and the supporting actors. I am at most a supporting actor, though some would say I am merely a prop. So, if I am who you claim I am, it is your work."

"Okay. What is on tonight's agenda? Is there any way to make these lessons less brutal? I need to get some rest so I can save Ralph."

She didn't reply, she just gave me a slight smile. She started waiving her arms about and slowly spinning around. Then she said, "Your dream, you can end any of this at any time."

"What do you mean?" I asked.

"All you need to do is ask it, or think it. This is your dream."

"So I could have ended my previous lessons?"

"Of course."

"Oh, I see," I said.

"Would that have changed anything?"

I thought about the past lessons. "No, I wouldn't have done anything differently."

She smiled again. "This lesson is on fisticuffs, boxing, and the martial arts."

"Okay," I said. "I have some familiarity with this, perhaps too much. This whole mess started when I punched Ralph. I am still going to be in big trouble for it, if I ever get him and me back home."

There was a break as she looked me over, and then she began.

"This lesson will be very limited. Only punching, evading, and blocking are permissible. No kicking, throwing, or other practices. Again, only punching,

268

evading, and blocking. For the start of the lesson, we will need specific equipment. You will be wearing a mouth guard, light gloves, and forearm and knee protection. I will be wearing forearm protection and a mouth guard." As soon as she paused they appeared. I was wearing a pair of small boxing gloves. Our forearms were covered by small light sequins of wood that overlapped each other in layers so they covered our arms completely. They tinkled lightly when they moved.

"Punch me," she said.

"You are going to block my punch, right? I don't want more trouble."

"I will block if needed."

"Okay," I said. "Are you ready?"

"Please punch me."

"You are ready?" I asked again.

"Of course. Please punch me," she said with a look of impatience.

So I did. She barely moved. My fist flew by her left ear. With the lightest of pushes I ended up toppling to the floor.

"I don't remember pushing being on the list of things that can be done."

Her smile broadened. "Yes, add pushing. If someone is off balance and needs some assistance in falling to the ground, pushing is permitted."

I glared at her. And I understood the need for the knee protection.

"Please punch me again," she said.

I threw another punch. She easily moved out of the way.

"You are projecting. That boy you hit must have been asleep for you to have hit him."

"He kept poking me. I wanted him to stop and he didn't get it. I guess he could not imagine that I would actually hit him."

"Please try again. Relax. Empty your mind. There are many ways for you to strike me and I know that you know some of them. Try to let your body decide and not your head."

I threw a few more punches. The last one she grabbed my fist.

"Finally, you are beginning to perceive. I was concerned we would be stuck here. Now you may punch me as you see fit."

"What do you mean, perceive? I asked. "I don't perceive anything."

"That is because you are limiting your perception to things you can think about. There is more. Let us begin again. Our time together is limited so we must stay focused."

As we continued she needed to block or step away more often.

"Good, she said. "Now the second part of the lesson will begin. For this I will be wearing heavy gloves." A large pair of boxing gloves appeared on her hands.

"And now I will throw punches at you. These gloves will prevent any major injury. At the start I will hold back a bit. Prepare yourself."

I got ready. I brought my arms up defensively.

She swung and hit me on my left cheek. I fell to my knees. I was glad she was holding back. I crawled my way back to standing. She offered me her arm but I waived her off.

"You need to pay attention to your opponent. You can't hold your arms in place and hope. You must see and anticipate. Prepare yourself once more. Relax. Even though you may soon be on the ground, you must relax."

I did my best. I blocked a piece of her punch and I didn't go down, but I was pretty shaken. I took a step away and a few deep breaths. *When Aunt Maybel taught me to fight, I can now see that she held back so she wouldn't hurt me. This woman says she is holding back, but she is all in on hitting me.*

The lesson continued. I improved, blocking more of the punches. I blocked a string of punches. She moved to punch but did not. She did this a number of times. It was like a dance, she would prepare a punch and I would adjust.

"Good," she said. "This lesson is at its end."

"Why did you stop throwing punches?"

"I could see by your reaction that you would block most or all of each punch. You have better things to do with your energy than to dance with me. And so our lesson is over," she said. The dream abruptly ended.

I woke up when something made a thunk on the roof. It was so cold, but the blankets pulled tight around me helped. The sun was being lazy and hadn't lit up the sky but I was too hungry to go back to bed. I wrapped a small blanket over my shoulders. My arms felt strangely tired, like lead. Some parts of my face were swollen and tender. I felt awful and I had no idea why. I dragged myself up to search the room.

What I thought was a sink was only a wash basin, so there was no water. There was nothing to eat on the shelves and nothing in the cupboards.

I built another fire in the pot-bellied stove. In a short while the fire was blazing and the chill had been driven out of me, but my hunger had grown. The sun had taken its good old time to show itself, but now it was dawn.

I went outside to see what I could find. The air was chilly and damp and there was dew on the ground. A little stream passed nearby. There was a small wooden platform that projected into the stream. On a post was a tin cup. I was hesitant to take a drink when from the bushes someone yelled, "Go ahead, the water is fine."

I scooped some water up. It was sweet. I cupped my hands and wet my face. The cold water felt good against it.

"Thank you," I said.

"Not my water," she said. "The water's not mine."

I looked around. "Is there anything to eat?"

"There's plenty of new leaves, and clover, and even some flowers behind the house."

I don't usually eat any of those so I walked around behind the house to see what I could find. There was what must have been a garden back there, long over grown. I saw some plants with berries, so I went to taste them. The bushes had big thorns and as I reached out the thorns circled and grasped my arm.

"You need to ask. Politely," said a small fawn that came out from its hiding place.

"May I please have some of your berries?" I asked. "I am very hungry."

The thorns moved away from my arm. I picked one and tasted it. It was familiar. It must have been a toffelberry. I picked a few more. The fawn was looking at me from a few steps away.

"No one has lived in that house forever. I have been told that long ago a crazy woman who always talked about flying machines lived there."

I saw that there was a pile of metal things nearby and walked toward it.

"This stuff is supposed to be part of her flying machine. She came from somewhere far away and crashed. They say that she needed all the medical help the local mechanic and wizard could give her to keep her alive. Half of her body needed to be replaced."

"How can you do that?" I asked.

"With good machinery and good magic, amazing things can be done."

I spotted pieces of a plane in the pile. A large propeller with a piece of a tip sheared off still attached to what must have been part of its engine. A seat. A yoke. Part of a wing. A wheel. Part of the rear section of the fuselage.

I went back into the house. The fawn followed me but stopped at the porch.

"It's okay, there's nothing dangerous in here," I said. As I entered I checked the nav ball once more. It remained blank.

"I've been curious about what's in here but I don't like closed spaces." The fawn followed me into the house and sniffed about.

I found a pitcher and collected some water so I could really wash my face. After I washed I looked around again. There was a small book shelf. The one bound book on the bookshelf was a pilot's flight log. It was the flight log of Amelia Earhart. The last entry was on July 3, 1937. There was another handwritten book titled "Airplanes and Flight." I turned the pile of paper that I had been reading from last night so I could see its front pages. The beginning pages were missing. I searched around the bookshelf area and found some loose pages nearby on the floor. On the cover page in large English script was written "My Memoir." So I now know the answer to the disappearance of Amelia Earhart. For everyone else it will remain a forever mystery.

I wanted to get more to eat so I walked back out to the berries. The fawn followed.

"What is your name?" I asked. "My name is Emily."

"I don't have a name yet. I will get named three moons from now, when I will be 13 moons old."

"It must be confusing to not have a name."

"I know who I am, so it's not confusing to me. That big willow tree is where they say the old woman was buried."

I walked to the tree. As I walked below its branches, a leaf fluttered down into my hand. I turned it over. In faint yellow lines on the underside of the green leaf "look under the blotter" was written in English script. I went back into the house and picked up the blotter. There were some hand written pages.

"What are these marks on this paper?" the fawn asked.

It was writing, writing in English.

"It's another language, English," I said.

"Do you read it?"

"I do," I said as I sat down in front of the little desk. The letter was written in English script in the same hand as the other writings. The dye used for writing wasn't dark, but it was enough for me to read.

"What's it say?" the fawn asked.

It said:

Date: Unknown
To Whomever Finds This:
I, Amelia Earhart, aviatrix, being rescued and saved by the inhabitants of this strange world, want to tell you of my life. In the nearby shelf, you will find a memoir of my final adventures. And you will find a small book, a dictionary that would assist an English reader in understanding the local language.
I, due to my physical condition, cannot return to my world under any circumstances, so in this house I will stay and in this land I will live. My life here has only been possible due to the generosity, friendship, and love that the people of this land have given me. May you find a place full of such inviting thoughtful people.
Whereabouts of my navigator, Fred Noonan, are unknown. I pray he survived and was recovered.
Amelia Earhart

I looked back on the first pages of her memoir and gave them a quick scan. It described her final flight in her airplane, a great storm that engulfed her, and her crash in Oz. Even though she knew she could never leave Oz due to all the magic and mechanisms that were used to save her life, she had tried to make a functioning

275

airplane. No matter what she did she could not get any of the airplanes engines to start and run. She said that she never could get a sparkplug to fire, even though the ignition parts looked to be in fine shape.

"Where do you come from?" the fawn asked.

"Far away. Where the woman who lived here came from."

"So you might be able to go back in her airplane?"

"It doesn't work. And the woman who lived here tried for a long time to get it to work. Apparently things don't work here in Oz the way things work where I come from."

"Too bad. I really wanted to see how it flew. Did its wings flap like a bird? They look sort of stiff for flapping."

"No, the wings don't flap."

"That must be pretty powerful magic to fly with no flapping."

"In a way, I guess so."

I put the memoir back and looked at the other sheets that were under the blotter. It was the start of a dictionary. It had three columns, an English word, an Ozish word, and how the Ozish word sounded using English letters. It had a number of cross outs and insertions. On the last sheet was an alphabet for Ozish. The list of words was really quite small but it would still be helpful to me if I wanted to learn Ozish. Then I could study Glinda's magic book at home. I folded the pages and slipped them into my pocket.

"You're going to take those?" the fawn asked.

"Yes, I am. I guess that I am her nearest living relative, in a very distant way. I think she wanted me to

276

have them, that's why her tree told me to look under the blotter."

"Well, they're not mine and I don't know anyone else who reads or speaks English, so I guess that's fine."

We walked to the door. There was a group of people looking at me.

"We saw the chimney smoke coming from Amelia's cabin and we were curious."

"Yes," I said. "I come from the same land as Amelia came from, though she was born long before me."

"Did her airplane really fly?"

"Yes, her airplane flew. She made long and dangerous trips in her airplane. She flew during the time that airplanes had just started being developed and she was very famous. I read about her in a book. Now there are even bigger, much bigger airplanes that fly very fast. Fast enough to go across a country in a few hours."

"I think the witches on their brooms go much faster than that."

"In the land I come from there are no witches and no flying brooms. If you want to go fast you need to take an airplane."

I answered more questions and the crowd started to leave.

"Does anyone know how to get to Oz, the Emerald City? I need to get to the Emerald City," I shouted.

Some people gave me suggestions, but no one had heard of Oz, or the Emerald City. In a short time most people had left. A man walked up to me. He wore a big smile and shook my hand with gusto.

"Hello, my name is Sam Likely and it is my pleasure to meet you."

"Hi, I'm Emily," I said hoping he wouldn't shake my arm off.

"I believe we can help each other. I am going to the nearby city of Ime and it would be nice to have someone to accompany me. Ime is a large and beautiful city and I am sure you can find help there."

That made sense to me. I looked at him. It's hard to describe him. The best that can be said about him is, "a little bit." He's a little bit taller than me. He's a little bit older than me. He's a little bit heavier than me. A little bit. Nothing about him stands out in any way. If you had to find him in a crowd you would be lost before he could be found. He looks like everyone.

He continued, "Not just any someone. It is very rare for me to have the company of a young lady who is so pretty. Your mother must be very beautiful. And your father very handsome. Do you have any siblings?"

"Yes," I said. "I have a younger brother, Jacob."

"What nice names your parents picked for you, Emily and Jacob. Your parents must be very smart as well."

"It was nice meeting you Emily," the fawn interrupted. "My mom and dad don't want me to leave this area so I can't come with you."

"Thank you for your help," I said to the fawn. Then I turned to Sam. "Sam, please wait for me. I need to do something before I leave." I went back to the cabin. I wanted to make sure the fire was safe and there were no glowing embers. It took a few pitchers of water to make absolutely sure. I laid the blankets on the bed as I had found them and put everything back in its place. I gave the cabin one last look. It looked good. I closed the door and walked to Sam.

"Sam, lead on."

"Is your family here? Perhaps they would like to come with us to Ime? Ime is a great place for a family to visit. The more the better."

"No," I said. "My family is not here. That's why I need to get to the Emerald City."

"That's a shame," he said looking disappointed, and we started our journey to Ime.

Chapter 23 Ime

The main entryway to the city of Ime was really a spectacle. There were jugglers. There were dancers. There were musicians playing all sorts of instruments. Young girls and boys handed out drinks of some cool sweet juice to all. Over the main entry was a large sign, "Ime, where all are welcome."

"Come this way," said Sam Likely, as he grabbed my arm and pulled me in. A young girl danced over to me. She wore a gossamer dress that flowed in the breeze and billowed as she spun around. She put a necklace over my head and danced away.

We walked to a small greenspace that had a lamp post and a bench on it. "Emily, please rest here," Sam said turning on his beaming smile. "I have to meet someone, but it will only take a few shakes."

I sat down. I watched him as he walked through the crowd. I decided to follow him. I saw him talking to a man who wore a dark green uniform. After a few words between them the man in the uniform took out a wallet and counted out a few bills to Sam. Sam turned to leave and I rushed back to the bench. Two young men now shared the bench with me. I waited. Sam soon arrived.

"Emily, great news," Sam said. "I met my contact and everything has been arranged. I need to do one more errand. While I am gone please relax here. One of my friends will come to meet you shortly. They will take you to a short orientation talk that everyone who first enters Ime is treated to. Follow them and you will get help going to Oz."

"Sure," I said. I watched him as he walked away. As he turned a corner he looked back at me. Our eyes met and he darted off.

A few moments later a woman approached the bench. "Hello to all of you. It is our tradition of giving all newcomers to Ime an orientation meeting and a welcome meal. If you would be so kind as to follow me we can get under way."

I looked around for Sam but he was nowhere to be seen. I assumed that this woman was who Sam meant, so I joined the group.

We walked down a wide boulevard. The road was split in two with a wide grass divide, with flowering trees that perfumed the air. Our little group proceeded along until we came to a grand tree that had a staircase spiraling around it. We climbed the stairs and entered a small dining room, with a round table, arranged with fancy place settings and bouquets of flowers.

"Please sit in comfort," our guide said. We all sat down. Over the table was a chandelier with many crystals twinkling in reflected light. Music played in the background. I was thirsty so I poured myself some water. We sat in silence for a short while.

"Hello newcomers," came a voice that reverberated throughout the room. "Greetings and welcome to Ime. I want to give you some important information that will make your stay in Ime more productive and enjoyable."

The voice reviewed a short history of the city, the primary agricultural and industrial products, the main cultural sites and museums. It told of where you could go to see a play, or listen to live music, or to dance. It continued on for some time and then the meal was served. It was a nice meal that made up for my sparse breakfast. After the final course the voice began again.

"I hope that you all have enjoyed this orientation and we hope that your stay in Ime will be long and memorable. As you leave please pay the entry fee of 1500 drumpys. Again, thank you and enjoy your stay."

I was flabbergasted. I didn't have any drumpys, whatever they were.

Everyone in our group got up, except me, and moved to the exit. They took out wallets and purses and counted out bills of what I can only guess were drumpys. I alone remained.

A man came to me. "Miss, is there a problem?"

"Yes," I said. "There is a problem. I have no drumpys and I had no idea that there was an entry fee."

"Oh, that is indeed a problem, but only a minor one. I am afraid that this sometimes happens. But do not feel low. If you have no drumpys, you may work to earn your entry fee. The economy of Ime is fast and dynamic. More workers are always needed. I am sure that a strong young woman such as yourself will earn her entrance fee in, say, three moons at most, perhaps even fewer."

"I came here with Sam Likely. I want to speak to him."

"Of course, once your entry fee is paid you can do as you wish and speak to whomever you wish. I assure you that Mr. Likely has properly received the customary seven percent facilitator's fee as was his due."

"Facilitators fee?"

"Why of course. Ime welcomes all and the more the better. To encourage people to visit we pay a facilitators fee."

I was angry, really angry. Sam had tricked me. But I decided to stay calm and see what unfurled.

"Okay," I said. "Where do I go to get work?"

"Follow me," he said. "Many people prefer to work for their entry fees, especially those from areas less wealthy than Ime. It is not unusual at all. There is always a nice group of people getting started in Ime and the housing facility is quite adequate."

As we walked to the living area I asked, "Do you know the way to the Emerald City? To Oz?"

"No, I have never heard of either. But I am not well travelled. There will be someone who can help you once your entrance fee is paid."

He brought me to the newcomers' facility and showed me around. As he said, it was adequate. It still was my prison.

After he left I went to the common space and began asking everyone if they knew the way to Oz. It was my plan to get out of Ime. They were all in small groups, talking about how they were doing paying their entry fees and what kind of work was available. They were in good spirits and for the most part they looked forward to staying in Ime. Some bragged about how nice Ime was.

I noticed an older gentleman by himself sitting in a chair. He had a cane nearby. I walked over to him.

"Do you know the way to Oz?" I asked.

"This is second hand, but a few moons ago one of the entrance fee workers told me of such a place. He said it was south-southwest of here, quite a long distance."

"Have you been here a long time?" I asked.

"Yes," he said. "I have been here for 27 moons and will be here for the foreseeable future. There is little need for an old man who can't see and walks with a cane. And they don't value people of science in this land."

"I am sorry," I said.

"They do take good care of me though."

"Is there magic in your world?" I asked.

"Such tripe," he cursed. "Otherwise sensible people who believe in magic. No, my world has no magic, nor does any other."

"I was testing you," I said. "I must make sure that I do not insult the local superstitions. There is no magic in my world either. My world is a world of science and engineering."

"It is a relief to meet a levelheaded person."

And now I hoped that I could improvise a spiel of technobabble that would be sufficient for this man. I certainly have heard enough while listening to my dad's favorite science fiction shows.

"Would you like to leave this place with me?" I asked.

"Of course," he said. "There is more to life than being treated well."

"My air car will soon arrive," I said. "We will have only a few heartbeats to get on and leave before a big commotion occurs."

"A space car? How is it powered?"

284

"Fusion."

"Very impressive. And how does it get lift?"

"We use the di-gravimetric effects of the, eh, poupon particles for lift."

"Hmm," he said. "I am not familiar with this technology."

I cut him off. "In my travels I have found that different civilization progress at different rates and each type of technology has its own rate. I have seen places with advanced communications, and simple transportation, as well as advanced transportation with simple communications. We do not have much time since my car will arrive shortly. I need to add that to minimize attention, my space car is cloaked."

"Cloaked?" he muttered.

"Yes, it will appear, at least to those who can see, as a broom, as a flying broom. Other space cars are cloaked differently, for example, I know of someone whose space car is cloaked as a police call box. But I prefer a flying broom. It is well respected by places where the belief in magic and witches is normal."

"I see," he said scratching his head.

I summoned my broom. *This will be my first test in flying with a passenger.*

The broom arrived. I whispered, "We must now depart. Please get on." I helped him on.

We were noticed. I jumped on. A group of people surrounded us, some shouting. I did a straight vertical lift. His cane clattered to the floor.

"Hold on tight," I yelled as some official looking people gathered below us. Off we went.

"Which way is south-southwest?" I asked him.

"Based on the time of day, and the position of the sun, I would say it is in that direction," he said as he pointed.

I spun us around. Nothing on the nav ball. I hoped we would get close enough to Oz to get a signal before too long.

I noticed we had company following us, and gaining fast. "Land now, or be prepared to be taken down," they commanded.

"Hold on tight," I yelled again. "Prepare for a bumpy flight."

I thought back to zooming around in that room in Oz with all the young witches and put the pedal to the metal, if that is what you say when flying a broom. We shot off.

I heard something fly past us on the left. "That sounded pretty close," my passenger said. "Does your space car have any protection?"

"Protection," I thought. "That's it, we need a force field." I imagined us inside an ellipsoid made of transparent aluminum.

Now things were hitting our shield. I got that set up just in time. *Eat your heart out Captain Kirk.*

"That's much better. How does that work?"

"Sorry for the delay," I said. "I had some trouble raising shields. I will have to discuss it with you later, once we are safely in Oz."

"Really impressive technology," he said. "I look forward to that discussion."

In no time we left the border of Ime. I didn't look back and they fell behind and broke off the chase.

Now that we were free of followers I went to a more moderate speed and altitude. Wrong idea. As soon as I let my mind drift anything that surprised me created chaos. A cloud floating by caught my attention, we did a corkscrew.

"Are you trying to kill us," my passenger shouted.

"Sorry, I, uh, the inertial dampers seem to be offline," I said.

"I hope you can get them online," he said. "The best technology is useless if it isn't reliable."

That pressure made it worse. I couldn't hold us at an even speed and direction. The harder I tried the worse my flying got. I knew I had to find someplace to land. The nav ball was still blank. I began to look for a good place to come down. That actually helped my flying a bit. I couldn't leave my passenger alone, abandoned without help, so we continued. I was sure he was as anxious as I was to land.

I scanned the ground, hoping to find something I could recognize, anything that looked familiar that might give me a clue where I was. We flew on and on and I constantly wished that I would get a hint of where we were. I had no idea of how fast or how far we had come. Then I spotted something familiar. It looked like Dr. Ulam's office. I wondered why my nav ball was still blank. We certainly were in its operating range.

I circled around and brought us down slowly. I addressed my passenger. "This is the office of one of this land's most renowned doctors. He is from a very advanced culture, a culture that excels in the medical arts. He will talk as if he believes in magic, but it is just a ruse. It allows him to help these superstitious people without creating conflict. He will swear everything he does is magic. If you push him, he will continue to swear it is magic. Remember, he has a cover that he needs to protect so that everyone accepts him. Please don't be rude to him and make everything awkward. Remember, it's all magic, no science."

"Okay, I understand," he said. "This sounds so difficult. How do you keep everything straight? How do you keep it from driving you mad?"

"It's something that becomes easier with practice. It's the cost of being able to visit this land. They may believe in magic, but you will find that many other things here are quite exceptional."

We set down and got off. I took him by the hand and led him into the doctor's office.

"Dr. Ulam, I hope that you can help this man. He has highly impaired vision and perhaps you can help him in some way."

"Of course Emily," Dr. Ulam said. "How is your inner ear problem? Do you need any gastro-intestinal aid? My specialist are in the office today," as he pointed to a petri dish that appeared to have some frothy blue-green slime in it.

"No thank you, doctor. I am fine. Please look after my friend. Uhm, sir, what is your name?" I asked the man I helped escape from Ime.

"My name is Dr. Umberto Splivia, doctor of astrophysics."

"Astrophysics?" Dr. Ulam asked. "I am unfamiliar with that course of study."

"Certainly you jest Dr. Ulam. As a man of science — "

He stopped when I grabbed his hand and squeezed.

"Yes that is fine, Dr. Ulam. Astrophysics is a course of study unique to my city. Which university did you attend?"

"I earned my doctorate from the Teaching Hospital of Zillyton."

"Is there really a place called Zillyton?" Umberto asked. I gave his hand another squeeze.

"Dr. Ulam, please give me some time to discuss this with Emily, if you please," Dr. Splivia said as he motioned me to exit.

We walked out of the office and around the building to a secluded spot.

"Am I to take this seriously? This ridiculous talk?"

"You must if you wish to be helped. Dr. Ulam is the best. His ways may be strange to you, but he is the best. How long has it been since you lost your vision?"

"It went slowly. For the last fourteen years I have been totally without vision." Umberto said looking down sadly.

"I suggest you play along with Dr. Ulam. He can work wonders."

"All the doctors in my land, even the most highly regarded specialist said there is nothing that can be done."

"That may be true, but technology advances at its own pace in different lands. I recommend that you work with Dr. Ulam."

"Fine," Umberto said. "You and your spacecar saved me from a life of endless tedium in Ime."

I helped Dr. Splivia return to the office. Umberto controlled himself.

"First we must run our standard diagnostic test, the diagnostic darts," Dr. Ulam said with Umberto grimacing. "Umberto, let me help you move to the scanning zone."

When Umberto was properly located in front of the body outline, Dr. Ulam moved to the throwing line and blindfolded himself. "Emily, if you would assist me in spinning me around?"

After being properly disoriented, he threw the darts, unblindfolded himself and moved to the body outline.

"Hmm," he said. "Very unusual, very interesting. And very specific. Dr. Splivia, I am going to repeat the diagnostic test to confirm your condition."

"Of course," Dr. Splivia said. "It is better to test than to perform unneeded delicate surgery."

"No, no surgery is performed in my office," Dr. Ulam said. It was the first time I ever heard Dr. Ulam say anything that sounded remotely like he was angry. "Such barbarism. How can even the best guided knife help on something as delicate as vision?"

"I apologize. I did not mean to offend. In my land surgery is the only option available."

"Fine," Dr. Ulam said. "I assure you that there is much that can be done before I decide to slice you open like a cantaloupe."

"Thank you, Dr. Ulam. I apologize again and I now have hope that at least some of my vision may be restored."

The doctors made up and the darts where thrown again. Dr. Ulam said, "The diagnostic testing is confirmed. There is a course of treatment with a good chance that some or all of your vision will be restored, but the recovery period is long. You will need to stay at the care facility nearby so that I can monitor your progress."

"Thank you," Umberto said. He had a smile on his face, the first smile I had seen there. "Please tell me about your plan of action. Please tell me what the diagnostic tests revealed."

Dr. Ulam spoke. "Avoiding unnecessary technical details, our brains are like beet roots, large beet roots. And our eyes are like Brussels sprouts. Each of our eyes is connected to our brains by a piece of spaghetti, the optical pasta. When some people are born, their optical pasta is not fully cooked, making it brittle and susceptible to damage. Your Brussels sprouts and your beet root are fine, it is your optical pasta. If you think back to when you lost your vision perhaps you will remember an accident, physical trauma to your head that you had."

Dr. Splivia paused to think. "Yes, I do. It was weeks before I started losing my vision. I had a skiing accident. I fell, quite badly. I quickly recovered and thought nothing of it. Then my vision slowly began to fade."

I had done what I hoped I could do, so it was time to leave. "Dr. Ulam, Dr. Splivia, I must leave. I wish you both the best, and perhaps we will meet again soon."

After a short goodbye I returned to my broom. The Emerald City beckoned, but my nav ball was still blank even though I was sure I was within its normal working area. I decided to do some visually guided flying. It had only taken the Tin Man and me a few moments to get from the Emerald City to Dr. Ulam so I knew I couldn't be far away from the palace. I was in luck. I soon found a spur of the yellow brick road, and a terminal for the JetBroom system. I landed and gave the bell a shake.

Almost immediately I spotted a witch on a broom descending toward me. I must have been near one of the departure points for the JetBroom system.

"Emily," Nadia said. I had met Nadia in my first impromptu flying lesson. "Where would you like to go? How have you been?"

"Nadia, it's nice to see you again. I need some help, more than a ride. My nav ball is blank and I don't know why or what to do."

Nadia looked it over. "Emily, you really bricked this thing. I heard this was possible but I never actually have seen it. You must have taken this thing on quite an adventure."

"I guess so," I said. "Is there anything that can be done to get it back right?"

"Yes, it should be easy enough to do. We must submerge the ball in naturally flowing water, like a stream. That is what's supposed to be the remedy."

We hopped on our brooms and flew to a nearby creek. I took my nav ball and submerged it in the water. As it hit the water, Nadia's nav ball let out a shriek, and then went blank.

"I'm not sure what we did but we seem to have taken down the entire system. It usually means there some important update going on. Don't worry, it will restart soon."

And indeed in a few measures both the nav balls did some kind of a turn on dance.

"Thanks Nadia," I said. "Now that I can navigate I am good to go."

"Any time Emily. Happy flying!" she said as she flew off. I watched as she did an overhead circle and then zoomed off like a bolt of lightning.

And now what was I to do?

Chapter 24 Right

I looked at my newly updated nav ball. It started back up in my broom flying lesson. I turned it off. *It's too late for me to learn to fly a broom, I either can or I cannot.*

I brought the area map up and decided to give it a good looking over. These nav balls haven't proven to be that reliable so I wanted to be able to navigate by memory. There were many familiar things: the palace, Dr. Ulam's, even Robotville and New York City. And many things I had never visited: Gings' home, the Riddle Writers Academy, the University for the Advancement of Random Speculation, the taffy pullers main factory, the S'mores S'myndicate, and on and on. I looked for where Sebastian might be, but I found nothing. I scrolled across the land, sector by sector. It became obvious there was much more to Oz than I could cover even at a high level in one short session. I gave up on a rigorous study and picked a few spots arbitrarily. As I was scanning one sector I noticed a dot that blinked into view. For an instant it was visible, and then it was gone. It appeared and disappeared at random. I watched and waited. There it was again, and then it was gone, again. And something told me that dot would be my next destination.

I rose up and stayed in place, waiting for it to appear. I waited patiently. And there it was, I swung around in that direction as it disappeared once more. I waited. When it appeared again I corrected my heading and scanned forward. It was gone once again. I spotted a landmark along the way, a large bush. I slowly flew to the bush. The dot appeared again. I corrected my heading again and moved on. I did this for some time, correcting, finding a landmark, and moving on. As I proceeded I noticed that the dot spent more time visible, which helped me pick up the pace. The picture on my nav ball resized and I could see more detail. There was a dot for Penelope Primrose Platypus, and a larger dot for Glinda's Castle, and a scattering of points nearby of houses. I flew closer. All this stuff was supposed to be missing. And then the nav ball went blank. The nav ball was bricked. Oops! I did it again.

But I could see where I was. I spotted Penelope's hut and I decided to visit her. I flew in low over the road where the carving of the Flyer had turned into the Golden Cap. I circled the hut and then landed by her front entry. I hesitated before I rested my broom against her hut. It all looked the same, but something was off. Just not right. I had a sense of lurking danger. I walked into her hut anyway.

"Penelope," I yelled. "Are you home?"

"Yes, of course I am home," said Penelope. "But you should not be here. You are too early. You are not ready to be here."

"What do you mean?"

"I am not at liberty to say, but I fear for you."

"Is it Sebastian?" I asked.

"No, Sebastian would not dare to enter the area around Glinda's castle. But he is not the only thing that is a danger to you. You need more time, more training. You should go. Go now while you can. Come back when you are called."

"Okay," I said. "But I was led here. I followed my nav ball."

"Please go," Penelope finished. Something was different. Last time she wouldn't stop talking.

I left the hut. Outside the hut was a large mob of young women, I guessed around twenty of them. When they saw me they surrounded me. They ranged in ages from young kids to early twenties.

"She is too weak," one shouted at me. "How can she be the one? She can't do what we need."

Another shouted, "She doesn't even know why she is here. She is asleep. Numb."

I tried to walk through them but they blocked my way. They shoved me back toward the hut.

"And she is a coward. Worst of all a coward. Run away. Hide, go ahead hide yourself."

I stopped and looked them over. There was a group of women who were older than me. They seemed to be the leaders. They were encouraging the others to block my way. They shouted insults at me, why I had no idea.

"Please, let me pass," I said. "I don't want any trouble."

"She doesn't want trouble. Well she is trouble. She brings trouble with her every step she takes," one yelled. Someone pushed me from behind. I nearly fell down. I spun around and everyone stepped back.

"I don't want trouble," I said. "But I do at times cause it. Let me be."

There was a murmur that went through the mob. One young woman started forward. She was not the oldest, and not the tallest, but she was tough-looking and she clearly was their leader. They parted and let her into the center with me.

"The prize for landing will be trouble," she said as she moved toward me and crouched for fighting. The other young women and girls tightened the circle around us so there would be no retreat. They began to taunt and jeer. They were expecting, were demanding a fight.

The crowd hushed as I felt something on my hip. It was Glinda's sword. I grasped it. It felt like it was part of me. I watched the blade glimmer as I moved it left and right. I looked at the young woman before me. Through her bravado I could see she was scared. *I don't understand what is going on but I will not carry a sword into battle against someone who is unarmed.* I said quietly to myself, "No one will die today." I put the sword back into its sheath and looked up at the mob.

I yelled out, "No one will die today." I took the sword belt off. I walked to my broom, the crowd parted as I approached, and I placed the belt near my broom. Then I turned and walked into the middle of the circle once more.

We both shifted, striving to obtain a positional advantage, always watching our opponent. I suddenly understood some things my Aunt Maybel had told me during my lessons. "Emily," she had once said, "you want to protect yourself, and hurt others as little as possible. But when you are truly being threatened, not just playing around, then the rules are different. In those times you must be violent enough to end the fight. And that means being willing to hurt people enough so that the fight can't continue. Do you understand what I mean?" she had asked. I had said yes, but I didn't really grasp what she meant, *until now.*

This young woman I was fighting was older than me and more muscular than me. I knew that the longer the fight continued, the worse it would be. So I would have to end the fight quickly. I had no other option than to hurt her, badly.

We exchanged a few punches and kicks. Nothing of any consequence, nothing that landed well, and nothing that created opportunities. We were well matched. And so I would have to do better.

She threw a punch and instead of blocking it, I grabbed her arm and threw her over my hip. I slammed her into the ground with all my might. She landed hard on her shoulder and in the instant her guard was down I hit her throat with the bony part of my wrist. Then I kneed her in the ribs. The sound could not be missed. The crowd paused its taunts.

I took a few steps back. "You are hurt," I said. "You need medical aid. I don't understand what you want, but it is no shame to end this here and now."

She quickly got back to her feet. I could see that she winced every time her weight was on her left foot. She prepared to continue. "You are a coward," she yelled. "I will show you what being hurt is like."

I prepared once more. We exchanged. She was excited, and that gave her the advantage. One of her punches caused me a misstep. She stepped in and I blocked and recovered. But I saw. I stepped in. This put me a bit off balance. She grasped the opportunity and knocked me down. This strange position gave me a path to deliver another blow to her ribs. I kicked up from the ground. She yelled in pain. She staggered and fell to the ground.

I jumped to my feet. "We must stop this now. You need help," I said. "No one will die here."

She dragged herself to her knees and then to standing. She was disoriented so that she had to look around to find me. She turned to me once again. "Coward," she yelled as she lunged at me.

I grabbed her arm, swept her legs out from under her and carefully placed her on the ground. She moaned in pain. Spots of blood saturated the lower part of her shirt. I looked at her. She did not look well.

"Where is your doctor?" I demanded

"We don't have a doctor."

This young woman was not going to make it without immediate medical help. Had I lied? Was someone going to die here?

"You and you, make a stretcher," I yelled as I pointed to two of the oldest looking. "Get her on the stretcher. You and you run ahead and open the doors of Glinda's Castle. Then follow me. The rest of you stay here."

They improvised a stretcher from clothes and fighting poles. We ran toward Glinda's castle. I sprinted ahead and caught up to the pair who were to open the door. I yelled at them, "Run faster. Is your friend's life not important enough for you to run? There is no time to waste. Open the doors and go ahead of us. " They must have finally understood the seriousness of the situation, because they sprinted forward at speed. They got to the castle and propped the doors open.

I ran along with the women carrying the stretcher, through the open doors and down the hallway.

"To the end of the hallway and down two flights," I yelled. We thundered down the hall and reached the stairs. The woman carrying the front of the stretcher

299

stumbled at the first step. The stretcher began to fall and the woman at the back end lost her balance and began to go down as well. I held the stretcher in the air and floated it down to those who had opened the castle doors. I could not stop the women from falling, but I was able to keep them from hitting the stones below. I took the first flight of stairs two at a time, bounded the platform, and took the second flight in a broad jump. Then I ran ahead of the stretcher and searched my hand along the wall. It was here somewhere. I reached through a rock and released a latch. A section of the rock wall pivoted out of the way.

"This way," I called.

We entered a long rock tunnel. Only a faint blue light guided the way. The tunnel sloped slowly downward. We ran the tunnel. At the end of the tunnel I recognized it. A surface opening of the Cold Spring.

"Unclothe her," I yelled. She reached up to me and grabbed my collar. "You must promise not to speak of this with anyone." She fell back into silence.

"We can't get her clothes off her without hurting her," they shouted back. I thought, "If we had scissors we could cut the clothes off her. But if we had scissors we would have a doctor".

"Put her on the platform in the spring," I yelled. I leaped into the Cold Spring with the others. We lowered her onto the platform. I would somehow take care of her clothes. As the water closed in over her head, a gasp went out among us.

I climbed out of the water. I knew I could do this, yet I had no idea how. I thought through my memories, and I had a vision of my town's public library. I ran down a row looking for what I needed. I came to the end and there was a chasm. I leaped the chasm. The book titles were now in Ozish. I ran down the shelves with my finger out, brushing the books as I went. I touch the memory I needed.

I closed my eyes and motioned. The young women gasped once more. Her clothes were gone.

I watched as she lay below the water surface. A blue glow spread across her body. She writhed in a painful seizure and the blue glow vanished. A faint blue film began again, spreading, growing over her. She twisted in agony. The blue was gone. And now blue, barely discernible, spread over her body. It spread and thickened. It covered her. She took a deep breath with a slow tremor and moved to silence. I could see that her body had relaxed. We had not been too late. We had not failed her. No one would die today.

But in that alien library of memories, another, less wanted memory persisted. The Cold Spring always exacts a price. It was worth the risk to save her. No matter the cost, I would have done what was needed to save her. I wished I could bear her burden, but I knew that the Cold Spring does not care for such sentiments.

I did not remember being told of the price I would pay for my time in the Cold Spring. I wondered what that price might be.

"She must remain submerged until she awakes of her own doing," I said. "Until that time, and I hope it is soon, you four are charged with watching over her. No others may enter the castle. You are sworn to secrecy. You must not talk of this place with any other. Not your friends, not your family, not your loves. No one. Do you understand?"

They looked at each other in silence. Then they looked at me and nodded.

"Oh yes," I added. "She will be hungry when she awakes."

I walked out through the tunnel, away from the young woman I had just fought. Away from a group of young women who had incited the fight. I climbed the stairs and walked again through the hall, past the rows of fading tapestries, and to the main entrance. I realized I was dripping wet. I had no time for being wet. I thought, and the water was gone. I closed the main doors. The remainder of the mob was waiting outside the castle. They parted as I walked through them. I walked to Penelope's hut and buckled on Glinda's sword. I took a few steps away from the hut and called my broom. All the girls and young women, some so young they were hardly past toddling, some old enough to have children of their own, and all of them were looking at me. And though they were silent their faces asked a question, begged a question.

I turned to them. "Sisters, there is much to do. So you must prepare. Prepare yourselves. A time will come and your friend will return in health. Until that time, wait and prepare. A sign will appear, and you will be called upon to serve, as you, your mothers, and your grandmothers have done in the past."

I got on my broom. I wanted to be alone. The weight of these events hung heavily on me. I shot off, heading for the nearest large cloud and obscurity.

I found the cloud and sat in silence. I realized my hands hurt, my arms hurt, my back hurt. Even my knees hurt. And I was the victor in that fight. And for what reason? For what cause? And at what cost?

"Would you like to join us?" I heard someone say. I looked around and I saw that I was practically at the edge of a large tea table all set for high tea. There were ducks all seated around the table sipping tea from dainty teacups, and nibbling on crumbly pastries. "We rarely get guests, invited or otherwise," one of the ducks said. "You look like your mind is troubled. Please take a moment of peace and join us."

And so I did. I took some tea, and I ate a few pastries as well. I ate more than a few so I was more a pig than a duck. I mostly listened as they chatted about the weather, and how things were growing in various gardens, and how there hatchlings were. At one point I noticed that the cloud we were in was dropping rain, and throwing bolts of lightning to the ground. I watched. The rain came down in sheets. And there were pauses between the sheets. The lightning came forth from the periphery of the cloud, and shot toward the ground. I had never seen a storm in this way, from this perspective. I watched until the lightning and the rain subsided.

It was a true break and I guess I needed it. The dark clouds from the fight parted over me and some sunshine broke through. I could dive into the storm clouds if I wanted, but I chose to feel the sunshine. I must have been lost in thought for some time because when I looked to the table I noticed that they were flying off.

"I'm sorry I didn't help you clean up," I said.

"That's fine darling. We could tell that you needed some me time and we were glad we could help you."

"Thanks," I said. *How is it that they were so thoughtful? Why do people scorn people who are thoughtful?*

I watched as the last of the ducks flew off. I thought of the young woman in the Cold Spring. She had been willing to die for what she believed. Was I that willing to die for what I believe? *I don't know and I don't think you can know until you are forced to choose.*

I got back on my broom. I circled slowly over Penelope's hut, and over Glinda's Castle. I flew over the houses and farms nearby. All so calm, all so peaceful. Each morning each of the inhabitants wake up and do their best. And at the end of the day they hug their loved ones, go to sleep, and hope they have the chance to do it once more.

But now something had changed. Now things seemed different, and I don't know why. I don't need the nav ball. I now know exactly where Sebastian is. And I know he has Ralph.

Chapter 25 Captured

I trudged down the rock strewn road that left the town, clutching the pouch of blue sand and hoping. Hoping it might work. I began to tire so I found a boulder along the path and took a seat. Blue sand. My life depends on the anti-magic effect of some blue sand. I put some into my hand and looked at it.

Then there was smoke in the air. There was a large boulder on the right of the trail ahead, shaped like an old fashioned clothes iron. A single strand of smoke trickled up from an empty crag in the boulder. The trickle of smoke grew and a pinpoint in the crag through off a blinding red light. I shaded my eyes. The pinpoint grew and burst into flame. The flame increased, roaring and cracking. Sparks flew in from all directions, joining the flame, making it surge. The flames grew higher and wider and the sound was so loud I covered my ears. A bolt of lightning struck the fire and bits of the boulder flew off in all directions. Where the fire had been stood the witch that I had seen in Creepman's room of horrors. She was one of the people he had stuffed. *And that was quite an entrance. How long did Creepman work on it? A little poof would have been sufficient.*

"You have given me a great deal of trouble," she said. "Perhaps if you were gutted and stuffed you would be more useful. You would certainly be more compliant. It's something for me to ponder. Like old Mombi here. Don't you just love this look," she said as she spun around like a fashion model showing off her dress. "She taught me her magic of transformation and then became one of my favorite styles. Taught me doesn't do justice to my part in the teaching. Between you and me, it took a lot of torture to make her generous enough to share her secrets with me, But in the end, share them she did. Now she is quite useful. Perhaps you will be as well. That's for a later time. If I had only planned ahead and collected all the necessary ingredients. But they are so hard to find. No matter. There is time for you. Now you must return home."

"But my, you are a slob," she continued. "I have seen swine that are more fastidious than you. Do you spend all your free time rolling in the mud? A little time away from me and look at you. Just look at you."

She snapped her fingers. The mud was gone from my clothes and my feet were no longer wet. *At least that is an improvement.* "Here goes," I thought. I walked toward her.

"Well, maybe you are trainable after all," she said as I approached her.

I tossed the blue sand at her and she was instantly gone. Apparently the blue sand was effective. *But it's not like Sebastian is dead. He disappeared too quickly for that. It's only a matter of time before he tries to collect me again.*

Now what? I sat down and thought. *Maybe this is all a nightmare. Or maybe I am laying on the floor in the nurses office convulsing. Maybe the best thing I can do is check myself in at the nearest facility that helps delusional people. But if this is a delusion, I may as well try to make it the best delusion ever.*

I began walking again, away from the town. Only one person in the entire town was willing to help me.

For that one person's sake I hoped Sebastian would not punish them.

After a while my feet were beginning to ache. I bent down to adjust my sneakers and smelled something good. I looked around and couldn't see where it came from. I followed the smell and my stomach rumbled. It was further down the road. Some kind of restaurant. I'd never heard of one before – Mother Hubbard's Cupboard. It looked like most fast food restaurant chains so I walked in.

"What can I do for you, sir?" asked the person at the counter who was dressed in an old fashioned frilly blue dress and on their head they wore a blue bonnet fringed in white lace. Over the dress was a white apron.

"I don't have any money," I said.

"Your name sir?"

"Ralph."

"And where are you from, sir?"

"Not from anywhere around here. Maybe an alternate dimension. I don't know."

"Please, in your own words, sir."

"North Carolina."

"One second, sir." The worker stepped over to a transparent bowling ball that was balanced on a needle point. They spun the ball left and right and waved their hands over the surface.

"Ralph of North Carolina, you say?"

"Yes," I said.

"Sir, you have a standing order per a decree by the Scarecrow, Regent of Oz. You may enjoy anything you would like as his guest."

I read the menu and ordered a large meal. *I don't know what to do, but I may as well not be hungry while I am waiting for Sebastian's next attempt to capture me.* I picked a spot off to one side so I could eat in seclusion. There was a steady stream of people entering and eating. I spent my time thinking in quiet. I slowly ate my meal, enjoying every bite. I looked up at the windows and I noticed that the sky had darkened. I walked back up to the counter.

"Is there a place to sleep nearby?"

"Yes, sir. A short way this way on the left."

I departed the restaurant and started walking. As described, on the left side of the road was "Three Bears Cottages and Campsites." I entered and walked to the counter.

"I'm Ralph of North Carolina," I said.

"Yes sir, I have been notified, and how may I help you sir?" asked the counter person. By person I mean an enormous grizzly bear that was easily half again my height.

"A room please."

"Cottage 273 is available." They circled a square on a map. "Follow this path," they said as they drew a line on the map. "Do you need any help with your baggage sir?"

"No, I'm traveling light today," I said. "Who is the Scarecrow?"

"The Scarecrow is the regent of the land of Oz."

"I'm not familiar with the term 'regent.'"

"A regent is someone tasked with the leadership of a country while a king or queen is not available."

Interesting. "And where would I find this Scarecrow?"

"The Scarecrow's main office, his throne, and his workshops are all located in the Emerald City."

Interesting. "And do you know where Emily of North Carolina might be?"

"No sir, I do not. I do remember reading the report a few weeks back about her arrival to the Emerald City. It was front page news. By the way, a newspaper will be delivered to your cabin promptly at sunrise."

"And how would I get to the Emerald City?" I asked.

"There is a JetBroom terminal nearby. We are quite far from the Emerald City, so the hours of operation are limited. Our terminal is not active presently but tomorrow morning you can call for a broom."

"Thank you," I said and I walked to the cottage. It was easy to find - the correct paths glowed green. *Call for a broom? I guess I'll just wait and be surprised.*

I opened the door. There were three beds, and there were three chairs, and there were three bowls of oatmeal, and in the bathroom there were even three rolls of toilet paper. Of course, I tried everything out until I found what I preferred. I was tired so I got ready for bed. I sat down and looked at the pouch. Anti-magical blue sand. It's very handy to have. Very handy indeed.

There's a saying, "Don't put all your eggs in one basket." I bet that applies to blue sand as well. I lay down and quickly fell asleep.

I was awaken by someone banging on the door. I didn't know what time it was, but the sun hadn't risen.

I walked to the door yawning and trying to rub my eyes awake. "What is it?" I asked as I unlocked the door.

They shoved the door open and threw a bag over my head. Then they tied my hands behind my back. I only caught a glimpse of them but they looked like monkeys. They wore vests and caps.

"Where's the pouch?" they demanded.

"It's on the table by the bed," I said. I heard some commotion as they pushed past me into the room.

"Now we're doing chores for Sebastian. He's pure evil," said one.

"There must be something's in it for us. Veeron always does what is best," said another.

"Veeron wants the sand in this pouch. Sebastian wants the contents scattered. I don't want to be around when Sebastian finds out we didn't scatter the sand like he demanded," added another.

"Give that to me," one said. I heard some pushing, followed by some rustling.

"Just like him. Take the easy job and take all the credit," said another.

"Oh, be quiet. Let's just get this over with," said another. "All we have to do is fly him back to Sebastian. That should be easy."

I felt them pick me up and carry me into the air.

"Right, all we have to do is return him to Sebastian," one said. "Can't we just drop him into Wolf Forest? That should be close enough."

"Be quiet," said another.

"Yeah, keep your bright ideas to yourself. Let's not get Sebastian angry. Hopefully, if and when he finds out we deceived him, we will be far away and Veeron will have to deal with it."

"Wolf Forest. I hate the wolves. They make my skin crawl. Even one is dangerous and in a pack, I dread to think of what they would do with one of us."

"Please be quiet."

The monkeys stopped talking. I couldn't tell what was happening but I knew soon I would be back with Sebastian. It was confirmed when I caught a faint smell of a recent fire.

There was some commotion and they seemed to slow. Then there was some pushing and some of the monkeys let go of me. It sounded like they flew off. We continued a short while and then the remaining monkeys dropped me and fled.

My face hit the ground. My pour nose smashed again. I felt the blood trickle out and across my face. I rolled on my side so I could breathe a little better. I must have been pretty close to the ground when they dropped me because beside my nose, everything else felt fine. I still had a bag over my face and my hands were tied behind my back, but I was alive.

"What are you doing down there, Ralph?" Nutmeg asked.

"I'm catching up on my sleep. What does it look like I'm doing?"

"You don't need to be nasty. I'm not familiar with the strange sleep habits of your kind. Do you always put a bag over your head when you sleep? Is it to block the light?"

"No, I don't put a bag over my head when I sleep," I said. "Could you help me by cutting the cord that binds my hands?"

"If I chewed through them, would that be acceptable?"

311

"Yes, thank you."

"You're welcome Ralph. There you go, all free."

In a moment I was free and on my feet. I tried to straighten my poor nose and wipe the blood away.

I looked around. I was at the edge of Wolf Forest, still a distance from Sebastian's campus of hovels. I turned and ran.

Two steps in front of me was Mombi. I couldn't move. I was stopped like a statue. "Not so fast," she said. "Back you go, dear Ralphy. I'm not surprised that the flying chimps didn't bring you back to me as we agreed. Don't worry Ralph, I will see they are properly punished. Perhaps some new looks for me? Did they take that nasty blue sand from you?"

"They took my pouch of blue sand," I said.

"They weren't a total waste then. No more tricks like that Ralphy."

She snapped her fingers and a chain bound my legs together and to a large stone.

"You know the way. Don't delay. I will be waiting for you."

I tried to turn but my legs weren't mine to control. I began to walk, dragging the stone behind me. I fell over and crawled forward. I felt the pain of the chains digging into my ankles and sharp stones scraping my hands but I could not fight it. I gave up fighting.

It went on and on. I stopped paying attention. I had no control so I turned my mind off. In time the smell from the after effects of the fire became more pungent. The area I had been trapped in became recognizable. The strange complex of shacks that Creepman lived in came into view. Where I had set fire was now blackened and looked like coals. I dragged myself to the door which opened as I approached. I crawled inside and the door slammed behind me. I crawled down the winding dark hallway, the stone scraping along.

I entered the main room. Sebastian spoke. "I don't understand why you treat me so poorly, Ralph. Haven't I shown you nothing but kindness? Yet you betray me by escaping. That is simply not fair to me. I am hurt. In return you will need to be punished. Yes, you need to be punished. Something painful. Something you truly dread. And fear. But in what way exactly, that is the question. You and your friend Emily are such strange creatures, from such a strange land. What really scares you? Who would be able to tell me that? You, my dear son can tell me. Oh, Glinda objected when I told her about this bit of magic. Don't look through people's memories. It's bad. It's evil. She was such a bore at times. So pretty, but such a bore. I won't do that, she would say. That is evil. She wouldn't work any magic that wasn't squeaky clean. But don't let that worry your head. Those limitations don't apply to me. I am without limits. Come here and give me your hand."

I tried to resist but I moved forward against my will. I extended my hand.

"This won't hurt a bit. Physically I mean."

He took my hand. In a flash I could see the things he had done, scenes from his memory. Some were so violent, so evil, so gruesome that my head was bursting. I wanted to vomit.

I must have fainted. I awoke on my back on an operating table. The other boy lay on a nearby table. My legs and arms were tied with leather straps. Sebastian was standing beside me, so close I could see the tiny bugs that crawled beneath his translucent skin.

"Ah, you return. I hope you found your nap restful. You indeed come from a strange land. I quite enjoyed your memories of nursery rhymes. The old lady that lived in the shoe, I liked how she beat her children before bed. And The Three Little Pigs. I'll bet that children wonder how well their houses are built. Or Little Red Riding Hood. Did you check your Grandma for signs of wolfiness each time you visited her? And how do you feel when out and about in Wolf Forest? Fe fi fo fum, I smell the blood of an Englishman. Be he live or be he dead, I'll grind his bones to make my bread! It must be nice to live in a land so cruel it teaches such things to its children.

"But the goal was to find a good punishment for you. You are not that afraid of pain. I see that you have experienced your share. After enough, you realize that you can endure. But you hate being laughed at, hate being embarrassed. How strange. You and I are alike in this way and in no others. How can I embarrass you? I asked and you told me.

"Another one of your childhood tales gave me the answer. Pinocchio. What a nice story. A boy of wood is transformed into a boy of flesh. I can only imagine how your friends will react when they see you. Please drink this."

He forced some liquid down my throat. It burned as I swallowed and the burning feeling spread through my body. I couldn't feel the straps on my wrists and ankles. I looked at my right hand. It was wood. I slid my arms free of the strap.

"Enjoy the new you. Go ahead, take some time, Look at yourself in the mirror. Now you may go anywhere you like. Feel free. Travel throughout Oz. Even return to your land. But remember only I can return you to flesh. But why would I?"

I rushed at Sebastian. I was stopped just short of him, frozen in space. I could just barely move my hand.

"Oh, you are learning. Anyway, I must leave. My visit with you has been pleasant but I have other places to spread my own unique joy."

Sebastian vanished with a bang and a plume of smoke. And I was left alone, a boy of wood.

So now I am Pinocchio. An interesting choice for Sebastian to make. When I was 7 or 8 I dressed as Pinocchio for Halloween. For a short while Pinocchio was my favorite. I don't get why Sebastian thought being made into Pinocchio would cause me any distress. I never planned to become Pinocchio but there are way worse things he could have done. Like call me son. Being his son, that would be distressing.

But my close fit like tents. I noticed a set of clothes nearby. I changed and did some experiments with my new body.

Hanging around and moping wasn't my plan. I considered all the things I had seen. And some of the things I had done. Some of them worked. Like setting fire to his mess of shacks. It stopped him, at least for a short time. *More fire.* But this time I wasn't going to set fire to his shacks.

First, I needed to do an inventory. I hastened around looking for things that could help me. I found a sling for carrying firewood. It would be a help. There was a bookcase full of old books. They would be useful in building up the fire. The fire was still burning in the fireplace, so I wouldn't have to start from zero. There were plenty of fireplace tools. A boy of wood needs to be careful when handling fire. There was that boy, and the stuffed people and animals in Creepman's room of horrors. I counted them up. I was ready.

I know that once things get going time will be critical. Once I start to spin this yarn, I will need to spin and spin.

So, I may not be able to win this war. But one thing is certain – I won't be moping around. I have a lot to do. I may not win, but I sure plan to mess him up.

Chapter 26 Tip

And to do what I planned I would need help. I walked over to the boy on the other operating table. He looked big, bigger than me, even before I was turned into Pinocchio. He looked strong as well. That would come in handy. I tried to wake him, but nothing brought him out of his slumber. I retrieved my pants. I didn't want to drop even one grain of blue sand so I held my pants over him as I emptied out my left pants pocket. I tried to wake him again. He shook his head back and forth like he was having a nightmare but then he returned to rest. I emptied the contents of the right pants pocket out on him. He shook himself violently and let out a shrill cry. I gave him a shove. A good hard shove. He let out a long low moan, sat up, and blinked his eyes. He looked at me.

"Where am I?" he asked. I expected some sand to fall off of him but there was none. Single use blue sand.

"You are in Sebastian's fortress of decrepitude," I said.

"And who are you?" he questioned.

"Ralph. I am Ralph. I don't normally look like this. Sebastian turned me into Pinocchio, a wooden boy," I said. "I need help fighting Sebastian, will you help me?"

"Why would you want to fight with Sebastian? He is the most thoughtful, caring person I know."

"Are we both talking about the same Sebastian? The guy with the jet black hair and white, nearly translucent skin?"

"Yes, that's him. He is like a father to me. He is better than my father. My father and mother abandoned me to the wolves of Wolf Forest when I was a small child. If not for Sebastian, I would have died there and then. Sebastian fought off the wolves and saved me. He took me in and has raised me like his own son. I could never hurt him. I could never go against him."

"Why are your hands and feet tied?" I asked.

He looked at his wrists, and then he looked down at his ankles. "I tend to toss and turn when I sleep. Sebastian ties me so I don't fall in my sleep."

"And you always sleep on an operating table?"

"Yes, it's funny, but I am so used to it I am not comfortable sleeping in a regular bed."

I couldn't believe what he was saying but I didn't want to fight with him and there were other ways to convince him. "That's okay," I said. "Sebastian asked me to move something for him and it's very heavy. I need help. Can you lend me a hand?"

"Sure, if Sebastian wants it done I want to help."

"Definitely. Sebastian would really like us to help him rearrange some of the things he has in his storage room so let me remove your bindings."

When he was free I walked him to Sebastian's room of horrors and I forced the door open.

"The door knob in this room is sticking," I said. "It's on my list of things to fix for Sebastian, but first he wants help reorganizing this room."

"Please help me move this over here," I said. I showed him to the stuffed image of himself.

When he saw his image he froze. One of him was stuffed and posed, and the other was frozen in shock. He stood in silence, looking at the stuffed version of himself. Then he put his head in his hands and began to sob.

"Hey," I said. "Are you okay?"

"No, I'm not okay. I'm not me. The memories I had a second ago are all false, all fake, planted into my brain by Sebastian. And here I am, looking at my stuffed image. And here, over here, the black dog. I have been the black dog as well. And the falcon. I have been the falcon. But most of all I have been imprisoned here. And I have tried and tried to escape. And failed every time. And then Sebastian began to wipe my memories and place false memories into my head, so I wouldn't even try. I wouldn't even know I was a prisoner. So no, I'm not okay."

"Will you help me fight Sebastian?" I asked.

"It's pointless, he will win every time. And then you won't even remember that you tried."

"I broke free once and now I think I have a way to harm him. I don't want to break free again. I can leave at any time, now that he has turned me into Pinocchio, but I don't want to leave. I just want to hurt him."

"You got free? I have been trying and trying."

"Yes, I made it to freedom, but I got recaptured, that's why I am here with you. I'm no longer trying to escape, it's a waste of time. Now I'm just going to make Sebastian suffer in any way I can."

"Yes, I will help you. Maybe we can repay Sebastian for some of his deceit."

I looked at the stuffed creatures. "Do you know which one is the real you?" I asked.

"No," he said. "Am I the dog, am I me? Am I the falcon? Or even someone else? I don't know."

"I hope you're not you, or the black dog, or the falcon, because —"

"Because they are all dead and stuffed. I see your point. I can only hope I am not one of these stuffed creatures. But I have no memories of being another."

"What's your name?" I asked.

"Tippetarius. My friends call me Tip. At least that's the last memory I have for a name. Is it really mine? Was it someone else's? I don't know."

"Well Tip, I'm the closest thing you have to a friend." We shook hands awkwardly, hand of flesh shaking hand of wood. "There is a large fireplace in the main room. I need a lot of firewood and a big fire in the fireplace."

"And you are not a boy of wood?" Tip asked.

"No. Sebastian turned me to wood. Normally I am a boy of flesh like you, but I am younger and smaller than you are."

"Yes," Tip said. "Some of my brain fog is lifting. Sebastian sometimes makes me gather firewood for him. And you are sure you are Ralph, and not one of his stuffed creatures?"

"I don't see me among the menagerie so I think I am me, except I'm Pinocchio, which is not me and not one of his objects."

Tip said, "Let's get the fire going and then you can tell me what the plan is." He found the fire wood sling and began collecting wood.

I worked a bit to revive the fire, crumpling pages from the books and blowing on the embers. In short order I had a nice blaze going, good enough so that I could let it be while I did other preparations. I rotated the caldron out of the fireplace; we were going to need every last bit of space to do what I planned. I broke up the wooden stand that stood beside the caldron, the stand that Sebastian used for his ingredients and tools, and tossed the wood in. Then I joined Tip in collecting wood. We filled the entire room with firewood. There was hardly a path to walk free.

"And now?" Tip asked.

"My plan is to burn the stuffed people and creatures in Sebastian's hall of horrors. Somehow Sebastian makes use of them, like he turns into them. I want to burn them. But that brings us to an important question: do we want to burn, and is it safe for you if we burn your image?"

Tip thought. "Let's leave my image out of it. I don't want to find out what will happen to me if it burns while I am it."

"Okay," I said. "That's your choice to make."

"Yes," Tip said. "I want to hurt Sebastian and I don't want to miss out if burning me means my early end."

"Then," I said. "Let's start with the falcon. It's small and I don't think Sebastian is using it."

I carried the falcon through the hallway and stuffed it into the fireplace. Tip dragged the wolf. "Just getting prepared," Tip said. At first the falcon didn't burn. We built the fire to a furious blaze and watched as the falcon slowly began to smolder and flame. It let off an awful stench so that we had to open all the windows to keep from gagging. Since the windows had been boarded up, we had to do a fair bit of smashing to get them open. The extra wood went onto the fire.

"On to the wolf," I said. I helped Tip stuff the wolf into the fireplace and we buried it in wood. *Was this wolf the sister of the wolf pack's leader? What did the wolf leader think when Sebastian came to him in the form of his sister? I'm sure he did. I'm sure he did and he enjoyed every bit of pain it caused.*

Only a roaring fire had any effect so we were quickly going through the wood that had once filled the room. "We need much more firewood," I said. We took turns getting firewood and keeping the fire roaring. Finally, the falcon began to crumble to dust.

"I think we can fit the winged monkey in the fireplace with the wolf. Let's get it."

We went to the hall of horrors to get the winged monkey. I had underestimated the size of its outstretched wings. We were going to need to break its wings to get it through the hall. I thought, "If I were stuffed, would I want my wings broken so I could be burned?" Then I thought, "I should be more honest with myself. The correct question is 'When I am stuffed, would I want my wings broken so I could be burned?'" The answers were yes and yes – We broke the wings. We dragged it through the hall. We pushed the wolf to the left and added the winged monkey to the right side. We needed more fire and more firewood.

We kept going. We burnt the buck, and then the black dog. The buck was a real challenge due to its size. We had to start burning it with half its body outside the fireplace.

I was saving Mombi for last. I was sure burning her would get Sebastian's attention since he was so proud of having her. We got the fire blazing and stuffed her in. We'd been burning Sebastian's styles for hours. Tip was drenched in sweat from the hauling and the heat of the fire. As a boy of wood, I didn't sweat. I guess that's one good thing about being Pinocchio.

Tip and I both hurried to collect more wood. The sun had moved across the sky and the area near Sebastian's lair was shrouded in shade. It always was unnaturally dark around Sebastian's shack, but now the shade made it darker. We brought our wood in and buried Mombi in it. The fire blazed around her but she didn't even begin to smolder. Not a bit.

"More wood," I yelled to Tip. We had already gathered all the nearby dry fallen branches so we were searching about when Nutmeg saw us.

"What kind of game are you guys playing?" she asked.

"We're trying to collect wood for the fireplace but we've used up all the nearby wood," I said.

"Follow me," she said. "See that shack over there? It's full of old sawn and split firewood. I sometimes store my nuts inside. That should keep the fire going for a while."

The shed was on the other side of Sebastian's menagerie of shacks. Tip and I knocked the door in and it was full with just what we wanted. We worked together emptying the shed, and then we knocked the shed down to burn as well.

I carried a pile of wood back in and then I worked the fire. When I came out Tip was out of sight, around back, at the location of the former wood shed. I could hear him breaking the boards into smaller pieces so they were easier to carry.

Sebastian appeared in front of me. He was angry. Literally fuming. It may have been due to our fire, but he had fumes coming off his skin.

"Ralph, you have gone too far. I have underestimated you. You are more dangerous than I thought possible. You will not due for being stuffed. Death is the only solution. Prepare to die," Sebastian yelled.

"It will not do to kill you as Pinocchio since I want you to experience every bit of pain. So first I return you to boyhood. First the clothes," and my clothes were replaced with my original clothing. "Then back to boy," and I returned to being flesh, along with the bleeding nose and bruised hands. "And now death," he said.

But he was interrupted. Tip had heard his shouting and took one of the boards of the wood shed, and swinging it like a baseball bat, knocked Sebastian's head clean off. It flew off his shoulders and landed a few steps from me. His body staggered forward to pick his head up. I ran forward as well and kicked his head with all my might. It rolled along the ground. I knocked Sebastian's body down and knee dropped on his chest. Just than the wolf pack appeared. I leapt off of Sebastian's body and ran aside.

"Well done Ralph," their leader said. "We will take it from here."

The pack leader snarled forward. "And now I will make you pay for what you did to my sister," he said.

"Pup, still wet behind the ears. Leave while you live," Sebastian's head said. The pack pounced on Sebastian's head and body.

But it didn't go well. Every wolf that bit into Sebastian's body or head and touched what once was his flesh instantly crumpled to dust. And as each wolf crumpled Sebastian seemed to get stronger. The wolves backed off. Sebastian's body righted itself and began to move toward his head. The wolves scurried off, less their leader and a number of the pack.

Tip took his board and tried to knock Sebastian's body down, but Sebastian caught the board and yanked it from Tip's hands. Sebastian swung the board about blindly but nearly clobbered Tip. Tip rolled under the swinging board and away from Sebastian's reach. Tip turned to attack Sebastian again.

"Tip, don't touch him," I yelled. "Escape if you can, save yourself."

I expected Tip to run away, though I'm not sure what good that would have done. But instead he headed straight into Sebastian's front door.

Sebastian's body picked up his head and placed it atop his shoulders. He turned to me. "Be still, your time is at hand," he said. I tried to turn, I tried to run, but I could do nothing. He flattened the skin of his neck against his body. He straightened out his hair. He tugged on his cuffs. He tried to fluff up two dents in his chest. The dents must have been from my knee drop. I guess I was lucky not to have touched his flesh. Or maybe it didn't matter since I was wood when I made them.

I'm not sure what Tip was doing, but Sebastian spun his head to his shacks. Then he returned to straightening himself up. He re-buttoned the top button of his shirt and flattened his collar down. He straightened his nose. Again he looked to his shack. Then he turned to me. But it wasn't me he was looking at. He looked to my right. Something had caught his attention, but I couldn't turn to see what it was. Then he smiled and looked at me.

"Tradition, tradition, tradition," Sebastian sang. "I am just such a traditionalist, Ralph. Tradition, tradition, tradition. I need to do things the old way."

Then he felt his hands along the bottom of his jacket, smoothing it out, and said, "You don't have the horse right here, the Wells-Fargo wagon is not coming down the street, and the sun will not come out tomorrow." Then he raised his hands and began walking toward my throat.

Chapter 27 Popcorn

I followed my instincts and flew to where they led me. It felt so familiar, yet so alien. I stood before a dome of dark clouds that enclosed Sebastian's place. The outside of the dome glistened in reflected sunlight. It was bright enough so that I squinted my eyes. I spread my hands on the surface of the dome, trying to determine if there was a way to enter. I grabbed Glinda's sword and stabbed the dome.

The dome thinned. I could see Sebastian raise his hands and begin to walk toward Ralph. In a panic I slashed Glinda's sword left and right and the dome vanished. The sunlight flooded the ground. Fumes drifted off of Sebastian's exposed skin. He fell to his knees and began to crawl to his door.

"Ralph," I yelled. "Turn around."

Ralph stood frozen watching Sebastian crawl and then he turned and ran to me. He stopped in front of me.

"What are you doing here?" Ralph asked.

"Saving your sorry butt," I said. "Be quiet and get on the back of my broom."

"Are you kidding me, a broom? Do I need to be afraid of black cats too?" he asked.

"Yes, a broom. And it wouldn't hurt you to be more careful around cats. And if you want to stay here, that's fine by me. I am leaving with or without you."

I got on my broom. "Get on behind me and hold me tight around my waist. The ride will be rough. And if you get wise and let your hands slip to somewhere they don't belong you will find that gravity works fine in Oz and I have no problem dropping you."

Ralph got on and we took off with a hard lurch upward. My flying hadn't gotten much better but that was just the way it was. I took us up and surged forward as fast as I could possibly go hoping to get some space between us and Sebastian.

We flew on just long enough for me to catch my breath. I thought we might get away without an incident, but incident there was. Some bolts of flame hit the back of the broom setting it to fire and knocking us around. The crystal ball fell off. So much for navigating. We were being jerked hard in all directions and flipped about so that I could no longer see where we were going. I tried to bring us down fast not knowing how this flying on fire was going to go.

"The broom's on fire!" Ralph yelled.

"Got it. Put it out," I screamed.

Ralph let go with one hand so he could try to snuff out the flame.

"I got it out but it's still smoldering," he shouted.

Just then another round of fire, stronger than the first hit the broom and the broom flared up worse than before.

My already limited control of the broom was slipping away. We were still way too high for a safe fall. The broom flared and then we started to fall. As the last bit of the broom's lift disappeared all I could think about was popcorn.

There would have been a hundred more elegant solutions, but I came up with popcorn. I envisioned

Ralph and me, each of us in the center of an enormous piece of popped corn.

The popcorn was the size of a house. I could hear the wind whistling by as I fell toward the ground. In all the other times that things got dangerous in Oz, I never had time to think about, you know, dying, but this time I had plenty of time. I saw Josh do his crash landing, and he seemed fine, but I'm guessing he had some protection spells on him. I'm no witch, and I know just enough magic to be dangerous, so all I could do was hope.

Besides the wind it was quiet, but I was tumbling erratically, being tossed about. Either way, I waited. Without any warning I smashed into the ground. I could hear the popcorn being crushed as I was smashed face first into the white fluff. My popcorn must have bounced a little because there was another lighter smash and I came to a stop. My head was mushed into the popcorn up to my chin. I pulled my head free. My ears got a rough pull on the way out. I blew some bits out of my mouth and nose as I started to claw my way free. I ripped my way through the popcorn and emerged, still way off the ground. I dug hand and foot holds and climbed down.

After I sneezed, sending little bits of popcorn flying all about, I started looking around for Ralph. He had landed and rolled quite a distance so I ran off in that direction. When I got there, he was just digging his way out of his popcorn.

"Nice trick, but you forgot the butter and salt," he said as he held a football size chunk of popcorn in his hand looking at it. "What do we do next?"

"We get out of here." Just as I said that a mass of putrid choking smoke jetted through the sky and landed nearby. We stopped in shock. As the putrid smoke cleared I could see Sebastian, looking bedraggled, but standing right in front of us.

"Don't be leaving so soon. I have plans for you both," he said.

"Emily, perhaps you would make a nice inclusion in my recently depleted collection. No, I think not. You are too annoying."

Sebastian raised his hands. "I hope this hurts you almost as much as it brings me joy."

A charging horse appeared behind Sebastien. As she passed Sebastian the horse kicked out, sending Sebastien flying. He landed in a crumpled heap.

"Get on," the horse said.

"Get on, Ralph," I yelled. "Get on, get on." He struggled to get on so I pushed him up. As soon as he was on I leaped on behind him and yelled, "Go."

The horse raced at full speed, but not fast enough. A bolt of fire ripped into the horse just behind me and the air was full of the smell of burning hair.

The horse galloped on and as it did the scenery flashed before us. With every step the entire surroundings were new. After many more places went by the horse slowed and stopped. It was obviously in great pain.

I jumped off. "Get off Ralph." He struggled his way off.

"What next?" he asked.

"Quiet please Ralph," I said. "I need to think."

"What's this?" he asked.

"Shut up, Ralph!" I screamed as I lost it. "I really need to think."

330

He shoved a book into my stomach. "Looking for this?" he asked.

I took the book. It fell open to a spell on healing. I read it over and then I read it again.

The horse lay down nearby. I could hear its troubled breathing and with every breath a spasm shook the horse's body. I walked over and closed my eyes. I imagined a crisp breeze over a snow covered field. A cold drizzle began to fall. The rain drizzled down and some flowers pushed their way through the snow. The sun came out and the snow quickly melted away leaving a meadow full of wild flowers. I opened my eyes. The horse was pushing its way up to standing.

"Thank you," the horse said.

"Thank you," I replied. "You saved our lives. How did you know we needed help?"

"One of your friends sent me."

"One of my friends?"

"Yes, you have friends, some who wish to remain unknown for the present."

"Then thank them for me."

"I will, but now I must leave. I have carried you far away, perhaps too far. I have never imagined such an empty place as this. This must be the edge of the great desert that surrounds Oz. Do not go in that direction. Do not touch the sand of the great desert. No living thing can survive it. But you are far enough away from Sebastian to be safe, at least for some time. And I cannot help you further. I don't have the strength. I hope I have enough strength to return myself. You must continue on your own."

I looked to the great desert. There was no sounds beside a faint hissing sound. Fumes drifted off the sand, floated into the air, spread, and dissipated. There were some bones. They looked like the bones of a bird that flew in, unknowing of the danger.

I scrutinized where we were. It was hardly more appealing than the great desert. There was no signs of life, only sand and rocks. The sun blazed down on the sand, through a perfectly cloudless sky. The sky seemed much less blue than usual.

Ralph interrupted. "Did that hurt? When Creepman fixed my nose it hurt more than I ever thought things could hurt. Even now, my poor nose is a mess."

"It didn't hurt," the horse said. "It felt like a cool breeze blowing over me."

I looked at Ralph's nose. "Did somebody else punch you after me?"

"My nose cushioned a fall. Can you make it better? I can't get a good breath of air."

I thought, "Is this an invitation to punch him again?" Another punch could really help how his nose looks. I decided to keep my thoughts to myself. I repeated the spell.

Ralph felt his nose. "It's a bit better, but I still can't get a good breath."

"Sorry. When we are back and safe we can visit Dr. Ulam. I bet he can help you."

Ralph looked around. "Hey, and where are we now? How did we get here? We rode for only a few steps and we're nowhere near where we were. That over there, that looks like hell to me."

"I did my best to turn space so we could get away," said the horse. "But now I must leave." It started to walk and as it walked it faded into a blue mist. In an instant it was gone.

Ralph shook his head in disbelief and then asked, "What's next?"

"I hope you are ready for a long walk."

"Anything is better than Creepman. That guy is seriously sick. If I told you about him, you would not believe me. He had people, stuffed people, in his house."

"Stuffed?"

"Yeah, stuffed and posed like mannequins. Mombi the witch was one of his collection of stuffed people. Tip and I burnt them, most of them. And what about him? Did you ever see him up close? His skin is like dried sunbaked mud. I mean, is he alive? He doesn't breathe."

I thought. "I don't know," was all I could say. After some silence I said, "Sorry about telling you to shut up."

"You can tell me to shut up a million times after saving me from Creepman." Without a pause he continued, "The desert looks a lot like hell, or perhaps like the pictures from Mars. Of course this can't be Mars because we would not be talking on Mars. We might be gasping, but not talking. Since it's nice and sunny we wouldn't be freezing, but we wouldn't want to spend the night, which would be deadly cold. Also, we would really be able to jump, well, except for the fact that we would be dead since we wouldn't be able to breathe. So this can't be Mars."

"How do you know so much about Mars?"

"I want to be an astronaut. Astronauts need to know this kind of stuff. There are two moons around Mars as well. Did you know that? What do you want to be when you grow up?"

"I don't know. I figure I will decide when I'm done being a kid. So for now all I want to be is a kid."

"Emily, the biggest, baddest witch in Oz," Ralph chided.

"I didn't choose any of this. I got chosen. I don't know why. Maybe it's just because I am curious."

"What do you mean?"

"I first came to Oz when I was hunting through some old stuff and touched a mirror that was owned by another girl who visited Oz."

"Cool. I mean, terrifying, I guess. So you know all about this place?"

"Not a thing. Everything seems to be churning. Everywhere I go is completely different."

I thought, "Now I have a book to carry. And who knows where my nav ball fell. Not that it would help, since it got bricked near Glinda's castle. If I only had my backpack, but that's in my school locker."

"Okay, let's walk," I said.

"Where to, boss?"

"That way." I pointed to a small outcropping of rocks that were farther from the great desert. "We may find some shelter there." All around us was sand and parched earth. Not a living thing in site, no animals, no insects, no sounds. It was so quiet I could hear our hearts beating.

In a few paces a flock of something flew over us. They were the strangest things I had ever seen. And I had seen some strange things while in Oz. They sort of looked like flying disks. Like looking at the bottom of an old sci-fi flying saucer. They wooshed by. Then one broke from the flock. It soared high into the air, circled back, and came down close to the ground, flying toward us. Ralph started running in the other direction.

"Are you coming?" he yelled back.

"We can't possibly out run it so we might as well save our strength."

We stood and watched as the thing approached. As it got closer to the ground it rotated so that it was rolling. It slowed and I could see that it was cartwheeling, like a pinwheel rolling along. It came aside us and stopped as we looked each other over.

"I heard that there are creatures that move by limbs that go back and forth but I never thought I would see one up close. Is it difficult to move that way?" it asked.

"No, it's quite natural to us," I said.

"You are welcome here, strange creatures, but you are far from everything. It is slow traveling by land."

"Is there anything nearby?"

"The nearest town is over there," it said as it pointed.

I looked in that direction and I could not see anything. "Your vision must be better than mine."

"Yes, perhaps that is true. Your eyes are so much smaller than mine." The creature had a bulge in its center that had five eyes, which looked off in different directions and worked independently. From its torso five legs, or arms, or wings, or some type of combination of leg, arm and wing, jutted. Between its legs spread a thin layer of leathery skin. While it was large there wasn't much mass to it. Obviously, they were meant to fly.

"Can I watch you walk? You are unique."

"Sure," we said. Ralph and I walked back and forth a few paces.

"Amazing. Thank you. Now I need to return to my flock before they are too far away. Good luck to you strangers," it said as it began cartwheeling away. It sped up and then rolled over on a side. It went fully horizontal, flying just above the ground. Then it flew off, rising high in the air. We watched as it grew smaller and smaller in the sky.

And so we began to walk. I was sort of day dreaming as we went. I was thinking about how I escaped from my room in the castle, how bold I was to get on any old broom and try to fly. But it saved my life so I guess I would do it again. I had bumped my way down along the wall of the castle, getting a bit more banged up and a bit closer to the ground with each bump. I was so relieved when I got to the ground. That old broom that had been left in that unused room, I had thanked it and carefully placed it into a tiny corner in the castle's wall. I wondered, "Is that broom still there? Is it mine?"

"Hold on Ralph. Let me try something."

"Sure 'nough Boss," Ralph said.

I wanted to call that old broom. I imagined it being in my right hand. I paced around waiting for the broom, but nothing happened.

"Okay, there is no easy way, so let's walk." We walked until we reached the rocky outcropping.

"Are we home yet?" Ralph asked with a joking smile on his face.

"I don't think so. This is no place like home. Ralph, can you climb to the top of this pile of rocks and see if you can find anything? The flying thing said the town was in that direction."

"Sure," he said. He climbed to the top and looked around in every direction. "I don't see any town, but there is something interesting in that direction. It could be something alive, maybe some trees."

We started walking again. I kept my thoughts to myself. We were at the end of the world, farther away from home than I have ever been. And we have a choice, be safe in this desolate place, or head to Oz and walk into danger. Danger ahead.

As we got closer I could see what Ralph found, a small stand of low stunted trees and some dried tall grass. My eyes searched around for something that might be a clue.

"I have an idea," I said. "We are going to make a broom. Ralph, search around and find a nice heavy stick about as long as you are tall. I'll cut down some of the dried grass and we will make a broom."

"You're kidding, right? Aren't these flying brooms special? I mean, don't they buy them from FlyingBroom.com? Or Aviation Brooms Inc.?"

"The first broom I flew by myself was just an old broom used to sweep floors. So yes, we are going to make a broom."

"Isn't there some special design for a broom that flies? Don't they have to download an operating system before they fly? Can they get hacked? Are there only two seaters? Are there broom airports? If a witch has a large family does she get one of those big push brooms? Is a push broom like a mini-van?"

"Ralph, less talk, more search."

I collected up a bunch of tall dried grass. Ralph returned with a nice stout stick.

"This ought to do," he said. "I think it's strong enough to hold us, if that matters at all."

"I don't know," I said. "I need one of your laces."

Ralph looked at his fancy sneakers with a pained expression. "I hope I get it back," Ralph said. "These are the only things that are mine that I like." He slowly took the lace out of his left sneaker. He looked at the lace in his hand and then handed it to me.

I laid the grass down and put the stick on top overlapping somewhat. I spread the grass around the stick and wrapped it into place with the shoe lace. A bunch of wraps and a tight knot and it was ready. Ready I hoped. Ralph looked at his lace. He didn't look happy.

"Okay," I said. "Let me test it."

I got on and lifted off to knee high. It seemed to maneuver fine. I lowered back down to the ground. "Get on, we have a long way to go." Then I noticed the book of magic left beside the tree. I picked it up and the magic book squirmed out of my hand. It fell open to a spell for making things small. After a few attempts I had the book of magic shrunk down so it was the size of a postage stamp.

"Ralph, do you have a good place to hold this for me?"

"Sure." He slipped it into his wallet. "Do you know how to read this tiny thing?" he asked. I didn't. And I hadn't learned the spell to bring it back to normal size. Another bridge to cross some other time. "No," was all I said. I got back on the broom. "Hop on Ralph."

"You've got to be the bravest person in the world. We are going to fly on that?"

"Sure are, unless you want to wait here for public transportation."

"No, I'm with you," he said as he got on.

While I didn't say anything I was plenty scared so I kept things low to the ground and slow for a while. That didn't last long though. When I realized we were fine I yelled out, "Hold on, we are going for a ride." In a second we were blasting along and I was whooping. We were going in the right direction, the land itself was growing more alive.

The scenery whizzed by below us. We passed over a large flock of geese. We were so high above them they didn't notice our passing. We flew over a large forested area.

"Hey, I think we are losing bits of the broom," Ralph said.

"Try to hold it together so I can get us down safely." I didn't want to find out what happened if it fell apart. We came down without a moment to spare. It didn't look like much of a broom anymore.

"Well, that's it for flying," I said.

Chapter 28 Broken

Ralph asked, "Do I get to have my lace back?"

"Yes," I replied as I handed it to him.

He straightened the lace and carefully relaced his sneaker. Snug on the bottom but laces flying.

"Why lace it if you aren't going to tie it?"

"It makes it look like you don't care. If you don't care than no one can hurt you."

"But you care about your sneakers so if someone wanted to hurt you they could take your sneakers away."

"Yes, but not without a fight."

"Let's keep going," I said as I pointed onward. We started walking. In a short while we came to a stream, two streams actually. At their closest point they were separated by a wide patch of sand. These little turtle-like creatures were walking upright from one stream to the next, if you could call it walking. They waddled clumsily along, swaying side to side in the sand. If they fell, and they often did, and it was on their front, they quickly pushed themselves up and continued. If they fell on their backs they worked frantically to set themselves right, but their fins just fanned the air. Large birds would swoop down and carry them off in their bills.

"Look at these goofy things," Ralph said. "If you tip them over they can't get up." He tapped one nearby and it fell over. A bird flew down a scooped it up.

"Stop it, Ralph."

He went into the path of the creatures and tipped another one over. "These guys as so clumsy," he said.

"Stop it. Please stop." Another bird whirled by and another turtle was gone. He knocked another one over.

"Ralph, what is wrong with you? Did your mom drop you on your head when you were a baby?"

"No, she didn't drop me on my head. And don't you talk about my mom."

I guess I got through to him. He stopped tipping then over. Then he saw a turtle that had just fallen over and righted it.

"Give me a hand if you care about these things. We can try to save them."

We set to, finding the turtles that were on their backs and righting them. There were so many we couldn't help all of them, but we helped some. We were moving among them, as carefully as possible, and as quickly as possible, setting them up and on their way. I was just about the reach down to stand up a turtle when a swarm of the birds flew down and carried Ralph off. I didn't have time to move before another swarm latched onto my arms, legs, and even my hair and lifted me into the sky.

I was afraid we were in for another drop from the sky. No more popcorn. But I watched as we flew along one of the streams. We followed the stream until we came to a great bog. Large turtles sat sunbathing on top of the mounds. We began to descend. We must have startled the turtles for many plunged into the water, enough to make a constant drum roll of splashes as they jumped in. The birds that carried Ralph and I lowered us gently to the top of one of the mounds and flew off.

A large turtle climbed up out of the water, followed by another, and then another. The largest one looked at Ralph and me and asked, "Why are you interfering with the migration of the children? Why?"

"We saw those birds eating the little turtles that fell over," I said.

"What did you see? Were any turtles eaten?"

"I saw them scoop them up into their bills" I said.

"And you concluded they were being eaten. Did you see any actually being eaten?"

"Yes, yes. I saw them go into their mouths."

"Not to eat them. To carry them. The ones who are not strong enough to cross the sand will not be strong enough to survive the migration they must make down the stream. Those birds, as you call them, carry the small turtles in their bills, here, to our nursery. Look," the large turtle said. Indeed the same birds we saw landed and carefully released the small turtles they had scooped up.

"I didn't know," I said.

"That you didn't know is not a problem. Not knowing and still assuming you knew better than everyone else, that is a problem."

"I am sorry," I said.

"It is of minor import. The migration is tough. Many of the strongest ones won't make it as well. The weak ones that you think you helped, these will surely not make it."

I was stunned. I had inadvertently hurt, possibly caused the death, of some of these creatures. I watched as more birds dropped their loads off and returned to the air. Again and again they flew.

"The birds are our grandparents," the turtle said. "You were thinking how the birds are part of all this. They are our grandparents. Few of us live long enough for the final transformation, but if you are blessed with enough time, you emerge from your winter hibernation transformed."

"That is amazing," Ralph said. "There are no creatures in our world that undergo so dramatic a transformation. How do you know they are transformed?"

"They have their memories," the turtle said.

I didn't know if that was true or not but I decided to listen rather than talk. In my silence I realized it was time for us to move on.

"Do you know the way back to Oz, back to the Emerald City?" I asked.

"This stream is one of the many tributaries to the River Oz."

"I don't recall any river in Oz," I said.

"The River Oz is under the ground in most of Oz. It flows directly underneath the castle in the Emerald City, I have heard."

"How are we going to get from here to there?" Ralph asked.

"I am open to suggestions," I said.

"Well, there are these little insects that float along in some creek, floating in half acorns. They use little sticks to keep from getting stuck," Ralph said.

"There's nothing here big enough for us," I said.

"Ain't you a witch?" Ralph chided.

"No, I ain't no witch."

"Didn't Plato say 'Necessity is the mother of witchcraft?'"

"That's not the way I remember it," I said.

"I'll get something we can float on, you figure out how to make it large enough," he said.

And he did. In a few minutes he had taken some reeds and roughly woven them together into a round mat, big enough to fit under a dinner plate.

"And now for some magic," he said.

We said goodbye to the turtles and walked along the stream to where it was wide and deep enough to hold something that would fit us.

I couldn't use the book of magic, since it was stamp size. I could try to make the magic book larger, but if I could do that I didn't really need the magic book. I decided I would use the shrink incantation, but say it backwards, which took me a few minutes to get my brain around, saying backwards and all.

"Okay, here goes," I said. I did the backward incantation and it worked. The plate size mat was now about the size of a large car tire. Still too small.

"Once more with gusto," Ralph laughed.

And I did. Now it looked about right. It was plenty big; we struggled to get it into the stream. We got on and pushed off the rocks and into the center current.

The stream went slow for some time but I could feel that it was getting faster. And faster. Now we were hurtling along with the stream, bouncing over rocks and jams, and spinning around. I tried to keep myself looking forward but I couldn't keep up with the spin. We hurtled along. And then an enormous tentacle reached out from the water and pulled me under. I held my breath. The tentacle had spikes and suction cups along its length, but I was not being hurt. I began to become faint. I knew I couldn't hold my breath any longer. Then I inhaled, the water filled my lungs, and …

And it was fine. I looked around and saw Ralph was wrapped in another tentacle. The bottom of the stream flew by, and then it suddenly became dark. My eyes adjusted and I could see again. Everything was illuminated by a blue glow. We raced along and then the beast, a squid I guess, tossed me up a vertical tunnel. I popped out of the water on the other side and gasped for air. It was the spring, the Cold Spring, below the castle in the Emerald City.

Ralph popped up, gasping for air. "Where are we?" Ralph asked.

"Just where we want to be," I said. "In the lowest level of the castle in the Emerald City."

"That was some ride," Ralph said.

We climbed out. Like last time, the water of the Cold Spring did not wet our skin, though our clothes dripped. I had done this once before. In a blink of an eye we were both dry.

"Nice one," Ralph said. "I thought I was going back to sloshing in my sneakers again."

"Follow me," I said. We climbed the stairs and headed to the Scarecrow's meeting room. As we approached I could hear him talking.

"I am not making any progress in breaking the spell of the Flying Monkeys. Gings, do you have any other ideas?"

"No, I don't," Gings said as we entered the room.

They paused and stared at us. I was surprised Gings had been helping but I decided to let it go.

The Scarecrow said, "Hello Emily, and welcome to the Emerald City, Ralph."

Now Ralph was doing his own bit of staring, at the Scarecrow.

"Hello Mr. Scarecrow," Ralph said. "Thank you for the hospitality."

"You are welcome, Ralph. As a good friend of Emily you will have every courtesy," the Scarecrow said.

The events of the day suddenly caught up with me and I felt exhausted. I must have gone to bed somewhere, but I don't remember it. And we must have been protected because my sleep was uneventful, except for a dream.

Glinda was young and vivacious and Sebastian, Sebastian was alive. Glinda said, "How could you do this? She is just a child."

"You have something I want, and I have something you want. It's very simple really," Sebastian said.

"The princess Ozma for Gings? Don't you have any morality?"

"No," Sebastian said.

Glinda said, "I will speak to Ozma. It is a lot to ask, to sacrifice your life for someone, but she feels responsible for all her people."

"Then we have an agreement," Sebastian said. "And anytime you break your half of the bargain I will find your dear Gings and —"

"I understand," Glinda said.

The scene faded and was replaced by Glinda talking to Gings. Gings was a young child.

Glinda asked, "Gingold, while Sebastian had you imprisoned, did he do anything to you? Did he hurt you in any way?"

Gings replied, "He went through my memories. I saw the things he had done. It was bad, awful."

"Gings, I don't like to do this, but I think I must. May I look through your memories? I am afraid of what Sebastian may have done to you."

"Of course. I trust you," Gings said.

Glinda held Gings' hand and closed her eyes for a moment. Then she removed her hand and opened her eyes.

"Gings, it is as I feared. I did my best to correct what he did, but it cannot be totally undone. He made sure you could never be a danger to him. He left behind fragments to prevent you from challenging him. In the future, you may want to fight against Sebastian, but you must not do so directly. He will know your plans and prevent you from being successful. No matter what you feel, no matter how necessary it may be, no matter who asks you, you must never directly fight Sebastian. You may help peripherally, but you cannot be part of the main battle. If you ignore this, all will be lost. All your effort, all your loved ones, all that you care about will be lost. Do you understand?"

Gings said, "I understand, but how will I know? And does that mean we can never rescue Ozma?"

Glinda said, "I don't know. You will have to remember and decide. And yes, we can never rescue Ozma. Others must bear that burden."

Gings said, "I don't like it. I don't like it at all. But I understand."

When I awoke one of the Scarecrow's attendants ushered me to breakfast. The Scarecrow, the Tin Man, Gings, and Ralph were all waiting for me.

"Good morning, sleepy head," the Tin Man said.

"Good morning," I said. "I guess I needed to catch up on some sleep."

Gings spoke. "Our agents say that Sebastian is greatly diminished, thanks to all the troubles meted out to him. You should be safe from him today, but do not go off and start any wars. You may also want to keep on the ground."

"Okay," I said. "My broom is destroyed, so ground travel sounds good."

Gings continued. "I will be preparing the necessary mixtures to send you both home. Also I have sent agents out to try and retrieve your lost nav ball."

"Yeah, sorry about that," I said.

"You can use the fusion cycle," the Scarecrow said. "It would be a good test of it and you will be able to go wherever you wish."

"Sounds good to me," Ralph said with glee. "Can I drive it?"

I shook my head yes and the Scarecrow agreed. In short order we were heading to Dr. Ulam, Ralph driving and me pointing directions. As we got there Ralph killed the power. The lag was still there; we had to circle the office once waiting for the cycle to stop.

It was early, before Dr. Ulam's office hours, but we were here already so I knocked on his door. I heard some shuffling inside and then I heard the door creak open.

"Emily," Dr. Ulam said with a yawn, "I hope you are well."

"I am, thank you. Dr. Ulam. My friend Ralph here needs your attention. He has trouble breathing."

Ralph didn't say a thing which is very unlike him. Perhaps it was Dr. Ulam's green with pink polka dotted pajamas.

"Come in, come in," Dr. Ulam said. "Give me a bit to get dressed and I will be happy to examine you, young man."

A short while later the doctor returned, this time wearing a green with pink polka dotted lab coat. "Please come forward and let me have a look at you." The doctor examined Ralph's nose squeezing it and pushing it side to side, sticking something up it and looking in.

"Yes, you have taken some damage to your nose and the healing has not progressed well. But before I address your nose I need to run a full diagnostic test. Young man if you would please step to that marker on the floor and face this way."

Ralph stepped to the marker and turned this way. Dr. Ulam handed me the diagnostic darts. "Please hold these as I prepare."

"What are you going to do with those darts?" Ralph asked.

"After I am blindfolded and properly spun about I will throw them at you."

Ralph jumped from the mark. "No you won't. They're sharp as knives. I'd rather sniffle then bleed all over."

"Do not fear Ralph. These are magic diagnostic darts. They will pass through you without causing any harm. They tell me where attention is needed."

"But you already know it's my nose. Just fix my nose."

"I need a full diagnostic test. Emily, please explain this to your friend."

"Ralph, they're magic. You won't feel any pain at all. Dr. Ulam did it to me to help me with an inner ear problem. They pass through without any pain."

"Yes," the doctor said. "Please cooperate. I will best be able to help you when I have the complete results."

"Okay," Ralph said quietly and slowly.

Dr. Ulam blindfolded himself and then spun himself around so much he could barely stand. I helped him to his marker and aimed him in the right direction. "The darts please, Emily," he said.

"You're sure about this?" Ralph whimpered.

"Yes," the doctor said. "Please show some courage."

Ralph calmed himself. "Okay, I am ready."

Dr. Ulam threw the darts.

We all looked at the display. The darts had landed in the same place, above Ralph's left eye.

"Young man, you have a serious brain ailment that is far more dangerous than your difficult breathing. You are lucky to be alive."

"Perhaps your mom did drop you on your head, and you just don't remember it?" I quipped.

"Emily, this is serious. Don't be glib," the doctor said.

"I am sorry, Ralph," I said.

"Oh no," Ralph said. "I am going to die like my uncle George. I never met him, he died before I was born when he was young. He was my dad's older brother, and a good student and athlete. They say his teacher thought he had fallen asleep at his desk. But that was it, he never moved again, a brain aneurism. One day he was fine and the next he was …" Ralph's voice trailed off.

"You are lucky you came to see me. We can get you fixed up as good as sunshine."

"But my dad told me that it couldn't be fixed."

"It is extremely rare, and often not diagnosed early enough. But with the diagnostic darts this is no longer a problem. I am sure my friends the vein otters will help us. I believe they will be happy to assist."

"Vein otters?" Ralph asked.

"Of course. The vein otters swing through your circulatory system removing blockages where they don't belong and patching up damaged areas."

"Emily, vein otters?"

"I had ants put into my ears and it worked out great."

"Come to the microscope and see for yourself," Dr. Ulam said motioning to us.

We stepped over. Ralph looked in and then I did. There were tiny otters swimming around. When they noticed me watching they all turned and waved.

Dr. Ulam took some water that looked like pond scum and scooped it into a capsule.

"Sit down over hear Ralph and swallow this."

Ralph sat down. He looked at the capsule and then swallowed it with a gulp.

"What's going to happen?" Ralph asked.

"We wait for the vein otters," Dr. Ulam replied.

Nothing happened for what seemed a long time. Then Ralph began to itch his head behind his left eye.

"They're crawling around in my head?" Ralph asked.

"Swimming actually," the doctor replied.

Ralph stopped itching his head. A moment later he took a deep breath.

"Wow, they must have fixed my nose. I can finally breathe again. Hey, now that they are done, how do they get out of my body?"

"I was going to mention that. The bathroom is over there," the doctor said pointing to a door. "Please urinate in this container."

The doctor handed the container to Ralph. Ralph took the container. Ralph's expression changed abruptly and he bolted to the bathroom.

"When they're done they don't like to stick around," the doctor said to me.

Ralph returned holding the container.

"You're as good as new. In your case, even better than new," the doctor said as he took the container of urine from Ralph.

"Thank you!" Ralph said as he gave the doctor a hug.

"Careful, Ralph. I don't want to spill my specialists."

Chapter 29 Dead

We said our goodbyes to Dr. Ulam and took the fusion cycle back to the Emerald City. This time Emily drove. I figured we were about halfway back to the Emerald City when the fusion cycle started to coast. It picked up again and then finally it coasted to a stop.

"Ralph, I don't know what's wrong with the fusion cycle," Emily said. "We are still a long way from the Emerald City and I am broomless."

We got off and began to look at it. It looked similar in many ways to a motorcycle. But in many ways, it was as different as it could be.

"How's it work?" I asked.

"I'll give you what I remember from the Scarecrow's tutorial," Emily said. "It fuses two metals to make heat. The heat makes steam. The steam drives a turbine. He said the limiting factor would be running out of water."

We looked the cycle over. We found the water reservoir and there was plenty of water in it.

"The Scarecrow said that the fusion would work for centuries, so it shouldn't be that," Emily said.

We went back to exploring the cycle. There was a vent that was releasing a small amount of steam. And there was another tiny horizontal tube that looked like it was plugged up.

"What's this?" I asked.

"That must be where the waste gold is disposed of," Emily said.

"Waste gold? How do I get some?" I asked.

"You don't, Ralph. You can't bring anything from Oz home with you. It's the only way to make sure you don't get pulled back to Oz."

"Too bad," I said. "Some gold would really help my family. Last year my dad got hurt and couldn't work for a while. Things got really tight. I wanted to find a job, but my mom wouldn't let me. 'Your job is to concentrate on school,' she said, but it's hard to concentrate on school when you're worried about your parents. My mom was working all the time, and my dad was stuck at home, his leg in a cast, with nothing to do. And you could tell he was just so sad. He would do anything for his family, and he could do nothing."

"I'm sorry," Emily said. "I didn't realize."

"It's not the kind of thing you talk about, you know? Things are better now, or at least they are getting better. But when everything is going good you think, wow, I'm so smart, so talented, and so strong. You don't realize you're also lucky. Just plain lucky. When thing go wrong you learn a painful lesson."

I found a small stone nearby and gave the tube a few sharp raps. A few fine grains of gold sand, more like coarse gold flour, fell to the ground. I blew into the tube and a bit of gold dust flew into my face. I brushed it off.

"Let's try it again," I said.

We got on and it seemed okay.

"I'll have to tell the Scarecrow he needs to look at the gold disposal system," Emily said.

When we finally returned to the Emerald City Emily gave me a short tour of the grounds around the palace. I've really never been anywhere besides around my home. I saw some pretty amazing things during our walk.

We stopped by some pools that were near the palace and some children came up to greet Emily. There was a man wearing an ornate naval uniform floating some models of old fashioned sailing ships. When he saw us approach he retrieved his ships and left.

After the tour we went into the palace's main cafeteria. We sat down with some of Emily's young witch friends. They were particularly interested in my and Tips battle with Sebastian. Time flew by and pretty much everyone left. We went to visit the Scarecrow in his meeting room. We sat for a short time waiting for him to enter.

"Sorry for the wait," the Scarecrow said. "The duties of office, you understand."

Emily cleared her throat. "It's time I destroyed the Golden Cap," she said. "How long should a people be punished for the foolish behavior of a few?"

"What is the plan?" the Scarecrow asked. "We have tried to burn it and to smash it. It is protected by a powerful enchantment. Gayelette was a formidable sorceress."

"I've got the solution to that," Emily said. "We need a large open place to do it in."

"I suggest the Central Amphitheater," the Scarecrow replied.

The Scarecrow led the way. Emily and I followed. Emily seemed comfortable with the strangeness of Oz, but I was not, and I wanted to get out of Oz. Even with a bloody nose, I preferred school.

Something glinted off in the distance. "What's that?" I asked.

"When the wizard built the new palace, there were a lot of extra cut emeralds left over. He had them piled in a big mound. The children call it Emerald Mountain and they slide down it on gliders," the Scarecrow said.

"Amazing," I said. "You toss away gold and have mountains of cut emeralds. And I can't borrow even a few."

"Not if you don't plan on returning," Emily said. "Sebastian would love to see you again."

"I'm sure he would," I said. "But it would still be nice to have some."

We arrived at the amphitheater. It was built along the side of a hill, so that benches were placed on steps cut from the earth. The seats looked upon a large flat center area, which was floored in white marble. The stage area was surrounded on all sides but the front by large columns. The columns supported an arched roof that shaded the stage. There was a large tables toward the center back and a few chairs nearby. The Scarecrow led us to the table.

"This is fine," Emily said. "This should suit the Flyers well."

"Must you call them?" the Scarecrow asked. "They are dangerous."

"Yes, I must," Emily said. "I have pledge to destroy the Golden Cap and I want the Flyers, particularly one Flyer, to witness it." Emily put the Golden Cap on her head and did some goofy little dance while she said some weird sounds.

After a short wait, I could see something approaching from the sky. As it got closer I could make out that a group of Flyers were carrying something large, and there were three other Flyers. When they landed, I could see that six Flyers were carrying something that had a throne upon which a large Flyer sat. The separate Flyers all carried wooden chests.

"You have called, and we have come. We are bound to fulfill your wish," the one seated on the palanquin said in a tone of disdainful boredom.

"I need you to bring a hammer, a large hammer, to break the golden band of the Golden Cap, and to build a fire to burn the cloth part of the cap," Emily said.

"None of this will work. You are wasting our time. The Golden Cap is protected from all physical attacks. It cannot be broken, it cannot be burnt, it cannot be melted, it cannot be ground away or chipped," the Flyer said.

"Veeron, this is my wish," Emily said.

"And so it will be fulfilled. It is your second wish, foolish though it is."

Veeron order three Flyers to fulfill the request. Shortly a fire was ablaze and a large hammer was placed on the table.

Emily took the Golden Cap off her head and placed it on the table. She drew out Glinda's sword and lightly tapped the Golden Cap with the side of its blade.

"Now, the protection is lifted." Emily said. "Break the Golden Cap and be freed from it curse."

Veeron walked forward. The six Flyers who had carried the palanquin stepped forward as well.

Pointing at one of his attendants, Veeron commanded, "Smash the golden band."

His attendant took the hammer from the table and smashed the golden band and replaced the hammer on the table.

Veeron said to another attendant, "Burn its remains."

The attendant took the cloth part of the cap and tossed it into the fire. The cloth burst into a high flame, sending sparks high into the air.

"I have promised and I have fulfilled that promise. You are freed from the curse of the Golden Cap," Emily said. She turned to the table and placed Glinda's sword down next to the hammer.

In an instant Veeron had grabbed the sword. He stabbed Emily deep in her back. The sound of the sword cutting through flesh, and hitting bone seemed to scream out against a backdrop of absolute silence. Veeron pulled back on the sword, but it was so deep in Emily that it partly lifted her off the table, so he used his other hand to hold her down, and yanked the sword free. A second time, he stabbed her. The sound of the blade rang out once more. And again, he wrenched the blade out, and stabbed with all his might. Emily lay face down against the table, with her mouth open, and blood trickling out. Veeron ripped the sword free once more and jumped to the air. I was frozen in horror.

"Thank you, Emily, for breaking the curse. Now that I am free and have Glinda's sword, I will punish you dust eaters in ways you cannot conceive. The Emerald City will be free of filthy dust eaters. You will pray for your death, beg to be killed, plead for a fast ending rather than the suffering I plan to inflict on you. You will say, 'Emily got off easy, only stabbed to death.'

"But first I must attend to the Nomes. I will not be subservient to the Nome King any longer. No longer will Flyers serve the Nomes and toil in their mines. I will rain pain and suffering down upon the Nomes light the storms of Minlee. Poems and books will be written of their suffering." Veeron yelled.

"Take him," he commanded his attendants, who charged at me and grabbed my arms and legs. I struggled to free myself, but these Flyers, even though they are small, are surprisingly strong. I fought to free myself. I continued my struggle and in only a few breaths I could feel their grip begin to ease. They seemed to tire. I pulled my right arm free of all but one Flyer. I bashed those on my left arm flat with my right arm, though it still had a Flyer hanging on. Then I bashed that Flyer good. Two Flyers fell on the floor and the rest flittered from me.

"Yes, the Nomes. Our friends? No, not at all. Merely a stone for me to step on during my path to ascendancy. Now I will revenge us upon there flesh."

Veeron cleared his throat, as if to speak again. Then silence, a vast silence. The silence was broken by a drop. A single drop of blood. A single drop of blood the hit the white marble floor. It was followed by a second. And a third, forming a small puddle. Veeron let out a gasping cough and dropped Glinda's sword, which clattered to the floor. He started to fall from the air and tried to flap his wings but they did not seem to work. He dropped to the floor. His wings and his limbs twitched about as he lay on the floor.

Veeron stopped moving. He lay still struggling to breathe. One of Veeron's attendants rushed forward. He pulled out a knife and ended Veeron's life. "Now, he is dead and I will take his place," the attendant said.

One of those who had carried a wooden chest leapt forward and grabbed Glinda's sword. She came at Emily and I grabbed a hammer from the table. But instead of attacking Emily, the Flyer turned, holding the sword as to fight off the other Flyers.

Another Flyer immediately leaped into the air and flew off. The remaining Flyers fell upon each other. They pulled knives from hidden places in their clothing and attacked each other. The two Flyers I had knocked down were killed where they lay. Another came at Emily and I clubbed him. He fell to the floor. Then he staggered his way to standing, looked at me once, and flew off. Two other Flyers lay motionless on the cold white marble, in pools of blood. Two more Flyers took to the air. One of them fell back to the floor, and lay silently.

The Flyer next to me, seeing that all the other Flyers had left or were motionless, turned to Emily. She placed Glinda's sword down beside Emily's body.

"Emily, trying to save everyone, even those who hate you. Fulfilling a gargantuan promise, and dying for your kindness. You saved, but when you needed us, where were we? Too distant, too full of hatred, to help. Your life, so dear a thing, paid to free people who hate you," the Flyer said. "And now you lay here, silent, growing cold, your life consumed.

"Emily, so different from me, yet we could have been friends. And now all I can be for you is a pallbearer."

Emily made a slight coughing sound. We all stared. She moved her hand to her head. Then she slowly pushed herself off of the table and stumbled. I grabbed her arm and helped her into a chair.

"Oh my head is pounding. And, and I can't see. Ralph, what has happened? What has happened to me?"

"There was a fight," I said.

"Are you okay?" Emily asked.

"Yes, I am fine," I replied. "But how are you?"

"My head is pounding. My vision, my vision, I can see some light. And some dark. I need to rest. But first, Scarecrow, how are you?"

"I am fine," the Scarecrow replied in a soft voice.

Emily sat silently with her eyes closed. And then she stared at her hands. She looked around and asked, "Why are all these Flyers on the floor?"

"They killed each other. After Veeron died the fought each other," I said.

"Once Veeron died, the way was free for his underlings to try to take power," the Flyer said.

"Is that you Hypatia?" Emily asked.

"Yes, I am here".

Emily held the sides of the chair and pushed herself to her feet, looking at the blood and the bodies on the floor. She swayed and I was scared she would fall, but she stood firm.

"I don't see Archimedes," Emily said. "Is he safe?"

"Yes," Hypatia replied. "As soon as Veeron fell he flew off. I never could understand him, but I never placed him as a coward."

"I would not assume he is a coward just yet," Emily said. Once more Emily looked over the bodies of Flyers, the puddles of blood, the empty throne on the palanquin, the wooden chests, the fire burning down, and the pieces of the band from the Golden Cap.

"Oh my. What are we to do with all these dead?" Emily asked.

"I cannot help you with this. I leave now. Without Veeron there will be a battle for power. And it is now clear why Flyers work the mines: There must have been

361

some corrupt arrangement between the Nome King and Veeron. I must leave to protect whatever I may. You will have to do what you must. Whatever you decide will do," Hypatia said as she hurled herself into the air and flew off.

"Ralph, are you okay?" Emily asked me once again.

"I am fine, not even a scratch" I said. "Even my nose is okay. And you? You looked like you were dead just a moment ago. How is your vision?"

"Besides a pounding head, I seem fine," Emily said. "My vision has fully returned."

"You have three cuts in your dress, you know," I said.

"Three cuts?"

"Where Veeron stabbed you."

Emily was silent.

"Where Veeron stabbed me?"

"After Veeron saw that the Golden Cap was destroyed he grabbed Glinda's sword and stabbed you. You looked dead."

"Well, I am not," Emily said. "And I am thankful for it."

The Scarecrow, who had been standing in silence through all the madness spoke. "Emily, I will see that this is taken care of. We need to get you and Ralph safely into the castle. We have all had enough excitement for today."

We walked back to the castle and to the Scarecrow's meeting room. After a short while we were ushered into an adjacent room. We had a quiet meal. Emily and I were given robes and slippers to change into so that our clothes might be repaired. The royal tailor shook his head as he saw our clothes.

"'First, I don't want anything besides what you are wearing. If you give anything else to me, it will go in the garbage.'"

I took my wallet from my pants. Emily took her stuff and strapped Glinda's Sword over her robe.

"You both are extremely hard on your clothes. Were you in a war that I didn't hear about? And I am given the impossible task to fix them without making any changes. 'Fix them but don't change them.' How do you do that? I cannot even fix the obvious errors in construction and poor fit. I will do my best. That is all I can say." He left still shaking his head and muttering.

"Ralph and Emily, I will now lead you to your rooms for the night," the Scarecrow said. I joked to Emily, "Emily, Warrior Princess."

She pulled Glinda's Sword and did some fighting poses along with some goofy expressions. Then she stopped.

"And what will prevent Sebastian from —?" Emily asked.

"We are adding special security measures which I dare not say lest they be compromised," the Scarecrow said.

"And is Gings involved?" Emily asked.

"No," the Scarecrow replied. "She is preparing to send you home. For you to be safe, your memories of everything in Oz must be removed. She is making the forgetting powder."

Emily was shown to her room and then I was led to my room, just a few steps further down the hall.

I thought about my time in Oz. Many terrible and some wonderful things have happened to me while I have been in Oz. I will remember none of it, not the bad, and not the good. I will not die of a brain aneurism, and I won't even know it was a possibility.

When I was a small child, I would say prayers each night before I went to sleep. It had been a long time since I said night time prayers. But that night I did.

Chapter 30 Forgetting Powder

A knock on my room door woke me up. I pulled myself out of bed and went to the door hoping I wasn't going to get an unwanted surprise. I opened the door and Nadia was standing there, holding the clothes I came to Oz in.

"Good morning Nadia," I said.

"Good morning Emily," she replied. "I am glad that you are healthy, and considering what I have heard you've been up to, is something to celebrate."

"Yes. Yesterday is a day I won't mind forgetting," I said.

"Here are your clothes. I will wait here and then escort you to the Scarecrow's ready room."

I took them in and closed the door. I looked over my dress. I could make out the very finest stitch work concealing three slits. Some things are best forgotten.

I got dressed. I put my change purse and the packet of sugar from lunch (this all started at lunch!) into my pockets. I put Glinda's sword on. And so my final goodbye to Oz drew near.

I opened the door. "Ready," I said.

"First stop, we need to secure Glinda's sword. Follow me."

I followed Nadia as we walked through the palace. Without breaking her brisk stride she said, "We are having difficulty finding your nav ball, in part because we believe it had been bricked before being lost."

"Yeah," I said. "I forgot to mention that."

"You have a rare talent there," Nadia said.

"Yup," I said. "I can be hard on things."

We wound our way through. Last time, it was Gings who brought me. We went to the same place.

"Please place the sword inside this container," Nadia said.

I did, and the sword was sealed in, locked in, and magiced in.

"Another link to Oz broken," I thought.

We walked to the Scarecrow's ready room.

Ralph was already there, talking to the Tin Man.

The Tin Man came over, smiling as usual.

"Emily, great morning to you," he said. I gave him a hug. I will miss him. And I will miss my memories of him.

"Tin Man, I am so glad you came. I didn't want to leave Oz and not see you. I do hope you have been good."

"Indeed I have," he said. "I was off venturing but I came back as soon as I heard you were here."

Some food was brought in for Ralph and me. I got the impression that everyone else had started the meeting long before. The Scarecrow went over the plan. We would be going by land en masse to Gings' home. I had noticed that Nadia had worn protective guards. Now it made sense. An attack by Sebastian was expected.

The Scarecrow gave a signal and we all moved to the palace's main entrance. All the doors were open and a wide carpet extended from outside to well inside. We all assembled on the carpet. At the far end of the carpet I could see Orlanda and Ungeira, followed by four towering elephants. Then a contingent of Glinda's Guard stood at the ready, each one covered from head to foot in armor that vanished them into invisibility when they stood still, so that only their eyes floating above the ground could be seen. The Scarecrow and the Tin Man came next atop the fusion cycle.

An old sorcerer came over. "Emily and Ralph, you will be enclosed in a protective cocoon for this trip. Are you ready?"

We nodded yes. I took a deep breath and swallowed hard. He cast his spell and I was enclosed by a thick pliable bubble. I stretched my arms out and pushed the wall. I could just barely make out anything on the outside. It was like fogged glass, so I can only imagine what the rest of the procession consisted of. My bubble bobbed above the carpet.

The procession started. We moved slowly forward. By looking down I could just make out that we were always over the carpet.

I couldn't tell what was going on, and I couldn't tell how much time had passed, but suddenly my head began to burst and I slumped to the bottom of my bubble. In my head I heard Sebastian say, "Emily, I'm coming for you. Soon you will be mine." A racking pain burst across my body. I became so angry, so angry. I wanted to strike back at Sebastian, hurt him the way he was hurting me.

And then I had a dream, if dream it was. I saw Glinda talking to a young Gings. Glinda said, "Gingold, because of what Sebastian has done to you, I must give you the tools to fight him off. He will likely test you again, and you need to be able to defend yourself."

Gings replied in a tentative voice, "I understand." She was so young.

"Gings, I am going to touch you and demonstrate what Sebastian will try to do. It will be painful. But it is the only way you can prepare for a real attack."

Gings replied again, "I understand." She was looking at her shoes.

Gings screamed, "Stop it. Please, please stop!"

Glinda asked, "Gings, beyond the pain, what did you feel?"

"I was angry. Angry. I wanted to strike you back, hit you, make you hurt," Gings said.

Glinda spoke. "Here is the choice you must make. You can strike back, and cause the attacker pain. But by doing so you strengthen the link between you and your attacker, and by strengthening the link, you allow them to hurt you further, and in more substantial ways. Or you can accept the pain. Accept the pain and not respond. By not responding you prevent the true danger of this type of attack. It is a tough choice, one your ego will tell you is weak, a mistake, and will fail. Do you understand?"

"Do you mean I must allow myself to be in pain and not do anything to stop it?"

"If you want to be safe, yes. If you do not respond, you will be safe, and your attacker will in time wear themselves out and stop. It will be painful, at least at first. If you can be calm, and not respond, you will see that the pain is just a mirage, make believe, imaginary, and cannot hurt you."

"Okay," Gings said.

"If you fight back, if you respond, you open yourself up to attacks that are truly dangerous. You will tire from the fight and you will be lost."

"What do you mean, be lost?" Gings asked.

"It is very bad," Glinda said. "You are too young to know of such things."

The sat in silence.

Glinda said, "So, you have a choice, you can react and fight back, which will give you a short break from the pain, but a truly terrible outcome, or you can be calm."

"I think I understand," Gings said.

"Gings, this is a bit like tic-tac-toe. If you play properly, you never lose, no matter if you go first or second. If you make a mistake, you can lose. But only by making a mistake. If you are attacked like this, fighting back is the mistake, and if you do, you will lose, and you will be lost."

The dream faded. I was back in my body, and my body was crushed in pain. I so wanted to fight back, I so wanted to strike out at Sebastian, to make him hurt and suffer.

As the pain continued, and it did continue without pause or relief, I found I could tolerate it more. I could experience the pain, but not suffer from it. I could watch what was happening without participating. In time the pain diminished. Perhaps Sebastian was growing bored. I decided to give him a taste of his own medicine and struck back at him hard.

He responded. The pain I felt before was trivial compared to this new attack. I fought down the urge to continue. I recaptured my composure. I would not try that again. But the pain abated quickly. I stood up in my bubble. No one apparently noticed the battle I had fought right in their midst. I wasn't sure when it actually ended because I had learned to ignore it.

We continued on and in time we came to a halt. Perhaps there would be no physical attack from Sebastian. The old sorcerer brought Ralph and I, in our cocoons, to Gings' front door. The sorcerer opened the door and our cocoons squirmed their way in, contorting so that they could fit through. The sorcerer made another incantation and Ralph and I were free.

"Gings, I leave these two in your care," he said. He turned to us and said, "May you be safely returned to wherever you call home." He stepped out and closed the door.

Gings quickly ushered us in and let us to her lab room. We stood around a heavy wooden table that had various pieces of equipment scattered on it. Things you might expect in someone's laboratory. She had some powder that she was crushing in a mortar and pestle.

"The powder is almost complete," Gings said. "Just a bit more crushing is required." She continued working the pestle around the bowl, meticulously crushing and turning the bowl.

"Done," she said. She measured out the powder into two identical small envelopes and handed one to each of us. "Here is the forgetting powder." "You need to take the powder, all of it, to forget Oz. This is the only way I can see that you will stop being drawn back into Oz. Take a glass of water, stir in all the powder, and drink it down. I will give time for it to take effect and then send you back. You will need to concentrate on where you came from."

"Okay," Ralph said. "I am happy to forget this crazy place and never come back."

"Okay," I said. I needed a few seconds so I asked, "Gings, why do we fly on brooms?"

"We fly on brooms because the first witch decided she would try flying on a broom. I am thankful that she didn't decide on a canoe, though flying might be a bit safer had she."

"You mean it really doesn't matter what you use?"

"It doesn't, but you can't have any doubt. Any doubt and you fall out of the sky. And since people are accustomed to seeing witches on brooms they have no doubt, and it's easier to have no doubt among people who support your beliefs. If you can have no doubt you can fly on anything, or nothing."

Ralph interrupted. "You mean you could fly on a bicycle? Or a motorcycle? Or a surfboard? That would be cool, flying on a surfboard."

"Yes, anything, or nothing. I've seen witches that prefer umbrellas, and some that prefer carpets. It's just a matter of having no doubt, which sounds simple. You can't require your attention to maintain your belief. If your attention is broken, and you have subconscious doubt, you can fall. Glinda was great at flying in new ways. Sometimes she would fly inside a bubble. Landing in a bubble makes for a great entrance. There would be lines of people staring at her with their mouths open. For less experienced witches a broom is safer. 'Want to zoom, take a broom' is a good motto."

"Thanks," I said. I was as ready as I could be.

We heard some commotion outside. Gings made a gesture she tried to conceal, and all the sounds from outside ceased. She tried to hide her expression as well, but I could see she was concerned.

Just then something fell in another room and Gings went to investigate. "Stay here and wait," she yelled as she left.

"Strange," she said as she returned. "A picture fell off the wall, and nothing else. I will have to fix it after you are gone. Bring up and image of where you were just prior to coming to Oz. Do you have the image in your mind?"

"Yes," I said. "I have an image of the nurse's room in school." Ralph nodded his head.

Gings continued, "Pour the powder in and give it a stir."

Ralph and I did as told.

"Drink the potion down in one breath."

Ralph and I did as told. Mine tasted a bit too sweet for my liking. The glasses vanished.

"Now, we hold hands."

Gings, Ralph, and I formed a ring holding hands.

"Hold the image in your mind," Gings said.

I imagined the nurse's office. Gings counted out loud. I grabbed tight to Ralph's hand so he wouldn't fall down on the other side.

Ralph and I were back. Ralph stood in silence for a second swaying a bit. Then he blinked his eyes open and sat down on one of the chairs.

"Ralph, can I have the thing I gave you to hold for me? It's in your wallet. It looks like a postage stamp."

"I don't remember that. Are you trying to pull something on me?"

"If you don't believe me just look in your wallet." He did and there it was. He handed it to me.

"I don't remember you giving that thing to me but I plan to remember to keep away from your fist."

The nurse walked back into the room. "Ralph, what happened to the bandage I put on your nose. Why did you take it off?" she asked. "Come over here. I will have to bandage you again."

Ralph walked over to the nurse.

"Are you playing a game with me? Your nose is fine."

"No ma'am," he said. "My nose was bleeding. I guess it healed itself."

"No one heals that fast Ralph. Come with me."

"Emily, don't you move a muscle," she shouted back at me as she left the room. I wasn't planning on being anywhere else.

Ralph and the school nurse returned. She gave us back our phone. She looked at me suspiciously. "Emily, walk over her," she said. "Turn around." She looked at the back of my dress. "Okay, I've got both of you hooligan's numbers. I'll be watching you. Don't try this stunt again."

Ralph and I waited in silence. My mother called me. "Emily, I don't know what is going on in your school but I just got a call telling me not to come in. Evidently everything healed itself, which I don't believe. But whatever happened, there is no plan by the school to discipline you. Don't think that I am happy. You are not to hit anyone, you understand?"

"Yes mom, I understand," I said. "I will not hit anyone else."

"Don't be funny. That's not good enough. You are not to hit anyone and that includes Ralph."

"Yes, that's what I meant. I will not hit anyone," I said.

"Okay," she said. "I will speak to you more about this when I get home from work."

The room phone rang. The nurse answered it and after a few uh-huhs and yeses she hung up. "Okay, she said with an icy tone as she opened the door, "Get out of my sight."

The rest of school passed in a daze. It was hard to concentrate and I kept drifting away in thought. When school was out I walked home. I usually walk home with my friends but I told them I needed to talk to one of the teachers so I could walk home alone.

When I got home my mom was waiting for me. "I want to hear everything in detail but hold it until your father gets here. I don't want to have two performances." She did not sound happy.

I went into my room and plopped my backpack on the floor. Then I took a shower and changed my clothes. I hid all the stuff in the back of my closet. When I get a chance I will wash the clothes myself, in secret, and keep my mom away from them. I don't want her to get pulled into Oz.

What day was it? Oh yeah, Monday, still Monday. I had some homework due tomorrow, even though it seemed so far away. After I started working on it everything fell back to normal. Normal, as long as I didn't think about what happened.

I heard my dad's car pull into the driveway.

"Tell me what happened and don't leave anything out," he said. My mom stood by with a stern look on her face.

I told them what happened, but I left plenty out. When they were satisfied with the story my mom said, "You know better than this Emily."

"I know," I said, though I am still not sure I would do anything different if it happened again. But perhaps, I could change something. I am not sure what. Anyway, smoothing things over and agreeing was better than fighting about things that might happen in the future.

My dad said, "Don't go beating on people, but I don't want any of my children to be punching bags either. Use judgement. Better judgement. Things may not always be obvious, that's why you need to think."

When my dad was a child he lived in a tough neighborhood. My dad and my mom don't always agree on everything. The need to defend yourself is one of those things.

After a long pause he began again. "We are going to visit your Aunt Maybel today for her birthday. So make sure you are ready at 5:30PM so we can leave on time. We are meeting her at her favorite restaurant."

"Okay," I said. I walked back to my room.

Just then Jacob ran into my room. He was breathing hard.

"Hey, I almost forgot to tell you about the excitement at school," he shouted. "You remember that dog that was walking with us to school?" My parents showed up just outside my door.

"Yeah," I said. "Big and a bit scary."

Emily of Oz

"Yeah that one. Well when we were outside during recess the dog attacked this old guy that was walking past the school. Turns out he wasn't an old guy but some criminal dressed up like one. When the dog attacked him he took off running. The dog dragged him down. It was right in front of all of us at recess. Then they cancelled recess and called us all back into school. I heard the sirens. This guy is someone the police have been looking for, hiding right here, right near the school."

"Jacob, did you see this man before?" My mom asked.

"Yeah, I've seen him. I've seen him walking near the school. Sometimes around recess and sometimes around dismissal. Everyone just thought he lived nearby and like to go for walks."

"And Emily, what about this dog?"

"When Jacob and I walked to school this morning this big dog joined us. At first I was scared but the dog seemed to be watching for something, if you can believe that. Anyway, he left us alone."

"Oh, yeah," Jacob added. "I heard that they tried to catch the dog but he got away. Pretty smart dog I would say."

"So this scary dog that attacks people is still free?" my mom asked.

"I'll drive the children to school for now," my dad added. "We can talk to Sam and Eva to see if they can drive the other way."

"Let me give them a call," my mom said. She picked up her phone. After a few minutes she said, "All set up. You drop off and they will pick up."

"Today has been exciting, too exciting for me," my dad said. "I am glad we are all home and safe." With that everyone dispersed, but I agreed silently. It is good to be home and safe.

Chapter 31 Aunt Maybel's Distress

We all file into my dad's car and take our prescribed positions. My dad's car reflects him well; functional, moderate, and solid. He's really a great guy and I'm lucky to have him as a dad. The only complaint I could have, and it is minor, is that sometimes you want a bit of information and you get a ton. It's like needing a glass of water and getting a bathtub full. Minor, right? And he is a teacher after all.

My mother is the person who says what needs to be said. If you are trying to avoid the elephant in the room, she will paint it green and add pink polka dots, like Dr. Ulam's pajamas. She is disciplined and industrious. Only a fool would bet against her when she decides to do something. I'm lucky to have her as well.

Together they make a formidable team. But today they are worried. Aunt Maybel is troubled. They have no idea what the cause might be, but I do. It all began after my last visit to her. I don't think that's a coincidence.

We head off to the Tarot Card. The Tarot Card is Aunt Maybel's favorite restaurant. The decorations are tarot card kitsch; cards of all sizes are hung everywhere. They decorate the walls. They hang from strings. The tables have cards scattered all about all sealed over in a clear coating. They have those paper placemats like other restaurants, but in the Tarot Card, in the middle of all the advertisements and puzzles is a single tarot card. I don't know how they do it but each seat gets a different card. The food is a mix of Southern, American, Chinese, and Cuban, so you have a lot of choices, and some of the fusion cooking can be surprising. Which is polite for strange.

Aunt Maybel makes a big deal about birthdays at the antique store, but that happens during the day with her staff. Then she gets together with her close family, which is just my dad, mom, Jacob, and me. She also goes out with her friends, but that she does separately, and doesn't include us.

As we walk in, we spot her sitting on a bench waiting for us. She doesn't notice us. She is wearing a troubled expression.

"Hey, Aunt Maybel," I say.

"Hey Emily," she says coming back from wherever she was. She replaces her troubled expression with a smile. I can tell it's for our sake.

After hugs and kisses we head to our table. We get there just as the utensils and placemats are put down.

Aunt Maybel is usually one of those people who just fizz, you know what I mean? She fills a room, attracts everyone's attention, is the center of the conversation, and always is laughing or joking. But she is quiet today. She's not herself.

We order.

Aunt Maybel gets up. "I need to go to the bathroom. I'll be back in a jiffy," she says. I watch her as she walks off.

After a few minutes she returns. We have some stilted conversation. Then Aunt Maybel excuses herself to go to the bathroom once more.

We are quiet. My tarot card is the hierophant. I notice that Aunt Maybel's tarot card is the tower. After a minute I get up. "I'm going to see if I can find out what's up with Aunt Maybel," and I leave for the bathroom.

She is half sitting against one wall, with her head in her hands.

"Aunt Maybel, is everything okay?"

"Oh, it's you Emily." She stands up and stretches. She tries to smile. "I hear you had some excitement at school."

"Yeah, I hit someone."

"I heard," she said. "Did it do what you wanted?"

"It stopped me from getting poked, at least for now."

"Was being poked so bad that you couldn't do something else?"

"I was really angry. I guess I could have moved away from him easy enough."

"You know how I feel about fighting. I don't have a problem with punching someone who deserves it, and it sounds like he may have deserved it. But doing it in anger, that's a mistake. You can't think properly or pay attention when you are angry. And you don't want to be fighting someone when you're not present and thinking."

My dad taught me how to defend myself. Aunt Maybel taught me how to fight.

"I know," I said. "I try, but I still get angry."

"That's okay. Everything takes time. You will learn to control your temper."

"But how are you, Aunt Maybel?" I asked again. "Are you okay?"

She tried to smile once more. Then she looked at me and trouble returned to shroud her face. "No, things are not okay. My trip to Oz has knocked the links of my life apart. I can understand love, I can understand pain, I can understand loss, but I can't fit Oz in. There is just no room for it. But it won't go away. I don't know what to do."

"Before our trip to Oz, you told me that there would be a time that I would need courage."

"Yes. From what I heard, you got tested and you passed."

"This is a test for you. Do you trust me?"

"Sure, I trust you."

"When I said that I understood that I could need to have courage at any time, you said that it was because I hadn't really thought about it. At the time, I hadn't. But now I have to ask again, because I fear you haven't thought about it, do you trust me? Would you put your life in my hands?"

She looked at me. "Yes, I do."

"Then wait here for me. I need somethings. I'll be back in a minute. Please be patient."

I hurried back to the table. I picked up my glass of water.

"I'm helping Aunt Maybel. She'll be back soon."

"Can I help?" my mom asked.

"No, we are good."

I walked back to the bathroom. No one else had entered.

"I am going to help you forget Oz."

"You can do that?"

"I believe I can, but you need to trust me?"

"Yes, I already said I trust you."

"Okay." I took her hand in mine.

I thought of the dark halls of Glinda's castle, as they are today. I envisioned us being there, with the thin rays of light beaming through the broken shutters, and the closed dank smell of rotting cloth. And there we were.

"You're a witch. How did you learn to be a witch? Where are we?"

"We are in Glinda's castle. I don't want to stay here long, so I can't explain. Hold this glass of water."

I took Gings' forgetting powder from my pocket and poured it into the glass.

"I forgot a spoon to stir it."

"I'll use my finger," Aunt Maybel said as she stirred the powder in.

"Close your eyes and drink all of it."

My Aunt Maybel said, "You know that when I drink this you will be alone, by yourself, solitary in your memories of Oz."

"I know," I said. "I don't know why I was sent to Oz but I think only I was selected. And I will not be alone, I have many friends in Oz."

"Emily, you can always talk to me," Aunt Maybel said. "You will never be able to share fully, but I am always here for you."

"I know," I said. "I love you and appreciate you for it. But time is something we don't have to waste."

"Okay," she said. She drank the potion.

I counted time as I remembered Gings did when she sent Ralph and I back. I took the glass from Aunt

Maybel and held her hand. I imagined us back in the restaurant's bathroom. And in an instant we were there.

Aunt Maybel stood silently with her eyes closed. Then she opened her eyes.

"I must have drifted off. Anyway, you will figure out your temper in time."

She smiled. "It's my birthday. A day to celebrate. And I am here with my silly little Emily," she said as she gave me a squeeze. "Let's get back and see what the food looks like. I hope it's not too weird. And when are you coming to help me again? The antique store doesn't run properly without my best worker. The furniture asks why no one is climbing on it."

"Soon," I said. "I have a big school project, but I should get myself free soon."

"I will hold you to that," Aunt Maybel joked.

We walked back to the table and I hoped everything would work out. Jacob must have spilled his water because a waiter was busy wiping up a wet mess at Aunt Maybel's spot. Now her tarot card was justice.

"Everything okay?" My mother asked.

"It's my birthday," Aunt Maybel said. "Of course everything's good. Where's that food? I know it is international cuisine, but I didn't think they were going to have to import it."

Well, she seemed better. It was good to have her back. And it was good to be with my family, enjoying each other. Everyone was happy, the food was good. We were all safe

It was late by the time we got back so I got myself ready for bed. I snuggled down under my covers. The door opened and my mom came in.

"Emily," she said as she pulled over my desk chair and sat down. "Through all the things that happened today, I haven't really had a chance to talk to you. How are you?"

"I'm fine, mom. Better than fine. I'm really good."

"You are such a wonderful person, Emily. I hope you know that."

"Thanks, Mom." Now was as good a time as any to ask. "Mom, did you have any dreams?"

"Sure. But I don't usually remember them. When I do they can be really odd."

"That's not what I meant. I meant dreams like what you wanted to do, or who you wanted to be."

"When I was very young I wanted a beautiful voice like my mom, your grandmother."

"But, you do have a nice voice."

"I have a good voice, but even though I trained it was soon obvious that I would never have a great voice. Don't misunderstand me, the time I spent learning singing improved my voice a lot, but I could see it would be limited."

"I'm sorry you didn't get your dream."

"That was only my first dream. Then I dreamed that I wanted to learn interesting things, and get and education. And I got that dream."

"Oh," I said.

"And then I dreamed I would be able to go to college. And I got that dream too. And then I dreamed I wanted to be a mechanical engineer and design things that would help people. And again, I got that dream."

"I see," I said.

"And then I dreamed I would meet a nice young man who I could love forever and who would love me forever. And I met your dad."

"And then I dreamed that we would have a family, and I had a beautiful baby girl."

"Whose name is Emily," I said.

She kissed me on my forehead. "Yes, whose name is Emily. And then I dreamed I would have a beautiful baby boy."

"Whose name is Jacob," I said.

She kissed me once again. "Yes, whose name is Jacob. So you see, I have had all the best dreams I've dreamed come true. I have been so blessed."

"I love you, Mom," I said as she got up and walked to the door.

"I love you, Emily," she said. "Sweet dreams."

Epilogue   Super Hero

"Mom, what if you hurt someone, and you didn't mean too?"

"Emily, people sometimes do the wrong thing. They don't mean to hurt someone, but they don't understand what's going on and they do what they think is right, but it turns out to be wrong. It's always a shame, but people are not perfect. If you do something like that you should try to make it right. And if you can't make it right you can at least apologize. Did you do something like that?"

"Yes mom. I meant to help someone, but I hurt them instead."

"Did you try to make it right?"

"Yes, but I couldn't fully fix it."

"You tried and since we are talking about it you learned you need to be thoughtful. You're a good person Emily. But even the best people make mistakes."

"And do you think it's okay to kill someone who is evil?" I asked.

"Emily, why do you think such things?"

"I don't know, I just do. I mean, if there was someone who was evil, really evil, would it be okay to kill them? Someone so evil, so malicious, and it didn't look like he would ever be stopped? Like, if you had the chance to kill Hitler, would you take it?"

She just looked at me. "This is just hypothetical, correct?"

"Yes, purely hypothetical."

"I guess if there was no way they could be brought to justice, and they would continue to do unspeakable things, it would be okay. Perhaps even necessary. But this is the last thing anyone wants to happen. It means every norm, every bit of the fabric of society has been ripped and shredded."

"Thanks, Mom," I said.

"Emily, I worry about you. Sometimes you seem to carry the weight of the world on your shoulders and I don't know why. You are too young to be responsible for everyone's problems. You know you can always talk things over with me. Are things at school really that bad?"

"No, Mom. School is fine. I just want to make things clear for me."

"Clear, how does that make it clear?" she asked.

"It's clear that when someone is evil and no one else can do anything, and, I guess, society can't do anything, then it may fall on an individual to act."

"Please don't do anything rash, Emily. No more punched classmates. Are you and Ralph okay?"

"Yes, Ralph and I are fine," I said.

"Good," she said giving my shoulder a gentle squeeze. I turned to look at my brother who was sitting next to me on the picnic table.

"Jacob, can I have that piece of chicken?" I asked. He had lost interest in eating and I hadn't. I was still pretty hungry actually.

"Sure, Emily," he replied. He was watching the people riding horses off in the distance. Dad and mom had brought us to this ranch for a few days so we could vacation and get some horse rides. It's very nice here on this sunny warm day. I loved it here in the past, but my mind is somewhere else.

I turned to watch the line of riders slowly plodding along. The horses know the trail and they do their best to ignore the riders, who are bouncing up and down in the saddles. For some reason one particular small boy in the parade of riders caught my eyes. He bounced atop his horse as the riders began to approach where they were helped off. I got up and walked a few steps away from our table so I could follow him with my eyes.

My dad must have walked over to me. He startled me when he said, "You know, Emily, you still have time to get a ride. We paid for them whether you take them or not."

This was our last day here. After the big picnic there was only a few more hours of time, enough for a ride, pack up, and check out.

"No thanks, Dad. I guess I am not into horses right now. They are enormous beasts and they pretty much do what they want anyway."

"Okay Emily, you don't have to. It's your decision."

We watched the line for a few more seconds and then my dad sat down at the picnic table. I was just about to do the same when the little boy came to where he would be helped off. Something must have happened because the horse whinnied, reared up and took off in a run.

The boy held on with a panicked look on his face. There were a few screams from the picnickers.

Small silvery disks shimmered into view, marking a line from me to the boy's horse. I began to sprint forward, putting each of my feet onto one of the silvery disks. Three paces on the ground, two on a picnic bench, and two across a picnic table, a leap to the next picnic table.

One on the back of the neck of a woman reaching for more potato salad, one on the top of a big beer mug. The last one on the head of a tall bald man. Then a flying broad jump to the horse.

I hit the horse hard, nearly falling off the side, and nearly taking the little boy off with me. When I pulled myself up I had the reins in my hand. We were now flying along. On the left was the fence that surrounds the corral and on the right, far below us, through trees and bushes, was the entrance road. The ledge we were riding on was getting narrower, the fall was getting steeper, and we were running out of time.

I leaned forward. "Okay, Athena," I whispered into the horse's ear. "You got this."

We leaped the corral fence and came down hard on the other side. The horse stumbled. I was so close to the ground. I thought we were going down. But the horse righted itself and sprinted around close to the fence. I swung myself off, half hanging on the horse and half running beside it slowing it down. When the horse stopped I lifted the boy off.

"How are you doing?" I asked him.

He didn't reply. The look on his face was confused. About to cry? Shock? Relief? I couldn't tell. We slipped through the slats of the fence.

I noticed that two adults had run toward us.

"Your parents are looking for you," I said. The boy scampered to them. I walked back to my family. I decided to hurry and see if I could get myself another piece of corn.

As I walked by the serving area I snagged myself one. I slipped back into my place and began eating it.

"Emily," my mother said.

I was in midbite and had butter all over my chin and fingers. I put the corn down and tried to wipe up a bit. I noticed that my mother and father were looking at me. I hoped I wasn't going to get a scolding for being sloppy.

"Yes Mom?" I asked.

"You saved that boy," she said.

"It was nothing, Mom."

"You saved that boy," she said again.

"I guess so," I said.

They stood there staring at me for a while.

"Jacob, did you see what your sister did?" my dad asked. "How she saved that little boy?"

"Sure," Jacob said. "But I always knew Emily was a superhero."

Well at least my brother wasn't making a big deal out of it. I got back to eating my corn.

A few more mouthfuls and another group of people came up. Some guy from the ranch. And the boy's parents. They all thanked me.

"Emily, that was impressive horsemanship. We could really use someone with that kind of skill. We would love to have you work for us," the man from the ranch said. "We could be flexible."

"Thanks," I said, "but I already have as much work as I want."

After a bunch more milling about and thanking me they finally left me alone. My corn was stone cold by then but it still was good. When I was done I looked up to notice another crowd heading to me.

"Dad, I'm going for a little walk. Tell them I vanished."

"Sure Emily," he said as I walked away.

I headed down the path that the horse had taken, but this time I climbed down the bank, among the trees. There was a nice secluded spot, away from everyone. I sat down on a large stone that was covered in lichen. My life can be strange at times. I looked around. It was a really pleasant place. It felt good to sit. I drank the place in. Leaves rustled slowly. Shadows danced here and there. Quiet. Wonderful solitude. But my heart was churning. I thought of my friends in Oz. And of Sebastian. He wasn't going to stop. How many of my friend will he hurt?

I don't like to run out on friends, but what could I do? What was the answer? How was this going to end?

I daydreamed. An old woman said to me, "Emily, I hoped to give you more. But you will be tested soon. Too soon. Be brave."

A breaking branch brought me back. What did that mean? Be brave?

I need to go back. Confront Sebastian. Make Oz safe. I felt Sebastian pull at me, pulling me to Oz, like I was surrounded by strings and when I moved and touched a string, I felt a pull to Oz. If I touched one and held on, I would return to Oz.

An idea formed in my head. It was clear. Everything had become crystal clear. I grabbed on to one of the strings with all my might.

I appeared in Sebastian's house. He was right in front of me, two steps away. He was working over a cauldron,

391

putting bits of various things in and stirring. He watched his potion intently. He pulled a lever and the cauldron swung so that it was in the fireplace, the very fireplace that Ralph described to me. The very fireplace that Ralph and Tip had used to burn Sebastian's stuffed people. I wondered how long it would be before he turned around and noticed me. Not long.

"Emily, I am so glad to see you," he said with his usual smirk. His face had patches of blisters and burnt skin. That seemed new to me. "So much effort have I put into catching you, and here you are accepting my invitation to visit. If I had known that letting you go home would bring you to me, I would have let you go sooner." He stepped forward and grabbed my wrist with his hand. My skin was on fire. Then I burned from the inside. I did my best to ignore the pain.

He started to laugh. I put my hand over his. He smile with confidence. He would win at this game, he thought.

Back to the cool secluded spot, among the trees, at the ranch. In an instant we were there. Sebastian tried to pull away but I held his hand in place. He was too late. He had played the wrong game.

A gentle breeze blew some of his hair off. The rest crumbled to powder. The tip of his nose fell off. Then his free arm fell off, caught for a second by his shirt. Then he fell and crumbled. I let go of his hand and brushed some dust off my wrist.

I sat back down. So this is it. Completed. Sebastian gone. I thought back on everything that had happened. Everything that had come undone and everything that had been renewed.

My phone rang. "Emily, it's time to go," my mom said. "We packed your things in the car."

"Thanks, Mom," I said. "I'll be there in a second."

I looked around. There was no trace of Sebastian.

I walked from the darkness and climbed the bank. I found my family standing by our car in the parking lot.

"Ready to go Emms?" my dad asked.

"Ready to go Dads," I replied as I climbed into the car.

www.ingramcontent.com/pod-product-compliance
Lightning Source LLC
Chambersburg PA
CBHW051549250626
47157CB00001B/230